THE IMPOSTER

A LEGACY OF LOVE NOVEL

MELANIE DOBSON

EMBER ROTH BOOKS

For Kinzel Shae (my sweet little pea)

*Your love of music and laughter brings
so much joy to our family.
I'm incredibly blessed to be your mom!*

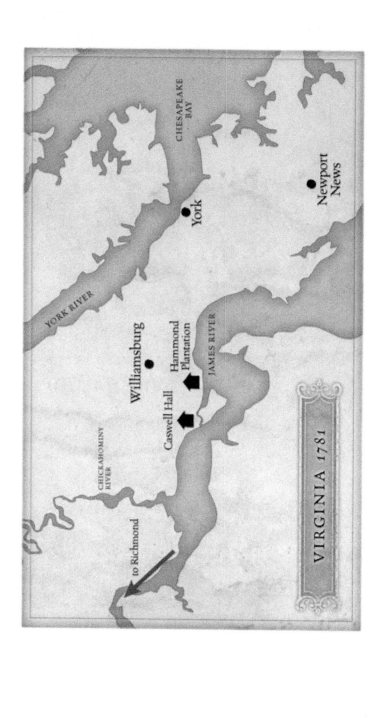

VIRGINIA 1781

CHESAPEAKE BAY

Newport News

York

YORK RIVER

CHICKAHOMINY RIVER

Williamsburg

Hammond Plantation

Caswell Hall

JAMES RIVER

to Richmond

PROLOGUE

JULY 4, 1826

*G*littering trails of firelight illuminated the champagne
in Lydia's glass. Leaning back against a sandstone
column, her stiff fingers curled over the worn crook of
her cane, Lydia sipped the Veuve Clicquot from its gold-
encrusted pool. The warmth from her drink fought off the coolness that stole through her silk gown and gloves.

Hundreds of guests gathered on the north lawn of the white
President's Palace as another round of red-and-blue fireworks
rocketed through the night, but only one of the guests interested her. She scanned the shadowed faces of cabinet members
and representatives from across the States, searching in vain for
their country's secretary of state.

The echoing boom rattled her bones, and the crowd cheered
as shards of light cascaded over the grass.

"Jubilee of Freedom"—that's what John Quincy Adams, president of their United States, called this day, but the celebration
in Lydia's heart blended with her memories, jubilation fading
away like the fireworks in the darkness.

Would their country remember the sacrifices the men and
women of the colonies had made as well as their triumphs?

She took another sip, looking again for the distinguished secretary. Fifty years had passed since their country had declared its independence from Great Britain—and almost fifty years since the man who became the country's secretary of state turned her and her family upside down.

After the last firework fizzled into the night, the strum of a harpsichord soothed the crashing sounds from the fireworks display. A flute followed the harp and then violins.

Lydia scanned the crowd again. This time she found him.

He stood beside the president, looking quite regal in his long black evening coat. The red-and-golden stripes on his waistcoat and cravat honored this celebration of independence, and his laughter made her smile. He usually didn't enjoy parties, but this was one celebration he loved.

The music stopped, and silence rippled across the grass as President Adams lifted his glass. Men and women alike lifted their glasses with him. Even though her champagne was gone, Lydia lifted her coupe as high as the others. Decades ago she would have been mortified about her empty glass, but she was much too old now to care about pomp and circumstance.

The secretary of state turned his head slowly until he found her in the lantern light. As the president toasted the jubilee, the secretary raised his glass to Lydia and she smiled at him. His love seemed to wash over her, cleansing the remnants of pain, and her heart fluttered.

Ages ago she'd been called beautiful, but now lines crept up her face even as the youth of her body slipped away. At sixty-nine, her hands were already speckled purple-and-blue, and her copper-brown locks had turned the same milky-gray color of the stone portico at her beloved Caswell Hall.

Yet when he captured her with his gaze, she felt beautiful.

The orchestra resumed playing, and the couples around her began to dance a minuet on the wide patio. How she wished she and the secretary could steal away from the lights and the people and the responsibilities that weighed heavy on them. How she wished they could go back to Caswell Hall and sit together on the wide porch, hand in hand, as they watched the ships parade up and down the river.

Louisa Adams stepped beside her and took her arm. Mrs. Adams's gaze wandered toward the secretary. "I think you still fancy him."

Lydia smiled at the First Lady. "Very much."

"And clearly he fancies you."

Lydia laughed. "I've cast a spell over him."

"I believe you have. A beautiful spell." Mrs. Adams let go of Lydia's arm and brushed her gloved hands over the ruffles of her pale-green gown. "How many years has it been?"

"Forty-four years since our wedding day."

"And you are still in love."

Lydia's heart stirred. "Madly."

As her husband slowly crossed the floor, Lydia turned away from the First Lady and welcomed him with her smile.

Mrs. Adams nudged her forward. "You should dance with him."

How she had once loved to dance. She and the secretary hadn't danced in more than a decade, ever since the doctor said a cane would be her companion for her remaining years, but tonight her husband gently set her cane against the wall and offered her his arm.

Her feet moved slowly to the music, her leg threatening to buckle. But she knew the dance, and she knew her husband's steps. She knew everything about this man who held her.

His arm anchored her back as they danced on the patio. He'd anchored her for most of her life. Through illness and the loss of her family. Through the birth of eight children and the death of two. Through the storms that raged outside their plantation and those that raged in her heart.

He bent toward her and whispered in her ear, "Do you remember?"

She looked up into green eyes that flashed in the light, and the years seemed to melt away. She was twenty-four again, and he was teasing her.

She tilted her head ever so slightly, their banter as familiar as the steps of the minuet. "Remember what?"

"That night by the river." He stopped dancing, and a curtain of skirts swirled around them. "I don't want you to ever forget."

"I—" she started, but she never finished her words. He rocked toward her and she clung to him, holding his limp body to her chest. Pain shot up her failing leg, but she wouldn't let him fall. He was saying something to her, and she tried to hear his voice over the music, desperately wanting to understand.

One of the senators—a doctor—rushed toward them, and the orchestra stopped playing as the senator helped lay her husband on the ground. Her husband opened his eyes and calmed her racing heart with his gaze.

The crowd circling around them seemed to vanish. All she saw were the eyes of the man she loved looking back at her.

His gaze transported her to that cold night so long ago when he'd searched her face. The night he'd asked her the question that changed her life. She could almost feel the dampness on her skin, the longing in her heart.

Her tears drenched her husband's fine coat as she pushed his hair behind his ears. He was so handsome. So strong.

She couldn't lose him here.

She reached for his hand and leaned forward so only he would hear her whisper. "We're going home, my love."

What we obtain too cheap, we esteem too lightly: it is dearness only that gives every thing its value.

Thomas Paine, *The American Crisis*, 1776

CHAPTER 1

FEBRUARY 1781, WILLIAMSBURG

wilight laced the snowy banks along the James River with orange and pink. The Caswell family had already retired for the night, each member warming by a fire in his or her bedchamber, but the King's Men hadn't retired.

Leaning against the pillows on her window seat, Lydia Caswell watched a parade of British ships steal past her family's home, the blue-and-red King's Colours glowing from a dozen masts.

Why was the British navy sailing up their river?

The last she'd heard from her father, the British soldiers who'd landed in Newport News last month had left for Charles Towne in South Carolina. They weren't supposed to return to Virginia.

She put down her sampler and slid off the cushioned seat, neatly folding the quilt that had warmed her lap. Part of her wanted to sneak down to the bank to enjoy a better view of the ships, but she wasn't fond of being outside—at least not like her friend Sarah Hammond.

Before the war, Lydia's family hosted hundreds of visitors each year at Caswell Hall for lavish dinners and balls. She preferred dances and teas to walks in the garden, but the winter and lingering war made the evenings terribly long. Sometimes it felt as if the paneled walls were beginning to close in upon her.

With a candle flickering in her hand, Lydia stepped into the dark hallway. Her parents' chamber was across from hers, and to her right was the door for the servants' staircase. Her sister's chamber and the one kept for her brother, Grayson, were to the left of Lydia's room. Beyond their rooms was the balcony that overlooked the grand staircase and hall below.

When her father built Caswell Hall, he meticulously crafted a manor that would rival his childhood home outside London, intending to raise his family in a colony ruled by the king. His father had helped him build this house, but the life of the senior Lord Caswell was stolen away much too early.

Lydia crossed the hall to her parents' door. If he hadn't seen them already, Father would want to know about these ships. After what had happened to Grandfather, Father kept his political views inside the walls of their house, but she doubted there were many in the American colonies more loyal to the Crown than he.

Her parents' door was cracked open, and she lifted her hand to knock but stopped when she heard her mother speak. "She cannot marry until after the war."

Lydia leaned closer to the door. Who was her mother talking about?

Everyone knew that Lydia wouldn't be married until after the war was over, and her sister, Hannah, had only just turned fifteen. Some families married off their daughters when they were fourteen, but Mother had told Hannah many times that they wouldn't even consider a marriage for her until she was at least sixteen.

"The war will be finished soon, Dotty. Perhaps before summer." Her father was probably sitting by the fire, waving a cigar in his hand as he spoke. "We must begin to make arrangements."

Perhaps they were discussing Lydia's marriage to Seth Hammond after all. While she had promised to marry their neighbor five years ago—and her parents approved of the union at the time—Father had since changed his mind.

Was he reconsidering his objection?

"There will be no wedding without a groom," Mother said.

Father sighed. "We must find an Englishman for her. Someone loyal to the Crown."

Lydia held her breath as she leaned closer to the door. Surely they were talking about Hannah, when she was old enough to marry.

"'Tis impossible to say who is truly loyal now," Mother replied. "When the fighting is over, it will be sorted out."

"But she is already twenty-four," Father insisted. "I fear we cannot wait much longer to find a husband for her."

Lydia sank back against the wall. They were discussing her.

Father continued speaking. "We know where the loyalties of the British officers rest. Perhaps one of them could marry her and take her back to England."

The strength in Mother's voice drained. "I do not want to lose her, Charles."

"Then one of the officers must learn how to run a plantation."

Lydia backed away from the door and fled down the servants' circular staircase. She didn't want to marry a stranger. Until Seth had gone to fight in this cursed war, she had planned to marry him and stay here, at Caswell Hall. But when he joined the rebels in their fight, Father swore she and Seth would never marry.

In the basement she retrieved a dark-blue cloak from the wardrobe along with a muff to warm her hands. She needed to get out of the house, if only for part of an hour. The war was making all of them desperate.

Great Britain had the most powerful army in the world. Once they stopped the rebellion among the colonists, all would return to normalcy. Seth and her father would reconcile, and she would become Mrs. Hammond.

Quickly she fastened the leather straps of wooden-soled pattens over her slippers to keep the satin dry. She reached for the long handle of the door that led toward the river, but before she turned the handle, someone stepped into the room through the kitchen door.

Both she and Prudence gasped at the sight of the other. Lydia reached out to help Prudence steady the silver tray in her hand.

Prudence was the oldest of their six maidservants, the only light-skinned one among them. Her hair was tucked back under her white mobcap, and her plump cheeks were always rosy, in both the hot and the cold. She had come to Caswell Hall almost twenty-five years ago to work as a nursemaid for Lydia and then Hannah. The girls were much too old for a nursemaid now, but Prudence had stayed on with the Caswell family to attend to all the women.

Lydia eyed the top of the silver platter. There was an oval-shaped teapot, hand-painted teacups, a wooden caddy for the tea leaves, and a plate of powdered cakes. "Is Hannah hungry again?"

Prudence shook her head. "Your parents called for tea in their rooms. Would you like to join them?"

Lydia stepped toward the door that led to the riverfront. "Perhaps when I return."

Prudence eyed her cloak. "'Tis too cold for you outside."

"I'm just walking to the river."

The teacups clattered with the shake of Prudence's head. Lydia may have outgrown the need for a nursemaid, but

Prudence still watched over her. "The river's a long way in the snow."

"Only a few steps, really." She tied the strings of her cloak. "I shan't be gone long."

"Aye," Prudence said. "I will take Lady Caswell her tea and then remain here until you return."

"Please don't tell them where I'm going."

Prudence hesitated before she agreed.

Lydia pulled the woolen hood over her cap as she stepped outside. Snow crunched under her pattens as she hurried away from the house down a pathway leading to the small wharf where her family received and shipped goods to England.

She breathed deeply of the crisp air, savoring the golden moments before the sunlight was completely gone. Father's office was on the left side of the house, its frosty slate roof matching the main house, along with a smokehouse and a barn. The kitchen gardens were to her right along with several other flank buildings: stable, coach house, washhouse, and summer kitchen.

The gardeners, laundry maids, and groundskeepers lived in the servants' quarters beside the coach house, while the rest of the Negroes lived in dwellings a half mile north, closer to where they labored. Prudence and the other fairer-skinned house servants lived in the attic of Caswell Hall.

The family's formal gardens wrapped around the east side of Caswell Hall, extending all the way to the river, and centered in the midst of the garden was a white gazebo and an ornate glass-and-brick orangery where the gardener grew fruits and vegetables in the winter. On long summer days, she and Seth had sometimes sat in the gazebo, before war began to rage in their colonies.

In 1775, Lord Dunmore, the royal governor of Virginia, stole the colonists' gunpowder from the magazine in Williamsburg and harassed those who rebelled against the Crown. But then, like the tides along the Chesapeake Bay, the power in Virginia shifted. Lord Dunmore and his family fled during the night, and the rebels began attacking those who remained loyal to the king. They boycotted businesses, imprisoned Loyalists, and administered a painful coat of thickset to the most outspoken opponents of rebellion.

Her heart ached at the memories of her grandfather, a distinguished member of the House of Burgesses, covered with the tar that burned his skin. He died from his wounds—or perhaps from the humiliation of being forced to walk through town clothed only in thickset and a degrading coat of feathers.

Lydia shook her head. That was four years past now, and Grandfather wouldn't want her to think about the tar and feathering. Even though he'd been treated dishonorably, he'd died an honorable man and he would want her to remember his strength. If he were still alive, he might have been on one of the British ships, fighting for the king.

Caswell Hall was four miles southwest of Williamsburg. She'd seen the British soldiers passing through the town last October, but neither the British nor the rebel soldiers had come near her family's plantation. She didn't know how her father had managed to keep the soldiers away, but the current Lord Caswell would do almost anything to protect their plantation.

It was only a matter of weeks, Father had said, before the Continental Army would fold anyway. When that happened, King George III would reward the Caswell family well for its loyalty.

She stepped to the top of the bank and looked upriver. Black willows drooped low to her right, their icy fingers dangling in the water. The ships had passed by, but on the other side of the willows, she could still see their ensigns in the fading light. With the British navy in Virginia, surely the British were close to restoring peace in their colony.

She burrowed her hands farther into the muff. Her father

might not be vocal about his politics in Williamsburg, but in the privacy of their dining hall, her father was as loyal to the Crown as General Cornwallis. And he wanted her to marry someone just as loyal.

She was so tired of this war that pitted neighbor against neighbor— the war that killed her grandfather, took away her brother, and drove the man she was supposed to marry to rebel against the country her family loved.

Peace was what she desired. A return to the days when neighbors trusted each other. When they were all working together to build up the colonies instead of tearing them apart.

King George III would eventually win the war—everyone of a reasonable intellect knew that—but like a child rebelling against his parents, the Yankees and their George, General Washington, persisted in demonstrating the little strength they had left. No amount of discipline from Great Britain had been effective enough to end the rebellion. The rebels stood on what they called "principle"—principles that would get them either hanged or shot.

She shivered. Every day she prayed that the rebels would buckle before Seth was killed.

At one time, her father had great admiration for George Washington, a hero for the British during the French and Indian War, but that changed when Washington stood against the Crown. Still, Father respected Washington, just as he should respect Seth.

She must convince Father to change his mind. When the war ended, Seth and her father would make amends—she was certain of it—and their lives would return to a steady pace of high teas and elegant balls and visits with the friends who now shunned them in Williamsburg and Richmond.

Stars began to peek through the darkness until a canopy of twinkling lights ceiled the wide river. She took a deep breath. Perhaps now she could tell her parents about the ships—and try to tell them that she couldn't bear the thought of marrying a stranger. She must make them understand.

She turned to retrace her trail along the starlit path, but before she took a step, she heard a sound in the willows.

A groan.

Her heart leaped in her chest. She froze, listening, but the only sound in the night was the steady current flowing over the rocks near the shore.

The darkness must be playing with her mind. An animal had gotten trapped in the branches. Or the water was driving a log through the leaves.

She began walking toward the windows that glowed with warmth when a voice cried out.

Her heart seemed to stop.

It wasn't an animal in the willows. It was a man.

CHAPTER 2

*E*verything within Lydia screamed for her to run. Back to her warm room, to her father who would do anything to keep her safe. Back to the brick fortress that had protected her for more than twenty years.

The man groaned again, and her mind flashed back to that terrible day when the three rebels dumped her grandfather outside the plantation door.

She couldn't leave anyone out here in the snow and hope the servants would find him in the morning. The cold would steal away his life long before dawn, and his blood would be on her hands.

She moved slowly toward the willows. "Who's there?"

No one answered.

She lifted a willow branch and stared into the tree's dark tendrils. Branches and leaves were all she saw in the starlight.

Perhaps it was her imagination. The sighting of the British ships had startled her nerves, creating people when there were none.

But then she heard another groan, and her nerves shattered. Lydia stepped into the branches and saw the man's shadowed form, hidden a few feet into the willows. His head and arms were on the shore; his legs dangled in the frigid water.

She lurched forward. There was no time to consider where this man had come from or whether he was friend or foe. She must get him out of this water before the chill of it killed him.

Leveraging her foot against the roots, she cupped her hands under his shoulders and pulled him a few inches up the bank. He was so heavy, his clothing weighted down by the river water.

She pulled again, dragging him out of the water a few inches at a time, away from the willows. Then she stopped, her lungs crying for air.

"Arnold," the man rasped, grasping her arm. "Arnold is coming."

She took another breath before prying his hand off her cape and placing it back at his side.

"Hush," she whispered.

His head thrashed from side to side. "You must tell them."

Who was she to tell?

"I shall," she assured him, and his head stilled at her words.

She examined the man in the starlight. His waistcoat was soaked, as were his trousers. And his long hair. No gentleman would venture out unshaven, wearing homespun trousers, but during this time of war, she could hardly criticize a Loyalist for his state of undress. If he was loyal . . .

His words were slurred, but his accent sounded British. Of course, it was impossible to judge one's loyalty by an accent. Plenty of rebels were from Britain.

Kneeling over him, she wiped the river water from his face with her muff. Then she removed her heavy cloak and covered him. If he was a Loyalist, Father would welcome him into their house, but if he was a Yankee, her father would probably put him right back out into the snow.

"What am I to do with you?" she whispered.

All she heard in reply was his heavy breath as he trembled under her cloak.

What if he was a rebel coming to hurt her family? Or a marauder intent on stealing their livestock?

She stared at him for another moment. It could be a ruse. He might be bait, to get inside their home. Or a band of Skinners— thieves—might be waiting in the willows to steal their food and livestock, hurt her family. Or he simply might be a poor soul who fell off one of the British ships.

If he was a Skinner, he was much too weak at the moment to steal or injure anyone. She could turn him over to the magistrate in the morning.

Lifting her skirts, Lydia turned toward the house. Others might fear the king, but she feared God. She would have to answer to Him if she left this man to die, and he would die, probably in a matter of minutes, if she didn't hurry. Peace would never come to their colonies unless people on both sides were willing to help each other.

She wished she could fetch Sarah—Seth's sister and her best friend— to assist her with this man, but there was no time. She must convince Prudence instead.

"I need your help," Lydia said when she found Prudence downstairs in the kitchen, the empty tray in her hands.

Prudence set down the tray on a counter. "What is it?"

"There's a man outside." Lydia hesitated, not sure how to explain. "He's unconscious."

Prudence looked alarmed. "One of the Negroes?"

Lydia shook her head. "A British man—or an American. He seems to have fallen off a ship."

Prudence pointed toward the staircase. "We must tell your father."

"We cannot." She twisted the muff in her hand. Her parents never explained themselves to their servants, but she wanted Prudence to understand. "What if this man is a rebel?"

"If he is—" Prudence hesitated. "Your father might avenge his father's death."

"That's what I fear." Lydia glanced back at the door that led outside. "I cannot be responsible for letting another man die here."

"He might not be a good man, Miss Lydia."

"That is not for me to judge."

Prudence still didn't move. "The Scriptures say we know a righteous man by his deeds."

"Then we should wait until he awakens before we pass judgment." She swallowed. "But he'll never awaken without our care."

Reluctantly Prudence joined Lydia outside, her hastily donned cape askew. By the light of their lantern, the two women stared down at the man's pale face.

Wet hair curled around the crown of his head, and icy drops clung to his eyebrows. He no longer shivered, and his stillness frightened her.

"We must take him inside," she insisted.

"There's no place to hide him."

Her parents might not find him in one of the spare rooms or the attic, but Hannah most certainly would. Her sister would burst before she kept a secret this big.

Prudence rubbed her arms under her cape. "Perhaps we could hide him in the servants' quarters."

But it was a risk to have him near the servants. One of them might turn him over, afraid of her father's retribution, and if this stranger was a rebel, Prudence's position would be in jeopardy.

An idea began to form in Lydia's mind. The head groom at the stables was an honest man, and he lived in a room above the coach house, with a view of the river instead of the house. He was also strong enough to carry this man.

She looked up at Prudence. "Do you think Elisha would

help us?"

"He's probably the only one who would."

And they could trust him to keep a secret.

"Should I fetch him?" Prudence asked.

When Lydia nodded, the woman set the lantern in the snow. Then she picked up her petticoat and ran toward the stables.

Watching her grandfather die had torn at the seams of Lydia's heart. The idea of another man dying beside her, a man whose story she had yet to learn, was terrifying. She didn't want him to die, didn't want anyone to die.

She knelt beside the stranger and reached for his hand, praying quietly that God would intervene. She didn't know what else to do except pray and warm his hand in hers.

He might perish on someone else's watch, but she prayed not on hers.

Elisha came back with Prudence, his dark skin blending in with the night. He swore when he saw the stranger. Then he looked up at Lydia, his eyes wide. "Pardon me, Miss Lydia."

"There is no reason for apologies," she said. "I was shocked as well."

"What do you require of me?"

"You must carry him to the coach house."

In the starlight, she could see the fear in his eyes. He stepped back, shaking his head. "If Master Caswell finds out—"

"You'll tell him the truth—that I insisted upon it."

Elisha examined the man's face as Prudence had done, as if he were debating whether it was more beneficial for him to listen to Lydia and incur the wrath of his master, or ignore her command and escape Lord Caswell's anger. His sigh was long, resigned, as he knelt down in the snow and lifted the stranger to his chest as if the man were a newborn foal.

Prudence rushed off to heat water while Lydia used the lantern to guide Elisha to the other side of the well.

Elisha climbed the steps of the coach house and set the

stranger on his narrow bed. Lydia knelt beside him, examining the stranger's face again.

He looked to be about Elisha's age, perhaps nearing forty years old. His skin was shaded like a gray winter sky, his jawline flecked with stubble. When his chest stilled again, she reached for his wrist, checking to see whether life still coursed through his veins.

His damp skin felt colder than the snow, and when she felt no pulse, she placed her fingers on his neck. The slightest knock of his heart tapped against her skin.

Elisha stacked three pieces of wood in the fireplace. "I'm afraid there isn't much hope for him."

Prudence was correct—they would know a righteous man by his deeds—but Lydia didn't know how long they must wait to discover the righteousness of this man.

Another scripture flooded her mind. *"Inasmuch as ye have done it unto one of the least of these my brethren, ye have done it unto me."*

Life was fragile for even the strongest of men, but they couldn't abandon this one, no matter how weak he was. God asked of them to care for His children.

"As long as there is some hope, we must fight for his life."

"If he lives—" Elisha looked up at her, hesitant to speak.

"What is it, Elisha?"

"I'm afraid you might not like what happens if he lives."

"Somewhere this man has a family." She pulled her cloak off the stranger. "If nothing else, we must attempt to keep him alive for their sakes."

"Yes, ma'am." He stood to help her peel off the man's drenched waistcoat. Then he reached for two blankets on a shelf. "You best turn your head."

She nodded, turning to face the narrow window, as Elisha removed the rest of the stranger's clothing.

What did one do to save a man half-frozen and perhaps half-drowned as well? Father usually sent for Dr. Cooper in Williamsburg, but Dr. Cooper was an outspoken Loyalist and one of her father's closest friends. He would certainly tell Father about this man.

Elisha gasped, and Lydia swiveled around. Her stomach rolled when she saw the jagged gash on the man's foot.

She'd been well-schooled in the arts of dance and conversation. She'd learned to serve tea and cake and stitch pincushions and samplers for gifts. But no one had taught her much about practicalities.

Or how to save a life.

Perhaps she should fetch Mother's laudanum. Mother thought the laudanum cured everything.

The fire began to warm the room, and Prudence returned within the half hour with a pot of hot water and rags. Steam curled toward the wooden ceiling as she poured the water into Elisha's white basin, dipped a rag into the hot water, and wrung it out. Leaning over Lydia, she covered the man's face and then his arms with more hot cloths.

Elisha produced a bottle of whiskey and Prudence helped lift the man's head. The stranger sipped the whiskey without urging. Then he began to mumble again about Arnold as Prudence and Elisha cleaned his wound and wrapped it with clean cloths.

Lydia felt so helpless, watching Prudence and Elisha work with ease.

Where had they learned to care for someone on the brink of death?

She stared up at Prudence, desperate to do something to help bring back his life. "Shall I get medicine?"

Prudence shook her head. "Whiskey and warmth are the only cures for him now."

Lydia looked back at the bed. "And prayer."

"Aye," Prudence replied. "Particularly prayer."

Elisha added several pine knots to the small fire. The room would be plenty warm soon.

Prudence pointed toward the door. "You should return to your chamber, miss."

She didn't move. "I cannot leave him."

"You mustn't worry," Elisha said. "I'll do my best to care for him tonight."

"But what about the morning?" she asked as she slowly stood.

"It's not likely he will survive."

She knew it would be a miracle if he lived until morning.

Thankfully, she still believed in miracles.

CHAPTER 3

*S*arah Hammond wrapped her shawl across her shoulders and stepped out into the cold as darkness fell. None of the servants inquired after her. Ever since her father had sailed away last summer, they'd become accustomed to her nightly strolls. They just didn't know why she must venture out each night.

She knew her servants often whispered in the basement about her oddities, as did the people in Williamsburg. How could they not? No other woman aged barely twenty-five was attempting to run a plantation in Virginia.

Her servants had no choice but to work for her, and she had no choice but to run this plantation until her father returned. Every night, she dreamed about sailing away with her father instead of trying to manage his property.

She tried to be grateful for the blessings of a home and plantation, but she held on to them loosely. What she clung to was the gift of freedom and her library full of books. The library whisked her away to places she might never visit, the pages of her book sweeping her off to islands and cities and long voyages filled with grand adventures.

The flame inside her lantern lit the wrought-iron railing her great-grandfather had constructed more than eighty years ago.

The Hammond family plantation house was one of the first built along the James River. It was small compared to the other nearby plantation houses—like those belonging to the Caswells and the Webbs—but her family's plantation had ushered in the growth of the colonies. In time, when her brother returned, it would grow as well.

Seth wanted to become a planter like their father, but Sarah had no desire to stay. One day she would visit some of the cities she read about in her books—Philadelphia, New York, and Charles Towne. Once this war was over, she would be free to go wherever she wanted, but until then, she and Thomas—her father's overseer—were left here to manage four thousand acres.

She'd never planned to run a plantation, and to her knowledge, her father—the renowned Commodore John Hammond—never intended for her to run it either. At his king's command, he had no choice but to go to the West Indies last year. With Seth already gone, her father didn't trust anyone else but her with his affairs, so she had been left with a man's job.

Sarah held up the lantern, and the light flickered on the iron, casting spindly shadows across the wooden steps, as she searched for the white ribbon. Nothing was tied to the railing tonight.

Sighing, she lowered the lantern again. Morah's four-year-old son, Alden, had spotted British ships out on the James tonight. She'd thought a messenger might arrive as well, so she could deliver a message after services tomorrow.

A coyote howled in the woods at the end of their long drive as she scanned the drive. Not that the messenger would parade up her snowy lane, but perhaps she would see the shadow of a man.

She wrapped her shawl closer to her chest as the skeletal arms of their elm trees swayed along the drive.

Maybe there had been a mistake. The messenger might have forgotten to tie the white ribbon around the railing. Or perhaps a servant had found the ribbon and snipped it. A message could have been delivered earlier this evening and she might not know it arrived.

The courier always hung a ribbon to alert her if he'd left a letter. She wasn't supposed to check the hiding place, at least not regularly, but tonight she would.

Snow carpeted each step, and she clung to the banister as she edged her way down to the lawn. Lifting her skirt, she hurried past the summer kitchen and the icehouse until she reached the circular stone building to the right of their house. The dovecote.

When she opened the door, hundreds of doves and pigeons squawked, but they didn't fly out the glover on the top. The birds were used to the cook opening the door, stealing away squabs for breakfast or dinner. Sarah reached her hand into the stone crevice to her right, but all she felt were feathers and straw.

Admittedly, it was a strange system of delivery to hide messages in the dovecote, but it worked well. She knew she could be hanged for treason if she was caught, but she had no intention of being discovered.

Holding up her lantern, she checked the nearby nests for the familiar leather pouch, but there was nothing here tonight. After closing the door, she turned back toward the house, laughing at herself as she walked back through the snow.

Who would have thought that she would be a link in the network spreading throughout Virginia? No one in Williamsburg would ever guess what she was doing. They thought her too shy, too quiet, too loyal to the king to do anything this risky.

She stepped back into the narrow entryway of their house, but she wasn't ready to put away her shawl. A fire roared in the parlor, and she moved close to warm her hands as she watched it dance.

Then she picked a book off the shelf—stories written by Madam Sarah Knight—and slipped into a rose-colored wing-back chair that Aunt Marguerite had given her parents when they married. Her aunt had gifted her with Madam Knight's stories when Sarah turned sixteen.

Sarah liked to think that her mother had named her after Madam Knight, the famous colonist who rode on horseback from Boston to New York in 1704 and wrote about her adventures. That was what Sarah longed to do as well—see the world, experience it in all its glories and discomforts, and maybe even write about it.

Grayson Caswell used to tease her about her obsession to travel, calling her Madam Knight. Yet in his teasing, she knew he understood like no one else. He might not have loved the pen as she did, but he loved learning about the world. Before he disappeared, his mind wandered often from the confines of Caswell Hall, and she'd loved wandering with him.

Someone walked into the parlor and she looked up to see Thomas, the overseer of her father's plantation. Father had purchased him in North Carolina when Thomas was a boy, and he'd served their family faithfully for more than fifty years. Her father trusted few people, but he trusted this man to look after his property and daughter while he was away.

"Will you be needing anything else, miss?"

She put the book in her lap. "I will be attending services after breakfast."

"I shall have the carriage ready for you."

"Did you secure the stables?"

"Aye."

"Thank you, Thomas." She took a deep breath. She would be lost without his help. "That is all for tonight."

"Good night, then."

As he left, her gaze wandered toward the dark window. It had been almost a month since she'd received the last message.

Was it possible that General Washington didn't know about the ships? Perhaps the courier had been detained. She would pen a letter herself so those Patriots in Williamsburg would be prepared for more soldiers.

She only hoped that the British wouldn't stop at her house. No matter what happened, she wouldn't—couldn't—entertain them. They could take all she had, but nothing could make her give up this fight for freedom.

~

Light crept between the shutters and stole across Lydia's bedcovering, taunting her for remaining in bed on a Sunday morning.

Lydia let it taunt. On the Lord's Day, Episcopals in and around Williamsburg put aside their political differences and worshipped together at Bruton Parish Church.

It took at least an hour for the Caswells' coach to drive into Williamsburg, but no matter the political dissension or the weather or even if it was planting season, Mother always insisted their family attend. Lydia enjoyed the trips into town, but she would not be going to service this morning.

Mother walked into the room and pushed open the paneled shutters before sitting down on the side of Lydia's bed. The elegant Lady Caswell wore a gown the color of the evergreen trees that grew along the road to Williamsburg. Her gown swept overtop a cream-colored petticoat, and the ribboned curls in her blond wig smelled of pomade and a trace of her lavender-scented perfume.

As light poured into the room, she pushed tendrils of wavy hair away from Lydia's face and placed the back of her hand on Lydia's forehead. "Are you unwell?"

Lydia shivered under her bedcoverings. "There are pains in my stomach."

Mother put her hand in her lap and sat straight. "We shan't attend church without you."

Lydia shook her head, her mind racing. Her family must leave this morning. "That would be unfair to Father and Hannah."

"They will certainly understand," Mother said.

But if Father knew the truth, he wouldn't understand at all. He would be furious if he found out what she had done.

She reached for Mother's hand and squeezed it. "You must go. You are already dressed."

"I will undress."

Lydia shook her head. "The house will be quiet, and I can rest this morning."

"But you need medicine and soup and—"

Lydia stopped her. "You will return before dinner. Prudence will care well for me while you are gone."

Mother's gaze traveled back to the door, where Prudence stood. "Get the laudanum."

Prudence nodded. "Yes, ma'am."

Mother held Lydia's hand tightly. "We will be home by one."

"I know."

"Stay in your bed."

This time Lydia didn't reply.

Her mother kissed her forehead and tucked the coverings close around Lydia before she left. Lydia wasn't ill, but she was plenty tired from being up most of the night, worrying that the stranger would die, worrying that her family would find him.

Had he survived? His passing might eliminate a number of complications, but even so, she didn't want him to die. Perhaps he would be well enough this morning to continue on his journey.

Or maybe he was already gone.

Prudence returned with the laudanum and a spoon.

"What shall I do with it?" she asked, holding it out as Lydia climbed out of bed.

"Perhaps we should take it with us to Elisha's room."

"But—"

"You may tell the servants I have recovered."

Prudence shook her head. "I shall take no part in this deceit."

"But I have recovered." Lydia glanced toward her window. "Has my family departed?"

"The coach just left."

She sat up. "We must hurry."

Prudence laced Lydia's cotton stay over her shift and helped her dress in her petticoat and a jacket before pinning her hair behind a cap that matched the light color of peach in her attire. Tucking the laudanum and spoon in the small pocket under her petticoat, Lydia climbed down the servants' staircase alone so as not to indict Prudence in her scheme.

The clear blue in the sky and white mantle of snow brushed a bit of color across the dull browns of tree limbs and the grayish blue of the river. She rushed across the melting snow, toward the coach house.

Elisha had driven her family to church. He would keep her secret, but some of the other Negroes might tell the overseer that she'd gone outside while the family was away. The overseer would surely report back to Father.

When she reached the coach house, Lydia looked both ways but didn't see anyone on the grounds. Taking a deep breath, she climbed the steps and knocked on Elisha's door.

CHAPTER 4

The room above the coach house had cooled this morning, the logs disintegrating into black stubs of coal. The stranger on Elisha's bed didn't stir with Lydia's presence, and for a moment, she thought he had indeed perished during the night.

But as she stepped closer, she could see the slight rise and fall of the blankets piled on his chest. Somehow this man had survived his frigid swim in the James.

She looked out the window at the thread of water winding in the distance. Was the Royal Navy looking for one of its sailors? And if he was in the navy, why wasn't he dressed in a red coat and white breeches like the men she'd seen passing through Williamsburg last month?

If he was a deserter, she would have to turn him in . . . but she'd heard terrible stories of what the officers did to deserters. After saving his life, she hated to think of his being shot or hanged.

The air might have cooled, but sweat continued to bubble on the man's forehead. He was younger than she'd thought last night. Perhaps just thirty years of age or even five and twenty.

His sandy-brown hair had dried with the fire, the gray pallor drained from his face.

It felt odd to be alone with a man sleeping in this room. A stranger. She lifted his head and spooned a teaspoonful of laudanum into his lips. She wished she could ask Mother how much medicine to give him, but it was better to err on more than less.

The sooner he recovered, the sooner he could leave the plantation.

When she fed him another spoonful, the man sat up straight in the bed, coughing as he flung the covers off his chest, scouring the room until he found her.

She started to step back, but it was too late. He clutched her arm. "Tell the men that Arnold is coming."

She struggled to pull her arm away, but he wouldn't release it. "Who is this Arnold?"

He shook her arm. "Tell them they must fight."

"But who must fight?" she pressed. "And whom must I tell?"

He released her arm and fell back onto the thin pillow. His eyes closed again, and he muttered as his head tossed. "Three across, two down."

"Three across, two down," she repeated. It was an odd statement, but she hoped the words would comfort him in some way, if only letting him know that she'd heard him.

He nodded in his delirium. Then he sat up again. "Go!"

She leaned toward him as he sank back onto his pillow. The laudanum must be working.

"Where should I go?" she whispered.

When he didn't reply, she nudged his shoulder, but he was no longer conscious, his pleas to her a mystery. If only there was some way she could help.

Standing, she covered him with the blankets and retraced her steps back to the house and down into the basement, past the colorful glass bottles of cherries, wine, and ginger beer that lined the kitchen walls along with wheels of hard cheese and brandied fruit.

The cook was hovering over a steaming pot of chicken soup, and the entire room smelled like garlic and thyme.

Viney looked up from the stove, her eyes filling with surprise. Lady Caswell was the only member of the family who ventured into the kitchen.

"The mistress said—" Viney stuttered. "She said Prudence was to bring soup up to your chamber."

"Aye," Lydia responded. "But I am feeling better and would like to dine in the hall instead."

"Of course, miss." Viney stirred the soup again. "I will have Joshua bring it to you."

Lydia's stomach rumbled. "Will it be ready soon?"

Viney leaned forward to sniff the aroma rising from the pot. "'Tis ready now."

"Then I shall eat now."

The windows of the dining hall overlooked the garden and the river in the distance. The large room seemed eerily quiet without her family. In fact, she couldn't remember a time she had been in the house without her mother or sister near her.

After she sat at the side of the long table, Joshua, her father's indentured manservant, ladled the hot soup into a bowl and placed a basket of warm bread beside her. She spooned the soup to her mouth, and the broth warmed the chill that had settled in her bones. Surely it would help the stranger in Elisha's bed as well.

But how would she sneak the soup to Elisha's room?

She turned toward Joshua, who stood by the sideboard. "You needn't stay."

He nodded and stepped back through the servants' door by the fireplace, leaving her alone.

She finished her bowl and refilled it with more soup. Then she eyed the open doorway into the great hall.

Years ago, when she was eight or nine, she'd hidden bread in the folds of her petticoat and fed them to a wounded duck she'd found near the pond on a neighboring plantation. Mother had caught her taking the piece of bread. She'd scolded her at first for stealing the bread, but once she found out what Lydia was doing, she explained that she didn't have to steal. For a week, there was an extra piece of bread beside her dinner plate.

Then the duck was gone.

In her silent way, Mother might approve of what she was doing to help the wounded man, but Lydia doubted she would risk their family's well-being to help him. This time Lydia would have to help on her own.

Lydia lifted the warm ceramic bowl from the table and covered it with her cape. She waited for a moment by the doorway, listening for footsteps, and then hurried through the great hall and out into the stair hall.

The split staircase in the entry hall swept up to the second floor balcony, and one of the maidservants was descending the stairs while the family was gone.

The girl stopped on the steps, but Lydia didn't acknowledge her as she walked quickly toward the front door. The servants could speculate if they wanted about what she hid under her cape. As long as Prudence and Elisha kept her confidence, the others would never find out the truth.

Stepping out onto the wide stoop, she eyed the drive below her. It circled in front of her house and then lumbered north under the shade of two neatly planted rows of trees. On each side of the trees were hundreds of acres for planting tobacco, and toward the road to Williamsburg were the barns to cure the tobacco.

She stepped outside, not bothering to wear her pattens this time. Her family's coach shouldn't return from church for another hour, but she mustn't delay. The wet snow might ruin the silk fabric, but at the moment, she didn't care. Shoes she could replace—after the war— but a man's life could never be replaced.

Soup splashed as she hurried across the walkway, splattering broth across her petticoat and sleeves. When she reached the coach house, she pushed open the door with her shoulder and found the man still asleep. If only he would wake and fight for his life.

Sitting down on the stool, she spooned the broth into the man's mouth as she had the medicine. His eyes opened and closed as he ate the soup, but they never focused on her.

What if she hadn't gone walking last night? What if she had ignored this man's groan?

He wouldn't have survived the night and probably not the hour, in the condition he was in. It was a cruel war, this meaningless plunder of so much life. Thousands were dying, and for what? A proper cup of English tea?

All of it seemed meaningless to her, as King Solomon said in his book. It was like chasing after the wind.

His head tossed again on the pillow, and she set the soup bowl and spoon beside the basin. Where had this man come from? He didn't look like a rebel, at least not like the cruel men who'd tortured her grandfather. In fact, he reminded her a bit of her brother, Grayson.

Mother had yet to part with any of Grayson's clothing or personal effects. Perhaps she could find some newer clothes for him to wear from her brother's closet.

Lydia picked up the bowl and spooned more soup into the man's mouth.

Often she wondered where both her brother and Seth were. While Sarah received letters from Seth, she herself hadn't received one letter since he'd departed two years go. Or if she had, Father had confiscated it.

The day Seth left to join the Continental Army, Father

ceased to talk about the man he'd once thought would manage Caswell Hall.

If Seth was wounded on the field, she hoped someone would care for him. It didn't matter to her the political leanings of the person who helped him. She hoped his rescuer wouldn't see a soldier but a man who needed compassion. A man with a future ahead of him, no matter who won this war.

Her parents' conversation from last night replayed in her mind, and she clenched her hands together. How could they presume to marry her to a man she didn't know? She and Seth might have departed on bitter terms, but when the war ended, surely he and her father would put aside their political differences. And if they didn't—

She might not marry Seth, but she would never marry a stranger.

If Seth and Father couldn't reconcile, there would be no wedding for her. And no marriage.

She leaned her head back against the bare wood, the sun warming her face through the window. As her eyelids began to droop, she propped up her chin with her hands. She would rest here for a few moments, just in case he awoke.

No matter what happened, she wouldn't regret what she'd done.

A loud bang jolted Nathan from his sleep. His eyes flew open and he scanned the surroundings.

There was a small fireplace to his right, bare wood walls, a basin by the window. Sitting beside him was a young woman, her eyes on the door.

And there was another lady, a middle-aged woman, wearing a gray housedress and a white cap. Her breath came in heaves as she shut the door behind her. "You must leave, Miss Lydia."

The woman beside him—Miss Lydia—hopped to her feet. "Are they home?"

The woman by the door nodded. "They're scouring the house for you."

His head pounding, he closed his eyes. Where was he?

Until he knew whether he was in a safe place, he'd feign sleep.

"Viney will tell them she fed me," Lydia said.

"She told Lady Caswell you took your soup bowl with you."

The younger woman groaned.

"Elisha or I will check back on him. You must stay away from here."

He heard the shuffling of feet and then the shutting of the door. The room grew silent, leaving him alone in a room filled with the oddest mix of smells—chicken soup and horse manure and—he sniffed again—the faintest scent of flowers.

Opening his eyes, he clutched his fists and then curled his toes. His left foot and calf burned, but thank God, he was still alive.

He never thought he'd survive the initial impact of the water, and certainly not the temperature of it. But it was much better to die in the river than at the hands of the British.

He shivered under the blankets. He might be forced into acts of valor for the sake of his country, but in his heart there was little courage. He remembered hitting the icy water off the side of the *Defiance*, but the memories after the plunge were blurry.

He'd been cold, colder than he'd ever been in his life, and he'd struggled for air even as his lungs froze within him. Death seemed imminent. It was time, he'd thought, to meet his Savior.

The next thing he remembered was a woman's voice.

He looked at the beveled glass on the window. Perhaps it was the same woman who had been sitting beside him moments ago.

He tried to push himself up on his elbows, but there was no strength left within him.

How long had he been in this room?

His pulse raced. After taking that fall, it was a miracle he was still here. The British, he hoped, thought he had perished in the river.

Now he must deliver his message before it was too late.

CHAPTER 5

A dozen people crowded into Mrs. Hester Zeigler's formal parlor. The narrow room was papered with a pale red-and-white-striped design from London and smelled like cinnamon and cloves.

Most people stood, conversing pleasantly with one another about the weather and such, but Sarah waited for the dinner meal on the settee, her leather-bound copy of *Gulliver's Travels* clutched in her lap.

She always brought a book to these weekly meals, and this one was a particular favorite among Tories. While she tolerated Mrs. Zeigler's company, she disliked these weekly Sunday gatherings immensely. Sarah suspected the woman invited her after services because she entertained notions of a future with Commodore Hammond when he returned from the West Indies.

The late Mr. Zeigler had been a good friend of Lord Dunmore's before the governor abandoned the palace and the town. Even as the political tide in Williamsburg shifted to support the Patriots, Mrs. Zeigler remained influential as a hostess and organizer of women.

It seemed that everyone in Williamsburg, of either political persuasion, wanted to be included on the list when she held a party at her fine house. Lord Dunmore attended her gatherings when he was governor, and Governor Thomas Jefferson and his wife attended them until last year, when the colony moved the capital and the governor from Williamsburg to Richmond.

Lately, Mrs. Zeigler seemed to entertain only those who supported the King's Men, and now it appeared she wanted to marry one again as well.

Even though Sarah could never imagine her father married to the widow Zeigler, it was most important for Sarah to spend time among the British sympathizers. So she attended these dinners each week without fail.

While Morah helped the other maids in the kitchen each Sunday, Sarah endured all sorts of meaningless talk from people who thought her father had lost his mind. No decent man, Mrs. Houser once said, would leave his daughter in charge of four thousand acres—as if Sarah would single-handedly ruin all her father and grandfather had built. She knew they doubted her ability, and even worse, she doubted it herself.

No one seemed to be whispering about her this afternoon. Information had begun to trickle in about the Continental Army fighting against the British occupancy in Charles Towne.

Sarah listened intently—and silently—to Mr. Pendell, a professor at the College of William & Mary, as he shared the information he'd gleaned.

"I heard they were trying to take back South Carolina," he said.

Mrs. Pendell fanned her face. "At least Washington's men aren't here."

The town doctor—Dr. Cooper—stepped forward, a black hat secured in his hands. "I wouldn't be so certain. I've heard Washington and his men might be leaving New York."

Mr. Houser put his hand on the edge of the settee, leaning

toward the others in their discussion. "It's about time our men showed the rebels in Virginia that the king is serious."

Dr. Cooper lifted his glass. "Long live King George."

"Hush," one of the women said, nodding toward the kitchen. "Not all the ears are sympathetic."

All the people in the room were Tories, also known as Loyalists. Or at least they claimed to be. It was impossible to know who was stalwart in their convictions and who would turn if Patriots took the town. With her father off fighting with the King's Men and her brother fighting against them, the people of Williamsburg weren't quite sure what to think about Sarah.

She never offered her opinion, and Mr. Pendell's wife offered hers sparingly. It was best for both of them to remain as indifferent as possible to this war.

"My dear Sarah," Mrs. Pendell said, both her arms outstretched as she approached her. She was a large woman who laughed easily and loved books almost as much as Sarah did.

After embracing Sarah, Mrs. Pendell handed over *The Old English Baron*, a novel she'd borrowed from Sarah's library three weeks ago.

"Did you enjoy it?" Sarah asked, perhaps a bit too loudly.

"Very much," Mrs. Pendell replied, eyeing the book in Sarah's lap. "Have you brought me something else to read this week?"

Sarah handed her *Gulliver's Travels*. "I fear you won't find much of interest in this one."

"Perhaps next week," Mrs. Pendell said before she tucked the book under her arm and turned to greet another guest.

Everyone in Williamsburg seemed to know the Pendells, but Sarah hadn't known Mrs. Pendell well until a year ago, when Seth informed Sarah that she and Mrs. Pendell were destined to become close friends.

Thankfully she enjoyed the woman's company, and Mrs. Pendell seemed to enjoy hers.

"Did you hear what happened to Benedict Arnold?" Dr. Cooper asked. When no one replied, he continued. "He was feeding information to the British, and when he was discovered, he ran off to the British army. Now he's an officer."

"I care not if a traitor is for the British or the rebels," Mr. Pendell declared. "Any traitor should be hanged."

Sarah swallowed and glanced over at Mrs. Pendell in spite of herself. The woman's smile remained frozen as she nodded in earnest beside her husband.

They might have to rely on deception to do their work, but they were helping deliver information to those who needed it. Information that would save lives, Sarah reminded herself. Besides, they were only conduits, so the British wouldn't discover who among them was gathering information for the Patriots.

Sarah didn't even know what the letters contained, nor to whom Mrs. Pendell delivered, but she was ready to assist in the fight for freedom however she was needed.

Sunshine poured through the dining-room windows, across the long white-cloaked table, as Lydia's father studied her face. His powdered wig, which he still wore from church that morning, matched the color of the tablecloth, and he looked as distinguished as any member of the House of Burgesses.

Father lifted his silver goblet and took a long sip of his Madeira wine before he spoke. "You have made quite a speedy recovery."

She pushed a bite of salted ham with her fork, mixing the ham with her sweet potatoes. "Aye."

He tilted his head, and the beads of sweat on his brow glistened in the light. "Dr. Cooper would be amazed."

41

"I did not sleep well last night," she said. "The fatigue over-powered me."

"Perhaps you should have remained in bed all day."

Lydia glanced across the table at her mother, who was sitting with perfect posture to Father's right. Mother dabbed the edges of her lips with her napkin before she spoke. "There is no reason to interrogate her, my dear. We should just be grateful to the Good Lord that she is well again."

Hannah raised her glass and winked at her. "Hear, hear."

Lydia clenched her heavy silver fork. When she'd hurried back from Elisha's room, she had seen Hannah's face in an upstairs window of the manor house. And she'd seen her sister lift her hand in a mock greeting.

She knew she must protect this stranger, but she hated being trapped inside this cauldron of deception. Even more, she hated that her sister knew she had been outside the house instead of in the library. If Hannah managed to keep her secret, she would make Lydia pay dearly for it.

Father cut a piece of ham and lifted it. "Your mother said you had fallen asleep."

Mother nodded. "She was curled up on the chaise lounge."

"But I checked the library prior to—"

Mother patted his hand. "You have been preoccupied, Charles."

Beside her, Hannah straightened the flatware by her plate. "A chair is a most unusual place to sleep."

Lydia shrugged. "I was tired."

Hannah smiled. "But apparently not tired enough to—"

Prudence stepped into the room, holding up a platter. "We have ginger pudding and macaroons for dessert."

Mother glanced over her shoulder, surprised. None of the servants ever announced the food. "Thank you, Prudence."

Prudence set the platter on the sideboard and turned to

42

place a silver bowl in front of Mother. "I know the pudding is your favorite, ma'am."

"Indeed it is."

Lydia flashed a smile at the maidservant for redirecting Father. Prudence had been with their family for so many years, Father would forgive her indiscretion.

Mother sampled the pudding. "Please tell Viney that it is splendid."

Prudence nodded. "Aye."

Father cleared his throat. "I have news."

Lydia sighed quietly, relieved that he had moved past the questioning about her time in the library.

Hannah lifted her spoon as Prudence put a bowl in front of her. "Do tell."

"I received a letter from Solomon Reed. His son has been commissioned a major in the British army."

Mother took a macaroon from the proffered plate. "What an extraordinary opportunity for him."

Lydia wasn't certain how extraordinary it was, considering that most British officers had to pay for such an honor, but there was no good reason to provoke Father.

"Who is Solomon Reed?" Hannah asked.

"An old friend from London." Father looked at Lydia. "You must remember him."

"I am afraid I do not."

Father sighed. "I suppose you were too young to recall everyone you met there."

They'd visited London when Lydia was twelve. Hannah would have been two. Lydia remembered the parks in London, the great river called Thames, and the older woman whom she was supposed to call Grandmother. The faintest memory remained of her parents' friends, but she didn't remember their names.

Prudence set the tray of macaroons in front of Father, but he didn't even look down at it.

"According to Solomon, Major Reed has arrived in the colonies. If I'm able to find him, perhaps we can invite him here for a visit."

Mother reached for a second macaroon. "What a splendid idea."

Hannah smiled, her blue eyes sparkling. "I'm sure he will be most interesting company."

Father looked at her. "You seem to find every bachelor interesting."

"That's because there are so few of them, Father."

Father glanced at Lydia. "I'm hoping you might find him interesting as well. Solomon's son would be a fine match."

"Indeed," Mother replied.

Lydia's eyes grew wide. It was one thing for her father to speak in general terms about her marrying a British man. It was quite another for him to pursue a specific man for her marriage. "You don't know what type of match he would be."

Hannah leaned forward. "Any Englishman would be more suitable than Seth."

Father's eyes narrowed. "You will not speak of that man at my table!"

"But Lydia is planning to marry—"

"Hannah," Mother interrupted, "your father said not to talk about him."

Hannah looked at Lydia from across the table and sniffed. "There are other things to talk about, I suppose."

She knew well that look in her sister's eyes. She was about to spill the news about seeing Lydia outside.

"There most certainly are other things to discuss," Lydia said as she turned toward her father. There was so much she wanted to ask, like who Arnold was, but then Father would inquire about where she'd heard the name and she could not tell him. It was better to steer him in a different direction, one that would trump anything Hannah said.

"Did you see the ships going upriver last night?" she asked.

He leaned so far forward that the white lawn material of his cravat brushed across the pudding. "What ships?" he demanded.

"The ones with British flags."

His spoon clattered onto the table. "Why didn't you tell me?"

"I didn't want to disturb you."

"You should have—"

"At least you know now," Mother said as she wiped the pale orange streak of pudding off his cravat. "There is no reason to badger."

Father sat back against the wooden chair and a slow smile washed across his lips. "The British are in Virginia."

"It appears so," Lydia replied.

"Where do you think they are going?" Mother asked.

Father lifted his wine again. "They must be sailing to Richmond."

Mother placed her napkin beside her plate. "Excellent news for us."

"Indeed." Father pushed back his chair and stood. Hannah left the room behind him.

Mother remained beside her at the table. "Viney said she's missing the soup bowl you used earlier."

Lydia's spine stiffened. She had rushed away so quickly from the coach house that she'd left the bowl on the basin. "I shall retrieve it for her."

Mother studied her face. "What are you hiding, Lydia?"

She hesitated. It was one thing to mislead her sister and Father, but she could never lie to her mother. Unlike Hannah, Mother knew how to keep a secret, but Lydia didn't want to pull her into the deception, not until she knew whether this stranger they were harboring was loyal to the Crown.

"Helping," she whispered, hoping her mother wouldn't pry further.

Mother sighed. "I don't suppose you're feeding a wounded animal, are you?"

Lydia shook her head.

"Then 'tis probably unwise for me to ask questions," Mother said, tempering her inquiry.

"Probably."

"Have you heard from Seth?"

She shook her head. "But I would like to go visit Sarah."

"We can't go visit," Mother said. "Not now."

"Sarah doesn't feel the same way as Seth."

"'Tis not wise," Mother insisted. "It would look like—"

"Like we are loving our neighbor," Lydia said.

"I wish it weren't so complicated." Mother wrapped Lydia's hand in hers. "You will be careful, my daughter."

"I will."

It was for the best, she supposed. A visit to her best friend would fill some of her loneliness, and she longed to hear news of Seth, but she couldn't leave the plantation until the man sleeping in Elisha's room was gone.

"You and I shall shop in Williamsburg soon. It will cheer you."

"Perhaps."

"Hopefully this Major Reed will come to Virginia. It's been too long since you have enjoyed the company of men your age."

Lydia looked down, wiggling her toes in her wet shoes. Was it possible that this Major Reed had already arrived at Caswell Hall? Perhaps he was the man she'd been sheltering outside.

"Lydia . . ."

She looked back up.

"I am certain that Viney would like the bowl back."

"Yes, Mother."

"Is it in the library?"

Lydia shook her head.

Mother sighed. "Please bring it back before one of the servants finds it."

If they found the soup bowl, they would also find the man who'd eaten from it.

Before she turned, Mother eyed the damp soup stain on Lydia's sleeve. "And you had best change your gown."

CHAPTER 6

*D*ust covered the dresser and bedpost in her brother's chamber. Lydia quietly closed the door behind her and looked around in the dim light. Mother had told the servants not to touch his room until he returned, as if Grayson would return on the morrow.

Four years had passed now, and there was still no word from her brother or even about him. How she missed him and his antics that made her laugh.

Grayson was only two years older than her, and yet she'd always thought him much wiser. He loved to solve problems, and during the early part of the war, Mother had relied heavily on him to find household items and fabrics that no one else could secure.

Someday they would have to accept that he was gone, that they might never know what had happened to him, but at present her parents refused to even discuss the disappearance of their son.

Perhaps after the war—

She had retrieved a yellow ribbon from her chamber, and in Grayson's room, she opened the wardrobe and scanned the navy-and-black breeches and waistcoats colored with light gray, sage green, and a coral that reminded her of the wildflowers that grew in their forest each spring. Her brother wouldn't mind if she used some of his clothes.

Grayson's silk stockings were in a drawer, and under his bed were two pairs of buckled shoes. She slipped out a pair to take to the stranger.

In the first months after her brother disappeared, she wondered why he—or an acquaintance of his—didn't send them a message. As the months and then years passed, she began to assume that he had passed on like Grandfather.

Before the declaration for colonial independence was published, Grayson and the senior Lord Caswell had spoken out for peace over patriotism in Williamsburg, and Grandfather advocated loyalty both to their neighbors and to a monarch. Neither man wanted war or death, but their sentiments for peace hadn't made them popular with either side.

She retrieved a tan-colored waistcoat and made a bundle of stockings, shoes, a blue-and-gray scarf, and a black cloak. As long as Mother didn't find Lydia with the clothing, she would never realize they were missing.

Father was meeting with the overseer in his office to the north of their house this morning, and last she knew, Mother was mending a dress in her chamber. She heard strains of the pianoforte in the drawing room downstairs, thankful that Hannah was occupied for the moment as well.

It was ridiculous, all this sneaking around, but her guest couldn't leave until he had decent clothing.

But then again, perhaps he wouldn't have to leave at all. If Major Reed had washed up on their shore, her parents would welcome him into their home.

Every bone in Nathan's body ached as he slowly pushed himself up from the bed again. He was almost upright, his hands balanced under his weight—but then his arms collapsed and his head crashed back onto the pillow.

His foot throbbed, and a terrible weariness seemed to chain him to this bed. He didn't know how long he had been here, but he must leave soon. He had to warn the colonists and rally the people of Virginia to defend Richmond before the newly commissioned British general, a traitor named Benedict Arnold, surprised them with an attack.

Richmond first and then Williamsburg.

He scanned the small room again. Sunlight beamed through the beveled glass and lit a cream-colored bowl beside the basin. In his last prison, he hadn't had a bed or a window—or food, for that matter. Someone had been taking good care of him here.

There was no time to linger in the comforts of this place. He must obtain a new disguise and travel to Richmond straightaway.

He sat up and forced his legs off the side of the bed. Perhaps if he could stand, the rest of his body would cooperate. He just had to make himself move.

But no matter how hard he pushed himself, he failed. It was as if his body was anchored to the bed.

How was he going to walk to Hammond Plantation if he couldn't even stand?

He fell back onto his pillow again. It was hopeless. He couldn't even walk as far as the window. He certainly couldn't stop Benedict Arnold from taking Virginia, nor could he deliver his message.

Something shuffled outside his door, and he covered his legs with the blanket. Closing his eyes, he prayed silently that the person on the other side of the door was a friend.

The hinges groaned as the door opened and footsteps padded toward him. For a moment, all was still.

A shadow crossed over him, as if someone was inches above, examining his face. He kept his breath steady, hoping the visitor would think he was asleep.

Did this person intend to harm him or care for him? Or perhaps he or she was just curious about who he was.

The person shuffled away, and he opened his eyes ever so slightly to see a woman in the room, her back to him as she rummaged through his coat.

He propped himself on his elbows, his mind racing. "Those are my things."

She gasped, whirling around to face him.

Her light chestnut hair hung loosely under her cap, and her eyes were the lavender color of the Virginia bluebells on his uncle's plantation. In any other situation he might be intrigued, smitten even, but he didn't care how pretty this woman was. She had no right to be going through his private affairs.

He sat up straighter. "What exactly are you searching for?"

Lydia swayed on her feet, her heart pounding. The stranger in Elisha's bed was awake, staring back at her.

She hung his coat back on the peg and took a shaky step toward him. He searched her face like Father had done earlier, as if he was trying to determine whether she would speak the truth, but she had no reason to hide anything from this man.

"I was looking for your name."

He edged back down to his pillow and rolled over to face her.

"What do you want—" A harsh cough interrupted his words. "What do you want with my name?"

She scooted the stool close to his bedside, and the ruffles and lace of her dress covered it as she sat. His English was educated, but it was not the British English she'd heard in London. Still, she had to inquire. "Are you Major Reed?"

The man sighed and then looked back toward the window. "My name is Nathan."

When he didn't offer his last name, she inquired again. "But are you Nathan Reed?"

He pressed his lips together in such a way that made her wonder. Either he didn't want her to know his name or he knew a man by the same name. A man he disliked.

"How do you know Major Reed?" he asked.

She shrugged.

He struggled again to sit up on his pillow. She leaned forward to help, but he rejected her assistance as he scooted himself up to a sitting position. "How long have I been here?"

"Since last night. I found you on the riverbank of our plantation."

"What is the name of your home?" he demanded.

"Caswell Hall."

His eyes closed. "I was hoping—" he began and then stopped, looking at her again. "Who are your neighbors?"

"The Webb family lives to the west, on the other side of the Chickahominy River, and the Hammonds own the plantation to the east." She paused. "Are you acquainted with either of them?"

He lifted his head and then rotated his body, placing his feet on the floor. "I must leave right away."

She watched him for a moment as he struggled to stand, but he wavered. She grabbed his arm and helped him return safely to the bed before he injured himself further. "There will be no leaving until you heal."

"You don't understand."

"I am aware that Arnold is coming."

He turned toward her, his eyes wide. "How do you know?"

"You kept saying it in your sleep."

His gaze wandered back to the window.

She picked up the bundle off the floor and set it on the edge of his bed before returning to her seat on the stool. "Here are shoes for you, and a waistcoat."

He eyed the bundle. "Where did you find the clothing?"

"The clothes belong to my brother." She held out the yellow ribbon. "And this belongs to me."

"Will your brother not miss his clothing?"

She shook her head, her voice barely a whisper. "I don't think so."

He eyed her with curiosity. "Where is he?"

She paused. "Grayson has been missing for four years."

"I'm sorry." He hesitated. "Is it because of the war?"

"I believe so."

"It's a brutal affair." He pushed himself back up on his elbows. "Which side do you find yourself on?"

"The side my grandfather was on." She paused. "He wanted peace."

"Aye. That is what most of us wish for, isn't it?"

She nodded. "It will come soon, will it not?"

"I pray it will."

She smoothed her hands over the lace on her gown. "Are you a rebel or a Loyalist?"

His shoulders straightened. "I am a Patriot."

"I thought you might be . . ." She slumped back against the wall. "You were on a British ship."

"I was a guest."

She blinked. "A willing one?"

"Hardly." He shifted his leg. "How far are we from Williamsburg?"

"About four miles."

"I don't suppose I could hire a horse to ride."

She cocked her head. "Do you have someone waiting for you?"

"In a manner of speaking."

"There is no livery near here." She studied him for a moment, wondering whom he needed to visit in Williamsburg. "Perhaps I could send a message to your friends."

He shook his head. "I fear I must deliver this message on my own."

"Lydia?" She heard Hannah call outside.

Why was her sister looking for her?

Lydia stood and backed toward the side of the room, away from the window. The finger to her lips warned him to be quiet, but he probably didn't need a warning.

"Where are you?" Hannah called, terribly close to the room. "I know you are out here."

Protocol demanded that family members not frequent the quarters of their servants, but Hannah seemed more concerned with Lydia's secret than protocol at the moment.

If her sister opened this door, there would be nothing Lydia could do. Not only would her sister find this man, she would find Lydia in his chamber. Father's heart might give out with that news.

She held her breath, praying silently that Hannah would continue searching for her on the other side of the building.

Seconds passed, and she glanced over at Nathan. He'd covered his head with the pillow, as if Hannah wouldn't see him when she walked into the room. Any other time it might have been funny, but Lydia couldn't find much humor in their plight.

If Hannah did open the door, hopefully she would see only a hump of bedcovers and think Elisha was ill in bed.

Lydia stepped toward the door, listening. When she didn't hear Hannah's voice, she propped open the door and glanced both ways.

"Good-bye," she whispered as she reached for the bowl beside the basin.

The sooner this man left the plantation, the better it would be for all of them.

54

CHAPTER 7

*S*arah dipped her pen into the inkwell and began to write in tiny lettering that only the eyes of youth could read. She had no choice but to write small. She could ill afford to buy any more paper, and even if she could afford it, it was almost impossible to obtain.

Before he left, Father had stashed a large box of linen paper among the other supplies in the basement. She could do without tea or sugar, but with her family gone and most of her friends occupied, she needed the companionship of her pen and paper. Now that her supply was dwindling, she cherished it even more.

In the afternoon light, she bled her heart onto the linen, pouring out all that was inside her. The compounding doubts of how much longer she could manage the plantation, of how she longed to travel somewhere— anywhere—beyond Williams-burg. And she wrote of how she loved Grayson. Oh, how she had loved him and still did to this day.

One day, when they found Grayson, perhaps she would give him the letters so he would know she had never forgotten him. That her heart had never loved another.

Everyone talked of Seth and Lydia marrying the plantations together. No one knew—not even Grayson—how much she had cared for him. He thought of her as Seth's younger sister, the girl who loved to dream.

They were both dreamers—not knowing or even caring a whit about how they would actually pay for a voyage around the world. He once told her he could secure her a passage to Europe or the West Indies or wherever she wanted to go, and she never doubted in his ability to do it.

She dipped her pen again and wrote how she missed him, how she anxiously awaited his return. She wrote the same thing in each letter and pretended the ending would be like the endings in many of the novels she and Mrs. Pendell exchanged. Where good triumphed over evil. Freedom triumphed over tyranny. And the man she longed for returned.

Wind beat branches against the windows, and the old house creaked. She signed her letter as she always did.

Madam Knight

The woman who longed to wander.

She sprinkled pounce on the ink and let it dry before she put her letter into a box and hid it behind two books on the shelf. She never said anything specific about her friendship with Mrs. Pendell in her letters to Grayson, in case someone discovered the letters. Nor did she tell him how she was assisting the Patriots.

It would be dark within the hour, and she would check then to see if the courier had come. Thomas told her there had been whisperings about more British soldiers coming into Virginia.

It was strange that she hadn't received a message about their arrival.

∾

"I know you're hiding something," Hannah whispered.

Lydia pulled blue thread slowly through the canvas sampler in her lap. "Whatever do you mean?"

She had visited Nathan only twice in the past week, in the evenings when Hannah was preoccupied, so she wouldn't jeopardize the life she had helped save. In her absence, Prudence and Elisha had cared well for him, but this morning Prudence said she feared Nathan was not eating enough.

Somehow Lydia would need to obtain more food.

"Why have you been frequenting the coach house?" Hannah asked.

Lydia looked up from her sampler. Mother might be embroidering a pillowcase nearby, but whispering in return would only make her seem guilty. "I have not been frequenting any place. I have been taking evening walks."

Hannah tilted her head. "You never take walks."

She shrugged. "I have decided to take up a new hobby."

Lydia turned the sampler. The scene was emerging of the river with trees along the bank. Eventually she would stitch Caswell Hall into the picture and then she would hang it in her bedchamber.

Father rushed into the room. "I have more news."

"What is it?" Mother demanded of him.

"The British—" he began and then stopped to take a deep breath. "They have taken Richmond."

The women all stared back at him.

"This is good news," he prompted as he sat in the chair across from them.

Mother spoke first. "Why, of course it is, dear. I'm glad they are close."

Lydia swallowed hard. "What happened?"

"Governor Jefferson refused to meet their demands, so they took over the town."

"Where is the governor?" Lydia asked.

"He fled along with most of the rebels," Father replied. "Unfortunately they managed to take a good bit of gunpowder and food supplies with them."

"The British will find their stash," Mother said confidently.

Father nodded. "I'm told that Solomon's son is among the army now in Richmond."

"If they are so close—" Mother placed the embroidered pillowcase on the table. "It would be beneficial to remind a British officer that we have remained loyal."

"Indeed," Father replied.

"But we must be cautious," Mother continued.

There had been rumors of British soldiers carousing and wrecking the houses where they lodged. Entertaining a host of soldiers might compromise their daughters' virtue, and if they decided to cause trouble, it would leave the entire plantation in disarray.

"I believe I shall send an invitation for Major Reed alone."

"Please do," Hannah said with a clap.

Lydia didn't clap, but neither was she opposed to the idea of a visit.

She had no intention of marrying this man, but it had been so long since they'd entertained. They would all welcome the company.

Father turned toward Lady Caswell. "The servants must prepare Grayson's room."

She secured her needle in her pincushion. "I don't know—"

He took his wife's hand in his. "It is time. We must provide Major Reed with hospitality meant for a loyal subject of the king."

Lydia's mind raced. Surely her mother wouldn't notice the few items of clothing that had gone missing.

Mother sighed. "None of us must tell our neighbors that we are entertaining the British."

Hannah didn't seem to hear her. "I wonder if he is dashing."

"You are too young to be thinking such thoughts," Father replied. "But Lydia—"

She shook her head. "I'm not interested."

Father didn't seem to hear her. "You and Solomon's son played well together when we visited London."

She didn't remember him; she'd played with dozens of children on their trip to England. "That does not mean we are suited for one another."

"Once you make his acquaintance again, that will change," Father said.

Lydia pushed the thread through her sampler again. "You and Seth will make amends when this war is over."

"I will never make amends with that man," Father said. "I will shoot him if he tries to step on my property."

Mother reached for Father's arm, resting her hand lightly on his sleeve. "Let us not talk of shooting, Charles."

"But I want an Englishman to take over the care of Caswell Hall!"

Mother patted his arm. "We can discuss it later."

"This war will be finished soon," Father declared. "And then we shall have a wedding."

Lydia groaned.

But at least he had stopped talking about shooting.

Nathan clung to the windowsill as he looked out at moonlight spread across the rugged brick buildings on the plantation. He had been stranded in this room for a good week now, failing miserably in his job as a courier.

From the moment he heard about the planned attack on Virginia's capital, he'd wanted to deliver his message and then ride into Richmond, warning the militia of what was to come, but his body had refused to cooperate. His foot was healing, but his left calf still throbbed from where he'd sprained it, and his legs were shaky.

His uncle would be disappointed at his failure.

The British had surely landed by now, and the questions of what was happening outside these walls plagued him at night.

Were the people of Richmond fighting? Or had they succumbed? He hoped to God that they kept fighting. Without every American—man and woman—willing to participate, they would never win this war.

He wished he could give Lydia his message to deliver, but even though she treated him with kindness, she was still a stranger. He could never trust her with this message.

Fire burned up his leg as he tried to take another step. Even if he couldn't walk far, at least he could get out of bed.

He'd been ill before embarking on the British vessel, but he had refused to let his fever stop him from doing his work. Once he was onboard, he heard the men questioning his loyalties. Even with his feigned accent and disguise, the officers suspected —and rightly so—that he was insincere.

Once the ships were underway and the British began talking about putting him in chains, he knew he had no choice. He would either die on the ship or he would die delivering his message. He preferred the second option.

With the bumpy waves, it hadn't been difficult to convince the guard that he was seasick. No one had suspected that he would jump into the icy river, and he'd jumped as close to the Hammond plantation as he could.

Unfortunately, he washed up at the wrong place.

He didn't know what the sealed message in his leather pouch contained, but his uncle was relying on him to deliver it. Since he'd been appointed to work as a scout and courier, he'd never once failed to deliver a message, and he didn't intend to fail now.

It was late, probably midnight by now, and Elisha hadn't returned to the room. Most nights Elisha slept on a blanket on the floor beside Nathan, but sometimes he didn't come back. Nathan didn't ask where the man slept those nights. He suspected an empty stall or the back of one of the coaches.

Prudence had been faithful to bring him food in the mornings, and Elisha brought him wood for the fire each evening, but Nathan enjoyed Lydia's visits most of all. Even though he was a Patriot, she cared well for him, and each time she came, he wished she could linger a bit longer. Yet he well understood how much she risked even with the briefest of visits.

He lay down on his bed and slept. He didn't know how much time passed, but when he awakened, Lydia was sitting again on the chair beside his bed. She had a cloth napkin with bread in her lap, and he could see the compassion in her eyes.

For a moment, he wished he saw something else there. Like admiration. Instead of a man, it seemed she saw him as a wounded animal, a puppy.

"I thought you might like some food." She held out a piece of bread and he thanked her. "Prudence says you're not eating enough."

"I am eating as much as I can."

"'Tis not enough to build your strength."

"I promise you, I am more anxious to leave here than you are to be rid of me."

"That is not what I mean—"

He took a bite of the bread. "You have been a most gracious host, but I must leave soon."

She nodded. "The British have taken Richmond."

He groaned. It was as he feared. "Did the Patriots fight?"

"Not well." She swallowed. "But they moved most of their supplies before the British could confiscate them."

He pushed himself up with his elbows and slid his legs over the side of the bed. "I must go."

He stood and tried to walk to the door, but his foot failed him. When he stumbled, she caught him and helped him back to the bed.

He stared at the window, humiliated. He couldn't think of anything much worse than a lovely young woman catching him before he fell.

A shadow crossed over her face. "There is something else I must tell you."

"What is it?"

"I fear it will be very poor tidings for you."

He took a deep breath. Only a woman would torment him so. A man would simply deliver the news and be done with it. "You do not have to cushion it, Miss Caswell."

She looked a bit startled at the use of her name, but he knew it well. Elisha and Prudence reminded him regularly as to why they cared for him.

"My father has done something—" She swallowed. "He has invited a British officer to be a guest in our home."

"Major Reed?"

At her nod, he groaned again. Dalton Reed was the man who'd questioned Nathan's loyalty on the ship. If he was discovered, he would never be able to convince the man that his loyalty rested with the king.

"I fear for my family's safety," she said.

"I will not let them harm you or your family."

"I know you mean well—"

He put his feet on the floor again. "The moment I can walk away, I'll leave."

"Thank you."

He shook his head. "I would not have survived without your care."

She stood. "I am glad you lived."

"Even if I am a rebel?"

"I see you only as a brother, not as a rebel."

He smiled as she left the room. At least she hadn't said "puppy."

CHAPTER 8

*S*arah yanked open the swinging door and rushed inside the stable. Thomas was supposed to have checked the door last night to make sure it was secure, but when she looked out her window at first light, the white door was banging in the wind.

Either Thomas had forgotten, or someone had paid them a visit during the night.

The stable was eerily quiet inside, void of the stomping of hooves and nickering that usually greeted her entrance. Their stalls were empty, the horses gone.

She kicked a bale of hay, and dried grass scattered in the air and across the muddy floor. There had been rumors of thieves roaming the countryside, stealing horses, but she thought their house was too far from the main road to be disturbed.

This was exactly why she shouldn't manage the plantation. Her father and Seth probably would have guarded the stable alongside several of their Negroes, but it hadn't even occurred to her to have several of their Negroes stand guard.

She had allowed herself to become distracted.

Leaning back against the wall, she wrapped her arms over

her chest. She'd already sold all but six of their best horses to purchase needed supplies. Now those horses were gone too.

How was she supposed to deliver messages to Mrs. Pendell now? And how could she till their land this spring? Between the thieves and the soldiers and her own ineptness, it would be nigh impossible to keep this plantation in order until her father returned.

Even if she had the money to buy new horses, there were none to be had. The King's Men bought—or stole—any available livestock.

"We'll track them down."

Sarah turned to see Thomas, his musket in hand. He looked brave enough to take on an entire band of outlaws, but with his arthritic knees, she knew it pained him to walk even the perimeter of the property. There was no way he could track down the horse thieves on foot. It wasn't like the thieves would stop along the road for tea.

"Thank you, Thomas, but they are probably halfway to South Carolina by now."

"I will gather up some men in town—"

She shook her head. "It is too far, and I need you here."

"But—"

"Please check the rest of our property to see if anything else is amiss." Father had left her in charge of the plantation, but he'd told Thomas to watch over her. Still, she must protect Thomas as well. He had no choice but to respect her decision.

He nodded, backing toward the door. "I will check right now."

Turning, she pressed her fingers against her temples as she hurried toward the house.

She glanced at the railing like she always did, but there was still no ribbon. It didn't matter much now. Without her horses, she had no means to take a message into town.

Leaning back against the doorframe, she closed her eyes and

listened to the gentle hum of Negroes singing as they worked in the washhouse. Her responsibility toward them weighed heavier on her than anything else at the plantation.

The Hammonds weren't like some families who starved or beat their Negroes. Every one of their Negroes was clothed and fed. As long as they did their work, their men and women had nothing to fear.

The thought of selling a single one of their house servants or field slaves was heartbreaking to her, but with the storehouses nearly bare, the flour supply quickly diminishing, and now the horses gone, she might have no choice. The sale of one Negro could feed the rest of them for weeks.

She sighed, weary from this war, weary of running a plantation where people must be bought and sold.

Opening her eyes, she surveyed the land Father had left in her care.

If only he would come home and resume his role of managing their plantation.

If only she could travel away as well.

But if she set sail from here, she knew that she might never return.

Prudence tightened the laces on Lydia's stays and helped her dress in an embroidered jacket with lace cuffs and an ivory petticoat. After brushing Lydia's hair, Prudence separated the locks and slathered them with a fragrant pomade smelling of cardamom and honey. Then she rolled the strands over a metal rod and held the rod over a candle to create tight curls that cascaded over Lydia's shoulders and down her back.

The household was in an uproar, servants and family alike scrambling to prepare for their important guest. Two hours earlier, as the family ate breakfast, a courier arrived with a message from Major Reed. Not only did he intend to visit Caswell Hall, but he planned to call that very day.

Hannah was ecstatic about entertaining a British officer and a gentleman. Lydia would have been excited as well, if she hadn't hidden a rebel in their coach house. It was poor luck on her behalf that she'd rescued a man her father considered an enemy.

She might only want to mend wounds, but Father would have no appreciation for her sentiments. Mother might understand—Mother would understand—but she would never directly oppose Father's convictions.

Lydia had no desire to become entangled in the affairs of this war. She wanted reconciliation. She wanted the colonists to respect the country where her parents were born . . . but that didn't mean she would let a rebel starve.

As long as she kept Major Reed away from the coach house, everything would be fine. There was no reason for the major to visit the coach house anyway, and if he happened to feel inclined to see their carriages, she would personally guide him so that he wouldn't accidentally stumble upon their hidden guest. If he found Nathan—

She shivered.

"Are you cold, Miss?" Prudence asked.

She shook her head. "It was just a chill."

Prudence stepped over to the fire and stirred it with the iron poker.

"Do you remember the last time we had guests?" Lydia asked.

Prudence shook her head as she reached for the metal rod once more. "It seems like a lifetime ago."

"It was the celebration for Twelfth Night two years ago." Lydia studied her image in the looking glass. "That was the last time I saw Seth."

Prudence looped another section of Lydia's hair around the

rod and held it over the candle. "We all miss Master Seth."

She wished she could say she missed Seth as well.

She had been just eighteen when the colonists declared their independence, so she scarcely remembered the balls and parties her parents hosted before the war—but Hannah had only been nine when the war began. While Hannah hadn't formally attended a ball, Lydia knew that she had spied on plenty of them from behind the servants' door in the great hall. Father had built the door to balance the appearance of the walnut door on the other side of the fireplace, and then he added a narrow hallway behind it to lead to the servants' staircase.

Lydia knew well the crack that lined the side of the door. When she was young, she and Sarah would spy on the balls as well, longing to be part of the frivolities. The view of the room was narrow through the crack, but she could hear the music and laughter and the stomping of feet on the wood. As girls, she and Sarah had often pretended they were guests as well.

It wasn't proper to talk of such things while there was a war, but she did miss the dancing. And she missed her long visits with Sarah.

When Prudence finished curling Lydia's tresses, she secured both sides with horn combs. Lydia turned her head and admired her maid's handiwork in the vanity glass. "It looks lovely."

Prudence smiled, and the wrinkles under her eyes crinkled like paper. "Major Reed will be smitten."

"I have no interest in smiting any man—except perhaps Seth." Lydia smiled, but when she looked back at the glass, she saw pity in Prudence's reflection. Seth might not return to marry her, but she still hated being pitied. "You needn't feel sorrow for me."

Prudence placed the brush back into the top drawer of the dressing table. "Sorrow is what one should feel when another is hurting."

Lydia forced a smile. "We should be feeling sorrow for Seth and the other men who are fighting."

Opening her jewelry box, Lydia chose a necklace of gold beads and held it around her throat. Prudence clasped it and then added matching earrings before she glanced over her shoulder, at the door still closed behind them. "Yesterday Joshua asked me why I've been visiting Elisha's room."

Lydia's heart sank. A rumor like that would spread like a grass fire. It wouldn't pay to have the servants talking about Prudence and Elisha, nor did she want to soil Prudence's reputation by asking her to visit one of their Negroes' rooms at night.

"Perhaps you can leave the food for Elisha to take to his room."

"Nathan must leave soon," Prudence said firmly.

"He is nearly healed." Lydia examined the necklace in the looking glass. The gold color didn't look right with her dark red dress. Or perhaps it was the dark bags under her eyes from the late night that altered her appearance.

"Did Nathan tell you his surname?"

"He did not," she said, reaching for a string of milky pearls.

Prudence changed her necklace and earrings. "I fear you are beginning to care for him."

"As a brother, perhaps, but no more."

In the looking glass, she saw Prudence raise her eyebrows in question.

"There is nothing more," she insisted.

The door to her bedchamber opened, and Prudence picked up a pot with rice powder. Hannah sauntered into the room, a smile on her face.

Lydia looked at her in the glass. "Did the major arrive?"

"No, but surely he will soon."

"I fear you will be disappointed," Lydia said.

Her sister had dressed early and spent the morning traveling from one window to another as they waited for the major.

"How could I be disappointed?" Hannah paced behind the vanity, and it wearied Lydia to watch her.

"If you do not stop moving, you shall be too tired to entertain."

Hannah shook her head. "I couldn't possibly be too tired."

"Well, you are exhausting me."

Hannah lowered herself into the upholstered chair next to Lydia. "You are still hiding something, and I want to know what it is."

Lydia's eyebrows spiked. "Why would I hide something from you?"

Hannah glanced at Prudence as she brushed the rice powder on Lydia's cheeks and forehead. "Do you not think she's hiding something?"

Prudence kept her eyes on Lydia's neck. "You girls have hidden all sorts of things from me since you were old enough to walk."

Hannah planted her hands on her narrow hips. "My sister has been carrying around this secret for a good week, and I intend to find out what it is."

Lydia rolled her eyes. "You need an occupation, Hannah."

"I have no problem occupying myself." Hannah looked out the window and turned back to her. "It is you who seems to require an occupation."

"You are talking in riddles."

"I have seen you visiting a certain Negro."

Prudence coughed, backing away. "With your permission, miss, I think I will take my leave."

"Of course," Lydia said. When the door closed, she turned toward her sister. "How dare you insinuate—"

Hannah shrugged. "It seems as if you have spent an awful lot of time near the coach house as of late."

"I—"

"Do not be coy, Lydia. Father may be distracted by this war, but you cannot pretend with me." Hannah paused. "What exactly are you doing over there?"

"Nothing that concerns you."

"I would prefer to judge whether it is my concern."

"You need not know everything, Hannah."

"I disagree." She laughed. "Knowledge is the prelude to power."

Lydia looked out at the gray sky. If nothing else, her sister was tenacious. She wouldn't stop until she found the source of Lydia's interest.

With the curiosity of their servants and now her sister—and the imminent arrival of a British officer—she must determine a way for Nathan to leave the plantation right away, even if he wasn't well enough to walk.

She pressed her lips together as she stared at the river. Where was she supposed to take him? And how could she transport an injured man?

She turned her head back toward her sister. "What would you do if Seth paid us a visit?"

Hannah shrugged. "Probably fetch Father."

"But Father would have him shot."

"After what he has done, he deserves to be shot."

"Hannah!"

"'Tis the truth." Hannah pushed her floral slippers out from under her dress. "Did Seth pay you a visit?"

"Of course not."

"Then why do you ask?"

Lydia brushed more powder under her eyes. "Right and wrong can be muddied during a war."

"You are talking like a rebel."

"I am doing nothing of the sort!"

"Well, you had better not let Father hear you talk about a

muddied right and wrong when he's convinced there is nothing muddy about this war."

The door to her bedchamber swung open again, and Prudence called to them. "A carriage is coming."

Hannah clapped her hands. "Is the major inside?"

"I do not know, miss."

She twirled. "Let us have no more talk of rebels or a war."

They might not talk of it, but Lydia couldn't stop thinking about how to help Nathan escape before Father or their British guest took a shot at him.

After Hannah slipped by, Prudence stopped Lydia. "Lady Caswell helped us clean Master Grayson's room."

Lydia groaned.

"When Major Reed leaves, she would like to have a word with you."

CHAPTER 9

*H*er head held high, Lydia slowly moved down the hall to the staircase. Hannah had already disappeared ahead of her, running down the steps.

Her sister had little appreciation for the finer arts of the gentler sex. A lady was never supposed to rush—or at least, she should never look as if she was rushing. Mother kept hoping that experience would tame Hannah and turn her into a lady.

Lydia had her doubts.

Inside the family's drawing room, eight wingback chairs and two couches were arranged in small clusters. The walls were papered with mint-and-white flowers, and a tall window framed the front lawn of their house. An elegant fireplace served as the focal point of the room, adorned with blue-and-white tiles, a limestone mantel, and ornate flowers carved into the overmantel. Plaster columns rose to the ceiling on each side.

Her parents were already seated in the drawing room, and Mother directed Lydia to sit beside her. As Father argued with Hannah about her conduct while Major Reed was here, Mother whispered to her, "There are several items missing from

Grayson's room—his shoes and favorite waistcoat and the scarf I knitted for him before he left."

Lydia smoothed her hand over her gown, suppressing her groan. It had never occurred to her that Mother might have knitted the blue-and-gray scarf.

"Can you retrieve them as you did the bowl?" Mother asked.

"I'm afraid I cannot."

Mother wove her slender fingers together before looking back at her, and Lydia could see the fear in her eyes. "I fear I will lose you too, Lydia."

Lydia put her arm around her mother's shoulders. How could she assure her of anything?

Hannah sauntered toward them, announcing as she walked, "I am going to look outside."

Mother stiffened. "You may not."

"What is the point of having a window—?"

"Hush," Mother insisted.

"I will not hush."

Father faced her. "Must I find a muzzle for you?"

When Joshua walked into the room, Hannah swirled toward him. "Is he—" she started, but Lydia reached out and took her sister's hand, squeezing it to silence her.

She stopped Hannah just in time. Several steps behind their manservant was a clean-shaven man wearing a powdered wig and a scarlet coat adorned with white lace and shiny pewter buttons.

He was shorter than she'd imagined, standing only as tall as Father's chin, but he held a tall hat in his hands. A black belt crossed over his chest in the shape of an X, and his smile was stiff, as if he hadn't been in the practice of smiling lately.

Father greeted him and then introduced him to the ladies.

Major Reed gave the slightest bow. "It is a pleasure to see each of you again."

"I believe you were but fifteen or sixteen when we saw you last," Father said.

The major nodded. "I remember your visit well. My father said I must call on you if I came to Virginia."

Mother stood and reached for both his hands, welcoming him. "Lord Reed has been a good friend to my husband."

The major bowed again.

Mother released his hands and pointed him toward the leather chair next to Lydia. "You must tell us all the news of London."

"I'm afraid, my dear lady, that my news is quite old. It has been six months past since I left our beloved country."

"Please, tell us what you remember," Mother implored.

A housemaid placed a platter with the silver tea set on the round table between them as Mother soaked up Major Reed's news from Great Britain like a sponge that had been sunning too long on the shore. Lydia didn't know any of the families of which he spoke, but she enjoyed hearing his stories.

Mother nodded toward Lydia to serve the tea, and she carefully poured tea into five cups and handed out each one. Then she offered Major Reed milk, sugar, and a biscuit. He took all three before enjoying a long sip of the tea. Then he set his cup back on his saucer.

"It has been much too long since I had the pleasure of a good cup of tea."

Father reached for a biscuit. "We serve tea only to our most distinguished guests. If word got out that we have English tea—"

"I shall keep your secret," Major Reed said and then picked up his cup, slowly draining it before setting it back on the saucer again. "If I might have another cup . . ."

"Most certainly," Mother replied as she refilled his cup. Even if the Patriots didn't have political convictions against drinking English tea, it was almost impossible to obtain. Mother refused to say where she found hers, though Lydia guessed at her supplier. She kept her mother's secrets just as she hoped Mother would harbor hers.

Lydia sat back against the firm seat, her teacup in hand.

"Have you news from Richmond?" Father asked.

"Aye," the major said before he took another sip. "General Arnold and our men have taken the capital under British control."

Lydia took a deep breath, trying to make her voice sound cheery. Naive. "I have not heard of this General Arnold."

"I don't suppose you would, with your devotion to the Crown." Major Reed straightened the belt around his chest, and she wondered if he felt as uncomfortable in his uniform as he looked. "Benedict Arnold was a commander with the Continental Army. During his time with the rebels, he was able to garner important intelligence for the British."

Lydia's lower lip dropped. Father might have heard of the man, but she hadn't heard of him until Nathan spoke his name. "How did he relay the information to the British army?"

"By hiding it in fancy letters, all written in code."

"Code?"

Major Reed nodded, seemingly impressed with himself for bearing this knowledge. "And some of the messages were written in invisible ink. They had to use a special wash to decipher them."

"Fascinating," Lydia said. "How does one obtain invisible ink?"

"Invisible ink?" Hannah coughed. "Dear me, sister, you sound like you want to become a spy."

"I want no such thing!"

"I am sure you do not." Mother's words were followed by a laugh that didn't sound the least bit amused.

Father set down his cup. "I can assure you that our daughters have no interest in spying—or in politics."

Lydia started to retort, but Father silenced her with his eyes. What was he protecting her from? Major Reed was an old family friend.

The major laughed. "At the moment, I have no interest in politics either."

Hannah's smile was forced. "May we please move on to a more pleasant topic?"

"Certainly," Lydia replied, even though she wanted to hear more about the ink.

Major Reed's smug smile reminded her of the picture Father kept of King George. "I enjoy conversing about almost any subject."

Hannah took one of the biscuits and nibbled on it. "Was your sea crossing bearable?"

"It was tolerable except for the fierce storms we encountered halfway across the Atlantic."

Hannah clapped her hands together. "How exciting."

"My men and I prefer the land to sea."

How ironic that he would be sleeping in her brother's room. Grayson had always preferred the sea.

"How many do you command?" Mother asked.

"One hundred and twenty soldiers."

Hannah's eyes grew wide as she sipped her tea. "That is remarkable."

He leaned in as if he were confiding in them. "Most days I am more nursemaid than commander."

"Will you be nursing your troops in Richmond for long?" Lydia asked.

Slowly he turned his head, his gaze settling briefly on each one of them before he turned to the next person. Once he had examined each face, he lowered his voice. "This is the strictest confidence."

"Of course," Father said, and the three women nodded their heads.

"We will only be in Richmond for a few weeks." He paused. "When our reinforcements arrive, we will be taking Williamsburg as well."

Tears welled in Father's eyes, and he turned away from them, wiping his cheeks with his handkerchief. A victory in Williamsburg might, in part, avenge the death of his father.

"Will they destroy the plantations?" Father asked.

"Not of those who remain loyal."

"I have had to remain quiet, to spare the rest of my family," Father said. "But you know where my loyalties rest."

"Our army will keep you safe."

Mother set her dainty cup on the saucer. "We've heard stories of the British stealing animals and crops for food."

The major's pride seemed to quell. "They are not supposed to steal, but some of our men disobey their orders."

Mother poured him another cup of tea. "We will rely on you, Major Reed, to protect our affairs."

Major Reed nodded slowly, brushing his hands over his breeches. "Most assuredly."

Father leaned forward. "You may stay with us however long you'd like."

Major Reed studied the contents of the drawing room as if he were noting the details of a fine painting. "Some of my officers are in need of shelter."

Mother glanced over at Father, and Lydia knew precisely what she was thinking. They couldn't refuse the man, though. There might be trouble if they didn't offer their hospitality.

"With a bit of notice," Mother said, "we will do our best to accommodate your officers."

"Splendid! I need accommodations for at least six of them." There was no request in his tone. Clearly he was used to commanding.

"You would be welcomed as a guest in our home, and we could house your men in our other buildings, so that . . ."

Father's voice trailed off as if he were searching for a reason the men couldn't stay inside Caswell Hall.

Mother finished his sentence. "So that we might prepare the house for your meetings and recreation."

"Of course," Major Reed said.

Lydia's heart began to race. "But what about our Negroes?"

"They will stay on the top floor of the house. Temporarily." Father turned back toward the major. "We have a dozen beds in our servants' quarters and can offer you fresh linens and food. You will find it much more accommodating than our attic."

"That would be more than acceptable."

Mother smiled with relief. "When should we expect your men?"

"Actually—" Major Reed began, but he was interrupted by Joshua opening the doors again.

He cleared his throat. "Master Caswell."

"Yes, Joshua?"

"We have some additional—" He hesitated. "We have more visitors on the front lawn."

Major Reed stood. "Perhaps my men have already arrived."

After the major departed, silence permeated the room as the Caswell family collectively tried to contemplate the turn of events. Then Hannah hopped out of her chair and raced toward the window.

She clapped her hands. "Come look at this."

Lydia's legs shook as she stood. It would be hard enough to try to hide Nathan from Major Reed, but to have a half dozen of his men snooping around their grounds as well . . .

One of them would surely discover her secret.

∽

Nathan swigged water from Elisha's canteen and brushed his mouth with his sleeve. Then he handed the canteen back to the man who had shared so much with him. "I thank you."

Elisha screwed on the lid before passing Nathan a small package wrapped in brown paper and knotted with twine.

"What is it?" Nathan asked.

"Some fruit leather and nuts and a corn cake for your journey." Elisha brushed his hands over his legs. "If you hike east about a half mile along the bank, you'll come to a stream that snakes back onto the Hammonds' land. About twenty paces north from the mouth, you'll find a canoe hidden in the trees."

Nathan pulled the package closer to him as he repeated his thanks.

The window was covered with a blanket, and Elisha opened the door to retrieve something else outside. It was a cane, carved and polished.

Nathan gripped the head of the cane. With his foot bandaged tight and the cane, he might actually have a chance of stealing away tonight. "Did you make this?"

Elisha nodded. "I used to carve toys for Master Grayson when he was a boy."

"He must have admired you greatly for it."

"Perhaps he did . . . until he was thirteen." Elisha seemed to contemplate his words. "Then Master Caswell made him whip me."

The thought of anyone beating this man—a friend who had helped save him—made Nathan's gut clench. "Why would he do that?"

Elisha shrugged. "It was long ago."

"If only—" He couldn't remedy what had happened then, but perhaps there was something he could do now. He lifted the cane. "I wish I could repay you for your kindness."

Elisha lowered his voice when he spoke again. "I've caught wind of a rumor."

"Rumors can be dangerous."

"But this one—" He glanced over at the door and then back at Nathan. "I'm told the British will free any Negro who arrives in their camp."

"'Tis not a rumor."

Elisha's eyes grew wider.

"They will free you, but they will require you to fight alongside them."

"I'm willing to fight for my freedom, as the Americans are."

Nathan brushed lint off his trousers. It was a strange world. The Americans fought for their own freedom while the British offered freedom to the runaway Negro slaves. "If the British take you along with the plantation, though, they'll sell you as property."

"Aye." Elisha nodded and sighed heavily as he sat on the stool. "It is what I feared."

Nathan had considered many arguments and approaches for freeing the colonists from the tyranny of the Crown, but he hadn't thought much about the freedom of slaves from their masters.

His uncle owned more than a hundred slaves, but unlike many slaveholders, Uncle George treated his Negroes well. In fact, he recently vowed to never again buy or sell another man or woman.

Looking at this man beside him, the man who'd cared for him along with Miss Caswell and her maid, Nathan understood his uncle's decision. He couldn't imagine buying or selling someone like Elisha, a man as dignified as any he'd known. His uncle might vow never to buy or sell another slave, but Nathan vowed to himself right there never to own one.

He leaned back against the wall. "What would you do if you were free, Elisha?"

"After I fought?"

Nathan nodded. "After the war."

"I'd free my wife and son."

Nathan shook his head sadly. It was indeed a cruel world. "Where is your family?"

Elisha slapped his hands on his thick legs and stood. "They are due east of here, at the Hammond plantation. Every Sunday night, I sneak up to see them. Miss Sarah knows about my visits, but Lord Caswell would whip me if he found out I left his property."

"Maybe you could take your wife and son to the British camp. Then you'd all be free."

He shook his head. "Alden is crippled. We would surely be caught if we tried to escape with him."

"Someday, perhaps, you will be reunited."

"Someday I will take them to a place where all men and women are free."

Nathan couldn't imagine what it would be like to be torn away from those he loved. He understood why Elisha would be willing to risk his very life to rescue them, and he admired him for it. "Those are good aspirations, my friend."

"Aspirations worth dying for." Elisha plucked his coat off a peg. "What will you do after the war?"

"I don't remember much of what I did before the war."

Elisha buttoned his coat. "Surely you had a position. A family."

"Most of my family lives north."

"What was your occupation?"

"I managed my uncle's business affairs," Nathan said. Much had changed since those days of sitting safely at his secretary, pouring over accounts.

"The war seems to change everyone."

"Indeed." It would be difficult for him to return to that occupation now.

At the time the work had seemed exciting, but now it would be drudgery.

"Lydia said you were on one of the British ships." Elisha spoke slowly, as if he were counting each word.

"I was."

"Could you—" He cleared his throat, his strong hands fidgeting with the lid of his canteen. "Could you direct me to their army?"

Nathan shook his head. "Last I knew, the British were in Richmond, but I do not know their exact position."

Elisha's eyes implored him. "When you leave, can you take me with you?"

"I am afraid my services are no longer needed in Richmond."

Elisha looked away. "I see."

Nathan hated to see such disappointment on Elisha's face. He wanted to fight for the freedom of all men, black and white. "You do not need me to take you. If you desire independence, then you must find the army on your own. Perhaps after you find them, you could secure freedom for your family."

Elisha's eyes sparked. "Of course."

"I believe you can do it."

"If Master Caswell finds me . . ."

"If Lord Caswell is a true Loyalist, then he should be glad of your freedom."

"My master is more concerned about what is best for his plantation, not his country."

Nathan heard the clip-clop of horses outside, and he stood and walked toward the window. Inching aside the blanket, he saw a flood of redcoats on the lawn. "It appears you won't have to search for the British army."

Nathan lifted the blanket higher as Elisha joined him by the window. "Master Caswell won't resist their company."

"They will not give him a chance to resist."

Elisha reached for the door latch. "You must leave."

Nathan didn't move. "When the time is right."

The soldiers outside slapped each other on the backs, pointing up at the mighty house.

Elisha cracked open the door. "I believe the right time is now."

The man was correct, but he was sure to be caught—and probably shot—if he tried to escape in the daylight.

Nathan sat down on the bed and put his head in his hands. What would his uncle do if he found out Nathan was again trapped among British soldiers? Even after his swim in the river, the leather pouch hidden in his waistcoat had kept his letter dry. Now he needed to steal away to the Hammond plantation before the British found him.

"Please thank Miss Caswell for her kindness."

Elisha opened the door. "Perhaps one day you will be able to thank her as well."

CHAPTER 10

*T*he courtyard in front of the plantation looked like it was ablaze, red uniforms sparking like flames against the white oyster shells along the drive.

At least twenty of the King's Men stood in neat rows, a haversack and a canteen attached to each of their backs. Six of them held the reins of horses in their hands.

Lydia tapped gently on the leaded glass. "Major Reed must be poor at arithmetic."

Mother leaned against the windowsill. "Indeed."

What else had the major neglected to tell them?

Hannah's smile stretched wide. "Is it not marvelous?"

"We must greet them." Mother turned from the window. "Let us hope we can accommodate all of them outside the house."

"This is good news, Dotty." Father buttoned his jacket. "The men will protect us."

Lydia's heart raced. What if they found Nathan? They would suspect Father of harboring the enemy, and the consequence of that . . .

She couldn't allow herself to think about the possibilities.

Father escorted them into the main hall, but Lydia turned

toward the back of the house.

Father stopped her. "Where are you going?"

"To find Elisha," she said. "He needs to help with their horses."

Father shook his head. "Elisha will come to us."

She swallowed. "Of course."

Prudence wrapped a shawl around Lady Caswell's shoulders and then helped Lydia and Hannah with their cloaks. Joshua opened the door, and Father led the family outside onto the portico. The sky was a pale gray, and the crisp air stunk of stale beer, manure, and sweat.

The men might have looked like gentlemen in their uniforms, but they smelled as if they'd been working in the fields all day.

Major Reed and another man stood on the portico above the rest of the soldiers.

"Welcome," Father said, shaking the hand of an officer named Captain Moore.

Captain Moore nodded his head. "We are very glad to be here."

Mother turned toward Major Reed, a forced smile on her face. "You have brought quite an entourage."

He didn't acknowledge the strain in her voice. "These are my best men."

"You are all welcome on our plantation," Father spoke loudly before glancing toward the servants' quarters. "Where is Elisha?"

Lydia hoped he was helping Nathan escape.

"I am here, sir." Elisha stepped onto the drive and took the lead rope of the first horse, guiding him toward the stable.

Lydia tried to catch Elisha's gaze, to see if there was any hope in his eyes, but he didn't look her way. He would suffer the most, she feared, if their guest was discovered.

Oh, why hadn't she found another place to hide Nathan?

Perhaps in one of the cabins of their field slaves, far from the house. Mother would never think to house the British officers there.

Hannah curtsied toward the audience of men. "We are delighted you're here."

Mother's smile remained intact, but Lydia watched her reach for Hannah's hand, a silent warning for Hannah to maintain her dignity. If Hannah wasn't careful, her foolishness would make fools of them all. Father remained on the top step of the stairs that led up to the front door. "We are all glad you are here. We will show you to your accommodations."

Even though her father was glad to host these men, her mother's lips pressed together in an unseemly way. She hadn't even extended an invitation for refreshment.

Lydia leaned toward Father, whispering in his ear, "Perhaps we should offer them tea and biscuits after their long journey."

He continued speaking. "After you settle, we would like you to join us for refreshments."

Her heart sank. She was hoping to warn Nathan while they were enjoying their food.

She spoke louder this time. "I can take our guests to the servants' quarters while you inform the servants of their temporary quarters."

Hannah followed right behind her. "I will come with you."

Lydia shook her head. "There's no need."

"You may both escort them," Father said and then faced the major. "We have a room prepared for you in the main house."

"I will accompany my men to their quarters first."

Hannah followed Lydia down the steps, and Lydia dared to glance over at the darkened top window of the coach house. Surely Nathan could see the soldiers. She would have to stall to give him time to escape. Slowly she guided the men toward the servants' quarters on the opposite side of the coach house.

She prayed Nathan would somehow find the strength to run.

She directed two of the soldiers into the first room. One man would have a bed and the other would have to sleep on a mat, she explained. Neither of them complained about the conditions.

"Where have you been staying in Richmond?" Hannah asked one of the men.

"In a barn."

That would explain the stench that clung to their clothes.

"I hope our plantation will provide better accommodations," Lydia said.

"We might not leave," the man said, laughing. Lydia didn't return his laughter.

Had Mother considered this possibility? Perhaps that was why she was so nervous. Not that Lydia could blame the soldiers, of course—she wouldn't want to sleep in a barn either —but she wasn't certain her family should entertain soldiers for long at Caswell Hall. The townspeople in Williamsburg were sure to find out, and the knowledge could be detrimental to their entire plantation.

Many Loyalists had retreated into silence, and it was impossible to know who was truly loyal to the Crown and who had changed their mind.

Lydia swallowed. She must keep her focus on Nathan, on giving him the opportunity to escape.

Opening the door to the next room, she lingered, explaining to the ten remaining soldiers the particulars of their quarters.

"Four fireplaces warm this building," she continued, "and the servants will keep those stoked for you. Breakfast is at eight each morning in the main house."

"We can discuss all that later." Hannah nudged her arm. "Come along."

"We will send one of the servants to bring fresh water for the bathhouse." She didn't want to command that they bathe, but she hoped they understood she was in earnest.

Hannah tugged Lydia's sleeve. "The others are waiting."

"You lectured me this morning on the importance of knowledge."

"They do not need to know every detail—"

Lydia continued. "The servants will also bring towels. And clean linens."

"Lydia!"

She scanned the faces of the men. "Are there any questions?"

Major Reed stepped up beside Hannah. "You have explained everything quite well, Miss Caswell. Shall we proceed?"

"Of course."

Two men occupied each room, and with every step they took, her heart rate increased. Surely Nathan knew they were coming, but what if he hadn't left?

There was no good scenario, and she despaired at the thought of his death. She didn't know his intentions after he left their property, but he had certainly done no harm while he was here.

When they closed the last door of the servants' quarters, two men remained along with Major Reed and Hannah.

Lydia shrugged. "I'm afraid you shall have to stay in a room with two of your fellow officers."

Hannah laughed. "You are frightfully silly, sister. They need not all stay in the servants' quarters. There's an extra room in your coach house."

In that moment, Lydia wished Father *had* muzzled Hannah. Or locked her in the attic and tossed the key into the James.

She shook her head. "Our driver resides there."

"Elisha can sleep in the stable," Hannah insisted as she guided the men away from Lydia.

Lydia's mind raced as she hurried to catch up, her stomach churning. Surely there was something she could do to deter them. Scream. Stomp. Pretend the house was on fire.

But all of those would bring suspicion on her and her family. There must be something else—

Hannah climbed the steps in front of her and reached for the door latch, the others trailing on the stairs behind her. Lydia reached for her sister's hand and smiled as graciously as she could muster. "Perhaps you might escort Major Reed to the main house."

Hannah shook her head. "I don't think—"

Lydia turned and spoke to the major at the base of the steps. "Mother will have the tea and biscuits waiting for you."

"I believe that is a splendid idea," Major Reed said.

Hannah looked at the blanket covering Elisha's window as if she would find Lydia's secret inside. Lydia watched her closely, wondering what she saw, if she saw anything at all.

Hannah climbed back down the steps and took Major Reed's arm, glancing once over her shoulder as he escorted her away. Lydia pointed toward the river, telling the two officers about the ships that traveled up and down from the bay. They didn't appear the least bit interested about the colony's shipping endeavors, but she didn't stop her lecture until Major Reed and Hannah were out of her view. Then she had no choice but to proceed.

Reaching for the latch, she prayed that Nathan had already made his escape, that he had strolled in leisure off the plantation and perhaps some friendly colonist had given him a ride to Richmond.

Her heart collapsed when she opened the door.

Nathan wasn't gone. He was standing in the room, dressed in his plain cotton shirt and waistcoat, the old linsey-wool trousers, and the scarf that Mother knitted. Her brother's black tricorn hat dipped low over his forehead; his hair was tied back in the yellow ribbon she had given him. In one hand, he leaned against a cane, and draped over his other arm was a blanket from the bed.

She wanted to yell at him to run—and she wanted to run with him— but she steadied herself, trying to make her voice strong.

"What are you doing in here?" she demanded.

"I'm sorry, Miss—Miss Caswell." He kept his head lowered. "Miss Prudence—she told me to fetch the blankets from the beds."

Slowly she processed his words, his demeanor. And then she breathed deeply. Nathan didn't have to run. If she could stop the trembling inside her, together they could convince these men that he was one of the indentured servants that worked on the plantation.

She swallowed a cough. "Then take that blanket to Prudence straightaway."

"Yes, miss." He scooted slowly around her, limping as he walked.

"After you are done, Elisha needs your help with our guests' livery."

He nodded again and slowly moved down the steps.

She whispered to the soldiers. "Please forgive his ignorance. When he was sixteen, an unfortunate accident with one of our horses left him lame and a bit slow in the head."

She glanced one more time at Nathan as he hobbled down the steps, and he winked at her before he moved toward the trees at the river's bank.

The soldiers inched around her, one sitting on the stool and the other on the edge of the bed. She thought they would ask questions about a white man cleaning their rooms, but they did not seem to notice anything amiss. Perhaps they were too afraid to ask a question of her, afraid she might bore them with her explanation.

Godspeed, Nathan.

After he delivered his message, she hoped he was well enough to return to his family.

91

CHAPTER 11

*N*athan ducked behind a tree and leaned back against the trunk, gulping in the fresh air. It had only been a short walk to the riverbank, but his foot was throbbing.

Thank God for Elisha's cane—and for Lydia's sharp wit and calm demeanor as she played along with his scheme. Thank God Major Reed and his men wouldn't think to look for him here. Unlike the bright-red coats of the Tories, his stained cotton shirt blended into the willows and underbrush.

He sank onto the ground, hidden by the barren branches, and watched Lydia stroll like a gentle lady toward the main house. Her beautiful chestnut hair was hidden behind the hood of her cloak, and she didn't make the slightest move to look his way.

Part of him wished she would look one last time, a parting glance between them. But even a single glance was risky. Anyone watching her might suspect his location if she had.

If only she was on the Patriots' side—

But she wasn't, and no amount of wishing would change Lydia or her family's loyalties. Still, he owed his life to her. Once

the Patriots won this war, he would do everything in his power
to keep her safe.

He glanced out at the wide river that drummed against the
banks. If Lydia hadn't found him, if she hadn't been willing to
risk her reputation and perhaps even her life, he would have
died by the river.

Elisha said to walk east to find his boat, but he would wait
until dark to retrieve it.

Checking inside his waistcoat, he found the small pouch
made of deer hide secured there, the letter safe and dry inside.
Then he patted the top of the blanket he'd used as an excuse to
escape.

Wrapped inside the blanket was the package of food that
Elisha had provided for him, along with the woolen scarf once
worn by Lydia's brother.

He smiled.

Perhaps one day he could return the blanket and clothing to
Lydia.

Lydia's hands trembled as she tugged on one of the pale-blue
gloves that matched her gown, even as Hannah chattered
endlessly about which of their new guests she thought handsome and which she'd already determined to be dolts.

Until now, Lydia had been too preoccupied to examine any
of their guests for their appearance or wit. There was only one
man who concerned her, and oddly enough, it wasn't Seth
Hammond.

Two years ago, after the family's last formal dinner, Seth had
stood with her and Father in the privacy of their library,
declaring his fervor for freedom. Father had been so angry that
he'd struck Seth across the cheek.

Seth tried to explain that he would never have killed the

senior Caswell, that not all men on the side of the Patriots believed that those who remained loyal to the Crown should be humiliated. Most of their men simply wanted freedom, not rebellion, and he couldn't understand why Lord Caswell didn't demand freedom from tyranny as well. Her father responded that the king should rule their nation just as he himself ruled Caswell Hall.

Then Seth had looked at her, imploring her with his eyes to take a stand. She remembered the moment as if it was hours ago. He'd reached for her hand, but instead of standing with him, she'd stepped away.

Everything changed in that one moment. His eyes no longer invited her to him. Instead, they seemed to dismiss her. He never broke their engagement, not officially, but in that moment, she knew he might never marry her, not unless she became a Patriot.

Even then, it might be too late.

She wished they didn't have to fight, neither the British nor the colonists. She wished she didn't have to choose a side.

Her parents entered the door to her chamber, and she took a deep breath. It was time to attend the dinner.

Father escorted the Caswell women down to the great hall. Their uniformed guests were waiting to sit at the two long tables provided to accommodate all of them. A hundred pale-green candles glowed, and the sweet fragrance of the myrtle-berry wax seemed to mask the stench of the men who hadn't bathed.

Viney served them wild duck soaked in wine, slices of salted ham, a platter of sweetmeats, crab from the nearby bay, cabbage with vinegar, bread pudding, and onion pie. As Lydia looked down the table, she realized some of the men were indeed handsome, as Hannah had said. Major Reed was probably the most handsome of all, but smugness enveloped his features like the gloves enveloped her hands. There was little she despised more than a man who believed his very presence to be a gift to others.

She sighed. The major's demeanor was so very unlike Nathan's, but then again, the pride of her previous guest had probably drowned in the river. Perhaps Major Reed had yet the opportunity to experience the death of his pride.

Breathing deeply, Lydia lifted her silver spoon and took a bite of some currants mixed in with the bread pudding. The men on both sides of her reveled in small talk with her family, but her mind wasn't on London or even on the siege in Richmond.

Her heart ached as she pressed her fork into a piece of soft bread. If only there wasn't a war. She could have invited Nathan to dinner along with the rest of their guests.

"Did you have any prisoners on your ships?" Hannah asked.

Lydia's fork clattered against her plate before she retrieved it. She didn't dare look up, but she listened intently.

"We took twelve prisoners back in Newport News. And one traitor."

Lydia turned toward the officer on her left. He was a slight man with a prominent nose and greasy hair that looked as if it had been dyed black. His fork and mouth were both stuffed full of meat, but thankfully, he smelled like lye soap.

She straightened her posture, trying to exude a dignified deportment as she cut a piece of ham with her knife and fork. Mother liked to say that the best way to encourage etiquette in others was to demonstrate the proper graces.

Lydia balanced the fork in her fingers as her neighbor shoved his fork into his mouth and filled his fork again. He didn't seem the least bit concerned about grace as he spoke before he swallowed in a most undignified manner. "Not all of them made it to Richmond, though."

The major nodded. "The traitor fell overboard before we arrived."

"How unfortunate," Mother said.

"I'm certain his demise was immediate."

One of the soldiers lifted his glass. "One less rebel."

"Hear, hear."

Lydia shivered. Nathan might be a rebel, but he also had treated her and Prudence with respect and gratitude for all they had done. "What will happen to your prisoners?"

"No one ever leaves a prison ship alive," Major Reed replied.

"Did you have to fight in Richmond?" Father asked.

He nodded. "More than a thousand of us marched on the capital."

Another man laughed. "The Yankees all fled, so we burned the town."

Lydia gasped. If only Nathan hadn't been injured, he might have reached Richmond in time to prepare their defenses.

Major Reed turned toward her. "We didn't want to burn it, but Governor Jefferson refused to hand over their supplies."

She mustered a smile. She was supposed to rejoice that the Yankees in Richmond had been defeated.

Mother focused her gaze on the major. "It's unfortunate we cannot host your wives for dinner."

The major glanced over at her in surprise. He would have to get used to her mother's art of directing conversation away from conflict.

Her neighbor lifted his fork, smiling at her again. "Perhaps before one of these dinners, I can invite my wife."

Surprised, Lydia glanced over at him. "Where is your wife?"

"With the other camp followers, back at Newport News."

Lydia's eyes widened. There was so much she didn't know about what was happening in this war. "How many women are following your army?"

He shrugged. "A number of them, like my Gwen, came over from England, and then there are the women who do laundry and cooking and . . . other things."

He dug a handful of dried fruit and nuts from the silver epergne before him and chewed them as if he hadn't eaten in a week.

She turned to look across the table and found Major Reed's gaze resting on her. "Miss Caswell is not interested in the particulars of our camp."

"On the contrary." She set down her fork. "I am interested in the plight of all women."

His eyebrows arched. "I do not believe our women are in any sort of plight."

"But the rebel women—" her neighbor said.

Several of the men laughed.

"Our enemy has their women fighting for them."

Hannah gasped. "Fighting for them?"

"I heard one of the women was even loading their cannons."

Lydia stiffened at the laughter that rippled around the table. If women believed in the rebel cause, what was wrong with helping?

"Perhaps she was using the heat to bake a cake," Captain Moore said. "It probably backfired."

Lydia watched her mother's lips press into a straight line. If the men didn't change the topic soon, it wouldn't matter who they served. They would be spending the night outside.

"Gentleman," Father silenced them. "You are in the company of ladies now."

The laughter quieted, and Major Reed spoke. "I would like to apologize on behalf of my men. We have only the greatest respect for our women. We would never let them fight."

Lydia glanced across the table at him. "Why not?"

"It is our job to protect the ladies among us, not put them into battle."

"An admirable outlook," Hannah said.

"The war is almost won," the major said. "And when it is, my married men will celebrate the victory with their wives."

Mother set down her fork. "Viney has prepared trifle with gooseberry jelly and fresh cream for dessert."

The men nodded their approval, and Lydia smiled at her mother's artful ability to steer a conversation in any direction she saw fit. The British could only wish women like her mother would fight for them.

Father scooted back his chair. "Shall we withdraw for sherry first?"

Lydia stood as well, for some fresh air on the back portico as the men drank their sherry. One of the officers trailed her out through the great hall.

"Your manservant never returned with our blanket," Captain Moore said.

Father waited by the entrance to the drawing room. "Which manservant are you referring to?"

"The white man with a limp."

Father looked back at her. "Has Joshua injured himself?"

She forced a most genteel smile. "Not to my knowledge."

"But you said—" Captain Moore started.

She gave him a curt nod. "I shall make sure one of our men brings you a new blanket."

Captain Moore looked as if he was going to say something else, but Lydia excused herself before he spoke.

Leaning over the portico, she rubbed her hands over her thin sleeves as she looked out at the dark river and prayed that Nathan was safe, wherever he was.

CHAPTER 12

The Hammonds' plantation house glowed like a beacon above the river, its warm light beckoning Nathan forward. He crept slowly through a grove of trees beside a field, scanning both sides to make sure no one saw him before he shuffled beside the wide trunk of an oak tree.

A chorus of song drifted across the field, emerging from a row of wooden shanties. He couldn't see any people in the sliver of moonlight, but their song was a welcome companion to him on this dark night.

His was a lonely occupation now, but he'd gotten used to this strange business of sneaking through forests and behind enemy lines.

When he was a child, he'd spent hours playing hide-and-seek with his many brothers and sisters on their plantation. His ability to hide well was one of the reasons he'd been appointed to work as a courier and spy. With the British now taking the capital of Virginia along with Charles Towne, it might be years before he returned to the life of a civilian.

If only he'd been able to convince Major Reed that he was a

Loyalist. The British might not have taken Richmond if he'd arrived early enough to warn them.

At the end of the tree line was a maze of flank buildings. Only one of the buildings interested him—a brick dovecote— and that was forty yards or so on the other side of the main house. Somehow he had to get to it without being seen.

He eyed the wooden plantation house in front of him. A civil person would tromp up to the front entrance and knock, but all the genteel manners he'd learned at Yale College were for naught here. It wouldn't be safe to knock. One of the servants might report him to the guests staying down at Caswell Hall.

His heart lurched again at the thought of Lydia surrounded by those soldiers tonight. They would be fawning over her, he was certain. Even if she ignored them, they couldn't help but be enchanted by her beauty and poise.

Nathan leaned back against a tree, groaning. He had to stop thinking about Lydia, he who was so distinguished that he'd spent last night in a corncrib alongside two barn cats.

His mother had attempted multiple times to find him a patriotic wife, but when he married—if he married—he wanted it to be for love, not for political positioning of any sort. In the meantime, he had plenty of family.

He snuck behind a small building and watched as someone moved around the stables. He felt his pocket—the pouch was still there. The sooner he delivered this message, the sooner he could return north to wait for his next assignment.

In the darkness, he crept toward the dovecote and jostled the latch until it opened. A hundred birds seemed to squawk and clap their wings from their tiny coops.

Three across, two down.

He counted the nests to the left of the door and the squab inside the designated coup squawked as he searched for a message from Seth's sister. When he didn't find a letter, he removed a pouch from the interior of his waistcoat and tucked it into the coop, beside the nesting squab.

Quickly he backed out of the dovecote and latched the door before someone from the stable or another place came to check on the noise. He wasn't certain of the time, but he guessed it to be nine or ten.

How often would Seth's sister check on the dovecote?

He rarely knew the names of those who delivered messages for General Washington, but he knew about Sarah Hammond. Seth had orchestrated this contact for the general and given both Nathan and his sister precise instructions.

He pulled a green ribbon out of his pocket and tied it around the iron railing that led up to the entrance of the house. Then he slid back into the shadows to watch the front door.

The hours seemed to crawl by as he waited, glad to be relieved of his message. If someone caught him now, they might think him a drifter or a deserter from the army. The note was safely where he'd promised to deliver it.

He knotted the scarf Lydia had given him closer to his neck, and with the blanket wrapped around him as well, he began to drift off. When he woke, he saw a flicker of light by the main house. His heart pounded in his ears as he watched the light move like an apparition across the drive.

At the door of the dovecote, a young woman held her lantern high to open the latch on the door, and before she disappeared into the dovecote, he could see the lace collar of her gown and her pale hair—the same color as Seth's. This must be Miss Hammond.

The birds greeted her with the same noisy welcome they had Nathan.

Seconds later, she reappeared and hurried back toward the house.

He waited a bit longer and then rechecked the tiny coop. The squab was still there, but the message was gone.

~

Four nights after their arrival, Major Reed and his band of officers crowded into the Caswells' parlor and huddled around Hannah as she played a British pub song on the pianoforte. With a shout, the men lifted their mugs in unison and then guzzled Father's prized beer.

Lydia sighed. The constant revelry exhausted her, but Hannah seemed to still be enjoying the company. These men certainly enjoyed the refreshment of being at a plantation while they waited for their next orders. Lydia was beginning to wonder how Britain would win the war if her soldiers weren't fighting.

Major Reed turned toward her. "Perhaps you might sing for us, Miss Caswell."

"Oh, I am not much of one for singing."

"Do not let her fool you," Hannah said. "She sings better than any of us."

The soldiers began clapping, cheering for her to entertain them. Lydia glared at her sister, but when she glanced over to her mother, Lady Caswell responded with a slight nod.

Reluctantly Lydia stepped up to the pianoforte and began to sing an old hymn—"When All Thy Mercies, O My God"—while Hannah accompanied her. The men quieted, listening to the words.

> *Ten thousand thousand precious gifts*
> *My daily thanks employ;*
> *Nor is the least a cheerful heart*
> *That tastes those gifts with joy.*
>
> *Through every period of my life*
> *Thy goodness I'll pursue;*
> *And after death, in distant worlds,*

The glorious theme renew.

The men clapped again, and when she looked up, Major Reed's eyes were focused on her. Then he smiled.

She moved toward her parents, trying to ignore him, but she could feel the major step up beside her. Father might want her to marry a British gentleman, but this man unsettled her.

Hannah joined them, looking between her and the major. "Did my sister tell you she is betrothed?"

Lydia nearly protested but stopped herself. She might be uncertain about her future with Seth, but perhaps it was best for her if these men thought she was promised elsewhere.

"I believe it's time for you to retire," Father said, but Hannah ignored him.

"She is planning to marry Seth Hammond."

Major Reed looked at her father. "Who is this Seth Hammond?"

"He is the son of our neighbor."

"But I thought—" The major hesitated, looking at her. "When are you planning to marry?"

Father cleared his throat. "She is not—"

"After the war." Lydia refused to look at her father. "We had planned to marry when the war was finished."

Father shook his head. "There is no reason to talk of marriage tonight."

Major Reed swirled his drink in the crystal tumbler. "Why does this Seth Hammond not marry you now?"

"Because he is off—" She stopped herself, afraid of what might happen if she told these soldiers about Seth.

Hannah, however, insisted on pressing the matter. "He is fighting, of course."

"Perhaps I know him," Major Reed said.

Lydia crossed her right hand over her chest, as if she could steady herself. "I don't believe you would."

Hannah gave a coy smile. "That's because he isn't fighting for the British."

"Hush, Hannah," Mother hissed.

Lydia hated the glee in her sister's words, the deviousness in her smile. It was as if she were trying to destroy their entire family along with Seth.

The major's eyes flashed. "He is a rebel?"

"He would not call himself a rebel," Lydia said.

Major Reed set his tumbler on the table, directing his question to Lydia. "Do you communicate regularly with this man you are to marry?"

"Oh, no," Lydia replied, trying to ignore the familiar ache in her heart. "I haven't heard from him since he left for the army."

"We have no communication with rebels or their cause," Father insisted.

Hannah tilted her head. "Except with Seth's sister."

Father filled the major's tumbler with more sherry. "Seth's father and his daughter are as loyal to the Crown as our family is. And my father was murdered because of his allegiance to the king."

Major Reed shifted his weight, leaning back against the paneled wall. "No one can be certain of another's loyalties."

When could they return to being neighbors again, without worrying who was on which side of this war?

Mother nudged Hannah toward the door, her lips set in a firm line. "It is time for you to retire."

"But I wanted to play another song!"

"To your chamber," Father commanded.

With a dramatic sigh, Hannah slouched from the room.

An officer sat down at the instrument, and as he played, Lydia heard her father change the topic to one she preferred even less than the topic of the Hammonds.

"What are your prospects for marriage?" he asked the major.

Major Reed stole a look at her again, and she felt a wave of heat creep up her face. She quickly fanned away her embarrassment.

He turned back to Father. "I have none at the moment."

"There are some fine young ladies on this side of the ocean who are quite devoted to our king."

Lydia stepped toward the fireplace and shuddered, pretending she couldn't hear their low voices over the din of singing.

Did Father really want her to marry this man? It seemed to her that Major Reed was much too pompous to be a planter. A man who didn't love this land would probably squander it, along with the house Father had worked so hard to build.

Of course, Father was getting desperate. Most of the local men of marrying age had joined General Washington's army, and Father was determined that neither of his daughters would marry one of them.

Her father and the major stepped closer to the fireplace.

"When do you intend to make your loyalties known?" Major Reed asked.

Father sipped his drink. "When the British have secured their win."

The major's eyes narrowed, his voice lowering. "Are you a coward, Lord Caswell?"

Lydia had never heard anyone imply that her father was a coward. With a quick glance toward her left, Lydia saw anger flash across Father's face and the twitching of his left eye.

"The rebels killed my father when he made his loyalties known, and they chased away my son." The sharp edge in her father's voice sounded like hail pounding their slate roof. "Many of our former friends already treat my family with disdain."

Mother moved toward him, and when she circled her gloved hand around his arm, his eye stopped twitching. Lydia admired the way her mother could diffuse her father's fury by a simple touch—the reminder, perhaps, that he wasn't alone.

"My husband is a survivor, Major Reed. A survivor and a protector of our family and plantation."

Father's tone calmed as he continued. "If I declare my loyalties now and your army is set back, the next time you come to Caswell Hall, there may be no house to host you."

Major Reed straightened the lace on his sleeves. "I suppose there is wisdom in that."

"It is common sense, my friend. If I speak up, my punishment would be swift. I would be forced to return to London with my wife and daughters, and there would be one less family in Virginia loyal to the Crown."

"We knew your father when he was much younger, Major Reed." The soothing lilt of Mother's voice broke through the tension. "But I did not have the pleasure of knowing your mother well. Where is her family?"

Major Reed looked startled at the change in direction of their conversation. "She is from Canterbury."

"I visited Canterbury when I was a girl." Mother's tone remained soft, her smile demure. "It was a charming village."

Major Reed mirrored her smile. "Aye. It is a beautiful place."

"You can understand, I suppose, how Caswell Hall means so much to all of us."

"I understand your sentiments, Lady Caswell, but my superiors may not."

"We are on your side," Father insisted.

Mother didn't mention Grayson, but Lydia knew the plantation meant so much to her mother in part because her son had grown up within these walls. He'd walked the fields and worked alongside Father. She wanted to protect her memories as much as Father wanted to protect his kingdom.

Lydia didn't want to return to London either. This colony was her home, a place where her father had prospered. She loved the beautiful landscape around Caswell Hall and their view of the river.

Father had given much of his life to the building of this house and to the planting and cultivating of the seven thousand acres that surrounded it. If they took Caswell Hall from him, if they burned it like they had so many houses . . . she feared her father would never recover from such a loss.

As Major Reed continued to ask questions, her mother urged Lydia to sing again. She moved to the pianoforte. Her heart wasn't in it, but she joined the men in a song about God saving their king.

CHAPTER 13

Sarah packed hard cheese, a small bottle of cherries, and two slices of bread in a small basket. She buckled her oldest pair of shoes and wrapped herself in her light-brown cloak.

It was already after eight in the morning, and the letter seemed to be burning a hole in the pocket under her petticoat. With the horses gone, she had no choice. She must walk the three miles to Williamsburg.

It might not be safe on the main roads with the British so close, but she would have to risk traveling over the footpath to deliver the letter.

She'd finished the weekly inspection with Thomas yesterday, walking the grounds to check on the buildings and the work of their Negroes. Winters weren't nearly as taxing as the summer planting and harvesting—nor were they as profitable—but the workers stayed plenty busy with maintenance and care for the livestock. The field slaves and house servants alike would be occupied for most of the day.

She found Morah dusting the banister over the main stairs, Alden playing with his crutch at her feet. Sarah assumed that Elisha had made the crutch for his son, but she never asked.

Alden needed his father, but Lord Caswell refused to sell Elisha to her. Now Sarah simply pretended that she didn't know Elisha paddled down the back river every Sunday night to visit his wife and son.

"When Thomas returns, please tell him I have decided to picnic this morning."

Morah stared at her as if she'd gone mad, and Sarah knew she must have a hundred questions about one picnicking in March, during a war.

"Yes, miss," Morah replied instead.

The gray skies threatened weather, but it was too warm for another snow. As long as she returned by nightfall, she would be fine.

Sarah walked the path along the riverbank east before turning north toward Williamsburg. In the distance she saw one of the few Patriot ships moving toward the ocean, probably going out to defend the Chesapeake Bay.

Not too many years ago, her heart had swelled with pride at the strength of the Royal Navy. At the time, her father hadn't been on a ship in many years, but he still regaled her and Seth with stories about his years traveling the world, before he and Mother came to run his father's plantation.

Mother had neither the strength nor the interest in traveling with him, but he'd seemed to settle well into the life of a planter until Parliament petitioned him to travel to the West Indies.

When Seth joined the Continental Army, it seemed that Father had been proud of his son for fighting. Father had once spoken out in favor of liberty, before the colonies wrote their declaration for independence, but he had withdrawn quickly, growing more dispassionate even as the world grew passionate around them. When he received his orders to sail, it seemed a mercy for him to escape all that confused him and his family.

She wondered if he still believed in any of the foundational blocks of freedom.

The path led her into a labyrinth of mud, leaves, and branches with snow quilted like patchwork between the trees.

Father would never approve of what she was doing. It was too risky to allow a messenger from either side to come onto their property, and he would fear for her life.

On the other hand, Seth wanted her to be safe, but he also wanted to win this war. Her brother had given his life for freedom; he would never be satisfied with defeat. Sarah would rather die than live under oppression, with the punishment that would inflict all those who had rebelled.

If she could fight on the battlefield, she would. She'd heard the story of Mary Hays, the woman who'd served as a "water girl" to cool down the cannons as the Patriots battled the British. When Mary's husband was injured in battle, she took his ramrod and kept loading the cannon.

General Washington designated Mary Hays a sergeant for her courage, but Seth said General Washington would never allow Sarah to fight—her role here as a courier was even more vital.

Or it had been, until they stole her horses.

She heard the sound of voices through the thickness of the trees, and she stopped walking. There were two or three men speaking, and they were close.

"No one must know of our intent," one of the men said. "We will search everyone who comes this way."

Sarah swallowed and then held her breath. Who were these men?

Then she heard the language of a German man, probably one of the Hessians the king had hired from taxes inflicted on the Americans. She wouldn't be able to pass without them hearing her, searching her. She shivered, her hand over the pocket that held a small book with the letter. It wouldn't be hard for them to find it, but the thought of them searching . . .

They might not be able to read the contents, but she couldn't risk it. The letter was still sealed and must remain so until it arrived.

She sat on a stump and waited, wishing the forest would swallow her. There would be no moving in any direction until the men were gone.

Blue and green threads on her canvas formed the path of a river. After weeks of work, the scene was finally finished, and Lydia took an old sampler off the wall by her bureau and replaced it with her new one.

Stitching usually calmed her nerves, easing her to sleep, but it hadn't worked tonight. The thought of having to leave Caswell Hall haunted her.

If she ever left here, this embroidered river would remind her of home.

The officers had retired for the night less than an hour ago, enjoying their time of refreshment to the fullest. Their household staff was showing signs of weariness at the men's demands. Lydia was exhausted as well, but she hadn't been able to sleep.

The officers talked tonight of the plantations they'd burned around Charles Towne and New York, and they told of a man—a Loyalist—who'd burned his family's plantation home even as his rebel brother looked on. It seemed outlandish to her, burning the places they were trying to secure.

What would happen if the British did win this war?

She closed her eyes and leaned back against the shutters that folded behind the window seat. If the Patriots won, her family would have to leave Caswell Hall, and the thought of leaving her beloved home terrified her. This place was her sanctuary, her fortress.

Some people, like Grayson, wanted adventure, but she had never felt the need to explore far beyond their plantation. Their trip to England when she was a child had cured her of any longing to travel. For the entire two months overseas, she had begged her parents to return home.

Unlike her, Grayson had loved their trip to Europe, especially the ride on the ship. He'd spent every waking moment Father allowed him on deck with the crew.

She and Grayson did have something in common when they were younger. Both of them preferred peace to conflict, like their mother. Lydia still craved peace in their colony, but it seemed as if it was much too late for that sentiment.

Grandfather's desire for peace had ultimately gotten him killed, and the irony of it still angered her. She didn't understand why anyone would condemn peace, but in the days after his funeral, she decided it was better to keep one's opinion to oneself than end up dead because of it.

She opened her eyes and looked out at the darkness.

Where had Nathan gone? Instead of choosing peace, he was risking his life for a freedom that seemed impossible to secure, especially now that the British seemed poised to take Virginia.

She didn't know what real freedom was like. Even though she'd been raised in the Commonwealth of Virginia, she'd always been a servant of the king. She never dared to wonder what it would be like if the colonies were independent.

It was almost as if the colonists had been children for well over a century now, obeying a demanding parent who lived four thousand miles away, a royal father who grew stricter instead of more lenient as his wards aged.

Could it be time for the colonies to mature? Perhaps they should unite and make laws on their own.

She shook her head. She must stop thinking such thoughts.

The very act of considering independence could be considered treason.

Her fireplace was blazing, but she still shivered, rubbing the cotton sleeves of her shift. Perhaps something hot to drink would warm her body and rest her mind. If Viney or one of the maids were in the kitchen, perhaps they could heat some cider or chocolate.

She wrapped her nightgown around her shift and then moved into the hall, eyeing the closed door of Major Reed's chamber before she slipped down the main stairs. Then she took the much smaller staircase down to the basement.

One of the maids was still cleaning and warmed up the cider for Lydia over the fire. After the housemaid bid her good night, Lydia sat in the dim kitchen by the remnants of the blaze, sipping her hot drink made of apple cider, nutmeg, and cinnamon. She wanted privacy, but she didn't want to return to her bedchamber. The kitchen was the perfect place for a respite.

Leaning against the counter, she enjoyed her drink until she heard footsteps behind her. At first she thought it was the maid returning but then realized they were much heavier steps, the steps of a man.

Fear sparked in her for a moment, and she chided herself. There was nothing for her to be afraid of. This was her home, and Father made sure it protected both his wife and daughters.

Turning, she saw Major Reed walk into the room, and as he eyed her nightgown, a smile crept across his lips. "Good evening."

She cringed and silently chided herself for leaving her room in this state of undress. "I thought you had retired to your room," she said.

"I have come to find food."

"There is plenty of food to be had. Take what you would like," she said, though she suspected he didn't need her permission to do so.

He moved closer to her. "Someone distracted me from eating enough at dinner."

She was glad it was dark, for she didn't want him to see her blush. "I fear you drank too much sherry tonight."

His eyes studied her in a way that made her want to run, and yet she wasn't sure what he would do if she fled. "I need not drink to know that you are beautiful."

She took a sip of her cider and stood, trying to appear much calmer than she felt as she backed toward the door. He stepped toward her, and while he didn't touch her, the way he surveyed her . . .

Perhaps she should be flattered, but it frightened her instead.

"I remember when you came to visit London."

She swallowed. "Do you?"

"You were twelve and already beautiful."

The stale alcohol on his breath made her cough.

"How old were you?" she asked, stepping away again. If she kept him talking, perhaps he wouldn't notice her moving backward.

"Fifteen." He leaned against the wall, his legs crossed, as he continued to watch her. "We spent time in our gardens chasing the rabbits."

An image began to form in her mind of a boy holding up a rabbit by the legs, her begging him not to hurt it. He'd let it go, but if she hadn't begged him, she didn't know what he would have done.

"I must go up to my chamber now, Major Reed."

"You used to call me Dalton."

"That was a long time ago."

When he stepped close to her again, she shuddered. He stood only a few inches taller than her, yet she knew he was much stronger.

Would they hear her upstairs if she screamed?

His gaze on her face, he reached out and caressed the thin material on her sleeve. "You might call me Dalton again."

She pulled her arm away, repeating her words. "It's time for me to return to my chamber."

Instead of discouraging him, her refusal made his smile grow even wider, as if the quest was as pleasurable as the plunder. "There's no reason for you to rush."

"But there is—"

He moved in front of her, blocking her way. "I don't want to frighten you, Lydia."

"Miss Caswell," she said, hating herself for the tremble in her voice. "And I have already promised myself to another."

His laugh was bitter. "The rebel."

"I do not think of him as such."

He pushed a strand of hair over her ear. "I'll care for you much better than any rebel could."

Lantern light filled the room, and she turned to see Elisha's wide shoulders emerge from the shadows.

"Lady Caswell sent me for you, miss," he said, his head bowed.

Major Reed took her arm. "I shall escort her upstairs."

"Of course," Elisha replied, but he didn't move.

Lydia shook off the major's grasp. "You haven't eaten yet—"

"My appetite has changed." He turned toward Elisha. "Leave us now."

"But Lady Caswell—"

"Thank you, Elisha." Lydia stepped closer to him, her heart warming. The major could have the slave whipped for his impertinence, and yet Elisha was willing to risk punishment to protect her. "You must take me to Lady Caswell's chamber."

Elisha followed her upstairs, and when they reached the second floor, he opened the door into the corridor for her. "Lock your chamber door, Miss Lydia."

Tears of gratitude filled her eyes as she thanked him again.

CHAPTER 14

*A*fter devouring a large breakfast, Major Reed and two of his men escorted the family's coach away from Caswell Hall. Mother sat on the leather seat beside Lydia, and she seemed just as eager to visit Williamsburg as Lydia.

The officers had been with them more than a week now as they waited for General Cornwallis and his army to join them near Williamsburg.

The Caswell family had enough food at the plantation to see them through the rest of the winter, but Mother still insisted on going into town today to obtain tea and other supplies. It was an excuse, Lydia knew, for her to escape their overbearing guests.

Hannah had stayed in her room this morning, saying it was much too early for her to say good-bye. They all knew she was pouting. With Hannah's tongue—and no muzzle—Father feared she would say something that might damage their family permanently.

A stream divided the land between the Caswell and Hammond plantations. On the other side of the water, Elisha stopped the horses.

"This is the end of the Caswell property," he told the officers from his seat high on the coach.

Major Reed opened the door beside Lydia, but she didn't speak to him. It seemed as if he wasn't even bothered about his behavior—or her rejection—two nights ago, but she could never pretend it away. If Elisha hadn't rescued her, her life might now be in ruins.

Instead of looking at Lydia, Major Reed addressed her mother. "The British are patrolling the forest between here and Williamsburg. I have given Elisha a letter describing your loyalty."

She thought it odd that the major hadn't mentioned the patrols to Father before they left home, but perhaps he feared that Lord Caswell wouldn't permit the trip if he knew about the guards. He wanted the tea and other items Mother would find in town.

"Can you not escort us the entire way?" Mother asked.

He shook his head. "We have other duties we must fulfill today, but you will want to return home before the night falls."

Mother clutched her beaded reticule in her gloved hands. "We won't linger any longer than necessary."

As their escorts galloped away, Lydia buried her hands in the warm folds of her cape and closed her eyes for a moment. Mother might be nervous, but relief washed over Lydia like a spring rain cleansing the ground. She felt a bit like a convict escaping jail—and her warden.

Caswell Hall, with its damask chairs, warm fires, and rich food, was hardly a prison, but this past week the house had been so crowded that she'd wanted to break free. Now that the kitchen was no longer a solace for her, her chamber was her only real escape. But the walls of her room felt as if they were closing upon her as well.

The snow had melted away, the ground swimming now with mud. The carriage wheels groaned and splashed through muck as the coach passed slowly under a canopy of barren elm trees. She didn't particularly care how long it took them to ride into town. She hoped they would be gone all day.

Of course, they must shop without raising any suspicions about whom they were hosting at Caswell Hall. Some of their former friends still scorned her family because of Grandfather's outspoken opposition against the rebellion. She didn't think the rest of her family was threatened, at least not with physical harm. Father must not think it either, or he wouldn't have let them go to town.

"Are you ready as I am for our guest to leave the house?" Mother asked.

Lydia nodded her head.

"Unfortunately, I do not believe your sister shares your sentiments."

"That is because she does not know better," Lydia said.

"Only by the grace of God . . ." Mother's voice trailed off. In less than a mile, they had neared the lane to the Hammonds' house.

Before the hostilities began, the Hammond and Caswell families had been not only neighbors but the best of friends, Lydia and Sarah almost inseparable as girls. When Sarah lost her mother almost twenty years ago, Lydia's mother had stepped up to help Mr. Hammond rear his only daughter, and Sarah spent more time at Caswell Hall than she did her own home.

But now Lydia saw Sarah only at church, and they rarely had the opportunity to speak together. Lydia knew Mother wanted to visit Sarah as well, but after Seth joined the Americans, the bond between their families crumbled.

Lydia looked over at her mother again. "Might we stop to visit Sarah?"

"There is much we need to do in town." Mother hesitated. "And the major said not to linger."

"Just for an hour, Mother, to make sure she is well."

As they drew closer to the Hammonds' drive, Elisha slowed the team. The coach was enclosed by windows, so he couldn't speak to them, but all Mother needed to do was open the window and ask him to turn.

If begging would work, Lydia would do it, but her mother had never been influenced by nagging. So Lydia waited silently for a response.

Patches of ice mixed with pools of water in the pond beside them. When they were younger, she and Grayson would meet Seth and Sarah for skating. How she missed those years, when they were free to enjoy their lives without worrying about war.

Mother finally inched open the window, cold air whisking into the coach as she cleared her throat.

"Elisha, we would like to pay a short visit to Miss Hammond."

"Yes, ma'am," he replied. Then he began humming as he turned the horses right.

Mother glanced over at Lydia. "We will not stay long."

"Of course not."

"And we had better not tell your father."

Lydia nodded her head.

They passed through the forest, and on the other side of the trees, dozens of sheep and cattle roamed the sweet-clover fields that led up to the Hammond house and the buildings surrounding it. The white plantation house overlooked the James River, and the windows were colored green by Venetian blinds.

Lydia missed the days of skating and dancing, and she also missed the days when she used to call on Sarah as an excuse to catch a glimpse of Sarah's older brother. Seth had come to their house as well, almost weekly, under the guise of visiting Grayson.

Both Sarah and Grayson accepted their role as conduits with

good nature, and they played along. In those days, what seemed like a lifetime ago, she'd often wondered if Grayson might have had hopes of winning Sarah's heart as well. Lydia never told her brother, but she'd entertained dreams of living in the Hammonds' house with Seth and visiting Sarah and Grayson at Caswell Hall.

As Elisha helped them step down onto the drive, Mother told him to wait with the coach, but when he turned to tie the horses to a hitching post, Lydia whispered to him to spend the hour with his family.

Neither Lady Caswell nor Lydia rang the bell at the top of the front steps. Instead Sarah opened the door and engulfed Lydia in her arms.

Her friend wore a pink kerchief around her neck and a creamy tan-colored gown. She was thinner than the last time Lydia had seen her, and with her pale blond hair and the yellow flecks in her green eyes, she reminded Lydia of a fairy who was more comfortable in the trees than cooped up in a house. The responsibilities her father had left for her must feel over-whelming.

After hugging Lydia, Sarah shook Mother's hand. "I am so glad you have come for a visit."

"Unfortunately, we cannot stay long," Mother said. "We are on our way to Williamsburg to buy some supplies—"

"You must come in first and have some—tea."

Lydia blinked, surprised. "You serve tea?"

"It is not nearly as good as real tea," Sarah said, "but I hope it will give you a little refreshment."

Lydia didn't mention that they served real tea at Caswell Hall. Only those faithful to the king drank tea, but even then it was almost impossible to obtain.

"Please come in," Sarah repeated.

Mother finally nodded, and Sarah motioned them toward her parlor.

Lydia and her mother sat across from her, on the black duvet where she and Seth used to talk about uniting Hammond Plantation and Caswell Hall. Where she used to dream of a houseful of children who would roam between the two plantations. She expected sadness to flood back with the memories, but all she felt was emptiness.

Lydia gave the slightest shake of her head as if it could erase the memories. She leaned forward. "How are you?"

Sarah's smile fell. "I was fine, until someone stole our remaining horses."

Lydia swallowed. "How many horses did they steal?"

"Six."

She shuddered at the memory of the six horses the officers brought with them when they came to Caswell Hall. She had no facts, only speculation, but that speculation frightened her.

"I am sorry," Lydia told her. "Truly."

Sarah sighed. "Many have lost so much more."

"It is the terrible cost of this war . . ." Lydia's voice trailed off. She'd wanted to see Sarah yet wasn't sure what to say to her friend whose brother and father were serving on opposing sides.

Morah set a platter with a pot of sassafras tea, milk, and sugar cubes on the table between the women. Sarah's maidservant was as elegant as any British gentlewoman and quite lovely with her light-brown skin and slender features.

Morah was only about five years older than Lydia, and everyone at their plantation knew Elisha loved her. When Sarah and Lydia were younger, Morah told them she and Elisha jumped over the broom together, and the girls thought Elisha and Morah needed a real ceremony. They conspired to throw them a secret wedding until Hannah found out about it. Hannah told Father, and he immediately put an end to their plans.

Soon after, Morah became pregnant and Father decided to sell her. It was Lady Caswell who convinced him to sell Morah to a nearby family so she and Elisha could visit on occasion. And with Morah nearby, Father probably figured Elisha would never run. Sarah had begged her father to buy Elisha as well, but Lord Caswell refused to part from his trusted driver.

Sarah nodded toward the door. "I believe you and Alden are needed outside."

Morah's brown eyes glowed. "I thank ye."

After she left, Sarah glanced out the window. "I was just thinking I wanted to go to Williamsburg."

Lydia nearly invited her, but when she glanced at her mother, Lady Caswell gave her the slightest shake of her head.

Sarah quickly recovered the awkward silence. "Will you be paying anyone a visit while you are in town?"

Lydia nodded. "We will be stopping to see Mrs. Pendell."

Sarah poured them each a cup of the light-pink drink, and Mother sipped hers without complaint. Lydia added a sugar cube, and the tea tasted a bit like the nutmeg that Viney put in hot cider.

Sarah picked up her cup. "I am sure Mrs. Pendell will be most glad for your company."

"Do you have news from your father?" Mother asked.

Sarah shook her head. "It is difficult to get correspondence from the West Indies."

Lydia added another cube of sugar to the tea. "He must miss the plantation."

"We miss him as well." Sarah smiled, but Lydia saw the strain in it.

"I can imagine." Lydia sipped her tea slowly, hoping Sarah would say that she'd heard from Seth as well, but she didn't mention her brother.

Lydia heard footsteps on the wood outside the parlor, and she turned to see Thomas, the Negro man who worked with Sarah to oversee the property and slaves. Thomas shifted his hat into his other hand. "Good morning, Lady Caswell. Miss Caswell."

"What is it?" Sarah asked.

"We found one of the Caswell canoes this morning, down by the stream."

Lydia's teacup clinked against the saucer. Had Nathan taken one of their boats here?

Mother cocked her head ever so slightly. "Why would our canoe be on your property?"

"I am not certain, but I can have one of our men return it to you."

"Lord Caswell would thank you."

Thomas nodded and backed toward the door.

"We must leave as well," Mother said.

Sarah stood. "Before you go, I have a favor to ask of you."

"What is it?" Mother asked.

Sarah motioned for them to wait and left the room. When she returned, there was a leather pouch in her hand. "Would you take this letter to Williamsburg for me?"

"Who is it for?" Lydia asked.

Sarah shrugged. "It is a note for Mrs. Pendell. I would like to visit her in person, of course, but with our horses gone . . ."

Lydia eyed the letter. She hadn't realized that Sarah and Mrs. Pendell maintained a friendship, but it was good for Sarah to have other women in her life, especially respectable gentlewomen.

Mother nodded. "We would be glad to take it."

Lydia took the pouch and hugged her friend. "I have missed you."

Tears welled in Sarah's eyes. "I have missed you too."

Mother thanked Sarah and moved toward the door. "I will meet you in the coach, Lydia."

She nodded.

Sarah lowered her voice. "Have you heard from Grayson?"

Lydia shook her head slowly. She wished she could tell her that there was news. "What about Seth?"

Sarah walked her toward the door. "It has been a long time."

"When you write him again—" Lydia started. She should tell him something, but what? That she still loved him, wanted to marry him? None of that was true. "Please tell him I asked about him," she finally said.

"I will do that." Sarah leaned against the doorframe. "Sometimes I think, I pretend, that Grayson is still alive. I know it is wishful thinking—"

Lydia nodded. "We cannot give up hope."

Sarah's voice grew soft. "I still hope you will marry Seth."

The strangest mixture of sorrow and appreciation washed over Lydia as she linked her arm through Sarah's. "No matter what happens, I will think of you as my sister."

"Aye," Sarah said. "And I you, as well."

Lydia squeezed the pouch. "If only—"

Sarah stopped her. "The people who killed your grandfather deserve to be punished, but Seth is not like them."

Lydia thought again of Nathan and his kindness to her. "I know."

"He only believes we should be free."

"The freedom comes at such a great cost," Lydia said as they walked through the entry hall.

"I suppose that is what we must wrestle with. Is this freedom worth it?"

Lydia looked out the front door, at the carriage waiting outside. "I know not the answer to that question."

Sarah held open the door as Lydia stepped out. "Thank you for delivering the letter to Mrs. Pendell."

Lydia nodded, squeezing the pouch in her hands. "I wish you could come with us."

Elisha helped Lydia into the carriage and then climbed up to his seat. As he drove them toward Williamsburg, Lydia watched both Sarah and Morah waving from separate windows of the grand plantation home.

～

Sarah lingered by the front window as Elisha drove Lydia and Lady Caswell away. Seeing the women together made her miss her mother, the lovely Mary Hammond from Philadelphia.

Her father rarely talked about the woman who'd died birthing Sarah's youngest brother, the brother who'd never received a name. He'd joined their mother an hour after she was gone.

A thread of guilt wove through Sarah as she watched the Caswell coach disappear into the trees. Just two days ago she'd waited for hours in the forest, until the British guards left, before she returned home. If she had continued to Williamsburg on foot, she would have been stopped and searched, the letter discovered.

Now the letter was in Lydia's hands.

She hated putting her dear friends at risk, but she didn't have a choice. Even if the coach was stopped by the British— and Lady Caswell told them that Sarah had given them the letter—she must risk it.

Sarah squeezed the back of a tall chair. She wasn't supposed to give the correspondence to anyone else, but if it wasn't delivered, hundreds and maybe even thousands of lives might be lost. She could think of no other way to get the letter safely to Williamsburg.

The British might have suspected Sarah with a letter hidden in her pocket, but she prayed they would not suspect her friend.

Lydia reminded her of Grayson, a calm presence whenever

Sarah was all in a flurry. Surely Lydia would be fine if someone stopped them. And she would truthfully say that the letter was for Mrs. Pendell, a woman respected by the British. If the British went to Mrs. Pendell, she could feign ignorance.

Sarah slipped a book off the shelf and thumbed through it as she tried to distract herself.

Minutes later, footsteps pounded across the hall and she heard someone yell her name. She returned her book, and when she stepped out into the entryway, she saw Morah. Her maid's cap was missing, her long hair askew.

Sarah rushed forward. "What is it?"

Morah turned to her, gasping for air as if she'd run a mile. "A British ship has docked at our wharf."

"Are they coming on land?"

She nodded. "I fear they're headed this way."

Her heart raced. "We must find Thomas."

Perhaps they would respect him more than a woman.

Sarah raced outside the door and down the front steps. He had been in the house an hour ago, but he could be in the fields now or in any one of their buildings.

As she shouted his name, Negro men and women watched her from the doorways of the washhouse, kitchen, and dairy. When Thomas didn't answer, she started down the avenue, toward the thousands of acres on this side of her house. He could be on any one of them.

"Miss!" Morah called behind her. "You must hide."

She turned. "I cannot."

"Master Hammond would want you to be safe, and so would Thomas."

She shook her head, though her heart began to falter. "Thomas and I will speak with the British together."

Morah pointed her toward the flank buildings. "You must let him do this alone."

"They will not respect—"

Her words were silenced by the sound of a musket blast near the riverbank. She swiveled and saw a swarm of scarlet—enshrouded in black smoke—marching toward her.

Her stomach rolling, she stumbled backward.

"Hide." Morah shoved her toward the dovecote. "I will find Thomas."

Instead of fighting, Sarah fled.

"Poor Sarah," Mother said as she watched the trees outside the coach windows.

Lydia tapped the pouch in her hands. "She is caught in a terrible place."

Mother nodded. "Even though she remains loyal, she may be persecuted because of her brother's choices."

Lydia turned the pouch over. "At least she has us to help her, if it becomes necessary."

Mother was silent for a long time. "It would be dangerous for us to visit her again."

"She is like family."

"Aye." Mother sighed. "'Tis a difficult situation."

"Her father is a commodore in the Royal Navy, and Sarah remains loyal."

"But now Major Reed and the others know about Seth."

"Whoa," she heard Elisha say as the horses stopped. Lydia looked out the window and saw four men, three in red coats and one dressed in blue. She sighed. It seemed the soldiers were everywhere.

One of the soldiers leaned against the coach, looking up at Elisha. "Where are you traveling?"

She heard Elisha's muffled voice. "I'm taking my master's wife and daughter to Williamsburg."

"We are in the midst of a war."

"The ladies are quite aware of that."

The men's eyes narrowed, and Lydia braced herself.

"Don't be impertinent with me," the soldier said.

"I'm only telling you the truth."

One of the men laughed. "We shall need a look at your ladies."

Mother's fingers circled around the door handle. They had nothing to hide, but the thought of these men searching her and Mother was appalling.

Mother opened the door and stood on the top step, overlooking the men. "What are you gentlemen doing on our road?"

"We are wreaking havoc on some rebels."

"Since my daughter and I are not rebels, you can wait until our coach has passed to wreak it."

A man with dark hair and the blue uniform laughed. He must be one of the hired German soldiers she'd heard about.

The Englishman stepped forward. "We have been ordered to search everyone on the road to Williamsburg."

Mother's chin inched up. "I am afraid we can spare no time for a search."

"You are too busy to serve the wishes of the Crown?"

"We are busy serving the wishes of the Crown," Mother replied. "Elisha, please give this gentleman our letter from Major Reed."

The man's eyes narrowed. "How do you know Major Reed?"

"He is a family friend."

The man laughed. "That is quite presumptuous of you."

"Major Reed is also a guest at our home." Mother climbed back into the coach and closed the door. She leaned forward to speak again through the window while the soldier skimmed the letter. "The major has sent us on an errand to Williamsburg."

The soldier took a step back. "You are helping him?"

"Of course," she said. "And he would appreciate it greatly, I believe, if you did not detain us another moment."

Lydia waved the pouch in front of her face as they rode away. The British army really should employ her mother to negotiate for them.

CHAPTER 15

The cobblestone streets in Williamsburg smelled like coffee beans and custard, pine and tar. The wooden sidewalks were crowded with people peering into the windows of the millinery, bakery, and wigmaker's shop.

Each shopkeeper displayed a painting beside his front door for those who couldn't read—a picture of shoes for the shoemaker, a loom for the weaver, a basin for the barber—and the doors were donned with evergreen wreaths of ribbons, pinecones, and winterberries along with wooden birds and other figures woven into the greenery.

It was almost as if no one realized—or perhaps they didn't care—that British solders were preparing to take over this town.

Down the alleyways were dozens of mulberry trees and whitewashed homes behind neat picket fences with gardens dormant through the winter months. Lydia loved the beauty of Williamsburg, though her nerves rattled with the hordes of people and the constant clanging of wagon and carriage wheels against the stone.

The bells of Bruton Parish Church rang out to announce the

hour of ten. She and Mother would have four hours in town before they must return home.

The coach passed beside the long lawn that led up to the vacant Governor's Palace. When Lord Dunmore's family occupied the palace, they hosted the most magnificent dinners and balls to celebrate the colony's bounty. He often invited members from the House of Burgesses, the men and women who owned businesses in their colony's capital and the influential plantation owners who lived around Williamsburg.

After Thomas Jefferson became governor, there were no more invitations for the Caswell family.

Elisha stopped the coach beside the millinery, near the old capitol building. Lydia followed her mother inside the shop to check on a spring hat her mother had ordered last month. Mrs. Reynolds, the milliner, had once been kind to Mother, but she'd stopped being friendly in the months before Grandfather's death and had been downright unkind ever since. The relationship with Mrs. Reynolds had evolved into a purely business relationship, and it saddened Lydia that they were no longer amicable.

Few people in town offered consolation for what happened to Grandfather. It was almost as if they believed he had deserved the tar and feathers.

Mrs. Reynolds sat behind the counter, her wide frame surrounded by colorful hats in an assortment of shapes and designs.

"I would like to inquire about my order," Mother said quite matter-of-factly.

Mrs. Reynolds pushed herself off the stool and retrieved the straw hat with a pale-blue flower on the back and a lovely display of yellow-and-white ribbons. Mother took it without bothering to compliment the woman's fine handiwork. Then she turned to walk back toward the door.

Mrs. Reynolds called out to her, "I'm afraid I will need the payment today."

Mother swiveled back toward the counter. "Lord Caswell comes in every month to reconcile the accounts."

The shopkeeper reached for the hat. "I can no longer sell you hats on credit."

Mother set the hat on the counter. Instead of arguing, she pulled two paper notes out of her reticule and set them beside the hat. Mrs. Reynolds took the money, and Lydia nodded to her before following her mother outside.

Mother set her new hat on her lap in the coach and pinched her fingers around the brim. "Dreadful woman," she murmured. "Just dreadful."

Lydia glanced back at the window of the shop, and she could see Mrs. Reynolds inside, working on another hat.

"Everyone seems to be struggling at present," Lydia said, trying to console her.

Mother shook her head. "She is not struggling. She is making a point that she does not trust our family to pay our accounts."

If there was another milliner in Williamsburg who made such beautiful hats, Mother would move her business, but Mrs. Reynolds replicated the most fashionable designs from London. Even though she had lived in the colonies for the past thirty years—and even though it was difficult to obtain the finer fabrics and lace—Mother still attempted to dress like a gentlewoman.

They strolled along the wooden walkway, purchasing sticks of cinnamon, gingerroot, and different colors of ribbon using the money in Mother's purse, since it seemed as if all the merchants had conspired against them to refuse the Caswell family credit.

They stopped shopping, but they didn't stop walking until they reached the long plaza that stretched to the palace.

The old steeple at Bruton Parish Church towered in front of them, and beside the plaza stood the Pendells' brick home. Mr. Pendell was a professor at the College of William & Mary and used to share the view that the colonies should submit to the king.

Lydia hadn't heard of any other supporters of the British being tarred and feathered in Williamsburg since the war began, but plenty had been plundered and some even killed for their beliefs. She often wondered how the Pendells escaped this, remaining in Williamsburg while many Loyalists from the university went back to England.

Perhaps Mr. Pendell also realized that he must keep his political views secret until after the war.

Mrs. Pendell had been one of Mother's closest friends since the Caswell family arrived in the colonies, but as Mother tentatively knocked on the door, it was as if she were afraid this friendship had dissolved as well.

A maid answered the door and escorted them into the parlor.

Mrs. Pendell rose when she saw them, her large arms outstretched— but her smile quickly faded when she saw Lady Caswell's face. "Oh, Dorothea, you look as if you are about to collapse."

Mother's resolve crumbled, and she pulled her handkerchief out of her small bag to dab at her tears. "It has been a perfectly awful day."

Mrs. Pendell guided her to a chair. "What on earth happened?"

Mother's story of humiliation surged out of her, Mrs. Pendell listening in earnest. Their host brushed her cheeks with her own handkerchief as Mother described the injustices done to her today and in the months and years past, interjecting words like ghastly, despicable, impossible. Mrs. Pendell sympa-

thized fully with her, but she didn't contribute any stories of
her own.

Were the Caswells the only family treated like this in town?

"We shall think of this no longer. We shall have some—"
Mrs. Pendell hesitated as if she were debating what she would
serve. She leaned toward them as if they were conspiring
together. "We can no longer serve tea here, you understand, but
would you like some chocolate?"

Lydia smiled. No one could argue against chocolate.

"Chocolate would be fine," Mother said.

Mrs. Pendell rang her bell for their refreshments and then
looked back at the women. "Have you heard from Grayson?"

Lydia shook her head. Part of her appreciated the sympathy
in Mrs. Pendell's eyes, while another part of her wished she
could refute the pity. Mother changed the subject, and they
talked of the weather and the plantation and the fact that Mr.
Jones's oldest daughter was planning to wed in spite of the war.

The chocolate arrived and Mrs. Pendell poured them each a
cup. Lydia sipped her drink slowly. The warm chocolate was
flavored with cinnamon and vanilla, and she savored each drop.

"I do hope the war will be over before Miss Jones's wedding,"
Mother said.

"We have heard the British might be close." Mrs. Pendell
leaned toward them again. "We pray they are."

"In the strictest confidence . . ." Mother began.

"Of course."

"We have eighteen British officers staying at Caswell Hall."

"Indeed!" Mrs. Pendell's look of alarm quickly turned into
one of joy. Lydia wished she felt as excited about the British
being in Virginia.

"They will not be at our home for much longer." Mother
turned toward the empty doorway as if to check for eavesdrop-
pers. "You and Herbert should leave Williamsburg for a season."

"Whatever for?"

Mother sipped her drink. "I believe they will be marching on Williamsburg soon. Even though your family is loyal, I'm afraid you'll be in danger."

"Herbert will want to stay and welcome the men."

"It still may not be safe."

Mrs. Pendell sighed. "Nothing seems safe these days."

"I suppose not," Mother said. "And it is difficult to trust anyone."

Mrs. Pendell reached for a wooden box and handed it to Mother. Mother reciprocated with the rest of her paper money. Even though they were friends, or perhaps because of it, the women never operated on credit. Mother held the box—filled with what Lydia assumed was English tea—close to her side.

"Please take care," Mrs. Pendell said, kissing Mother's cheek.

"I nearly forgot." Lydia reached into her pocket. "Sarah Hammond sent you a letter."

"Oh, she is a dear, isn't she?" Mrs. Pendell took the letter from Lydia and clutched it in two hands. "I wonder why she didn't bring it herself."

"Her horses were stolen last week."

"I certainly hope this madness will end soon." Mrs. Pendell patted her arm. "Might I bother you with one more errand?"

"'Tis no bother," Lydia said.

"I wonder if you could deliver my reply to Sarah on your way home."

After Mrs. Pendell wrote her reply, Lydia linked arms with her mother and set off, with Mrs. Pendell's box and the letter, to the livery to find Elisha and their two horses. The church bells rang three times as they rode away from the town center. Thankfully they would be home before dark.

~

Elisha pressed the horses forward to reach home before night fell, and Mother rested quietly beside her, though sleep was impossible with the fierce rocking. Lydia figured she was processing all that had transpired in Williamsburg.

While Mother trusted Mrs. Pendell with her thoughts, it was almost as if she were afraid to talk about all that was on her mind with her daughter. Maybe she feared appearing weak when she wanted to be strong.

As they neared Hammond Plantation, Lydia closed her eyes. She wished they could stop at Sarah's house to assure her that Mrs. Pendell's letter had been delivered and to give her the response, but it was too late in the day now for even a short visit. She would send Elisha over at first light with Mrs. Pendell's return message.

The earthy smell of wood smoke drifted into the coach when Elisha slowed their carriage. She glanced out the window and saw a man walking along the side of the road, a tricorn hat askew on his head.

The man looked like a vagrant, with his black cloak draped over his arms. One hand held some sort of satchel, and the other clutched a wooden cane.

At the sight of the cane, her gaze shot back toward his face. Surely not. Nathan should be far from here by now.

But when he glanced up, his gaze met hers and she gasped.

"Stop staring," Mother insisted.

Lydia turned forward quickly, afraid Mother would inquire whether she knew this man. Was her imagination playing with her? Why would Nathan be on this road?

As they approached the avenue to Sarah's house, the smoke grew thicker inside their coach, the smell rancid.

"What in heaven's name—" Mother coughed, trying to fan away the smoke with her hand. When that proved unsuccessful, she reached over and opened the window, but instead of letting the smoke out, more poured inside.

Elisha turned toward the Hammond house without being directed, and neither she nor Mother questioned him. There was no time to think about Nathan now. They must find out what was burning.

Mother leaned toward the open window. "Hurry, Elisha."

Had the kitchen caught on fire? Or another building? Whatever had happened, she prayed Sarah was safe.

As they drove toward the house, the smoke grew black, and Lydia's stomach rolled at the terrible stench. It smelled of death and dirt and fear.

Elisha slowed the carriage at the end of the lane, and Mother gasped. A burned shell had replaced the elegant home where they'd sipped sassafras tea that morning. Smoke from the dying flames rose to the sky, leaving only blackened scars.

Major Reed and the others had discussed burning houses around Charles Towne and in Richmond, but why would they burn houses here? Especially a plantation home like the Hammonds'? With the exception of Seth, the Hammond family was loyal to the Crown.

There must have been a terrible accident. She couldn't think, couldn't fathom, that someone might have done this intentionally.

Two Negro men sat beside the drive, staring at the coach, their faces blank from shock. Lydia hopped down and ran toward the cluster of four remaining buildings that flanked the house.

"Sarah!" she shouted.

When she turned back, she watched Mother step out of the carriage and begin calling Sarah's name as well. Elisha rushed toward the two Negroes.

Lydia cupped her trembling hands, her voice shaking as her shout turned to a question. "Sarah?"

Then she listened, praying for a response.

To her right she heard the creak of a door, and she swiveled on her feet to see her friend emerge from the family's dovecote. Her fairylike dress was covered in soot and hay, and her eyes bore the same blank stare of the Negro men.

Sarah tripped and then leaned back against the stone building, gulping great breaths of the smoke-laden air as Lydia rushed toward her. Then she led Sarah back toward Mother and the Negro men, wishing she had the perfect words to ease her friend's distress, to comfort her, but she had none. Only questions.

"What happened?" Lydia asked.

"The British came," Sarah murmured. "They set it on fire."

Even though she'd suspected it, Lydia still felt as if someone had struck her. She wished so badly that she had been wrong.

Sarah began to shake.

When Lydia looked up, she saw Elisha's eyes wide with fear. "Where is Morah?" he demanded.

"She must be near—" Sarah said.

The man next to Elisha interrupted her. "The British took the rest of the slaves with them."

A horrible noise surged through Elisha's lips, the guttural sound of despair. When he dropped to his knee, Lydia's skin turned cold.

What happened to his wife? His son?

In that moment, Elisha wasn't their family's Negro. He was her protector, her friend.

"I am so sorry," she whispered.

Elisha buried his head in his hands.

When Sarah spoke again, her voice cut like ice through the smoke. "What about Thomas?"

"He tried to stop them by the river." The taller man spoke again. "They shot him."

Sarah tilted again, and Lydia steadied her. She wished there was something she could do to comfort all of them.

"What—" Sarah's voice cracked. "What will they do with the rest of our servants?"

"I am afraid they'll sell them, miss," one of the men said.

Sarah collapsed onto the ground and Lydia sat beside her, wrapping an arm around her friend as Sarah's tears soaked her shoulder. For a moment this morning, everything had seemed normal again. They had been two friends simply talking over tea.

But nothing was normal.

The blunt brutality of this war came crashing around her. There was no safe place for any of them, Negro or gentleman.

"You must come home with—" Lydia stopped before she finished her invitation.

What would happen if Major Reed and the others had set Sarah's house on fire? They couldn't take Sarah home with them, and they certainly could not leave her here.

She looked over at her mother. "We can't leave her alone."

Mother eyed the unburned flank buildings around them. "There's no suitable place for us to spend the night."

Sarah sat up, and Lydia took her friend's hand as darkness began pouring over them.

"Perhaps we can all go back to Williamsburg," Lydia said. The soldiers might still be patrolling the roads, but Mother could concoct a story for them.

Sarah shook her head. "Elisha can't drive. He must grieve his loss."

Lydia looked up at him again, at the devastation etched into his face. If only they knew where the British had taken his family.

Another Negro man ran up to them. "Four more British soldiers are coming from the west."

Lydia's heart quickened as Sarah turned to her remaining two men. "Can one of you take us to town?"

The younger man stepped forward. "Aye."

Mother spoke. "You must walk home, Elisha."

His nod was inconclusive.

Mother kept talking. "Tell Master Caswell that we will return on the morrow."

Lydia's legs trembled as she climbed up into the coach. How could her mother ask Elisha to do anything?

But perhaps her mother needed to take charge of this situation in her own way. It was almost as if she couldn't allow herself to empathize with the loss of a son.

With his cane in one hand and a shaving kit in the other, Nathan moved slowly along the road. While he needed to stay hidden at times, often he avoided suspicion by remaining in plain sight. He couldn't have come up with a better way to escape notice. A crippled man, with a passable British accent, posing as a barber.

Even though British soldiers frequently stopped him, none kept for him long. He charged two pence for a shave. Some paid, some did not, but they always let him on his way.

Months ago, a barber near Fredericksburg had given him a basic lesson on shaving and letting blood. The barber tried to teach him how to pull teeth too, but heaven forbid if someone actually asked him to do so.

He hadn't expected to see Lydia Caswell. Even though she'd been mostly hidden by the coach, she'd looked even more beautiful than he remembered. She had seen him, and he had seen the surprise on her face.

Ah well, it couldn't be helped. She would keep his secret, he was sure of it, but suddenly he wished for a more dignified occupation for his disguise—a physician, perhaps, or a shipbuilder. But a barber required only minimal supplies easily obtained by Patriot sympathizers, and all the British soldiers needed barbering services.

Smoke clung to the air as he turned toward the Hammond plantation. Sarah's men must be burning debris before the next rain. Tonight he would sleep in one of the Hammonds' flank buildings and then retrieve any return messages in the morning. He already had two messages to deliver to his uncle. Once he checked the dovecote, he would acquire some sort of transport north.

Another carriage rumbled up the lane, and he crept to the edge of the trees to make room for it. A Negro he didn't recognize drove the horses, and when the driver stopped at the intersection, Nathan saw the profile of Lydia's face and two other women through the window.

Then he saw Lydia's tears.

Instead of turning toward Caswell Hall, the driver turned back toward town.

Why were they still traveling after dark? And what had happened that made Lydia cry?

With his cane, it would take him another fifteen minutes to walk to the Hammond house. Then he would search for Lydia in town.

CHAPTER 16

*Q*blaze roared upstairs in the Pendells' guest chamber.
From her bed, Sarah watched the lashing and twisting
of the flames in the fireplace. Once, she'd sought comfort and
warmth in fire, but now all she saw was destruction, the black
bones of her home left for dead.

Everything happened so quickly—the terrible stomping of
feet as the British drew close to her hiding place. The heat and
the ashes. Birds flapping against her in the dovecote before they
escaped through the roof.

If only she could have flown away with them.

Morah had been right. Those soldiers probably wouldn't
have respected her role, and no matter what she said, they
might have decided to make a spectacle of her.

Still, she wished there had been something she could have
done to stop them.

Kneeling in the dovecote, struggling for breath, she'd wanted
the smoke to take her life. But then it was as if she heard
Grayson whispering to her, telling her to fight. So she fought
with every breath until she heard Lydia calling her name.

The British had killed Thomas and destroyed all that he'd

helped her and her father build. And then they'd stolen away dear Morah and Alden and the others.

She should have given the few Negroes who remained some sort of instruction before she left for Williamsburg, but there had been no strength left within her.

Perhaps they could live off the land until Seth returned. Her brother might love the plantation, but she would never go back. Everything she cherished had been devoured by the flames—her treasured books, her mother's furniture, her father's papers, her letters to Grayson.

She hated the British for making her hide in the tiny dovecote while they plundered her house and property, hated herself for cowering before those soldiers and her servants.

Never again would she cower.

Her father and brother would be devastated by the loss of their home and Negroes. If Father had been there, he would likely have made her hide, but neither he nor Seth would have cowered. Surely they would have respected Father's position in their navy.

On the table lay the letter Lydia had given to her from Mrs. Pendell. Seth had asked her to deliver the messages for Washington, but how was she supposed to do that now? The next courier would realize the moment he arrived that this link in their network was broken.

How would they deliver the messages without an intermediary? The courier couldn't call on Mrs. Pendell directly. It would give away everything they'd work so hard to keep secret, and it would jeopardize Mrs. Pendell and her family.

A light tap on the door forced her thoughts away. After the door opened, Lydia moved quietly across the small room and placed a glass bottle and a spoon on the nightstand. Sarah closed her eyes, glad for the company but much too tired to entertain.

Lydia sat on a chair beside the bed and leaned forward. "Are you well?"

Sarah shook her head.

"Of course you're not." Lydia reached out, but Sarah couldn't grasp her hand.

Her voice trembled when she spoke again. "How can you be on the side of those—of those tyrants?"

Lydia placed her hand on Sarah's arm. "I do not condone what those men did to your home or servants."

Sarah could no longer pretend to be loyal. "But destruction is what they want—what the king wants. Destruction of our freedom and our property and our very lives."

"The rebels have also destroyed things."

"But they do not burn our homes."

Lydia took her hand away, folding her arms over her chest. "Perhaps not, but they've taken innocent lives."

Sarah stared at the blaze. How could she forget those dark days after the death of the senior Lord Caswell, the days after Grayson disappeared? "I am sorry, Lydia. My mind is not right."

Her friend dabbed at her eyes. "I love people who have remained loyal, yet I hate all that the British have destroyed. How am I supposed to choose a side?"

Sarah studied her friend's tears. Lydia reminded her so much of Grayson. He had pleaded for peace instead of destruction.

Lydia held up a glass tincture. "Mother said the laudanum will help you rest."

"I do not wish to rest." Part of her wanted to numb her pain, but another part wasn't ready to let go of it. The men who burned the plantation, they deserved her hatred. Thomas and the other slaves deserved her grief.

"You need your strength," Lydia said. "Tomorrow you must leave Williamsburg."

Sarah's stomach clenched. She hadn't begun to think about where she would go next. But what if the British were looking for her? What if they discovered that she hadn't died in the blaze?

Finally she took Lydia's offer of medicine and, after her friend left, pulled the covers over her chest and closed her eyes.

Lydia was right; she must leave as soon as possible. She wouldn't cower if the enemy found her again, but she had promised her father that she would do everything she could to survive this war.

Perhaps tomorrow she would finally sail away.

CHAPTER 17

*L*ydia rushed across the grassy plaza in front of the Pendells' house. The laudanum had coaxed both Mother and Sarah to sleep, but she couldn't rest. She needed a place to calm the racing in her mind.

Some people might find it odd, but the only place in town where she would find some sort of comfort was at her grandfather's side.

The houses along the plaza were dark, the residents unaware of what took place three miles from them.

What would happen if the British did take Williamsburg? She prayed they wouldn't burn it as they had Sarah's home.

Had the British set fire to the house because Hannah inferred the Hammonds were Patriots? Father had defended Commodore Hammond and his daughter, but Lydia had not joined him to defend her friends— nor had she denied her betrothal to Seth.

A thought came to her, and she shuddered. Would Major Reed retaliate because she had refused him in the kitchen? She had thought her engagement to Seth might deter the major, but instead, it seemed her deception had pushed him to destroy.

How could she tell Seth that she'd compromised his family's loyalties and the British had retaliated by burning down his home?

She opened the iron gate behind the church and hurried under a brick arch. The steeple loomed above her, and in front of her stood dozens of headstones, some tucked back among the trees.

Grandfather's tombstone was beside the brick wall. His epitaph said he was resting in peace, but how could he be at peace when the world seemed to be falling apart? Bitterness welled in her heart against the men who killed her grandfather, the men who drove her brother from their family.

But Sarah was right—not all Patriots were evil. Men like Nathan hadn't killed her grandfather, nor had Seth.

She stared at the epitaph of Lord Henry Caswell. "What shall I do?" she whispered.

Answers swirled in her mind, warring with each other.

If only King George would visit the colonies and see that most colonists were reasonable people. Perhaps it wasn't too late to negotiate a compromise. They could stop all of this death and destruction before any more homes were burned or lives lost.

Until then, how was she supposed to support the king while his men ravaged the colonies?

A twig cracked, and she turned. Had the soldiers come for her next? She was too numb to feel even fear.

"Who is there?" she demanded.

There was a long pause before she heard an answer. "It is Nathan."

Her heart lifted. It *had* been him walking on the roadside. "How did you know I was here?"

"I saw your carriage in town."

Now she could see his face in the moonlight, his steady

smile. He leaned against his cane, but he appeared much healthier. And stronger.

"So you followed me here?" she asked.

"I fear I'm guilty on that account."

She gave him a slight smile. Even if the two men were on the opposite sides of this war, Nathan reminded her a bit of her father, wanting to keep her safe.

"I'm glad you are well," she said. "After you left—I was worried."

"I was pleased to be your servant." He held up his satchel. "Just as I am pleased to serve the British as a barber."

"You're not really a barber?"

He shook his head. "I am dreadful at it."

She laughed and then felt guilty for her laughter.

His voice grew serious. "You played your part well, Miss Caswell."

"Thank you," she whispered, grateful that she had been able to help him escape. "Nathan . . ."

He tipped his head slightly. "What is it?"

She hesitated before she spoke again. "Why won't you tell me your last name?"

"Someday I would like to tell you, when the war is over."

Her heart warmed. It seemed as if he was trying to protect her, but even more than that, he wanted to see her again. Nathan had become a friend, and friends could ease their formalities.

"If I am to continue calling you by your first name," she said, "then I would like it very much if you would call me Lydia."

He smiled. "I would like that."

She smiled in return. Except for Seth and the members of her family—and Major Reed, in his presumptive liberty—no other man called her Lydia.

He looked down at the tombstone in front of her. "Who is this?"

"My grandfather."

"Was he on the wrong side of this war?"

"He was at the time." She glanced back up at him. "But the sides keep changing."

He traced through the grass with his cane. "A man must stand for what he believes, no matter what."

She had been angry with the rebels who killed her grandfather, but until the British swarmed their house, she hadn't thought much about supporting the Loyalists or Patriots. Her faith had been in God, her father, and Caswell Hall. And not always in that order.

"What if—what if one is not certain of what one believes?" she asked.

"Oh, Lydia." He motioned to a stone bench. "Shall we sit?"

She nodded before sitting beside him.

"Did something happen?" he asked.

She hesitated before she spoke. "My friend—"

Tears began to rise again. She wanted to confide in him, but he was supposed to be the enemy.

Yet Nathan knew where her family's loyalties lay, and he had done nothing to harm her. Even if others failed her, she desperately wanted to be able to trust him. "The British soldiers burned down her home."

"Who is your friend?"

"Sarah Hammond," she answered.

The curse that slipped from his lips surprised her. And eased some of her sorrow.

He felt her pain—Sarah's pain. Perhaps he could help her understand why men would do this, why they would hate so much.

"Is your friend safe?" he asked.

"She is alive, but they killed her overseer and took away most of the slaves." She leaned closer to him, imploring him. "Why would they burn an innocent person's home?"

He was slow to answer. "In war, Lydia, many innocent people die."

She glanced back at her grandfather's stone. "They die, and no one seems to care."

"That's not true," he said, his voice tender.

"The Hammonds didn't do anything to deserve this."

It was her words, hers and Hannah's, that had indicted them. With their words, she and Hannah strung the noose.

The British just finished the hanging.

Nathan wanted to kick something, but the gravestone of Lydia's grandfather—or any gravestone, for that matter—would hardly be an appropriate target for his wrath.

In his mind's eye, he could see the British avenging Seth's position—and perhaps Sarah's role as a courier—by burning down the Hammond house.

How would they have known about Sarah, though? He had taken every precaution to ensure secrecy, but sometimes the network failed. Money, promises—there were plenty of ways to coax a seemingly loyal person to talk.

He hadn't actually met Sarah— Seth was the connection between them—but Seth swore they could trust his sister, and Nathan trusted Seth implicitly.

Thank God, they hadn't killed Sarah Hammond in the process, but she must be devastated. And Seth would be as well.

Hammond Plantation had been a key link for their intelligence since last summer. The river allowed them easy access to bring the messages, and then Sarah delivered the messages inconspicuously.

What was he going to do without her help?

He could not visit the homes of their connections in town. In his barber's disguise, he would stand out like a blot of ink on parchment. Without Sarah, Mrs. Pendell would have no way to return her messages to Nathan's uncle.

"It was my fault they burned Sarah's house," Lydia said.

He leaned toward the beautiful woman seated beside him. "It could not possibly be your fault."

"My sister told them I am betrothed to Seth Hammond, a soldier in the Continental Army. They retaliated."

His mind raced in the silence. Lydia was betrothed to Seth? Why had his friend never said he was engaged to marry?

He cleared his throat. "They already know who is loyal to the Crown and who is not."

"But the rest of the Hammond family is loyal."

Shadows from the branches danced over the gravestones as Lydia breathed softly next to him. He wondered what he should say to comfort her, but the words eluded him.

Not only had they lost a vital link in the network, but the woman next to him—the woman who had saved his own life— was betrothed to one of his best friends. Nathan couldn't even hate the man she planned to marry.

Seth had spent the previous summer at Colonel Fielder's plantation in Maryland, and he'd spent much of the past year talking about the beauty and wit of the colonel's daughter. Nathan never confirmed a marriage proposal, but he had assumed that Seth would marry Fielder's daughter after the war.

How had the detail of Seth's engagement to Lydia escaped him? For a scout, he had done a rather lousy job of obtaining that important bit of information.

More than anything, he wanted to draw Lydia into his arms and tell her that everything was going to be fine . . . but no one could guarantee that, especially not him. And he would never intrude upon the woman Seth would marry.

Instead of holding her, he sat quietly beside her in the darkness, wishing he could do something else to ease her pain.

MELANIE DOBSON

The breeze fluttered the ruffles on her gown, and she shivered. "Do you believe in this war?"

"We have no choice but to fight if we want freedom and peace."

Her gaze fell to the tombstone. "Grandfather thought the best way to maintain peace was to remain loyal to the king."

"The colonists have been trying to do that for a long time. Unfortunately, it has not worked well."

"We should pay the taxes to prevent the loss of more lives."

He tapped his cane on the ground. "It's not only about the taxation, Lydia. It's about being taxed even though no one from the colonies represents our interests. About a king four thousand miles away being able to mandate whatever he wants on a place he's never visited."

"And that's worth a war?"

He understood her question. He'd wrestled with the same one for years. While some had pushed for war, many had attempted a peaceful pact with Britain—and failed. It seemed the colonists had no other recourse.

"When we declared our independence, we hoped King George would relinquish in a reasonable way. If we surrender now, the British will crush us—and any hope of our being free."

"Freedom sounds so appealing." She paused. "And utterly impossible."

He examined her face for a moment before he spoke again. "It is not impossible. Not if we continue to band together. They can hire thousands upon thousands of Hessians and send them over to fight against us, but none of those soldiers care about freedom. The Patriot soldiers are fighting with their hearts."

He leaned closer to hear her soft reply. "What would it be like to be free?"

He rubbed his hands together. "We would no longer be forced to answer to the whims of a stubborn king, and any taxes we'd

152

pay would fortify our own country rather than the most powerful empire in the world. We would live in peace, create our own laws to protect the colonies, and speak freely about what we believe."

She shook her head. "I don't care much about any of that."

"But you must care about something."

Her gaze rested again on the tombstone of her grandfather. "I care about my family. And about our home."

"When this war is over, the king might very well take away your family and your home."

"He would never—"

"He does what pleases him, and if we don't stop his men, they will do to Williamsburg what they did to Richmond and the Hammond plantation. Not even Caswell Hall will be safe."

She looked at him, her eyes wide. "But my father remains loyal . . . and there are still Loyalists in Williamsburg."

"Not as many as you think."

She rubbed her hands together. "I don't want our colony to change."

"I fear change is inevitable for all of us."

An idea flashed into his mind, and he considered it for a moment. Some might think it risky to trust Lydia with his secret, but she had cared well for him even after she discovered he was a Patriot.

Even if she wouldn't help him, he felt certain she wouldn't do anything to harm him or his work if he asked.

He swallowed hard. "I need your assistance."

She looked over at him again. "What can I do?"

"There are certain—there are messages that must be delivered to people in Williamsburg."

She hesitated. "What sorts of messages?"

"Messages that will stop the destruction of our colonies."

She scooted away from him. "Why would you want me to do this?"

"No one would suspect you," he said, drumming his cane against his hand.

"But it would be dangerous."

He nodded. "It would."

It was his job to protect the colonists— including Lydia Caswell—and he would do everything he could to prevent her from getting hurt.

She stood up and straightened her petticoat. "I'm not certain."

"Consider it," he said. "I must go away for a while, but I will obtain your answer upon my return."

A piece of hair slipped over her shoulder, and he almost reached out to push it back over her ear. Instead, he dug his hand into the pocket of his coat.

She twisted the strand of hair. "How will I find you?"

"You won't need to look." He stood and then stepped away from her. "I will find you."

CHAPTER 18

*S*moke lingered in the air as the Caswell coach passed by the Hammonds' land. Lydia hadn't wanted to leave Sarah in Williamsburg, but Mrs. Pendell promised to help her find transport to her aunt's home in Philadelphia. Lydia had no choice but to return home.

Mother looked out at the fields beside them. "I should have invited Sarah to come to Williamsburg with us yesterday morning."

"We had no idea this would happen."

Mother shuddered. "I am tired of this war."

"Me too." Lydia paused. "Do you think the officers at our house started the fire?"

Mother's response was swift. "We can't allow ourselves to think it. We must stay in the good graces of the king."

Lydia wished she could be like Mother, focusing more on what she knew than on what she suspected.

Nathan was right. Change might be inevitable, but she didn't even know who she wanted to win this war.

Even if she did choose the Patriot cause, even if she did agree to deliver messages for Nathan, how much of an asset would she be? It was too dangerous for her to leave the plantation, and the house was swarming with British officers who might harm her family if she did as Nathan asked.

And if the officers didn't guess about her involvement, Mother would.

The coach turned onto their long drive, and when it slowed, she looked up at the beautiful home her father and grandfather had built. If she chose the wrong side, it could all be gone in an afternoon, like the Hammonds' house.

But if Nathan was correct, their remaining in the king's good graces might not save Caswell Hall anyway.

No wonder so many had rebelled.

Father and Hannah rushed outside as the coach drew near to the house, but none of their guests greeted them.

Father swung open the coach door. "We were so worried," he said, wrapping his arms around both of them.

Mother glanced toward the coach house. "Did Elisha not tell you where we went?"

Father looked up at the man driving the carriage and then back down at Mother. "Where is Elisha?"

"He was supposed to return home—"

"He is grieving, Mother," Lydia said. "We can't expect him to come right away."

Father's eyes grew wide. "What is he grieving?"

"The loss of his family."

"What happened to his family?"

Instead of answering, Mother eyed the house. "Where are the officers?"

"They left yesterday and have not returned."

Lydia clenched her father's arm. "Perhaps they are gone for good."

Father shook his head. "They will be back."

Lydia released his arm, but her mother leaned on him as they walked toward the house.

"It was ghastly," Mother said.

Hannah stepped close to her. "What happened?"

Lydia didn't want her sister to know what had happened, afraid she might gloat in some way, but as Mother explained the story, even Hannah seemed sad at the loss. Father didn't seem sad as much as he seemed—

Afraid.

Father was cautious, but she never thought he would be afraid of anything.

Lydia was finishing her dinner when she heard the laughter of the officers in the hall, and their joviality infuriated her.

She glanced at her parents and then stood, rushing toward the servants' staircase. She must escape before she saw Major Reed, before she said something that would hurt her family much more than it would him.

When she heard her father's voice, she stopped beside the staircase to listen.

"Where have you been?" he asked.

"We have been fighting," Major Reed said.

"Did you know the Hammonds' house was destroyed?"

"The home of Lydia's rebel?"

"The home of John Hammond, a commodore in the Royal Navy."

Silence followed Father's words, and Lydia peeked out from behind the door. Two men flanked the major, seeming to wait until he spoke. "Miss Hannah said Lydia is promised to a rebel."

"Hundreds of families in Virginia are divided in their loyalties," Father replied.

The major looked toward the doorway, and Lydia scrambled up the steps, all the way to the third floor. She hadn't been in the attic since she was a girl, but she knew exactly where to hide.

She rushed past the doors to the servants' chambers until she reached a storage room. Inside, she pushed a trunk in front of the door and slipped to the floor beside it.

The sunshine from a rounded window above her lit the small room, and she looked at her surroundings. A wooden horse from her childhood. Old paintings. Trunks filled with clothes and her family's heirlooms.

Tears burned her cheeks.

She had once thought the British Army would stop the rebels, restoring peace to their colonies. But perhaps they needed to rid themselves of this army before the peace in their colonies was completely destroyed.

*The necessity of procuring good
intelligence is apparent . . . .*

For upon secrecy, success depends.

George Washington, 1777

CHAPTER 19

MAY 1781

The fragrance of cherry blossoms stole through the gazebo, and the vines shading the walkways shuddered in the wind. Hollyhocks, daffodils, and Mother's prized English roses had begun to bloom in the meticulous formal gardens around the arbors, and the sweet aroma of the flowers blended with the cherry blossoms.

As she leaned against the gazebo's seat, Lydia glanced back at the coach house. Elisha never returned to their plantation, and Sarah's remaining Negroes had walked away. Father was furious about Elisha's desertion, but surely her father would do the same thing if his own family had been taken by the British.

Breathing in the fragrant evening air, she watched a schooner slip down the river. In her visits to the gazebo in the past few months, she'd prayed for wisdom. Their guests had left, but when her family attended church last Sunday, she'd heard rumors that General Cornwallis and thousands of his men were on their way to complete their occupation of Virginia. The British officers had left in April to meet Cornwallis, but their presence lingered in Caswell Hall.

Father was counting on the protection of Major Reed and

his men, confident that the British would soon retake the colonies. Then their plantation would be safe.

But if the Patriots won . . . perhaps they would still be safe.

Lydia looked over at the willows along the bank, and her heart stirred. Almost every night she wandered outside to the gazebo, waiting and hoping that Nathan would return.

Three months ago, she'd found him down by the river. Now she wished he would find her.

In the past three months, she'd tried to avoid the officers when they were quartered in her home, entertaining herself instead with her stitching and frequent walks in the garden. As she walked, she often prayed for her friends— Sarah, Grayson, Elisha, Morah. And she prayed for Nathan too.

She longed to do something to end the war. Back in Williamsburg, she shouldn't have told Nathan she would consider his request. She should have told him she would deliver his messages.

As she rocked back and forth on the seat, the breeze moved through the gazebo again, this time smelling of mint and dill and the ripened fruit from the plum trees.

Something shifted behind her. "A lovely night, is it not?"

At the sound of Nathan's voice, her heart felt as if it flipped. She glanced over her shoulder at the rhododendron bushes behind her and tried to calm her voice. "It is indeed."

"You must pretend I'm not here."

She turned back toward the river. "The servants think nothing of me talking to myself."

He laughed quietly. "Do you have long conversations?"

"Sometimes. There is no one else to talk with."

"All your guests are gone?"

"They left three weeks ago to meet Cornwallis."

He paused. "Very good, Lydia."

"Is it?"

"You have a keen ear." The bushes shifted again behind her. "The last time I saw you, you were considering my request."

She took a deep breath. "I have decided."

"What is your decision?" he asked, hope lacing through his words.

"Will you truly protect my family?"

"There is no way I can promise, but if the Patriots win this war, I will do everything I can to make sure your family is safe."

It was a gamble to trust him, she knew. But the idea of freedom had begun to stir in her heart, the hope of escaping the men who brought destruction with them.

"Lydia?" he prompted

"I shall help you on one condition." Her gaze roamed over her mother's flowers on one side of her and the extensive kitchen gardens to the right. "If the British win the war, I want it to be known that I acted of my own accord. My family does not know what I am doing."

"The British are not going to win."

She contemplated another moment, wishing he could promise her and her family protection, but she knew neither he nor anyone else could make that promise. She must decide for herself what was right and then pray she made the correct choice. "How do I help you?"

The bushes moved again, and she knew he was close to her. It was good that she couldn't turn around. He might be able to read what was stirring in her mind, her heart, and he couldn't guess that her heart was wandering. She had told him she was betrothed, and that information would keep her focused on her work. There would be no question of personal intentions.

"Did you know there was a loose brick on the river side of your orangery?"

She took another breath. She must reveal nothing with her words. "I did not."

"It is the fifth row from the bottom. The eighth brick over."

The bushes rustled again. "There is a letter behind it for you to deliver."

"I will retrieve it tonight."

"When I leave a message, I'll tie a white ribbon beside this bench. If you have a message to give me, hide it behind the brick, and I will retrieve it when I return."

"What shall I do with the letters?"

"You must take them to Mrs. Pendell in Williamsburg."

She swiveled around. Mrs. Pendell was supposed to be as loyal to the king as Lydia's parents.

"Lydia—"

She sighed as she turned away from him again. It seemed the shapes of the people around her kept shifting. But she supposed it made good sense. Mrs. Pendell supplied Mother with her tea, and Lydia had long wondered how the woman managed to obtain tea when no one else could. With her secret stash, the Loyalists who remained in and near Williamsburg trusted Mrs. Pendell and perhaps told her things of keen interest to American ears.

A memory returned to her—Sarah had asked her to deliver a letter to Mrs. Pendell, and Mrs. Pendell had sent one in return. Had her friend been supporting the Patriot cause as a courier as well, before her home was destroyed?

Was no one who they seemed to be?

Lydia tapped her toes on the floor of the gazebo. "Is my friend safe?"

He paused. "Which friend?"

"Saying her name could bring more harm . . ."

"Yes, she is safe in Philadelphia."

She sighed with relief. At least Sarah was with her aunt now. "Before she left, she had a letter from . . . from the woman you just named."

"She delivered it to me."

"I am glad of it." Lydia tapped her toes again. "Has my friend found her slaves?"

"There is no word."

Her gaze roamed over to the pink blossoms that bubbled atop the cherry trees. Could Elisha have found Morah and his son by now? She prayed so. No family, black or white, should be torn apart.

"How will I deliver the—"

He stopped her. "She exchanged the messages in books."

Sarah had an entire library of books, but Lord Caswell's library didn't contain nearly as many, and her father would miss any she borrowed. Perhaps she could think of another way to take them to Mrs. Pendell.

His voice grew serious. "You must be careful, Lydia. They may search your person."

She thought of the British officers that had detained their coach in March. "I shall not let them—"

"You may have no choice."

She pressed her hands together. "Nathan?"

"Yes."

"Thank you for watching over my family."

"Without you, Lydia, I would not be alive."

"I am glad you survived."

She wished they could linger here for hours, but Mother called her name from the portico. When she turned back, Nathan had disappeared.

In the last moments—in the last weeks, really—she hadn't thought much about Seth. What would he think if he knew what she was going to do to help the Continental Army?

It didn't matter, she supposed. She wasn't doing it for him.

When Mother called her name again, she shouted back, "I am coming!"

"Good-bye, Nathan," she whispered, hoping he heard.

Nathan snuck back through the trees beside the river to his waiting boat, but he didn't row away yet. By the starlight, he watched Lydia walk back to her house.

She was a beautiful young woman with a penchant to heal what had been destroyed. And to help those who had been wounded. He admired her greatly for both.

As he climbed into the boat, his heart twisted within him. He hated having to ask her to risk her life. She'd already risked so much when she rescued him.

If he'd met her before the war—and if she wasn't promised to another man—he would have requested to court her. A decade ago it wouldn't have mattered if her father was a Tory. A decade ago they all respected the king.

He should avoid her and this place, but his uncle needed him to do this job. He must focus on his task and be grateful for someone who could take his messages into Williamsburg. Lydia Caswell might be beautiful, but what mattered most was that he trusted her to do this job.

He stayed a moment longer before paddling into the night. He would sleep near the shipyards and then travel north tomorrow by horseback to await his next assignment.

CHAPTER 20

A carriage driver shouted at Sarah, and she hopped back onto the sidewalk, her heart pounding as a horse rushed by. It seemed a lifetime ago that she would step out of her house and hear the sound of crickets instead of carriages, smell the sweetness of the curing tobacco in the wind.

There were no crickets or tobacco fields in this city, but it seemed as if everyone in Philadelphia was a Patriot. She was grateful for her aunt's hospitality in hosting her until her father or brother returned.

Aunt Marguerite's three-story brick home was inviting and immaculate. With the exception of English tea, they lacked no other comforts. Even so, Sarah couldn't stay inside the narrow house for long, especially on a beautiful spring day like this.

While she missed the promise of the James River to take her far away, here in Philadelphia she felt safe, and she loved the busyness of the city. Everyone seemed to have an important occupation, and she was intrigued by it all.

Her aunt didn't have many books in her small library, but this new adventure had calmed Sarah's need to escape. The British had taken much from her, but she'd shackled the hope of freedom to her heart. No matter what happened, they couldn't take that from her.

This spring, she had stitched coats for the soldiers alongside dozens of other Daughters of Liberty, but she longed to do something more for the army than make coats.

Aunt Marguerite reminded her regularly that they were doing an invaluable service for their soldiers—and she knew her aunt was right—but when she had delivered the letters, she felt as if she were impacting the outcome of the war.

If General Washington would only allow her to fight on the battlefield beside her brother, she would take up a gun and never look back. All that she saw now anyway, when her mind wandered home, were the burning walls of her family's plantation. And the faces of those she'd loved who were now gone.

People conducted business in this town as they did in Williamsburg, as if there was no war outside. Now that the British no longer occupied these buildings, the people of Philadelphia pressed for freedom. Most of the workingmen had joined the ranks of Washington's army, leaving the women to work in the shops and manage the town. Those with husbands who remained at home kept busy with sewing jackets and knitting socks for the soldiers.

The spring air had parched her throat, and she turned back toward the house for a glass of water. As she opened the back door, she heard the voices of several women and she sighed. Some days, it seemed, were an endless display of socializing and stitching when she wanted to roam.

Thankfully Aunt Marguerite seemed to understand her need to escape on some afternoons.

Sarah paused at the door to the drawing room, listening.

"He's been gone for almost three months," one of the women said. She recognized the voice of Mrs. Benson, a sprightly woman who seemed to know everyone in Philadelphia along with their business.

Mrs. Benson's daughter, Amity, spoke in a loud whisper. "I heard he's supposed to return by the month's end."

Sarah smiled. Amity was at least five years older than her and still unmarried. They must be discussing the visit of a bachelor, a novelty these days.

"Perhaps he will be back in time for the Miltons' ball."

Ball? Good heavens. Aunt Marguerite would want her to attend, but Sarah hadn't danced since 1776. Even though she enjoyed the bustle of the city's busyness, she wasn't fond of the social gatherings her aunt insisted upon. During a war, Aunt Marguerite thought, it was good to keep oneself occupied—but distractions like these only seemed to weary Sarah.

Even though she was Marguerite Hammond's great-niece, the women in Philadelphia still didn't trust her. Nor did they really know her.

When she first arrived in the city, Sarah quickly learned that her running the plantation in her father's absence embarrassed Aunt Marguerite. Oddly enough, it didn't seem to embarrass her aunt in the least that John Hammond worked for the Crown.

Louisa came upon her eavesdropping on the women just then, and Sarah quickly handed the maid her parasol before stepping into the parlor. Mrs. Benson and Amity and another unmarried woman named Victoria Pittman greeted her as she took a chair by the tray of tarts and lemonade. The women sat in awkward silence, as if they were unsure what to say now that she was here.

Amity shifted on the settee beside her mother. With her auburn hair and lovely fair skin, she had probably had suitors lining up outside her door before the war.

"Who is coming to the dance?" Sarah asked as she lifted a glass of lemonade and drank it.

Mrs. Benson patted her hand. "No one you would know."

"How was your stroll?" Aunt Marguerite asked.

"Quite pleasant, thank you."

"We shall go up to Chestnut Hill soon to escape the summer heat," Aunt Marguerite said. "Do you like to dance, Sarah?"

"I do, but I am not particularly fond of crowds."

Victoria's pleasant smile reminded her of Lydia's. "You will have a marvelous time."

Sarah smiled back at her. "Are there any men left in Philadelphia to dance with?"

"Aye, but all of the gentlemen are married."

Sarah reached for a tart. "I'm not seeking a husband."

Victoria's smile turned sympathetic. "Of course not."

Mrs. Benson eyed the tart in Sarah's hand. "It's a good thing you are not."

Sarah held the woman's gaze as she took a bite of the tart. Then she looked above the woman's head to Louisa, standing in the back, and lifted her empty glass. "Would you fetch me some more lemonade?"

"Certainly," Louisa said.

"Gracious," Mrs. Benson said, eyeing the glass as Louisa took it. "Did you guzzle your entire glass?"

Sarah shrugged. "I'm always thirsty after I walk."

Mrs. Benson tilted forward. "I've heard rumors of your frolicking through town."

Sarah couldn't stop her laughter at the woman's words, as if her walks had caused some sort of disturbance in Philadelphia. "I don't believe that touring the city in the daylight is considered frolicking."

"It is if you don't have an escort."

"Then perhaps I shall have to marry after all, so I have a handsome escort."

Mrs. Benson sat back in her chair, looking properly offended.

When the women left, Aunt Marguerite settled back into her chair. "Don't mind them. They don't know what to say to you."

Mrs. Benson knew exactly what to say, but Sarah didn't wish to air her offense since Aunt Marguerite was her friend. "Victoria and Amity don't trust me yet."

"The young women are overwrought," Aunt Marguerite said. "One of our privateers is due back in town soon."

"I'm sure it will be good to have the supplies."

"Oh, it is not because of the supplies he brings. He is a fine-looking gentleman, and the unmarried ladies are smitten with him."

"They are enamored of a pirate?" She'd imagined privateers to be unshaven, burly men lacking any sort of social grace.

Aunt Marguerite shook her head. "His name is Porter, and he is no pirate. He steals only from the British, and he takes supplies for the war and our women."

"And this Porter shall come to the ball?"

"There is a rumor that he will attend. If so, all the ladies will be swooning."

Let them swoon. The only man she wanted to see was the one who had disappeared.

Darkness settled around Lydia like a heavy mantle as she pretended to stroll down toward the river. She wished for a light, but she didn't dare even take a candle with her to the orangery.

It was one thing to enjoy the view of the river from the gazebo, but quite another to be sneaking outside at midnight to find a hidden letter.

It had been two nights since Nathan found her at the gazebo. Even though she wanted to retrieve his message, she had resisted until tonight. Tomorrow they would attend services in Williamsburg.

Goose bumps pricked her arms again, and she drew her

shawl tight around her arms. Father usually escorted them in and out of Sunday services before they had a chance to speak with anyone including Mrs. Pendell.

How was she going to talk to her mother's friend without raising suspicions?

When Lydia reached the orangery, she counted the bricks with her hands and moved the loose brick out. Just as Nathan had said, a sealed letter was set inside, and she quickly stuffed it under her shawl before replacing the brick. Then she rushed back through the gardens and climbed the steps to the security of her chamber.

After hiding the letter under her window cushion, she collapsed on her bed and stared at the ceiling. Sleep was fitful that night as she dreamed about Nathan, letters, and fire.

Prudence helped her dress in the morning, and then she filled an embroidered reticule with scented powder and slipped the letter inside. Mother always took a sweet bag filled with potpourri to church to ward off the variety of smells that clung to the air, but Lydia never carried one.

None of her family members questioned her about the reticule when she stepped into the coach, and she clutched it in her lap along with her prayer book on their drive to church and through the entire service. If the British stopped them, they would have to pry it out of her fingers.

Mrs. Pendell sat in the boxed pew to the left of the Caswell family's pew. Lydia couldn't focus on the music from the organ above or the words of the rector before her, not even when he prayed for peace.

She fidgeted with her sweet bag through the service until Mother nudged her. Then she pushed her toes against the tops of her brocade slippers. How was she supposed to deliver this message?

Instead of having to seek out Mrs. Pendell, the woman found Lydia after the service and enveloped her in a tight hug.

As Mrs. Pendell released her, Lydia slipped the bag into her hand.

Mrs. Pendell moved to embrace Lady Caswell, and when Lydia looked back, Mrs. Pendell held the bag to her side as if nothing was amiss.

It was official.

The daughter of Lord and Lady Caswell had betrayed their king.

CHAPTER 21

*T*he British officers returned to Caswell Hall on a warm day in July. Rumors abounded about their plundering across Virginia and the other colonies, and although Lydia wondered of their plans, she didn't dare ask. She needed to appear as oblivious as possible to the affairs of this war.

Major Reed greeted her with a smile, and she cringed at both his friendliness and the friendliness she must feign in return.

"We shall have men arriving throughout the day," the major informed her father.

"Of course."

"There is much for us to discuss."

As the men arrived, Lydia helped the servants prepare their rooms.

They had no idea how many would turn up, but Mother feared that if they didn't provide the officers with places to sleep, they might opt to take the family's rooms.

The men came by foot, horse, and wagon. A good thirty of them. Major Reed said the officers had been staying in homes across the region, some hosts more willing to have them than others. Part of her was glad that Sarah was in Philadelphia. At least she didn't have a horde of soldiers overtaking her house with no husband or father to protect her.

Viney and her staff rushed to prepare a large meal for the officers, and it seemed to Lydia as if they were preparing their great hall for a celebration. Except this was no special occasion. The men didn't bathe this time, and they smelled like animals that had rolled in ashes after a fire, smoke clinging to their uniforms. Instead of lingering over the meal, the officers devoured every morsel served to them and slurped cup after cup of Mother's prized tea.

Her parents insisted that Lydia and Hannah join them at the table for dinner, and Lydia watched enviously as the servants carried platters in and out of the room. She wished she could escape down to the kitchen with them.

She glanced over at her father, at the gray that rimmed his dark hair. He'd aged much since Grayson left and even more so since the British came to Virginia. He maintained that he wanted the British staying here, and yet the strain they caused was unmistakable.

If something happened to her father, what would she and Hannah and Mother do? Mother wouldn't want to run the plantation as Sarah had done, and Lydia couldn't imagine doing it. Perhaps if Grayson heard of Father's death, he would return. The men who'd killed Grandfather were no longer in Williamsburg, and those Patriots who remained no longer threatened with tar and feathers.

Two new officers walked into the room, and the other men quieted. Major Reed's voice was brisk. "What did you find?"

The two men stood before him, their red uniforms soiled and wet. "A storehouse of supplies hidden near their shipyard on the Chickamee River."

The *Chickahominy*, Lydia wanted to say—but better to let them think she wasn't paying attention.

One of the new officers glanced over at Lord Caswell. "Perhaps we should wait to discuss this."

Major Reed shook his head. "No one here will talk."

Heat rose to Lydia's cheeks, and she stared down at her hands so they wouldn't see her face burning. The major might have meant it as a compliment—the fact that they were all Loyalists—but she felt insulted. How dare he declare what she would or wouldn't say?

"What sort of supplies do the Yankees have at the shipyard?" Major Reed asked.

"Food and clothing and gunpowder."

Major Reed inched closer on his seat. "How much ammunition?"

"At least a dozen tons," the man said. "Much more than we captured at Richmond."

"This must be where they hid it." The major took a long drag on one of Father's cigars. "How many men are guarding their supplies?"

The officer shrugged his shoulders. "A pittance."

Major Reed leaned forward. "How many, exactly, is a *pittance?*"

"Ten or fifteen at the most."

"The precise number, lieutenant," Major Reed clipped.

"Fourteen," he replied, clearly making up a number to appease his superior.

Major Reed pounded his fist on the table. "Details like this are critical to winning this war."

The lieutenant took a step back. "Yes, sir."

Major Reed regained his control. "The Yankees must be preparing for the arrival of their military. We must move quickly before their men retrieve these supplies."

Several men stepped toward the door as if they were anxious to march out at any moment, but Major Reed raised his hand to stop them as he seemed to consider his next step.

Did this mean that General Washington and his men were on their way to Williamsburg? She wanted to move closer so she wouldn't miss a single detail, but feigning indifference was the only way to gain more information.

"We shall gather our men and go up the river on Friday night," Major Reed said. "Before sunrise, we'll confiscate all of their supplies."

Lydia memorized the details of the raid as Major Reed delegated them. Nathan had only asked her to act as a courier, but surely he would want to know what the British had planned.

Late that night, guilt swept over her as she transcribed the details she'd heard onto two sheets of Father's paper. Part of her was convinced that she was saving her family, but in other moments, it felt as if sharing these secrets would destroy them.

If only she knew where to find Nathan, she could deliver this information to him without writing it down.

The moon was high in the sky when she strolled out toward the orangery to deliver the letter she'd written. Then she sat in the gazebo for a spell, hoping to deter any suspicions.

If the Patriot army was indeed on its way to Williamsburg, would Seth be among them? Her heart should leap at the thought of seeing him, but she felt nothing. She hoped he was safe, for Sarah's sake, but could no longer marry him. Not when her heart had begun to pine for another.

Her gaze wandered back toward the orangery.

Was Nathan out there tonight? Perhaps he was in the trees now, watching her.

Hopefully, he would check for messages before it was too late.

The bricks on the outside of the Hammonds' summer kitchen were blackened, but the inside made an excellent hiding place for Nathan while he worked near Williamsburg. He lit a candle on the table and read Lydia's message twice, impressed by her attention to the necessary details.

With his injured leg on the mend, he'd left his cane here earlier tonight and followed two of the British officers back to the Caswell home, hoping to obtain intelligence as he trailed them. He'd heard the men talk of what the Caswells would feed them and then about their families back home, but not of their journey to the shipyard.

Lydia, however, had been able to obtain the information he needed, and she'd delivered it well.

The Patriots had managed to sneak most of their supplies out of Richmond and hide it in an abandoned mill near the shipyards. They'd stopped building ships for their fledgling navy this winter because no matter how many ships they built, they couldn't compete with the Royal Navy. Instead, they'd decided to focus on the land battles and contract with privateers to raid British ships and run supplies for them.

There was no time for delay. The Patriots didn't have enough soldiers nearby to defend the supplies, but Nathan could muster up enough people to transport them. He only had to determine how to move them. And where.

Nathan blew out his candle.

Perhaps they could hide the supplies somewhere on the Hammond plantation until the military arrived.

The British might have discovered where the Patriots had hidden supplies, but he hoped they didn't know that the Continental Army was in the process of marching north from Charles Towne. The King's Men were wreaking havoc on the east side of Virginia, and the Patriots refused to let the British ravage this colony as they had South Carolina.

He leaned back against the hard wall.

Lydia had done an amazing service for them. Seth was a blessed man indeed.

~

Lydia helped her mother decorate the dining table with candied flower petals, and then they began to build an elegant centerpiece with ribbons and fruit. Lydia reached for a cherry, but instead of pinning it to the pyramid, she accidentally pricked her finger.

Holding a cloth to her finger, she sat down on a chair. She'd barely slept during the night, worried that Nathan might not receive her message, worried as well that he would find it—and worried that the major or his men would discover her treason.

Mother held up a pear decorated with a silver ribbon. "Do you think I should use a red ribbon instead?"

Lydia glanced over. Red ribbon or silver—it seemed so trivial. And yet in spite of the foul-smelling men, in spite of the devastation, she knew her mother desperately wanted to preserve some beauty in the house.

"I like the silver," she said.

Mother patted her hand. "You are distracted."

"I feel as if I am living in a dream, Mother. As if one day all that is secure around me will collapse."

"The major and his men might not be the best-behaved guests, but they have certainly kept us safe and will continue to do so."

Lydia reached for a pear out of the bowl and took a bite. Mother swatted her hand. "You must not eat the table décor."

"If I do not, someone else will enjoy it tonight."

"Let them enjoy it. If they remember nothing else, I want them to remember all the good things we have done for them."

Lydia took another bite of the fruit in her hand. "What if they forget?"

"In Matthew, Jesus tells us to feed the hungry and shelter strangers in need."

Lydia nodded her head. Those verses she remembered well.

Mother cut another piece of silver ribbon and looped it. "These men need nourishment and a place to sleep. Even if they forget our hospitality, I will know that I did right in caring for them—as you did with a stranger before the British arrived."

"Aye." A stranger who had become a friend.

Mother pinned the ribbon on the pyramid and then looked up at her. "Is this visitor gone?"

"He is no longer on our property."

Mother studied her face. "What was his name?"

Lydia swallowed. She couldn't lie to her mother. "Nathan."

Her mother's eyebrows rose at her use of the man's first name. "I am glad this Nathan survived."

Lydia fought back the smile that welled within her as peace flooded her heart. "Me too."

CHAPTER 22

*T*he formal dinner was served at the Miltons' mansion at precisely six o'clock. Afterward, the host and hostess danced a proper minuet.

At Aunt Marguerite's urging, Sarah joined the others in the country dances that followed, her feet remembering well the steps to the familiar reels and jigs.

Around ten, Sarah retreated to the side of the hall for something to drink. She wished Lydia were here to enjoy the night with her. They'd had such fun as girls, learning to dance at finishing school and then watching the dancers from behind the servants' door in Caswell Hall.

After they turned fifteen, Lydia and she joined the dancers in the festivities, but between dances, they still huddled at the sides of the room to laugh together.

Sarah stepped up to a serving bowl filled with rinds of lemons and limes swimming in rum punch. A servant handed her a cup, and as she sipped the warm drink, she recognized Victoria and Amity nearby. The women didn't seem to notice her as they continued their discussion, their eyes focused on the enormous doorway that led into the room.

"Father said he was to arrive by nine," Amity said.

Victoria scanned the room and then looked back at the door. "He is always late."

"Do you think he will bring his crew with him?"

Victoria shook her head. "None of them enjoy the dances like Porter does."

Amity fanned her face. "I don't think he enjoys them at all. He comes to talk to the men about business."

"But he will dance."

Sarah took another long sip of her punch. This Porter sounded like a few of the men who had once tried to court her. They pretended to enjoy her company, but they were clearly more interested in the Hammond property than in her.

When she married—if she ever married—it would be to someone who hadn't the slightest interest in being weighed down by four thousand acres.

The women hushed suddenly, and their silence rippled across the crowd as heads turned toward the door. Sarah looked as well and saw a tall man walk in, his black hat dipped low over his eyes.

She stared at the man along with the others. His confident stride seemed familiar. His stance.

Was it possible?

Victoria and Amity laughed nervously as the man moved toward them. He removed his hat and offered Amity his hand.

Sarah's mouth fell open, her breath catching in her throat.

She had no idea who Porter was, but one thing she did know — Grayson Caswell was in Philadelphia, about to dance with Amity Benson.

Her hand dropped, searching for the table, and she tried to steady herself. Grayson had always loved sailing, but he had been a Loyalist like his father, not a privateer.

She tucked her chin, her gaze falling to the floor as she

struggled to breathe before she made a spectacle of herself by fainting.

The man she loved was back from the dead, and it seemed as if all of Philadelphia craved his attention.

As the orchestra played, she watched the man she loved dance with another woman across the floor. She had remained devoted to him for the past four years, written hundreds of letters declaring her love. She'd thought he might love her as she had him.

Oh, how foolish she had been.

The music stopped, and she thought she might be sick. All her dreams about him returning, her dreams for their future—everything she'd hoped for was gone.

"He's looking this way," the woman next to her whispered.

When Sarah looked up again, Grayson's eyes found hers. And locked on them.

Then the governor was beside him, and Grayson turned away to shake the man's hand.

Sarah lifted her skirt. She must leave here before someone introduced them. Others might be able to hide their feelings, but she could not.

Major Reed raged behind Lord Caswell's desk, his face the same powder white color as his wig. Three officers faced him, and the major's fury silenced them along with the entire Caswell family. Not even Hannah spoke.

His men had knocked on their chamber doors in the middle of the night, demanding that the family join the major in the library. Standing in her robe and nightcap, Lydia felt exposed, but she was more worried that the men would expose what she had done. If they found out she was the one who sent the message about the Patriots' supplies, they would hang her and perhaps her entire family.

The major's gaze wandered out the window to the night, as if someone might be listening to their conversation from outside. Then his eyes snapped back to her father. "Do any of your slaves sympathize with the rebels?"

"Of course not," Father insisted.

The major's hand slammed into his fist. "Someone talked."

His eyes searched each face in the room, stopping on Lydia.

"Talked about what?" she asked, widening her eyes in feigned distress.

He and his officers scrutinized her and her family members as he explained that the rebel supplies were no longer at the shipyard.

Father stepped forward. "No one in this family has any contact with rebels."

"I do not suspect your family," Major Reed said. "But one of your slaves—"

"Our Negroes have had no opportunity to speak with rebels." Father was clearly angry at the accusations. "No one leaves this plantation unless they are traveling with me or my family, and we have not gone anywhere since we attended church services last Sunday."

Major Reed sat in a chair. "I know you are loyal, Charles."

"As loyal as King George himself."

"Is there anyone else—?"

"Everyone in my household is loyal to Britain."

Major Reed studied him for a long moment before he spoke. "One of my men must have discussed our raid outside this house."

Father bowed his head slightly. "I would not accuse anyone."

He stood. "Leave my job to me, Charles. I do not tolerate treason."

The major's eyes rested on Lydia again. She felt as if she

were about to melt from the heat of his gaze, but she didn't falter. "As you should not," she said.

"I will find the traitor among us," he declared. And then he departed the room.

She sank into a chair, pleased that Nathan had received her message in time to save the ammunition and food of the Patriots. It was one thing to deliver information to save her family— and quite another to enjoy its success.

Had she become a rebel in her heart as well as a traitor?

Major Reed would probably be more cautious with his discussions in the house.

And she would have to be more cautious, as well, about distributing the information.

It took the entire night for the shipyard to burn.

When the King's Men discovered that the rebel supplies had been moved, they retaliated by burning everything down. Hidden behind a tree, Nathan had watched them light piles of wood, the wharf, and the deck of an abandoned ship.

The ships docked here would never again travel up the river. Not that the Continental Army could win the war with these ships, but their privateers or French allies could have used them. Though now that the Tories held Charles Towne and Norfolk and New York, even the French ships had trouble penetrating the British lines.

His uncle must arrive soon, or the rest of Virginia would be taken as well.

He sank into the river, the water cleansing him. It was much nicer to take a swim here in warmer weather.

The ships might be gone, but thankfully Lydia had saved the ammunition and other supplies for their army. He would have to find General Washington and his men soon to tell them about the supplies, but before he left, he must pay Lydia one more visit.

He massaged his temples. It would be dangerous to speak with her again, and he didn't want any harm to come to Lydia or her family. Yet if they lost the war now, terrible harm might come to her. He wanted to see her again—he couldn't deny it—but he would never put her at personal risk because of his selfish desires.

It would be the last time they would meet. From now on, she would be well-prepared to carry on her work without ever seeing him again.

CHAPTER 23

*S*arah hardly slept. She'd promised herself she would never run again, and yet she had done it last night. Instead of remaining strong and composed, she'd fled from the ball.

Over the past four years, she had often thought Grayson might be injured or deceased, or that he had sent letters that never arrived. But he was here in Philadelphia, healthy and well and dancing with other women, not bothering to write or return home for a visit.

Grayson had surely seen her just as she had seen him, and yet he hadn't offered even the simplest of greetings. The unmarried women likely spent the evening fawning over him, and how could he not enjoy the attention? He had probably been glad to see her run away.

At first, Aunt Marguerite had tried to coax her back into the ball, but when she saw Sarah's tears and disheveled hair, she went to offer their apologies for leaving early.

It was the last ball Sarah would attend in Philadelphia.

At half past seven in the morning, Aunt Marguerite knocked

on her chamber door before she slipped inside. "Louisa will bring breakfast to your room."

Sarah nodded.

Clutching the pearl handle of her lorgnette, Aunt Marguerite studied Sarah's face. "You still look as if you've seen a ghost."

"I believe I have."

Aunt Marguerite sat on the window seat. "Pray tell?"

"Why hadn't you told me Grayson Caswell was in town?"

Aunt Marguerite looked concerned. "Who is Grayson Caswell?"

"The man who came late to the ball." The man who'd made her run.

Her aunt's eyebrows rose in question. "You mean Porter?"

Her head throbbed. "I don't know who I mean."

"I didn't realize you might know him."

"He was my neighbor back in Virginia." She swallowed. "Was he the pirate—the privateer—you were discussing?"

"Aye." Her aunt paused. "Were the ladies as fond of him in Virginia?"

Her heart ached. "I don't know."

"Excuse me, miss." Louisa stood at the open door. "There's a gentleman to see you this morning."

"A gentleman?" Aunt Marguerite exclaimed from behind Sarah. "Why on earth would a gentleman come calling at this hour?"

The maid shrugged. "He said his business with Miss Hammond was urgent."

Sarah's heart began to race. Had Grayson come for her after all?

She threw back the covers from the bed.

"Please tell the gentleman that he may call at a more respectable hour," Aunt Marguerite said with a wave of her lorgnette.

"But—"

Her aunt turned toward her. "Assuming, of course, that you would still like him to call."

Mist clouded Sarah's eyes. "I believe so."

"Good." Her aunt looked back at Louisa. "Please tell him that we will be available at ten o'clock and he had better not be late. Miss Hammond has a very busy social calendar."

Sarah managed a smile at her aunt, praying she was right and Grayson returned. She ate a few bites of toast and drank two cups of coffee before Louisa helped her bathe.

Perhaps Grayson thought of her as a younger sister, a dear old friend. If he did, she would tell him that her sudden departure last night had been due to illness. All her letters to him had been lost in the fire. No one else knew what she had guarded in her heart.

At a quarter to ten, Louisa sprayed perfume on the front of Sarah's pearl-and-dark-blue gown. Red had been Grayson's favorite color, but even if she owned a red gown, she wouldn't cater to him as the rest of the unmarried women in the city seemed to do. He already knew almost everything about her. The only secret between them was her love.

She glanced again at the tall pendulum clock beside the window.

What would she do if he didn't come?

Minutes later the bell rang below, and her heart leaped. Louisa poured her a glass of water from the pitcher, and she took a long sip as she waited for Aunt Marguerite to summon her.

When her aunt stepped into her chamber, she looked as smug as a lioness who had captured her prey. "Your friend has returned."

Sarah stepped toward the doorway but then stopped. She had always known what to write, but after all these years, she had no idea what she would say to him.

"He wants to see you, Sarah," Aunt Marguerite prodded her. "There is no reason for concern."

How could she not be concerned?

She shadowed her aunt to the parlor, and Aunt Marguerite welcomed the man she called Porter to their house. Then she excused herself, leaving the door partially open behind her.

Sarah stared at the man standing in front of her, at his tanned face and dark hair tied neatly behind his neck. He'd matured since he left Caswell Hall, his rugged features even more handsome, his shoulders broader. No wonder the women in Philadelphia swooned. There were so many questions she wanted to ask of him, but she wasn't certain she was prepared for his answers.

He tried to smile at her, but his lips shook slightly. Gone was the confidence he'd displayed last night as he paraded into the dance. He looked more like a nervous boy who had stolen something from her.

He took a step toward her. "I didn't know you were in Philadelphia."

She wanted to run again as she had last night, but she remained. He mustn't discover the feelings she had for him. "I didn't know you were here either."

"I haven't been here long."

"Your family and I—we all thought you were dead."

He nodded. "It was better that way."

How could he say it was better? "You were— They imprisoned you for talking out against freedom."

He shook his head. "I never spoke out against freedom, only the route proposed to obtain it."

She clutched the table, trying to understand. Grayson was supposed to be a Loyalist like his family. Like her father. "But after your grandfather was killed, you said—"

His blue eyes clouded. "Those men who killed him were as tyrannical as King George."

As tyrannical as King George? When had he changed his views?

"I wish you would have told me what you thought." Her words spilled out. "I wish you would have said good-bye."

"I regretted it every day I was gone, but I could not place my family in jeopardy." He stepped toward her. "Please tell me about them."

She slowly released the table. "They are well enough in this war. Your parents have never given up hope that you are alive."

He paced toward the window and then looked back at her. "Do they remain loyal to the king?"

"Immensely."

"You see why I couldn't return."

"I see why you couldn't return to them."

He stopped. "I could not place you in jeopardy either."

Was it possible he did care for her?

She joined him near the window, smiling in spite of herself. If only he knew how much jeopardy she'd placed herself into. Even as she wanted to keep her feelings walled up inside her, those walls were beginning to crumble. "You think you know me, Grayson, but you know nothing about me."

His smile returned to reflect hers. "I would like to learn."

He reached out, taking one of her hands, and his touch sent a tremor coursing through her. Had he felt it as well?

His eyes met hers, and she saw the questioning in them. If only she could fall into his arms.

But she must force herself to remain the slightest bit aloof, at least until she found out where he had been and whether he felt as deeply for her as she felt for him. She refused to be one of the women of Philadelphia who longed for a man who didn't love her in return.

She stepped away, and his smile dropped. "I want to hear your stories."

"I have all day, if you want to listen. And tomorrow." He

placed his hand at the small of her back, directing her toward a seat. "What would you like to know?"

"Where have you been, Grayson?"

He started at the beginning.

Lydia walked toward the washhouse on Saturday morning to retrieve fresh linens for herself and her parents. She'd never been inside the washhouse, but one of their maidservants had run away during the chaos of the officers' latest arrival and it had been this woman's job to retrieve linens for the main house.

After Elisha left, they had lost five more slaves, including two who did not return from their work in the fields just last night. Neither Father nor the overseer had located those two men, and Lydia doubted they ever would. Until Father could purchase more Negroes, she and Hannah would be required to help with their work.

When she opened the door to the washhouse, steam poured over her and she gasped at the blast of heat. Two Negro women looked up at her in surprise, sweat dripping off their faces as they scrubbed clothes on a board in wooden tubs filled with boiling water. Clothes and linens hung on lines around them and lay in piles near the tubs.

She'd never felt so out of place in her life.

"I—I need some bed linens."

The women stared at her.

Lydia pointed at one of the presses where the folded blankets set. "Shall I take one from there?"

The younger woman, who was probably around Hannah's age, ran toward the press. "I will fetch them for you."

She retrieved two sets and brought them to Lydia. "Would you like me to carry them?"

"What is your name?" Lydia asked.

"Deborah." She said with a curtsy. "It's a Christian name."

"Hush," the other woman commanded.

Deborah bowed her head. "I'm sorry for my impertinence."

"You needn't be," Lydia said. "It is a pleasure to meet you."

"I can carry those, ma'am," Deborah said.

Lydia shook her head and smiled. "I will do it."

Deborah held the door open for Lydia as she scooted back outside with her arms full. How did these women stay in the washhouse all day in this heat, standing over boiling cauldrons of wash water? It was a wonder they hadn't fainted away on the ground.

Lydia looked down at the clean linens in her hands. Every night she slept on sheets like these without even thinking about the women who had washed them. She thought she was being kind to Deborah, volunteering to carry the sheets for her, but it occurred to her suddenly that it probably would have been a much greater kindness to allow Deborah to escape to the coolness of the house.

Sighing, she turned to go back to the washhouse. This new world of hers was difficult to navigate.

Someone whispered her name from behind the smokehouse, and she whirled on her feet, dropping the clean linens on the ground. Bending over, she scrambled to pick them up and balled them in her hands.

"Who's there?" she demanded.

"Your river friend."

Her heart leaped. What was Nathan doing, visiting her in the daylight? If someone found out that she knew him—

His presence risked both of their lives.

She looked both ways, but there was no one on the drive. She could keep walking, pretending that she hadn't heard him. Or she could speak to him quickly so he would leave.

The sooner he was off Caswell property, the better it would be for both of them.

She slipped behind the smokehouse and caught her breath when she saw him. After he'd recovered, she had seen him only in the darkness.

Now his green eyes glistened in the light, and his face was shaven clean. His sandy-brown hair was tied back with her yellow ribbon, and in his gaze, she saw a strength that unnerved her.

Had he been this handsome when he lay on Elisha's bed? If so, she hadn't noticed. He certainly wore his health well.

"What are you doing here?" she demanded.

"I must speak with you," he whispered.

"I go to the gazebo every night."

"They have set up a guard around your property after dusk. One of your friends has begun shadowing you in the evening."

Goose bumps bristled her arms. She'd been sitting out there alone with one of the officers near her. Thank God she hadn't gone back to the orangery to deliver a message.

"They are not my friends," she said.

"Neither are they friends to your father."

She thought of the major's anger when he'd discovered the Patriots had moved their supplies. Even though her father knew nothing of her treason, Major Reed would still punish him if Nathan was discovered on the property.

She pressed her fingers against his arm, urging him away. "They mustn't find you here—"

He glanced over her shoulder and then leaned close to her ear. She shivered in spite of the heat. "Take a stroll into the kitchen gardens after dusk. I shall meet you by the river."

The clip-clopping of horses startled her, and she looked behind her.

"Go," she hissed, but when she turned back to Nathan, he was already gone.

Her heart racing, she stepped back onto the drive, the soiled sheets cascading from her arms. The rider stopped his horse beside her, and she scrambled to pick up the sheets. She didn't recognize the man, but he looked like a British messenger.

He examined her and the muddy sheets in her hands. "What happened to your linens?"

She sighed. "You startled me."

"I am looking for Major Reed."

She nodded toward Caswell Hall. "He should be in the main house."

The rider prompted the horse forward, leaving her in his dust.

With the dirty linens bunched in her arms, she turned back to the washhouse. Her intention had been to help, but now she'd created even more work for these women.

This time she would ask Deborah to help her bring clean linens back to the house.

Shadows from the bell tower above Pennsylvania's State House stretched long across Chestnut Street. The bell had rung five years ago when their nation declared independence, and it continued to ring when the Continental Congress met in hopes of securing their proposed freedom.

Carriages clattered beside Sarah and Grayson, and the aroma of sweet pastries drifted from the door of a bakery as they skirted through the rows of shops, taverns, and narrow brick homes that overlooked Philadelphia's busy streets.

Aunt Marguerite had sent Louisa to chaperone them this afternoon, but Grayson never checked to see if the older woman remained behind them. If he could pretend Louisa wasn't following them, Sarah could pretend as well.

With Grayson at her side, Sarah couldn't stop smiling.

In her aunt's parlor, he had described the night his grandfather was killed in Williamsburg, how the men had threatened to kill Grayson as well. When he told his mother, Lady Caswell not only begged him to flee but helped him to do so. She elicited his promise that he would tell no one he was leaving, for she feared the news might somehow leak to those who wanted him dead. And now there were many more who sought his life.

Grayson and Seth had already been discussing in secret the ideas that had been brewing in Philadelphia and Boston. They both knew how critical it was to stifle their passions for the safety of themselves and their families.

His grandfather, Grayson said, felt he must speak up for the king before the colonists lost their control, and he felt compelled to protect his grandfather by standing beside him. But then his grandfather's speech ignited a tirade of colonists who were tired of the mandates placed on them by supporters of the Crown.

Sarah was surprised to learn that Grayson had sympathized with the Patriots before the war, but she was even more surprised to discover that Lady Caswell knew of Grayson's departure. Her admiration for Grayson's mother swelled at how she helped her son leave in the night and then harbored this secret to protect him. Sarah couldn't imagine, though, what Lord and Lady Caswell would say if they learned that their only son was assisting the Americans. She admired Grayson as well, for protecting those he loved.

Cobblestone winded down to the Delaware River, and they ceased to talk of the past and laughed together at the names of Philadelphia's streets—Cedar, Walnut, and Spruce. It sounded as if they lived in a forest instead of a city.

Those passing by stared at them. In a city with few men under the age of forty, Grayson and his crew were novelties. And today he had chosen to walk with her.

As they came upon the river, the stench from the docks swelled in the summer heat.

"There is my ship," he said, pointing at the long wooden ship with two masts rising tall from the deck.

"What's her name?"

Instead of answering her question, he said, "She has been all over the Caribbean and up and down the Atlantic."

She smiled at the pride in his voice. If only she could have gone with him. "How did you secure your own ship?"

He looked back at her. "When I first left the plantation, I didn't know where to go. A man in York asked me if I wanted to sail with him, and I agreed. We overtook two British frigates on that trip and sold the supplies to the Patriots. I worked a year for him and made enough money to purchase my own ship."

"I never expected—" she started. "A pirate, Grayson?"

He bristled. "A privateer. I aid the Patriots by relieving the enemy of their goods, and then I transport the supplies to our soldiers."

"You steal the supplies they are bringing to their own men."

He tugged on the hem of his jacket. "I'm not suited for soldiering."

"I wish I were."

He laughed and then stopped and looked down at her. "I have missed you, Sarah."

She swallowed. "I wasn't sure whether to miss you or not."

"If only we were on the same side—"

Perhaps soon she would tell him that she wanted freedom for their country as well. Freedom to speak what she believed. Freedom to worship in a way she saw fit. But she stayed quiet. If she spoke now, he might think her aim was only to impress him.

"I leave for sea again in the morning," he said.

The familiar sadness returned to her. "I had hoped you might stay longer."

"If you see my family, I beg of you not to tell them what I'm doing."

"Can I tell them you're safe?"

"Only my mother—and only if you do not tell her my new name." He paused. "If my enemies found my family, they might harm them in order to stop me."

Sarah understood and admired him for it.

He pulled her to the side, in an alley. A rat skirted by her feet, and she jumped away from it. Louisa must be near, but Sarah didn't care. She was alone with the man her heart longed for.

"Remember when we were but children," he said, "I would visit Seth in the evenings."

"I do," she replied. "I would slip into the parlor and help myself to the food the servants brought for you."

A nervous smile replaced his confident gaze. "I wasn't really coming to visit Seth."

She tilted her head, studying his face. "Nor was I particularly interested in the refreshments."

His smile grew. "I cannot leave again without telling you how I feel." He took both her hands and her fingers trembled in his. "I do not want you to keep slipping in and out of my life. I want you to stay."

"I would like to stay," she whispered above the noise outside. A wagon rolled by the alleyway, clattering on the cobblestones.

"My biggest regret these past four years was leaving you."

Her heart swelled. Perhaps Grayson did love her as she loved him.

He pulled her closer to him and leaned his head down. "I don't want any more regrets, Sarah."

"Nor do I."

Heat flushed her cheeks as his lips drew close to hers. Then she heard a scuffling noise behind her, and she turned.

Louisa appeared in the alley, her hands on her hips. "Miss Marguerite told me to keep my eyes on you. How am I supposed to watch you when you keep hiding away?"

Grayson groaned. "I was about to kiss her, Louisa."

The older woman swatted him. "Get back on the street."

He winked at Sarah, and the two of them obeyed.

Sarah grinned as she walked beside Grayson, her hand secured in his arm. He would have to leave again, but he would return to her. Perhaps next time he would be able to steal a kiss.

They hadn't walked far from the docks when someone shouted, "Porter!"

They both turned around.

"What is it, Zadock?" Grayson asked as the younger man approached them. He was dressed in a fancy orange-striped vest with gold buttons and green pantaloons, a bandana knotted around his neck. His black hair blended with the color of his skin.

Zadock eyed her skeptically before he spoke to his captain. "We must prepare to leave within the hour."

Grayson looked back at her before focusing on Zadock again. "But we do not depart until morning."

Zadock shook his head. "You must come to the shipyard at once."

Grayson turned toward her, and she wished his comrade had the courtesy to look away. Still, he took both her hands again as he leaned down to whisper in her ear, his steady voice calming her. "We will finish our conversation at a later date."

"I hope so."

Louisa waved her hand. "Come along."

"I shall be back by August first."

She released his hands. "I shall be waiting."

CHAPTER 24

*L*ydia waited by her window until moments before the
sun slipped behind the veil of darkness. Then she
moved out into the warm night, using a simple candle
instead of a lantern to light her path.

Usually she visited the gazebo later at night, but apparently
her guests were already acquainted with her evening strolls. If
she saw the guard, she would simply say she had chosen to walk
earlier this evening.

But what if the man still shadowed her through the kitchen
garden? And what if he found Nathan with her?

She would have to trust Nathan again tonight, trust him
with her life and the lives of her family, trust that he kept his
promises.

Instead of taking the path left toward the gazebo, she veered
right toward the acre planted with neat rows of cabbages, leeks,
parsnips, onions, potatoes, and beans. The hollyhocks, sweet-
briar, and English roses in the formal garden seemed like
paradise to her, but there was beauty in the kitchen garden as
well, with the dark-green stalks of radishes, crimson rhubarb,
and tassels of corn.

As she strolled toward the garden, the shadow of a man emerged from behind the well, and when he moved toward her, she tried to quell the panic in her chest. She and Nathan were much too close to the house to speak here. One of the British soldiers would surely discover them.

"Na—" she began, preparing to tell him to move away.

But the man's louder voice overtook hers. "It's a pleasure to see you this evening, Lydia."

She closed her lips, her fingers trembling. It wasn't Nathan there to greet her in the gardens. It was Major Reed.

And she'd almost said Nathan's name.

"It's a pleasure to see you as well," she said, trying to sound as if she meant it.

He walked toward her, and she saw his white ruffled shirt in the candlelight, a lump of tobacco below his lip. He didn't look quite as powerful without his red jacket, but she knew his power among his men was great. And his anger frightening.

After the major's confrontation with her family, she'd heard the men talking about how they'd burned down the shipyard. But there'd been no more talk of the missing food and ammunition. Should she ask him if they'd found the supplies, or would she appear too eager? And yet if she didn't ask, he might wonder about her indifference.

Perhaps she should just run.

"What are you doing out tonight?" he inquired.

She smiled as casually as possible, attempting to calm her nerves. "Taking a stroll."

"It's not safe for a lady to be out by herself these days."

"Perhaps not in the countryside, but Caswell Hall is plenty safe with you and your men here."

"I should hope so," he said. "Any rebel who dared to step on this property wouldn't leave alive."

She shuddered. Nathan would be shot or hanged if he was

discovered. And if they found out who he was visiting, she might be as well.

She prayed Nathan was far away at the moment.

The major pointed toward the walkway. "I shall stroll with you."

The memory of his confrontation in her basement rushed back to her, and everything within her wanted to decline. But if she did, Major Reed or one of his men would continue to follow, and they would surely discover Nathan when he approached. Perhaps if she walked beside the major, not far from the house, Nathan would stay away.

Major Reed offered her his arm, and reluctantly she took it. When he patted her hand, the candlelight flickered on its pewter stick. She cringed. If he tried to harm her, she would scream. His men, she was certain, were nearby this time.

"Your family's hospitality has been most appreciated," he said as they walked past the rows of vegetables.

She didn't want to engage the man in casual conversation, but then she realized she must keep him talking to warn Nathan that she had an escort.

"How do you like Virginia?" she asked, her voice a bit louder than normal.

"I like it very well," he replied. "So much so that when the king regains control, I intend to stay."

"Indeed?" If the Americans won their country, there would be no welcome for any of the King's Men.

"The king, I believe, will grant me a governorship." He paused to spit tobacco juice onto the melon plants. "I am going to ask him for Virginia."

She couldn't imagine this man as a replacement for Thomas Jefferson, but if the British won, she was beginning to realize that the colonies would no longer be a home for her.

"The king must be quite grateful to have you as such a loyal subject," she replied, determined to keep him talking.

"Aye, I will be forever loyal." He stopped walking and turned toward her. "And I will need a good, loyal wife to help me in this endeavor."

She held her candle in front of her, the fire a small barrier between her and this man she disdained. He thought she was betrothed to Seth and yet he disregarded it.

He looked quite serious. "I have spoken with Lord Caswell, and he agrees that you and I would make a formidable partnership to lead this colony under the king."

"I—" she said, stumbling over her words. She didn't want to anger him, but she refused to let him entertain the idea of matrimony. "I cannot marry you."

"But your father said—"

"Major!" an officer yelled, and she turned to see the man running toward them. Relief at the interruption washed over her.

Captain Moore bent over, his hands on his knees, as he heaved deep breaths.

"What is it?" Major Reed demanded.

"Someone has released all the horses," Captain Moore said. "The stable hand is frantic, trying to round them up on foot."

Lydia pressed her lips together. Had Nathan spooked their horses?

Major Reed waved his hand, dismissing him. "Help him retrieve the horses."

"We cannot find them in the darkness."

"Imbeciles," the major muttered. "I must escort Miss Caswell back to the house, and then I shall assist you."

Captain Moore glanced her way. "I can escort her."

How was this out-of-breath man supposed to protect her from any harm?

"Please do not concern yourself with me," Lydia said as demurely as possible. "I have no need of an escort."

"No—" Major Reed began, but then another of his men interrupted him.

"I am sorry, sir, but there is a fire in the washhouse."

Major Reed scanned the gardens. "Someone is toying with us."

"You must stop them." Lydia clutched the candleholder, her eyes wide. "we need our horses."

"It would not be pru—"

"Please, go!" she begged.

He spit out his tobacco and ran, Captain Moore and the other officer rushing behind him. In that moment, it seemed as if they had forgotten about her.

As she lowered her candle, relief flooded over her. She took a deep breath and continued her stroll toward the river, hoping Nathan would find her before the men returned.

She meandered down the path, crossing by the stalks of corn, when someone blew out her candle. It dropped to the ground.

"Come with me," Nathan whispered, taking her hand. Then he pulled her into the narrow rows of corn.

She trembled. "They are searching for you."

He held her hand a moment longer before slowly releasing her fingers. Then he leaned down to speak into her ear. "They will not find me."

The cornstalks towered around them, shielding them from the house and Major Reed. Nathan's face was inches above hers, and in the starlight, she could see the intensity in his eyes. She trembled again, but she did not know if it was because of fear or because of the way Nathan was gazing at her.

Her voice quivered when she spoke. "Did you have to burn our washhouse?"

"It was only a small fire." The warmth of his breath against her ear made her feel faint. "Your message saved our supplies."

"But not the shipyard."

"Soon we will have enough men to fight them." He moved his head back to study her face. "Lydia—"

When Seth proposed long ago, she had felt an obligation to marry. With Major Reed, she felt only fear. But here with Nathan, hiding in the garden, she felt something else. Longing, perhaps. And—love.

She was falling in love with a Patriot spy.

She searched his eyes and wondered at the admiration in them. "Yes?"

"I—"

Someone shouted in the distance, and her heart quickened. "We must hurry."

He reached for her hand again, and this time he placed some sort of package in it. She clutched it to her chest. "You must write me in secret now, in case your letters are found."

"But how—?"

He spoke quickly. "There is a letter in this booklet that explains what you must do next. Memorize it tonight and then burn the instructions."

She nodded. "I shall."

She wanted to stay hidden here with him forever, but it wasn't safe for them to linger.

"You must go," she insisted.

His fingers brushed over her hand again. "Lydia, I—"

Voices near the garden interrupted him, and she pushed him away. "Go."

He leaned toward her again, and for one moment, she thought he was going to kiss her lips. She froze at his nearness, not knowing what she should do. But then he kissed her cheek, and she inhaled sharply, the sound of it like a cannon blast in the night.

He met her eyes one last time and then turned. In seconds, he had vanished into the stalks behind him.

She lifted her hand to her face, the touch of his lips searing her skin. Her feet seemed planted into the dirt as her mind warred against her heart.

She ought not feel this way about Nathan. He had likely kissed her in gratitude for her work as a courier and a spy.

Still, she should be drowning with guilt for deceiving her family, their king, the man she once planned to marry. But she didn't feel guilty at all.

The stalks rustled to her left and she heard the voices of the men again as they searched through them. She tucked the small package down the front of her gown and stepped back out into the gardens. Her head lifted high, she strolled toward the house.

Captain Moore stopped her. "I thought you had already returned."

"There wasn't any danger in the gardens," she said.

His eyes narrowed. "Did you see anyone?"

"Indeed." She nodded. "Your men seem to be everywhere."

His gaze traveled over her shoulder, scanning the gardens, and then he looked back at her hands. "Where is your candle?"

She looked down at her hands as if they had swallowed the holder and flame. "I must have dropped it."

"That was quite careless of you, Miss Caswell."

The captain was right; she had been careless. "I suppose it was."

She stepped around him, wanting to run, but she held her composure as steady as possible, walking up the stairs and into the house before climbing up to the third floor. Then she stepped out on the small patio overlooking the gardens and clusters of lantern light that moved over the lawn.

Wherever Nathan hid, she hoped he would burrow down until they stopped searching. She couldn't bear the thought of losing him.

CHAPTER 25

*D*aylight lingered far into the evenings as the summer progressed. The long nights reminded Lydia of her childhood staying up as late as possible to play in the colorful gardens and fruit trees before the sun finally slipped over the horizon.

She had no information to deliver to Nathan, but she still walked every night at dusk to check the gazebo.

Each night she was disappointed at the absence of a ribbon, but she prayed as she walked, asking God to keep Nathan safe wherever he was. And she prayed that Grayson was still alive and would return to them one day.

Ever since she'd refused his proposal of marriage, Major Reed had ignored her, and the officers no longer spoke of anything significant in front of her family. But when the time came for her to listen, she was prepared. She'd hidden the small bottle of ink Nathan gave her by stitching it into the cushion of her window seat. In his letter, Nathan had said the ink was invisible.

Outside her bedchamber, Lydia heard Hannah's laughter echo down the hall, filtering into Lydia's room along with music from the hall below. She opened her door and saw the major looking down upon Hannah as if she were a sweet cake prepared just for him.

Hannah ignored Lydia's presence, continuing to laugh as if she were aged five instead of fifteen. The major turned toward Lydia, satisfaction flickering in his eyes.

Her hand on the banister, Lydia glared at the man who had proposed to her in the garden. "Hannah must return to her room."

Hannah's eyes flashed. "You can hide behind your door, Lydia, but I will not."

She ignored her sister's words. "Do you know how old she is, Major Reed?"

"Old enough to marry when others will not."

Hannah placed her hand in the crook of Major Reed's arm. With a swift nod toward Lydia, the major escorted Hannah toward the stairs.

Then he turned and looked back at Lydia one more time, as if she might change her mind.

Would it keep Hannah safe if she did?

She doubted it, and she had no power over that man or Hannah. Her sister would never listen to her.

Lydia pounded on her parents' chamber door until Mother answered. A glass of Father's Madeira sat on the stand beside Lady Caswell's bed. Lydia eyed the drink as she sat on the window seat. She'd never seen her mother drink wine in her chamber.

Lydia drummed her fingers on the cushions beside her. "Where is Father?"

"In the fields," Mother answered before taking a sip of the wine.

Lydia pointed toward the door. "Hannah is flirting with Major Reed, and unfortunately he is reciprocating."

Mother set down her glass, her voice barely above a whisper. "Do you want to marry the major?"

"No."

Mother lifted her glass again to her lips. "Then it's for the best."

Lydia clenched her fingers together. She knew how important peace was to her mother, but was she really willing to sacrifice one of her children for it?

"It is not best for Hannah," Lydia insisted.

"Major Reed will protect her and all of us."

"You don't even like the man!"

Mother sighed. "It matters not who or what I like. What's best for our family is most important."

"Hannah mustn't marry him. She is too young, and he is too—"

"Hold your tongue, Lydia." Mother nodded toward the door. "Someone might hear you."

Lydia folded her arms over her chest and lowered her voice. "You know he's not best for her or for our family."

"I do not know anything anymore."

The major might be kind to them as long as there was a hope for the future, but she wished her sister didn't pine for the man, wished Hannah was merely playing this terrible game to protect their family.

Unfortunately she had never known Hannah to bother herself by caring for another.

Footsteps pounded in the hallway, and Father rushed into the room. Her heart sank at the look of distress on his face.

He crossed the room and turned, continuing to pace as he spoke. "We have lost two more house servants and ten field slaves."

Lydia leaned back against the glass panes. The loss of their remaining slaves would be a blow to Father as he prepared to harvest their crop.

"Perhaps Major Reed and his men will help you find them," Mother said.

Father opened the door, and Lydia followed him down the main steps until he found the major with Hannah and the other officers in the drawing room.

Major Reed looked up from his cards. "What is it?"

"I fear some more of my Negroes might have joined your army."

The major tossed a card onto the table. "The king has permitted them to do so."

"But I bought these men."

Major Reed shook his head. "I understand, but there is nothing I can do."

Father leaned back against the banister. "Who will harvest my tobacco?"

"Surely there are other workers you could hire."

"All the younger men are off fighting." Father stepped toward the door and then turned to look at Lydia. "Tell your mother that I will return."

"Where are you going?" she asked.

"To retrieve my Negroes."

Outside the drawing room, she stopped him. "Hannah is consorting with Major Reed."

"That is the only good news that I've had today," he said before he retreated toward the front door.

"It is not good at all," she muttered, but he had already left.

It seemed as if everything was upside down. Without this war, Father would never entertain such a match for his youngest daughter, but he was as desperate as Hannah.

Perhaps they were all desperate.

Some for victory. Some for peace. And some for freedom.

Father returned three nights later, while Lydia and Mother were upstairs stitching in the quiet. When the door to her parents' room flew open, Lydia jumped.

MELANIE DOBSON

"Charles," her mother exclaimed, and she rushed forward, her arms open.

When Father embraced her, holding her close, Lydia looked away. She knew her parents loved one another, but she rarely saw affection between them.

Mother's tears demonstrated how much she loved her husband. That was what Lydia wanted, to love and to be loved.

"Did you find our slaves?" Mother asked.

He shook his head. "But General Cornwallis and his men have taken over Williamsburg."

"Are the Pendells safe?" Mother sounded alarmed.

"Indeed. It seems the army is only resting before they march again."

"How many soldiers are stationed there?" Lydia asked, trying not to sound as alarmed as her mother.

"Mr. Pendell said at least seven thousand."

Lydia straightened the edges of her skirt. Did Nathan know there were so many?

"The number of soldiers is good news, is it not?" Mother asked.

"It is good for the king, but our plantation will not survive if we cannot get our crop in."

It was too bad the soldiers couldn't band together while they waited to build up the colonies by harvesting the land.

"Someone in Williamsburg must know what happened to our slaves," Mother said.

"I met with Cornwallis himself, but he said that hundreds of slaves have joined their ranks in the past month. I searched for two days, but I think our Negroes must have moved up north quickly."

Mother sighed. "Did his men indicate when this war would end?"

Father shook his head.

"Surely the British could take over Virginia now," Lydia said.

210

She hated hounding her father for information, but she must find out what was happening, for the good of all of them.

"It may not be as easy as we once believed," he said. "The French have sent more troops and ships to help the colonists."

"The British must have more!" she insisted.

"They are not certain of it." Father's eyes grew worried again. "The Marquis de Lafayette is leading his men this way along with General Washington, but Cornwallis does not know how many soldiers they have."

Laughter filtered in through the open window, and Lydia turned back toward her father. "If Cornwallis is in Williamsburg, why are Major Reed and his men still here?"

"They will not be needed until the battle begins."

Lydia tried to steady her racing heart. She must get Nathan the news right away.

Lydia used the invisible ink to write her message, but delivering the letter was not as easy as she thought it would be. She'd attempted her delivery last night, but an officer had stopped her on the portico, begging her to dance.

She'd concealed the message inside the pocket under her gown, and throughout the miserable dance, it felt as if it might burn a hole in the fabric. Nathan needed this information, and yet she could not continue to throw suspicion on herself by escaping while the others were entertaining themselves.

Most of the officers didn't seem to think a woman could be smart enough to collect and share intelligence—and she would give them no cause to think otherwise—but Captain Moore continued to watch her closely.

As she finished breakfast this morning, the letter for Nathan remained in her pocket. Hannah hadn't joined them for the meal, and many of the officers were already gone, patrolling the countryside by foot since most of the horses hadn't been recovered.

After she stood, she spoke to her mother. "I shall cut flowers for the table."

"Do fetch some English roses," Mother instructed.

"Of course."

Lydia picked flowers from the garden and then slipped around the side of the orangery. With her back to the building, she loosened the brick behind her and slipped the message inside.

Once, she'd been afraid Hannah would find her secret, but the stakes were so much higher now.

She'd taken a few steps when a flash caught her eye. She turned, hoping it was Hannah. "Who's there?"

An officer stepped out, and she caught her breath. She didn't dare turn toward the orangery.

"You frightened me, Captain Moore."

His eyes narrowed. "Only the guilty are easily frightened."

She forced her eyebrows up in surprise. "Or those who are being stalked."

"Major Reed might not think you are capable of treachery, but you do not fool me, Miss Caswell."

"Are you accusing me of being a traitor?"

"Your actions have proved quite suspicious."

An angry huff escaped from her lips. "You eat our food and drink our wine, and now you suspect me of treachery?"

"We would eat your food and drink your wine whether or not you allowed us."

"We have been nothing but gracious to you, Captain." She held up the flowers. "And now I must return to the house to help the servants prepare a meal for you and your fellow officers tonight. Or would you prefer to eat our food without preparation?"

"You had best be careful, Miss Caswell."

"And you had best be careful as well, Captain. Major Reed would not like to hear that you were harassing the woman he has asked to marry."

A strange look crossed the man's face. "The major proposed marriage to you?"

"He has."

"And you have accepted?"

She swallowed. "I have considered it."

"Then I suppose he is right. You're not nearly as smart as I first believed."

CHAPTER 26

*N*athan waded through a riverbed along Virginia's coast at twilight, swatting the cloud of mosquitoes that bombarded his head.

The mosquitoes had been following him since this morning when he hopped off the wagon of a fellow Patriot who'd transported him to the outskirts of Manassas.

Nothing would deter these mosquitoes, just as nothing would deter him from finding where the Continental Army had gone so he could deliver Lydia's message. When he last left the army, soldiers were encamped in Connecticut, but in the tavern last night, he learned they were rumored to be along the shores of the Potomac River.

He must deliver this message before they marched farther south.

He was tired of tramping across the colonies with no knowledge of where he would spend the night. He couldn't imagine going back to his job as a business manager, but he would never again take for granted the benefit of a full stomach and a feather bed. One day he would like to have a home of his own and a family to return to at night. Perhaps even a wife like Lydia Caswell.

He never should have kissed Lydia in her garden three weeks past, even if it had only been on the cheek. It had been impulsive, and a man in his position couldn't afford impulsions.

Instead of clandestine meetings in the cornstalks, he wished he could return to her home in proper form and knock on the front door. If only she weren't planning to marry Seth, he would wait until the end of this war and then ask her father for her hand in marriage.

With a quick slap, he killed a mosquito on his neck.

These long nights alone were clouding his heart and his mind. Once he was back among the officers and soldiers, surely his longing for Lydia would diminish.

He unrolled his blanket and settled under a tree for the night. At first light, he would continue his search for the army. If they marched south and attacked the British now, they would surely be defeated. He must stop them until they were able to wait for more soldiers and ammunition. The supplies he had stashed at the Hammonds' would help, but there weren't enough to defeat the army that was accumulating in Virginia.

After he built a small fire to ward off the mosquitoes, he pulled a linen cloth out of his haversack and ate a piece of salted beef and a hard biscuit.

When he found the army, the first thing he would request was fresh meat and some coffee. And perhaps he could purchase some fresh bread from one of the women.

Trying to deter his thoughts from Lydia and his own hunger, he pulled out his prayer book and began to read how the Lord brought the Israelites out of Egypt: *"But made his own people to go forth like sheep, and guided them in the wilderness like a flock. And he led them on safely, so that they feared not: but the sea overwhelmed their enemies."*

Even when the Lord delivered His people, they disobeyed

His laws and grumbled in the wilderness. Nathan prayed that when this was over—if they were victorious—they would not dishonor the God who had rescued them from oppression, as the Israelites had done.

Leaves rustled behind him, and he took a stick and held it over the fire until it started to burn. He knew little about fighting men with anything except wit, but he could ward off a bear or a cougar.

He stepped forward, facing the unknown with as much courage as he could muster. "Who's there?"

The shadow of a man stepped out, and Nathan held out his torch. "'Tis I, Master Nathan."

He squinted again. "Elisha?"

"It is."

Nathan slowly lowered his knife. "What are you doing here?"

"I've been watching out for you."

"You followed me all the way here?"

Elisha sat on a log. "'Twasn't easy."

"But I was on a wagon—"

Elisha shrugged. "The wagon didn't move very fast."

Nathan threw the stick into the fire. He was impressed by Elisha's ability to track him, but he would have to be more careful. He hadn't even an inkling that someone had been trailing him.

Nathan nodded at the blaze. "Are you hungry?"

"Yes, sir."

Nathan opened up the linen cloth. "I've got some lousy-tasting biscuits and a little beef left."

Elisha took what Nathan offered and ate quickly. "I could catch us some squirrel or perhaps a deer in the morning."

"My stomach would thank you." An owl hooted in the tree above them. "I thought you had run off with the British."

Elisha shook his head, grief heavy in his voice. "I can't join them. They stole away my wife and son."

"But you cannot return to the Caswells, either."

"I must find Morah and Alden."

"You trust the Patriots?" Nathan asked.

"I don't believe I trust either army, but I trust you."

The weight of his words settled on Nathan. "We would have to wait until after the war."

Elisha rubbed his hands together. "Hope can propel a man like me forward for a long time."

Nathan threw his stick into the fire. It was hope that kept him fighting for freedom. "Are you going to ask where I'm going?"

Elisha brushed a small pile of leaves together and lay down on them. "It don't matter much to me."

Perhaps it didn't matter because Elisha believed Nathan could keep him safe.

Nathan wished he believed it as well.

Lydia heard laughter coming out of the great hall and glanced in to see if her sister was among the officers. She didn't see Hannah or Major Reed, but several men swam like fish around her pianoforte, lifting their mugs and singing a song about the Yankees and their Italian finery.

She wasn't certain if she was more angered or saddened by their display. The officers were mocking brave men like Seth and Nathan, men who might not dress as finely as the British but who had courageous hearts and lives they were willing to sacrifice to free others from oppression.

The smell of her father's ale wafted into the hall. There couldn't be much of his drink left in the basement.

One of the officers motioned to her. "Come and join us."

She shook her head. "I'm too tired."

Mother stepped up next to her, wrapping an arm around her shoulders. "They will leave soon," she whispered.

"Not until Father's ale is gone."

Mother scanned the room. "Where is Hannah?"

"I do not know."

One of the men held up his glass and shouted, "Long live King George!"

Everyone lifted a cup.

The keys from the pianoforte banged again, and one of the men set his glass on a pedestal. Another man knocked it off, but the crash was muffled by the music. The player paused and turned to look at the shards of glass on the floor. Then he continued playing and the others returned to their singing.

They didn't seem to care one whit what they destroyed.

Mother clutched her hands together. "I lost track long ago of how many glasses they have broken."

"We will replace them," Lydia said.

"I'm not certain that we will."

No matter how hard her parents tried to cling to the security of the past, nothing would be the same after this war, and Lydia feared the damage the major and his men inflicted on their family would last long after the war as well.

"There's Hannah," Mother said, and Lydia turned to look.

Her sister's hand clutched the major's arm, and she giggled as they strolled through the entry toward the great hall. Hannah would not make a good governor's wife, at least not until she matured, but she would dote on this man as Lydia never could.

As they drew closer to the hall, Hannah glanced over and flashed a victorious smile at Lydia.

Major Reed didn't seem to notice her at all.

～

Continental guards found Nathan and Elisha before the two men found the Patriots' encampment. The sun had just begun to rise as the three soldiers questioned Nathan and the man he brought into camp. Finally one of the men escorted them toward the general's tent.

As they walked, Nathan searched the rows of men cooking pork over small fires and making ash cakes from the flour provided by the military. The aroma of coffee mixed with smoke, and Nathan wished he could have just one cup. It would help him shake off the webs in his body and mind.

But first he had to deliver Lydia's letter to his uncle.

The guards outside the tent recognized him immediately. They eyed Elisha, but neither of them made any effort to question him. They probably thought he was Nathan's slave.

What would they think if he told them that Elisha was his friend?

General Washington stood with two officers from his elite General's Guard, hovering over a portable writing desk. He was a tall man who demanded the respect of both colonists and the British with whom he came in contact. He wore the dark-blue wool uniform of the Continentals with scarlet facings and white stockings under his buckled shoes. His hair was powdered white and pulled back with a blue ribbon.

Washington looked up. "Nathan—why are you here?"

"Hello, General Washington." He'd stopped calling him "Uncle" when he began working as a courier and spy.

The advisors simply nodded at Nathan. They tolerated him as General Washington's nephew, but they thought he would be better used as an officer. His uncle, however, believed that as long as their network didn't falter, the intelligence his spies gathered would win this war.

Washington glanced over at Elisha. "Who is your companion?"

"A friend to whom I owe my life." Nathan looked down at

the map of Virginia spread out on the desk. Then he handed Lydia's letter to the general. "I have news you must see."

A solution revealed what had been written in invisible ink, and General Washington slowly read the words.

Lydia confirmed what other spies had been reporting: although the Americans believed they had enough soldiers with the French recruits to defeat Benedict Arnold's troops, they did not have enough soldiers to defeat the troops led by Cornwallis. They needed to send for reinforcements before they engaged their enemy.

General Washington looked up again. "Whoever wins the colony of Virginia may very well win this war."

"Aye," Nathan said. "And there are too many British soldiers for us to fight right now."

"Too many soldiers," another officer said, "and not enough food for our men."

While the Patriots had recovered tons of much-needed ammunition from the shipyard, there was very little food among the supplies. General Washington had mandated that his army would not plunder the colonists as their opponent did.

"We have sent for supplies from our man in Philadelphia," the officer said. "They will be delivered to a hiding place near the town called York, at the mouth of the Chesapeake Bay."

His uncle turned back to Nathan. "You must go to York to oversee the delivery of these supplies."

"But I have established an invaluable source near Williamsburg." He hesitated. "This person can deliver information we need to recover Virginia."

"I shall send someone else to check for messages." He paused. "Captain Hammond knows that area well."

Nathan cringed. "I fear he would be recognized."

General Washington considered his words before he spoke again. "Then you will go straight from York to Williamsburg."

"Yes, sir."

Nathan searched the camp until he found Seth drinking coffee over a small fire while he and his men waited for direction. His friend was almost as tall as Washington, and he looked a lot like Sarah with his blond hair and light-green eyes. Nathan glanced down at his own ragged trousers and attire. Seth outranked him in multiple ways.

He reached for Seth's hand and shook it. "How are you?"

"We have been worried about you." Seth handed him a tin cup with coffee. "Do you have news of home?"

"Unfortunately, the news is not good."

Seth's eyebrows furrowed. "What happened?"

"I regret to say that the British have burned down your house."

Seth cursed. "What of my sister?"

"She went to your aunt's home in Philadelphia."

Seth swirled the coffee in his cup. Nathan couldn't imagine all the emotions that must be warring inside him.

"And our Negroes?"

"Some were taken by the British, and others seem to have run away."

"'Tis to be expected, I suppose." Seth looked off into the forest. "I hope those who ran, ran far."

Nathan sipped the coffee. "Aye."

"I'm glad Sarah is safe."

Nathan waited for a moment, expecting Seth to ask about Lydia and her family, but he didn't. And he couldn't tell Seth or anyone else what Lydia was doing.

CHAPTER 27

*N*athan found a cave in the bluffs north of the town called York. Two soldiers guided him and Elisha to York—Privates Lemuel and Benjamin from the First Virginia Regiment—and the four of them quickly unpacked their haversacks and settled inside the cave to watch the bay for the supplies.

It had taken them four days of walking to locate the town, and then they had to sneak by several camps of British soldiers as they hiked up the coast to find the place where the supplies were supposed to arrive by tonight.

He prayed they hadn't missed the boat. If they didn't secure these supplies, they wouldn't be able to fight well for Virginia.

Another soldier—a young New Jersey man named Micah—remained closer to the water with a wagon and a team of horses he'd secured from a trusted family in York. They would quickly transfer the supplies from the schooner to the cave, and then Nathan would leave behind the three soldiers who'd escorted him, to guard the supplies until they were needed.

It was his responsibility to return to his uncle with the news that the supplies were ready.

Clouds covered the stars as Nathan listened to the rain patter on the dark waters in front of him. A man known as Porter was supposed to meet them before dawn, and then they would secure the ammunition and weapons.

Once the troops had the supplies, they could march on the thousands of British troops gathering on the east side of the colony.

He balled up his blanket and leaned his head against it. The thought haunted him of Lydia in that big house with all those men, many who had no good intent. Lydia's heart might belong to Seth, but Nathan's heart belonged to her.

He might not be able to do anything about her heart, but he could help the Patriots rid the colony of the enemy. And the sooner the better. When the world righted itself, he would return to Caswell Hall to thank her for her courage. The soldiers fought hard for freedom, but it was women like Sarah and Lydia who would win this war for them.

Elisha sat down beside him. "Are you thinking about her?"

He glanced over with surprise. "About whom?"

"Miss Lydia, of course. Neither of you can fool me."

Elisha's words dawned slowly on him. "How is Lydia fooling you?"

"Seth Hammond is a good man, but he ain't good for her."

Nathan looked back at the water. "I wouldn't be good for her either."

"Now, I don't know about that. It seems to me you got a heart about as big as she does."

A light blinked on the bay waters, and he elbowed Elisha. "Did you see that?"

"I believe I did."

They watched it blink again in the rain and then two more times. It was the signal that the boat had arrived.

"Wait here," Nathan told Elisha and the two privates. He had to make sure it was safe before he put all their lives in jeopardy.

He scrambled from the cave and hurried down to the shore. With the tide lapping against the rocks, he couldn't hear the rhythm of oars or the sound of voices, but his eyes searched the darkness over the water.

The light blinked thrice again, but this time it was much closer. "Who are you?" he whispered into the darkness.

"A friend of the great king," a voice replied. "And I hope your friend as well."

"Aye," Nathan said. "I am your friend."

Then he heard the sharp swish of oars cutting through the bay waters and saw an outline of a rowboat pressing toward the sandy shore.

The man at the helm of the boat wore a tricorn hat dipped low over his forehead, and the moment his boat ran ashore, he stepped onto the sand.

Nathan held his musket at his side. "What is your name?"

"Porter." The man spoke so low that his voice blended in with the lapping of water. "And you are?"

"Nathan."

Porter responded with a sharp nod. "We have a delivery for your men."

Elisha guarded the cave while he, Lemuel, and Benjamin retrieved the supplies conveyed from the schooner by the rowboat. In the darkness, they helped five of Porter's men unload barrels of ammunition, crates with muskets, and bags with flour and coffee. Micah drove the wagon full of supplies up the hill, ten yards from the cave, and the team of men transported the supplies up to Elisha in the hiding place.

They worked in silence for hours, the rain making mud out of their tracks as they loaded the wagon and then unloaded the supplies by a dim light in one of the cave's side chambers. It wouldn't be long now before Porter and his men would have to leave, under the cover of darkness and rain. They couldn't risk being caught at dawn—for the sake of their ship and the supplies.

Nathan took a damp crate from Lemuel, and it rattled as he hauled it to the room at the back of the cave. Elisha had stuffed supplies high against the wall—there were barrels of flour and salted meat alongside crates that carried bottles of cherries and drink. The supplies would dwindle quickly once the army reached York, but it seemed to him that there was enough food and ammunition for ten thousand men.

When Nathan stepped back toward the mouth of the cave, he heard someone shout down by the water, and he cringed at the break in their silence. He had to quiet the man before the British heard them. Their lives— and the colony of Virginia— were relying on their stealth.

He rushed to the mouth of the cave, but instead of jumping outside, he listened for a moment. The crack of a musket ricocheted through the rain, and it felt as if his insides ripped into two.

Elisha swore as Nathan reached for his musket, but neither man left the cave. If the British found Porter's ship, they would search for the supplies. Nathan needed to guard them with his life.

More muskets blasted, and he heard shouting from several men. He and Elisha waited inside the cave with their muskets loaded, waiting for the British to march up the hill. He would do everything he could to protect the supplies.

The shouts dissipated suddenly, like vapor on a warm day, and he strained his ears to hear what was happening on the beach below.

Voices—he heard them outside, near the mouth of the cave. A small group of men with British accents were talking about the supplies found in the wagon. They weren't using a lantern, and he was grateful of it. If they looked up the hill, they would discover a whole trove of food and ammunition.

The rain fell harder, and Nathan held his breath, afraid that even the sound of his breathing would alert them to his position. He and Elisha might be able to fight this group, but he had no idea how many soldiers were behind them.

The men's voices began to fade, and Nathan breathed in the cool air.

What happened to Micah and the other men?

"You'd best stay here," Nathan said as he stepped outside the cave.

Elisha placed his hand on Nathan's shoulder. "The general said to protect you—"

"It's more important to protect these supplies."

Gray light began to seep over the horizon as Nathan hopped down to the ground. He carefully skirted through the tall grasses until he was five yards from the shore. Scanning the beach, he saw no sign of British soldiers or the wagon that had carried the last of their supplies. The schooner was gone as well.

But there was something lying on the sand, at the edge of the water. He rushed forward to see what the British had left behind.

His stomach turned.

They didn't leave something behind. They left someone.

Micah lay face down in the water, the tide rushing over his back. Nathan rolled him over, but there was no breath left in him.

Nathan sat down on the beach and pressed his fists against his forehead.

He hated war, hated the lives lost for no reason, hated that young men passionate about doing right were swept away at the onset of their lives.

Light illuminated the beach now, and he scanned the rocks and murky water for Lemuel and Benjamin—and the crew of the schooner—but it seemed as if they had disappeared.

Would the redcoats return this morning to search the area?

For the sake of those soldiers who remained alive and the colonists who were relying on him, he must act quickly.

The rain fell harder as he dragged Micah's body out of the water and hid it in the tall grass. He couldn't stay any longer, not even to bury this brave soldier in the sand.

When he climbed back into the cave, he sat down beside Elisha. "Micah's dead," he said.

"What about Lemuel and Benjamin?" Elisha asked.

Nathan leaned back against the wall. "I couldn't find them."

"It don't matter much to me who wins this war, but I hate seeing the lives of good men taken when they're so young."

Nathan unrolled his blanket beside Elisha and covered his wet clothes with it. Micah was one of thousands of casualties, but like Elisha, Nathan hated that anyone would have to die, even if he died a hero.

Once they had succeeded in obtaining freedom, he would never forget to celebrate the lives of the men who'd made it possible.

A breeze swept into the cave, and his eyes began to droop. There was nothing else they could do until the sun went down again.

Aunt Marguerite eyed the plate of raspberry tarts with her lorgnette and then gingerly lifted one to her lips, taking the slightest nibble off the edge. Sarah watched with fascination as her aunt's lips puckered and her eyes crossed ever so slightly.

Aunt Marguerite waved her eyepiece. "We cannot possibly serve these to our guests."

The cook stepped forward. "There is no decent sugar to be had in the markets."

"Then we must borrow some from our neighbors."

"I fear no one will loan us any more."

Sarah's aunt had a terrible sweet tooth and kept the staff busy, trying to accommodate her penchant for sweets. None of the neighbors were willing, it seemed, to part with any more of the sugar that was so difficult to obtain.

"Take it away," her aunt commanded, and Louisa swept the plate out from under Aunt Marguerite's hand and rushed it away so quickly that Sarah barely had time to swipe a tart off the plate. They tasted, well, a bit tart, but other than that, she thought it would be a wonderful treat for the women attending Aunt Marguerite's luncheon.

"If I may," the cook said, "perhaps we should consider serving dumplings with molasses."

Aunt Marguerite reached for her fan and propelled liberal amounts of air over her perplexed face as if the thought of serving dumplings and molasses to their guests might be the death of her.

"Or I could use applesauce to make a cake," the cook offered.

"Nonsense," Aunt Marguerite said. "I will personally go and ask Mrs. Richter for a loaf of sugar."

The cook bowed her head, backing away. "Of course."

Sarah finished the rest of the tart. "The women shouldn't care whether they are served a fancy dessert."

Her aunt looked at Sarah as if she'd lost her mind then turned and followed their cook toward the kitchen.

Sarah glanced out the window, searching the street as she'd done a hundred times before, hoping to see Grayson walking toward their house. He was supposed to return three weeks ago, but there was still no word of where he was or when he would be back.

Her heart trembled. When he returned, she hoped they would resume the conversation they'd started down at the docks. If Grayson did propose marriage, Sarah knew her brother would be happy for her, and Father would try.

Commodore Hammond had always supported men who stood by their principles, and Grayson had stood firmly behind his.

She was proud of Grayson for supplying the Continental Army with the rations they needed to survive and ultimately win this war. Now, instead of hiding away in her plantation, perhaps she could convince him to let her join him in his work.

When Aunt Marguerite returned, she moved to the window beside Sarah. "I'm certain he will come soon."

In the midst of her excitement, Sarah couldn't help but worry. Grayson had disappeared from her life before. It was possible he would do it once again. And if he disappeared without telling her where he had gone, she didn't know how she could ever let him back in.

How many times could she let him break her heart?

The front bell rang, and she leaped.

Aunt Marguerite wrung her gloves. "I must procure the sugar before our guests arrive."

Sarah nodded as her aunt bustled toward the back door, and then her gaze returned to the window. Seconds later, a man was escorted into the parlor, his vest and pantaloons dirty and torn, his long hair ratty over his shoulders. She struggled to remember where she had seen him before.

Then she remembered—she'd met him with Grayson down near the docks. Zadock was his name.

She reached for the arm of a chair, balancing herself. Why had this man come without Grayson?

"He insisted on seeing you," Louisa explained, distraught.

"It's all right," Sarah assured her before she turned to Zadock. "What happened?"

"Our boat was attacked in Virginia."

"Where is—" Her voice cracked. "Where is Porter?"

"The British have taken him and his boat along with most of the crew." Zadock paused. "Porter said if anything happened to him, I must find you."

She released her grip on the chair. Thank God, he was still alive. "Where have they taken them?" she insisted.

"I'm not certain," Zadock said. "But there was a wharf nearby, outside their camp in York."

She hadn't been able to save Thomas or the others from the British. But perhaps it wasn't too late to save Grayson.

Tyranny, like hell, is not easily conquered;
yet we have this consolation with us, that the harder
the conflict, the more glorious the triumph.

Thomas Paine, The American Crisis, 1776

CHAPTER 28

SEPTEMBER 1781

*S*arah insisted that Zadock and his small band of men escort her to where Grayson had lost his schooner. Aunt Marguerite protested as she left the house, but if she lost Grayson due to her fears, she would never forgive herself.

She didn't know how Zadock had secured the sailboat, but it served the four of them well as they traveled the waterways down into Virginia. As she helped the men sail, she imagined herself as Madam Sarah Knight traveling into the unknown—except that Madam Knight wasn't searching for the man she loved.

Sarah Hammond wouldn't stop searching until she found him.

When they stopped at a port in Virginia, another privateer told them that he'd seen a new prisoner ship at a camp a mile south of York. The information came for a hefty price, but Zadock had the gold to pay for it.

Sarah asked him about the money, and he explained that a shrewd privateer always carried extra funds, reserved for intelligence and bribery. Information that cost nothing, Zadock explained, was usually worthless.

Zadock left Sarah and the other men north of York for an entire day. When he returned, he had three other men with him. One was a soldier named Lemuel, who was searching for his comrade, and another was the courier named Nathan, who had secured her travel to Philadelphia. It took her a moment to recognize the third man.

"Elisha?"

"Miss Sarah," Elisha said, reaching for her hand to shake.

Tears wet her cheeks as she engulfed him in a hug. It was so good to see the husband of her beloved maid. "You are free?" she asked.

Fear flashed across his face. "It's of my own doing."

She nodded. "Then we shall keep it that way."

"Have you any word of Morah?" he begged.

"I am afraid there is none." She paused. "But we cannot stop hoping."

"Aye. I will not stop until I find them."

She understood. She would not stop either, until she found the man she loved.

Nathan said he knew where the ship was, but he also said it would take a miracle to recover Grayson and his men.

She would pray for a miracle.

They left their boat and the two hired sailors north of York and continued their journey south on foot. Nathan led them far around York, through a dense forest, before they crossed over a small footpath and an abandoned mill by a stream. Wind rushed through the leaves, tangling her skirt and the ribbons on her cap, but they pressed on until they reached the edge of the trees.

Elisha waved her forward. "Be careful, miss."

Peering through the trees, she saw the two masts of Grayson's schooner on the shoreline. The privateer had told them the truth—the ship was docked south of York. But he'd neglected to mention the hundreds of British soldiers crawling like red ants on the grassy hills nearby.

Any survivors of the attack were probably being held on the ship— and Sarah refused to let herself believe in anything except Grayson's survival.

To the left of the tents were the camp followers—hundreds of women and children clustered together around campfires. The smoke rose, and she could smell boiling meat. Her stomach ached from hunger, but there was no complaint in her. Grayson and his men would be much hungrier.

She backed away from the edge, retreating into the safety of the trees. She doubted anyone would see her in her brown gown among the tree trunks, but Nathan had warned them about guards roaming through these trees. If they were caught now, she might see Grayson, but only as a fellow prisoner. Then, she feared, all hope would truly be lost.

A half mile into the trees, Sarah and the men set up their bedding and ate the hard biscuits they'd brought from the ship along with berries she'd collected on their hike through the forest.

After unrolling her sheet and blanket, she stared at the dark tree limbs above her. She'd always wanted to travel, but she'd had no idea that her desires would take her here, sleeping beside four men in the forest. If her father knew, he would pretend to be perturbed with her, but she suspected he might actually be proud of her courage.

The men were silent, their best defense in the darkness. Sarah closed her eyes, remembering Grayson's small kindnesses to her when they were young—the plums and grapes and apples he used to pick for her. As she drifted to sleep, she prayed that God would give Grayson the sustenance he needed until they could find him.

She awoke to the smell of smoked applewood and opened her eyes to an animal roasting on a spit over the fire. She started to sit, wanting to help the men prepare breakfast, but she stopped when she heard Zadock say it was impossible for them to stage any kind of rescue.

She refused to entertain the word impossible.

"I might be able to sneak into camp," Nathan said, lifting up the barbering kit he kept in his satchel.

"But what then?" Zadock asked. "The guards will never let you on that ship."

"I could think of a reason—"

Zadock stopped him. "Even if you found a way on, Porter and the others will be too weak to swim away."

Lemuel stirred the fire. "And it would be impossible to sneak them back through the camp."

Sarah's mind raced. If the men were caught, both rescuers and prisoners would likely be shot on the spot. But there was little hope for Grayson's life if they left him on the ship.

"There must be a way," Elisha insisted.

"We could take them food and water," Nathan said. "Enough to keep them alive until we can rescue them from the boat."

"It is impossible." Zadock shook his head, resigned. "We'll never be able to get them off the boat."

Sarah sat up. "It's not impossible."

The men looked over at her.

"You might not be able to get into camp." She took a deep breath. "But I can."

Silence met her words as the men glanced at one another. She held her breath as she waited for their reaction.

Nathan spoke first. "We cannot let you go into the camp alone."

She took a long sip of water from her canteen. "You said it would be impossible for any of you to go."

"But that does not mean we allow you to do so," Nathan said.

She glanced at the trees around them. Who knew how many British scouts were roaming the forest, looking for invaders? "I will be as safe as I am out here, probably safer. I shall simply pretend to be one of the women living outside the camp."

"Perhaps it is possible," Elisha said, and hope began to well in her again.

Zadock cleared his throat. "I'm sorry, miss, but you don't look much like a camp woman."

While she appreciated his sentiments, she didn't believe him. Over the past week, her dress had become torn, her hair tangled in knots. After sleeping outside again, she probably looked more ragged than many of the women who camped for weeks in one place.

"I doubt they will question my appearance," she said. "But I shall need a good reason to venture into the camp."

"There are plenty of good reasons for women to go into the camp," Lemuel said. "You could bring in food to sell or ask to wash clothes."

Zadock crossed his arms. "Porter would never forgive me if something happened to you."

Sarah's mind flashed back to her hours in the dovecote, hiding as the enemy ravaged her house. Her own life had been spared, but she had been too cowardly to rescue Thomas and her other Negroes.

Her cowardice wouldn't stop her again. She wouldn't run from the chance to rescue the man she loved. "I would never forgive myself if something happened to Grayson."

Nathan looked up. "I thought the man's name was Porter."

Sarah licked her lips. "It is—now."

"Did you not meet him in Philadelphia?" Nathan asked.

"I saw him in Philadelphia, but I have known him since childhood."

"Grayson," Nathan said twice, as if he were trying to recall where he had heard the name before. His eyes narrowed. "You haven't told me the entire truth."

Her glance shifted from Nathan to Elisha, whose eyes had grown wide. "I told you both what you needed to know."

"Is Porter . . . ?" Elisha started, but his voice trailed off.

Nathan untied the ribbon from his hair, and his long hair fell across his shoulders. "Grayson is her brother."

Lemuel leaned closer to them. "Whose brother?"

Sarah pulled her knees toward her chest, her gaze still on Nathan. "His family mustn't find out. He is protecting them."

Nathan looked down at the yellow ribbon in his hands, and Sarah glanced at the other men, gauging their reactions. Then she looked at Elisha. "You must understand that I have no choice but to try this. You risked your life every week to visit Morah and Alden. You would risk it again to save them if you knew where they were."

Elisha's gaze rested on the fire. She knew he understood her pain, her need to rescue Grayson, but she also understood his hesitancy. Lord Caswell was the reason Elisha's wife and son had been sent away in the first place. Now Sarah was asking him to rescue his master's son, a man who'd lashed his back long ago.

Her voice softened. "Grayson is not his father."

Elisha closed his eyes for a moment and then nodded. "I know."

"I must do this," she insisted. "I would rather die than know that I might have rescued him but didn't dare try."

Zadock shook his head, as if he wasn't certain he believed her. "Porter is one lucky man."

"I have loved him since I was but a girl."

Zadock stirred the fire. "And he loved you as well."

She closed her eyes for a moment, savoring his words. Her eyes were wet with tears when she opened them again. "Then you must understand."

"But he might not even be there," Nathan said. "Or he might not be—"

"He is alive." She shook her head vigorously. "Now, what must I do when I find him?"

Elisha spoke first. "I can help you with that."

Hope stirred in her. "What will you do?"

Elisha pulled the blackened meat off the fire. "We can cause some sort of diversion," he said. "As Gideon did against the Midianites."

She well remembered the story from the book of Judges. Gideon and his small band of men broke pottery jars and sounded trumpets, and their enemy ran in fear. She looked around their simple camp. They had neither jars nor trumpets. "How will you divert them?"

"I have an idea," Nathan said.

CHAPTER 29

*L*ydia's knees ached as she scrubbed the floor of the great hall. How had the officers managed to leave behind such a disaster? Each time they visited, it seemed, they had less regard for her family's home. And each time, her mother had less regard for them.

The officers finally went to join Cornwallis, but they left behind a trail of dented furniture, torn upholstery, and broken doors. And mud— it was as if they'd released a passel of hogs to roll around on the floor.

"They took no care," Mother said, shaking her head as she scrubbed beside Lydia.

"Indeed they did not."

Mother leaned back against the wall, sweat dripping down her slender face as she surveyed the chaos left behind in the room. "How is it possible for them to do all of this damage?'

"They were expecting our servants to clean it," Hannah said.

Lydia shook her head. "They know our Negroes have fled."

"Some have remained."

"A dozen is not enough to work the fields and the house."

Hannah looked up, her eyes blazing in defense. "They don't

know how many slaves it takes to run a plantation."

"They have servants in England," Lydia retorted.

"When this is finished, Dalton will rescue us."

"You will call him Major Reed," Mother said.

"But he told me to call him—"

"I do not care what he said, Hannah. He is an officer in the British army, and you will address him as such."

"Major Reed," Hannah said, emphasizing his name, "will procure us more slaves."

Lydia wasn't so certain. Most of the house servants were already working in the fields. If they didn't harvest everything in the next week, Father had said that Lydia and Hannah might have to join them.

On Monday she'd worked with Deborah in the washhouse. After enduring the stifling heat, Lydia didn't think she would mind laboring in the fields. At least there might be a breeze from the river.

She doubted Mother would allow them to work the fields, though. Not because the work was beneath them—there was no work beneath any of them these days—but because she needed their help in the house. Mother had been educated in household management but she'd never been taught how to clean a house on her own.

Even if she didn't revere Caswell Hall as Father did, Mother endeavored to care well for their family's home, and Lydia loved her for it. It would have been easier for them to leave the work behind and board a ship back to England.

Mother longed for England, and her family would welcome them there, but as long as the hope remained for a return to British rule, Father wouldn't leave Caswell Hall. And Mother probably wouldn't leave anyway, not until they found out what had happened to Grayson.

It was useless to try to fix all the damage in the house until after the war, but Mother wanted the house clean, even if the officers returned soon. Or perhaps because of it. Even though the officers had no regard for the Caswell home or possessions, Mother still contended with her silent pride. They were British gentlemen, and even if they had caused the damage, she would not entertain a gentleman or gentlewoman in such a state.

Lydia brushed her sleeve across the sweat on her forehead.

How had their maids done this work every day without complaint? Or perhaps they had complained but she never heard.

It seemed like a lifetime ago that they were hosting balls here at Caswell Hall, wearing their finest gowns imported from France and England. She'd hardly noticed the men and women who worked tirelessly to organize the balls. Her family's role was to host, and Lydia had proudly considered her work to be just as difficult as that of their servants. Only their attire was different.

How haughty she had been to think her work just as difficult.

In those days, she'd concerned herself mainly with preparations to become Seth Hammond's wife. There were the endless lessons about etiquette and dancing and music at her finishing school—things that had little use now.

Lydia scooted several feet toward the open window before dipping her rag into the soapy bucket again and washing another layer of crusted dirt off the wood.

Who knew where the mud had come from? The men seemed to be storming all through the backwaters of Virginia as if they'd already declared themselves the victors of the entire colony.

At church on Sunday, she'd heard that Cornwallis had taken all his men to rest for the winter on the Chesapeake Bay. She put the information in a letter, behind the brick, but as far as she knew, Nathan hadn't returned. She wished there was something more she could tell Nathan if he returned—when he returned. Some way for her to help stop this madness and return Virginia to a state of peace.

Besides the retreat to York, she didn't know what the British were planning. Any strategy they discussed here must have occurred behind closed doors, because she hadn't been privy to it. With their frequent comings and goings, it seemed as if the officers were waiting to see what the Patriots would do next. Perhaps they were simply confident in overtaking the colony, as if they regarded their enemy with the same disdain they'd had for this house.

Every night she continued to walk out to the gazebo, hoping that Nathan would find her there, but it had been more than a month since she had seen him last. If only she knew he was safe. Then at least her heart would find a place of peace.

How was it that she was thinking more about Nathan than she'd ever thought about Seth?

A breeze flowed through the window, and she closed her eyes, facing the wind. She was glad the two women working beside her couldn't read her thoughts. She'd once proclaimed her faithfulness to Seth Hammond, and yet she hadn't been faithful at all. Her heart had declared itself for another man, and she couldn't seem to stop it.

Still, she must try. Seth might have left on bitter terms, but what if he continued to hold their commitment with esteem? It was only honorable for her to tell him about the change in her heart before she allowed her thoughts to dwell on another man. Not that Nathan had any intent toward her.

She sighed. Even if Nathan cared for her, Father would never consider any sort of alliance between them.

The door to the servants' staircase opened, and Prudence stepped into the room, the handles of a basket looped over her arm. After the disappearance of their cook a fortnight ago, Prudence had been attempting to care for the kitchen as well.

"Would you like me to carry food to Master Caswell?"

Prudence asked.

Hannah stood up, wiping her hands on her soiled petticoat. "I will go."

Mother shook her head. "'Tis Lydia's turn."

Lydia dipped her dirty rag into the water and wrung it out before she stood. Prudence held out the basket, and Lydia accepted it with gratitude. She would welcome a bit of a retreat.

She took a wide-brimmed hat from the wardrobe. It felt strange to be wearing ribbons and lace after sweating over a dirty floor, but it was a reminder to her of what had been and the beauty of what still might be.

The sun was hot when she stepped through the back door, but the breeze cooled her skin. Standing under a tree, she set down the basket and tied the ribbons of her hat under her chin. If their Negroes had tasted freedom, she could understand why they would have run away.

She picked up the basket again and retrieved the one horse in the stable that the British had left behind for their use, a bay thoroughbred named Restless.

How was it that her father remained loyal to the King's Men when they had no respect for his personal property? Father might believe he was master of Caswell Hall, but if the British won this war, all Father owned would belong to King George. The king might very well disdain all the colonists whether or not they had remained loyal.

But Father didn't see it. He was certain the king would triumph, so he aligned himself with the victor.

Her eyes on the stalks of corn, Lydia wondered if Nathan was nearby. Shaking her head, she continued to ride through the fields, searching for Father. She must stop herself from thinking of Nathan. It was likely that she would never see him again. She had given him the information he needed, and now that the British officers were gone, there was no reason for him to return.

Her heart ached. It seemed the last four years were nothing but loss after loss. Everything must be held loosely—her home, her family, her friends, and her heart. Would she ever be able to love deeply again?

She leaned back, allowing a whisper of sunshine to settle on her face. No one but Mother cared any longer if her skin turned brown.

She saw Joshua and the field slaves working alongside her father, and in her father's face she saw desperation. Like Mother, he was struggling to keep all they had worked for.

She admired the optimism that drove him forward but wished she could convince him that freedom was the only way for him to embrace the future. It was impossible to dream about freedom when his security was placed with the king.

She slid off the horse and walked toward Father with the basket. Opening the lid, she took out the jar of lemonade, cooled with the ice that remained in their icehouse. Sweat beaded on the glass, and she held it up to her neck for a moment to cool her skin. Then she gave it and another jar to her father so he could share with those who worked in the fields alongside him.

As she looked over the green fields of tobacco, her heart ached at all her father was about to lose. Then she thought of Hannah helping Mother in the hall.

Her father thanked her for the refreshment, but before he could walk away, she stopped him. "Would you like me to help?"

He shook his head. "It is hard work."

"I have no aversion to hard work."

He studied her for a moment. "Are you certain?"

When she nodded, he eyed her a moment longer as if she might change her mind. Then he handed her a knife and showed her how to slit off the leaf of the tobacco plant and set it carefully on the ground.

CHAPTER 30

*G*rayson felt like the dark walls of his tomb were closing in upon him. One of his men sang a hymn, while another muttered to himself. He had known the consequences of what would happen if the British found him, but he had become arrogant. Careless.

Now the British had stolen their remaining cargo and locked them up in the bay.

He had lingered much too long on that shore, not wanting to leave until every last box had been delivered. His risk—his pride —would cost them their lives. If only their captors would have mercy and kill them quickly instead of torturing them to death.

This was what he fought against, this inhumanity. The men who killed his grandfather had been inflamed at the tyranny that oppressed them. Although what they did was wrong, Grayson at least understood their passion against tyranny.

The British soldiers were more calculating in their cruelty. They had no love of freedom, no hope for the future. They just wanted to stop those who did.

He moved the shackle an inch up his leg to relieve the pain where it had rubbed mercilessly against his ankle. His lips and tongue were parched; his stomach no longer craved food. In the time they had been here—he had no idea how long it was—the guards had brought a bucket of water but twice, ladling a few meager drops into each prisoner's mouth and then pulling it away before the man's thirst was quenched. It seemed almost a sport to them, prolonging the death of their prisoners.

Grayson thought of the wide river that flowed behind his house. He had taken it for granted, the drink it offered and the current it delivered to be able to sail away. The irony struck him now; he was on his boat but unable to sail anywhere.

If only he had stirring words to offer his men, to encourage them to fight. But they all longed for death, their greatest hope now resting in the life after this one.

He closed his eyes and thought again of Sarah. He had said he would return for her, but there would be no return from this prison. Why hadn't he told her he loved her?

He would never forget the day almost fifteen years ago, when he realized how much he loved her. She had been visiting his sister when she found him alone, crying in the smokehouse. He was only thirteen when he had been forced to whip Elisha— the man who was only a decade his senior, the man who had been more of a father to him than the lord of Caswell Hall. After ten lashes, he had not been able to finish the beating. Lord Caswell was enraged, demanding that he do ten more, and Grayson's heart had twisted in shame for disappointing his father. And for beating the man he admired.

Even in her youth, Sarah hadn't condemned his weakness or his tears. Instead, she had said that the Savior would forgive him even if he wasn't able to forgive himself.

Days later he discovered the reason for the beating. One of their slaves had run away, fracturing his horse's leg as he tore across the field. Elisha recovered the horse but not the slave, so Father punished him.

Looking back, Grayson wondered whether the punishment

was for much more than Elisha's inability to recover the man. It was almost as if his father was trying to destroy the friendship between his son and his slave. Grayson had been too ashamed to speak with Elisha again, and for years, he had been too embarrassed to speak with Sarah as well. He and Sarah rekindled their friendship in the months before the war began, but he had loved her from the moment in the smokehouse when he saw love instead of blame in her eyes.

He couldn't understand how a woman as wise and kind as Sarah could align herself with his captors. Or how his family could support the king as well. They must not understand what tyranny meant.

Perhaps this separation was for the best. Grayson's heart longed for Sarah, but she was loyal to his enemy. If he returned to Philadelphia, his desire for her would be like this shackle around his ankle.

"I'm sorry," he whispered again to the men near him, his remaining crew and the soldier they called Benjamin.

Silence was the response.

Had they already passed on? Perhaps God in His mercy would take him soon as well.

Sarah smeared a pinch of dirt on her face and dress. Instead of securing her hair with pins, she left it long under her cap. Hopefully none of the soldiers would notice that her skin wasn't as brown as that of the women who had been following the army for months.

She purchased a loaf of bread from one of the camp followers and drank a cupful of water before she tucked the bread beside the canteen in her tattered basket. Then she moved easily among the hundreds of women and children who followed close behind this regiment. Some of the women,

Nathan had told her, were loyal colonists, while others had traveled with their husbands from England.

No one questioned why she was wandering through the camp. Perhaps the other women supposed she was a wife or mistress of one of the officers. She didn't particularly care whether they thought she was a woman of propriety. As long as no one stopped her, she would be fine.

She reached the perimeter of where the camp followers lived. Instead of stopping, she continued her walk into the British encampment. There were three schooners docked on the other side of the field, but only one had two masts.

She prayed Grayson and his crew would be onboard.

A guard stepped in front of her, eyeing her for a moment, as if he were trying to determine whether he knew her. "How can I help you, miss?"

She forced a smile on her face. "I'm here to see my husband."

He studied the dirt on her face and then her clothing. "I don't believe I've had the pleasure of making your acquaintance."

She didn't like the way he was looking at her. She held up her basket, trying to ignore his insinuation. "He asked me to bake him a bit of bread."

The soldier sniffed the basket. "Perhaps I shall take a bit of the bread before you find your *husband*."

He drew out the last word in such a way that she wanted to clobber him over the head with her basket, but she breathed deeply instead. Self-moderation and ingenuity were the only things that would help her rescue Grayson.

"He is my husband—" she insisted. "Or at least he will be soon."

"So you're not married, are you?"

"Not yet."

"I supposed as much." He towered over her. "Did you ask him whether he has a wife across the Atlantic as well?"

She swallowed hard, shifting the basket between her hands. She hoped he thought it was his questioning that made her nervous. "I did not think to ask."

"A hundred to one, he is already married." He laughed. "Why don't you just marry me instead?"

She secured the basket behind her back. "Did I mention that my father is a commodore? And my intended is a lieutenant. He helps guard the prisoners."

The man took a small step back, lifting his chest as if he hadn't been hovering over her seconds before. At least the prison guards seemed to receive some sort of respect. "What is his name?"

"Commodore Hammond."

"I know no such commander."

"My father is at sea."

He shook his head. "Not your father. What is the name of the man you intend to marry?"

She stood a bit taller, refusing to cower now. Nathan had told her to make up a name, but that was before she'd ranked her future husband. There were probably only a handful of lieutenants in the camp.

She swallowed hard and muttered a name.

"Speak up."

She mumbled again and then added, "And he will not be the least bit pleased that you are detaining me."

He looked as if he was going to insist again on the name, but perhaps the thought of punishment by an officer deterred him.

He pointed to his left. "The prisoners are on the middle ship."

She lifted her skirts. "I thank ye."

"He won't be marrying you any time soon," he called after her.

She scrambled through the grassy field, past tents and soldiers who barely glanced her way. The first hurdle had been crossed, but it would be the easiest one. She prayed no one else stopped to inquire about her business.

At the end of a long wharf stood two guards, one near the bow of Grayson's ship and another at the stern. She wanted to look back at the trees, to make sure everything was ready, but she couldn't hesitate. Instead she clenched her fingers around the handle of her basket and marched forward like a soldier.

Nathan had said many of the British were hungry, and many of them didn't even want to fight this war for the king. She just had to figure out which of these guards was more desperate.

The guard on her right looked like a Hessian, with his golden colored hat and cobalt-blue coat. The other guard was barely a man, probably seventeen or eighteen, and he looked quite forlorn in his position. The Hessian probably didn't speak much, if any, English, but she hoped the younger man would understand well her plan and be amiable to it.

Perhaps he was as much a prisoner as the men onboard the boat.

She stepped up to the young soldier and held up her basket, speaking loud enough for both men to hear. "I am looking for mending work."

He shook his head. "I do me own mending."

"I can wash clothes too," she said, desperation lacing her words.

She didn't have to pretend.

He pointed up the hill at a canvas tent. "Go see the colonel. He'll tell you if there's work to be 'ad."

She glanced up the hill and then eyed the schooner, catching her breath when she saw the dull white name of the ship painted on the side: *Madam Knight*.

Tears pricked her eyes. Grayson had named his schooner after her and her silly dreams. He had even believed in her dreams. Today she needed the courage he saw in her. Without it, she would run back into those woods and hide.

She shifted her basket into her other hand, trying to compose herself. "This is a new ship, is it not?"

He stood a bit taller. "Took it from the Yanks, we did."

"You captured it?" Her eyes grew wide as she pretended to be impressed by his feat. "What happened to its crew?"

He shrugged. "The ones that survived are still onboard."

"How many survived?"

His eyes narrowed slightly. "Now why does 'at concern ya?"

"It concerns me greatly." She nodded toward the forest. "Up in those trees, there's a regiment of Yankees watching you and me."

Fear flashed across his face. "Why're they watchin' me?"

"They've sent me here to see if my husband is on this ship."

He glanced at the forest, and she saw the skepticism when he looked back at her. "I don't see nothing."

"They know how to hide well."

He looked over at the guard on the other side of the wharf. The man didn't seem to concern himself with either of them.

"Why don't they attack?" the young guard whispered.

"They're not here to cause a skirmish." She opened the basket and held up her canteen. "I'm here merely to check on my husband's health."

The aroma of the bread rose from the basket, and she saw the desire in his eyes. Her heart pounding, she lifted the loaf of bread from its linen wrappings and showed him the trousers and homespun shirt underneath. Then she opened the pouch at the bottom of the basket and let him peek at the shillings inside it. "There is clothing here and enough money for you to settle well in the colonies."

He stared at the pouch, and she thanked God that he was considering her proposition. Just as she suspected, he didn't want to be in this army.

But she was still asking a lot of him. Everything, really. Deserters were rewarded with a firing line.

"I don't know—"

"They will cause a diversion, and with this money, you'll never have to fight again."

A blast rocketed the air, and the Hessian guard at the other end of the wharf swore. The soldiers on the bank turned, and when they saw a blaze of fire, they began clustering together into columns.

The Hessian guard hurried past her, but the young soldier didn't move, staring at the pouch in her hand instead.

Another blast sounded from the trees. "It's time to decide," she whispered.

He reached for the money, but she pulled it back. "Are they in shackles?"

"Aye," he said, his gaze shifting between her and the trees with urgency.

"Then I must have the key."

He reached up and slipped a chain over his neck before he handed it to her.

She clung to the key as she handed him the basket. "If this is not the right key, my men will find you."

He followed the others toward the forest, and she hurried onto the ship, praying that Grayson was still alive.

Lydia searched among the ripening plants for leaves that had thickened and turned the color of yellow moss. A light-green hornworm crept up one of the leaves, and Lydia watched it for a moment. She glanced up and scanned the rows of tobacco for her father. He was four rows down, supervising the work of their remaining two field slaves.

She leaned forward and examined the white threads across the back of the worm. It looked harmless enough, but Father talked of these creatures as if they came straight from the pit of hell.

Hannah clutched her hands to her chest when she saw the worm. "That is disgusting."

Much to Hannah's dismay, Father had recruited her to join Lydia in helping with the harvest. The muddy floors, he'd told Mother, would still be there in the fall, but the tobacco leaves would not. Even as her sister complained, Lydia was glad to be out of the house.

Leaning forward, Hannah flicked the worm off with her knife and ground it into the black dirt with her heel. "We should be preparing for a ball this afternoon, not picking worms off tobacco leaves."

Lydia leaned over to the next leaf. "Without these leaves, there won't be any money to dress for a ball when the war is over."

Hannah tugged on her hat, pushing it further over her nose. "Next year I will be married."

"You are much too young to marry." Lydia cut off one of the mature leaves with her knife and laid it carefully on the ground. Father said he would collect the leaves later, after they'd wilted. Then he would cure them in their barn.

By the end of October, if they could keep the worms away, the plants would be ready to be twisted and spun into ropes to ship to England. While the harvest would not be as great as it had been in years past, Father was relying on the income it would bring for the next year.

Hannah stood. Her gloves and petticoat were stained with dirt, but fire danced in her eyes. "You may have lost your opportunity to marry, but that does not mean I must remain unmarried."

"When you are seventeen or eighteen, Father will find you a proper husband."

Hannah shook her head. "I can find a man without Father's

help. And I do not want a proper husband. I want a dashing man, like Dalton Reed."

Lydia sighed. "Father would consider him a proper husband for you in a year or two. Or when the war is over."

"I may be an old maid before this war is over," she whined, holding up her gloves. "And completely ruined by field work."

Compassion mixed with irritation for her sister. Hannah's future did look rather bleak at the moment. She had never even attended a proper ball, never been courted. The most important years of her young life had been ruined by this war. Lydia cut off another leaf and held it up. "This is for a new pair of gloves."

Hannah eyed Lydia's leaf and then leaned down to a plant that climbed up past her knees. She found a ripe leaf and clipped it. "This is for a hat."

Laughing, Lydia searched for another mature leaf among the shoots and, with much grandeur, sliced it off. "Satin shoes."

Hannah joined her laughter. "Pearl earrings."

"A loaf of sugar."

Hannah found a large leaf several plants down and sliced it from its root. "And this is for my wedding gown."

Lydia rested the knife at her side, her tone turning serious. "You will be a lovely bride, Hannah."

Hannah smiled at her, and Lydia had no doubt her sister would marry well—in the proper time.

A shadow fell over her heart as she cut another stalk.

Perhaps Hannah was right. Perhaps it was too late for her to find love as well.

CHAPTER 31

*S*arah climbed to the top of the ship and lowered herself through an open hatch. Then she pressed through the stench inside the bowels of the schooner. Nathan said she had five minutes to retrieve the men and another five minutes to get them off the boat.

There was no time for hesitation, no time to calm the heart-beat that slammed against her chest or quench the thirst on her lips. Her body felt weak, but in her weakness, she prayed that God would prove strong.

Clutching the guard's key in her hand, she hurried through the shadows. Light swept through the cargo space from the hatch, and in the dimness, she saw a man on the floor. He was but a skeleton, lying in filth, and she wondered for a moment if he was still alive. She nudged him gently with her foot, and he groaned.

Thank God, there was still life in him.

His eyes opened and he held out his hand, his throat rasping when he spoke. "Have you any water?"

She untangled the canteen from her shoulder and gave him a long swig. Then he leaned back against the wall, whispering his thanks. How long had it been since these men had any nourishment?

She moved from him to another man, searching the faces of two other prisoners, but neither of them was Grayson. Her heart began to despair when, in the shadows, she saw one more man. She rushed to him, but when Grayson looked up, he didn't seem to recognize her. Her heart broke as she looked into his vacant eyes.

Even if she got him off this boat safely, would he survive?

She couldn't worry about that right now. She must rescue them first.

She pushed the key into the shackle that chained Grayson and twisted it, praying that the soldier had given her the right key to free them.

Thank God, the claw of iron clanged to the floor, but he still didn't move.

"Grayson." She shook him gently. "I am here to take you away."

His eyes seemed lucid for a moment. "Sarah?"

"It is I."

He reached out to touch her hair. "A beautiful apparition."

She pressed her hand into his. "I'm no apparition."

He stared at her as if he still wasn't certain she was real.

She stood. "You and your men must get off this boat before the guards return."

He shook his head. "There's no place for us to go."

"You must trust me."

She lifted the canteen to his lips, and he drank deeply. "I forgot the taste of water."

She understood well the craving for something to drink. "There is plenty more outside, and food as well."

He passed the canteen to the man beside him as she unlocked the shackles of the four other prisoners. Pointing up at the shaft, she urged them forward. "We must hurry."

Grayson stood slowly at first, rallying his crew to stand as well. Her heart raced. They had to move faster if they were to flee before the King's Men realized what was happening. She took one prisoner's arm to help him up the steps, and then she turned back to help another.

The men began to walk more quickly as she guided them up toward the stern. She wished she could stop her heart from racing, but it gave her the strength she needed to lead them away from their dungeon.

Crawling across the deck, she searched for a rope ladder until she found one tied to the bottom of the mast. She tossed it over the side and then scanned the bay from the deck. The first rays of moonlight glistened on the surface as she searched for Elisha's rowboat, praying that nothing had deterred him from this task.

She couldn't ask these men to jump into the water—they were too tired to swim, and the British would surely shoot them before they reached the shore. And if she couldn't get them off the boat, they would all face the British muskets before dawn.

"Please hurry," she whispered, a tremor of fear shooting through her.

What if Elisha decided not to come? No one could blame him after what Grayson did to him so many years before, but she'd felt so certain Elisha had forgiven the past. Perhaps Elisha was afraid that if Grayson were rescued, he would be forced to return to a life of slavery at Caswell Hall.

"What is happening?" Grayson begged of her, and she heard the fear in his voice as well.

"The boat will be here soon," she said, trying to assure him.

In the moonlight she saw admiration in his eyes, and for a moment, she reveled in it. "It's all right if it doesn't come, Sarah. You've been so brave—"

"I'm scared to death."

"But it hasn't stopped you, my dear. That is true courage."

She didn't feel courageous, not with the trembling inside her, but it didn't matter. Grayson thought her courageous, and he'd called her his dear.

Then she heard the soft paddling of oars in the water. And she saw the form of the whaleboat glide up beside the ship. Relief showered over her fear.

Grayson squeezed her hand. "Well done."

Her heart soared.

As Elisha helped lower the first three men into the large rowboat, Sarah's legs started to sway. At first she thought it was the boat's listing, but it wasn't the boat. Her body was too warm. The world too blurry.

She waited for Grayson, but he refused to climb down until she did. He helped her onto the rope, and with Elisha's assistance, she dropped into the rowboat. Grayson was last. As he lowered himself, Elisha offered Grayson his hand.

"Come along, Master Caswell," he whispered.

Grayson pulled his hand back. "Elisha?"

"Yes, sir."

"They call me Porter now. And I am no longer your master."

Elisha paused. "Aye. I thank ye, sir."

Grayson hesitated, and then he reached out his hand again. Elisha helped him into the boat.

She saw the tears in Grayson's eyes. "No," he said. "I thank you."

Sarah leaned against Grayson and prayed the soldiers wouldn't check on their prisoners tonight. She also prayed that the young soldier who'd helped her was able to run far before dawn.

The men took turns helping Elisha row the boat away. One of them whispered near her, but she didn't understand his words. Blackness seemed to engulf her and she drifted away into a blissful sleep.

Grayson was free. She could rest now.

~

Lemuel blasted his bugle again, and Nathan lit another fuse with his torch, the cherry bottle exploding from the gunpowder siphoned into it. Fire sparked the pile of leaves under it. Holding his torch high, Nathan ran farther back into the woods to light the final bottle.

Darkness was over them now, and he could hear the British muskets firing into the trees. When Lemuel first blasted the bugle, he and Zadock had run separate ways, setting off the grandest display of noise and fire they could muster to draw the British troops away from their camp and Porter's ship.

General Washington might question why they used so many of their supplies to rescue the prisoners, but Nathan knew they needed Grayson and his men to continue securing food and ammunition for this war. And he had promised Lydia that if she gave them information, he would do whatever he could to keep her family safe.

Another round of musket shots jolted him. The soldiers were much closer, hopefully fearing a serious threat in the forest. The three men were far outnumbered, but the British didn't know it. They only needed to hold their attention long enough for Sarah to find a way onto the boat and for Elisha to paddle the boat around the schooners.

Darkness and—he hoped—confusion would keep the soldiers at bay for the remainder of the night.

He, Porter, and Sarah had all known what could happen if they were caught, but they had chosen to gamble for the sake of freedom. He wasn't responsible for Porter's capture, and yet it still troubled him. Lydia's brother, he prayed, was free tonight.

Three horses waited by the creek. The people of York weren't thrilled about having the British camping in their backyard, and they had been kind to Nathan and the others by giving them horses to use.

He hopped onto one of the horses, hoping that Zadock and Lemuel were close behind him, and glanced back over his shoulder one last time. Muskets continued to pop in the darkness, but he still couldn't see anyone.

He would ride west while the others went north. Or at least, he hoped they would.

It might be weeks before he found out whether their operation had been a success.

Grayson hovered over Sarah as she rested in the army tent, studying with wonder the beautiful woman who had saved his life. No other women he knew would have marched onto a British prison ship and rescued five prisoners.

The camp physician hadn't wanted to hinder Grayson's recovery by discussing the details of their rescue, but somehow she had done the impossible and succeeded.

Sarah Hammond had stolen his heart that day in the smokehouse, but she had intrigued him for even longer, back when she was just Seth's little sister, the girl who liked to pretend she was Madam Knight as she read about faraway places. Unlike the members of Grayson's family, she understood his desire to explore.

As a younger man, he'd tried to control his growing love for her, but it poured out now. He had thought he was protecting her, that his work would contradict her loyalty to the Crown—a loyalty he didn't agree with but would never condemn.

Yet as he gazed at her in the coming daylight, at her fair hair tangled around her face, he didn't want to live another moment of his life without her. He was still weak, but the remedies the camp physician prescribed had breathed life back into him.

The morning light seeped through the flap in the tent, and Grayson heard soldiers bustling outside. They had met with a regiment from Maine on their way to join Washington's army. The soldiers had rested here these past five days, but now they were preparing to march south.

After Sarah rescued Grayson, Benjamin, and the crew, Elisha guided them west to the protection of this army, and Zadock met them here. One of the men from his crew succumbed to the grave, but the others survived and were nearly healthy enough to return to work.

Elisha's forgiveness was balm to Grayson's soul, as Sarah's gentle care was a balm to his body. Even as she recovered from her own long journey, she had rubbed a salve that smelled of lemon and honey onto his wounds and cooled his face with a cloth as he drifted in and out of sleep. Now as she slept, he wished he could care for her as well, as a husband would a wife.

He dared to lean forward and kiss her forehead, and her eyes fluttered open. "Hello, Porter."

He reached for her hand, weaving his fingers through hers. "You may call me Grayson."

She scanned the narrow tent. "You're not supposed to be in here."

He grinned. "I had to make sure you didn't run away."

"Oh, Grayson, I am not the one who runs."

He gently squeezed her hand. "I never ran away from you."

Her smile warmed his core.

"May I have some water?" she asked.

He slowly stood beside the cot, his body still weak. "Of course."

He dipped a tin cup into a pail and brought it back to her. She sat up, pulling the sheet over her shift as she drank.

He reached for her hand again. "How did you get into the British camp?"

"The doctor said we mustn't discuss it."

"I'm well enough to know."

She pondered his words as she studied him, as though

searching for any sign of lingering illness. "I told them I was looking for the man who was to be my husband." Her words seemed to dangle in the air, a light flush coloring her face.

He leaned closer to her, whispering, "It was the truth, then."

The color rushed across her cheeks. "Perhaps."

He sat back, the reality of this blasted conflict rushing back to him. "If only we were not on opposing sides—"

This time she laced her fingers through his. "We're not opponents, Grayson. My brother convinced me long ago that we must choose for ourselves whether we desired independence or British rule."

He slowly processed her words. "You chose independence?"

"Indeed."

He kissed her hand. For so long, he had thought the barrier of their beliefs would keep them apart until after the war, but it seemed there was no longer any barrier. If she supported freedom, they could marry. Perhaps she could even assist him.

He held her hand tightly between both of his. "Would you be willing to work with me for the cause of the Patriots?"

Her laughter sounded musical. "Oh, Grayson, I have been working for the cause of the Patriots for years."

His eyes grew wide. "You have?"

She laughed again, and then he listened in awe as she told him about delivering the letters in secret for General Washington. Sarah was no longer dreaming about adventure. She was living what she had dreamed.

"I have desperately missed the work since I left Virginia."

"Perhaps we could remedy that," he said. "Do you think there is a minister nearby?"

She returned his smile. "I believe we could locate one."

"Then I would be honored, Sarah Hammond, if you would become my wife."

CHAPTER 32

*N*athan studied the overgrown gardens on the Caswell plantation and then the outline of the grand brick house. The slate rooftop glowed a dusty yellow, and a pale hue of red settled over the fields in the distance. No red uniforms clashed against the warm colors of the setting sun, but he would wait a bit longer to make sure the British officers had taken their leave.

This was the same place he'd watched Lydia rush away from Elisha's room back in February, when he'd felt every bit like a wounded soldier. As he traveled through the colony, the seasons had blended together, the cool of winter melting into spring, spring giving way to summer's blistering heat.

Autumn would be upon them soon, and as he glanced past the house, toward the fields, he wondered if Lord Caswell had been able to harvest his tobacco. He knew the crop well after helping his uncle plant it years ago.

Tobacco was a demanding crop on a planter's land, and an unforgiving one as well. If one didn't harvest the leaves immediately after they matured, the loss of income could be catastrophic.

Even as Nathan had little sympathy for those in the Loyalist party, he didn't want harm to come to Lydia. Her brother was a hero, and so was she. In spite of the war, in spite of the loss of their labor, he hoped the Caswell family would succeed.

Perhaps when the war ended, Porter would come home to help his father.

Five days had passed since Nathan fled from York, but he had received no word that Porter and the others had made it. He couldn't yet tell Lydia anything about her brother or Sarah or Elisha, but when the time came, he prayed the news he delivered would be good.

The supplies were almost in place for the approaching Continental Army. If all went well, their men would be assembled by mid-September, but they needed Lydia and other spies like her to help.

After the sky darkened, he checked the loose brick in the orangery. He reached his hand far back, pressing on each side in hopes of some word from her. Inside was a letter, and he secured it in his cloak. Slowly he wove through the trellises and hanging vines in the formal garden until he could see the lines of the gazebo in front of him.

Lydia sat on the bench.

He crept closer, the silver moonlight reflecting the white in her dress. He stopped under the grape arbor and admired her beauty for a moment. If only he could rush forward and take her into his arms . . . There was so much he wished he could tell her.

He ducked behind the bushes. He didn't want to startle her, and yet there was no better way.

"Lydia," he whispered.

Through the leaves, he watched her jump and then scan the garden before her. "You have returned."

He smiled at the welcome in her voice. "I have."

"I thought you had left for good."

"Unfortunately, I was detained."

"Until this war is over, it seems we are all detained from going where we please," she said. "The letter I left for you is quite old."

"Have the officers moved on?"

"Aye," she replied. "But they will probably return. They seem to think that Caswell Hall is their home."

"One day they will be gone for good."

"I pray so."

He remained still for a moment. He was inches from her, close enough to reach out and take her hand. He wished he could tell her where he'd been and offer news of her brother. He didn't have trouble keeping secrets, but he hated keeping them from those he loved.

He cleared his throat. "We need something of you."

She turned her head ever so slightly, her profile stunning in the moonlight. Why couldn't he have found a courier who was elderly or plain or already married? Instead, he'd found the loveliest woman in all the colonies.

He closed his eyes. He couldn't do this anymore. The next time he saw General Washington, he would insist they find someone else to courier messages out to Caswell Hall.

"What is it that you require?" she asked.

"We need information passed along to the men who have been staying in your house."

"What type of information?"

He leaned closer to the gazebo. "There is a rumor that General Washington and his men are preparing to take New York."

She inhaled sharply. "New York?"

"That is the rumor."

"Ah," she said, as if realizing his intent. "And so the British must send troops north."

"In earnest," he replied. "You must be subtle about this information but very clear."

"I know not when our guests will return."

"The timing will be perfect when they do."

She straightened her skirt. "What if they do not return?"

"They shall," he said. "Much of their army is preparing to winter at York, though the officers would probably prefer to winter here. I have heard your family has been quite hospitable to them."

She sighed. "My father still believes our family will be given special treatment when the British win."

"He will be most disappointed at the outcome of this war."

"I fear we will all be disappointed in some way."

"Perhaps." He paused. "Will you do this?"

"When is the rumored date of this attack?"

He watched a light blink on the river and wondered if the officers would return here this night. "You have heard that Washington is preparing to attack New York immediately, before the armies in the South can help defend the city. A fleet of French ships will be joining the Americans in their fight."

She leaned back against the bench. "Where would I have received such news?"

"You must say that you heard it from Dr. Cooper."

"Dr. Cooper?" she asked, startled.

"Aye."

"Is our doctor a Patriot or a Loyalist?"

"I'm afraid I can't say, but you must use his name."

"No matter." She took a deep breath. "The doctor would never discuss such a thing with me."

"What would he discuss?"

"I don't know—"

"Perhaps he is inquiring about Seth Hammond, to see if you have heard from him."

She turned slightly, speaking over her shoulder. "I have heard nothing from Seth."

"Then you may tell them that as well."

"I will do as you ask." She looked back toward the river and stood. "I'm glad you have returned."

"And I as well." He balled his hands together, wishing he hadn't replied. "I'll check the orangery for your news."

"And I will continue my evening strolls."

From his hiding place, he watched her slip into the night.

Thomas Paine wrote about the high price people were willing to pay for what they valued, and the British paid dearly for their information. Dr. Cooper had worked hard to develop a reputation among their top ranks as a man knowledgeable about the workings of Virginia's government and her defense. A few British officers believed Dr. Cooper to be a Loyalist willing to secretly sell information he learned from his patients—minor intelligence that proved to be reliable but not detrimental for Patriots.

What the British didn't know was that the good doctor also sold them occasional—and critical—misinformation. If Lydia played her part the officers would act quickly, and the doctor was prepared to verify her story to the British—for a fee. Information like this would not be valuable to them unless they were required to pay a hefty price.

If it worked—and he prayed it did—the British occupying Virginia would march north to defend their hold. If not, he didn't know how much longer the Continental Army would survive. It would be a terribly hard winter for all of them.

CHAPTER 33

*G*rayson pounded on the narrow door of the parsonage, and Sarah's heart fluttered at his urgency. This man loved her just as she loved him. One day they could celebrate their marriage with her father and brother and the entire Caswell family.

None of them would approve their marriage now, but she knew, more than anything she'd known before, that she and Grayson were to become husband and wife before the end of the war.

The Continental Army had departed this morning, leaving her and Grayson behind with a sympathetic family who had but one small room for them to share. They said he could sleep outside in the barn, but Grayson didn't want to leave her alone. And she didn't want to be left alone.

There were no candles lighting the windows at this late hour, but he persisted in his pounding.

"The hour is too late," Sarah said, resting against the cradle of his arm.

"They will wake."

She had waited for years to be his wife. If they must wait for a few more hours, it would be all right. "We could be married at first light."

He glanced over at her and then pounded again.

Seconds later, the door cracked open. A sprightly man stood on the other side, the flame from a candle lighting his knobby nose and balding head. He wore a long nightdress, and his feet were bare. He examined them for a moment. "What is it that you need?"

"You must marry us," Grayson said.

The slightest of smiles tugged at his lips. "I see. Perhaps we can discuss it on the morrow?"

"That's not possible," Grayson insisted. "I fear the temptation is too great."

Sarah almost laughed. A man as strong as Grayson could conquer any temptation—but the man she loved was in earnest.

The minister examined them both. "Where do you come from?"

"Williamsburg," Grayson said. "We have known each other since we were children."

"And yet you chose this very night to marry."

"She has rescued me, you see, and I can't let her go again."

"What of your family?"

Sarah spoke. "My father is a commodore with the British army, and my brother is fighting alongside the Patriots."

"And my father is a staunch Loyalist," Grayson added.

The elderly man stroked his chin. "Ah, I see the conflict. What is your name?"

"Porter." He hesitated. "Grayson Porter."

The minister looked at Sarah. "And you desire this marriage as much as Mr. Porter?"

She smiled. "Perhaps more."

The minister sighed. "Then I suppose I cannot put asunder what God has brought together."

"Thank you, sir." Grayson reached out and shook the man's hand profusely.

"I must wake my wife as well."

A shadow moved behind him, a soft but sharp voice speaking clearly. "I am already awakened."

The minister turned to her. "Do you approve?"

Her silence was deafening, and Sarah feared for a moment that the minister might defer to his wife's opposition.

Then she finally spoke. "I believe I do."

Sarah sighed with relief.

The minister opened the door wide, and Sarah accompanied Grayson inside to become his wife.

Major Reed and two of his officers entered Caswell Hall just as the family was preparing to eat breakfast. Father welcomed them to their table, but Mother didn't acknowledge their presence at all. It had become strangely routine to have these men come and go as they pleased. They no longer even knocked upon their arrival.

Hannah smiled at the major. "Welcome."

He nodded toward her but didn't return the smile.

Lydia sat at her place at the table. Her hands trembled slightly in her lap, from anger at their audacity and from anxiety about what she must do. She hated the division these men caused in her family, but at least this time their presence might serve some good purpose. She would pass along Nathan's message and be done.

The men scooted out chairs and sat with the family at the table. Before them were runny poached eggs and bread toasted too black. The huckleberry jam, Lydia had learned, hid much of the burnt taste. There was no butter, as they had no one to churn it.

The major eyed the food on the table. "Is there nothing else to eat?"

Mother bristled. "Not unless you care to utilize the kitchen."

The major looked toward the doorway. "Where are your slaves?"

Father pressed his fork into a poached egg. He had already been working in the fields for several hours this morning.

"Our cook and most of our other Negroes seem to have found refuge with your army." He pointed at the remaining food with his fork. "This was prepared by a lady's maid and our washwoman."

"I see." Major Reed reached for a piece of toast and began to slather it with jam. "There is nothing I can do to bring back your freed Negroes, but perhaps I could arrange for you to purchase new slaves."

Lydia bit her lip, and it felt as if her skin might boil. How dare this man try to negotiate a sale with Father when he and his fellow officers had already taken so much from them?

Mother's face turned a light shade of red. "Perhaps you gentlemen could discuss business after our meal."

Major Reed gave a slight bow of his head. "Of course."

The scent of fried bacon preceded Deborah, and the men looked toward the doorway as she entered. She set the platter of steaming meat on the table, and the men confiscated most of it.

Lydia eyed the window as she reached for one of the remaining pieces of toast. Were the rest of his men waiting outside while the three officers ate?

"Will you be staying with us?" Hannah asked in the midst of clattering forks and knives.

"Aye," the major replied.

Mother sipped her tea slowly and then set down her cup. "And how long should we expect your company this time?"

"Until we secure Virginia."

Lydia dipped the knife into the jam and spread it on the

burnt toast. Nathan said to be casual but intent in her delivery of his message. If it would lure these men away from Caswell Hall, she was even happier to deliver it.

Her eyes focused on the toast as she spoke. "When will you leave for New York?"

Major Reed shook his head. "We have no desire to return to New York."

She chewed a bite of toast and swallowed. "I thought you might be defending it with the others."

He chuckled as he lifted a piece of bacon, as if she were a young girl needing to be amused. "We have already secured New York."

"Oh, what a relief." Her breath slipped from her lips. "I'd heard there was to be an attack."

"There is no attack." Then he leaned forward slightly, his eyes narrowing. "What exactly are you referring to?"

She gave the slightest of shrugs as she sat back in her chair. The less interested she seemed in the affair, probably the better. "I thought the Americans were preparing to invade the city."

All the men turned toward her.

"Where did you hear such a thing?" Father demanded.

She took another bite of her toast before she replied. "At church on Sunday."

Captain Moore leaned forward. "The Americans have already tried and failed to take the city."

"That is exactly what one of the men said, but then another said they hadn't tried before with the French."

The major searched her face. "Who said this?"

"Well, I'm not quite certain." She sipped her water, making him wait. "One of the shop owners, I suppose."

Major Reed pressed her. "Do you remember no one in particular?"

"I didn't know it would be of any importance." She tapped her fingers against the water glass. "There was one man—"

Chairs creaked as the men leaned closer.

"Who was it?" Captain Moore demanded.

"I believe Dr. Cooper was among them."

The major sat back in his chair.

"There have been other rumors about New York," an officer said.

Major Reed glared at him. "Quiet."

Her glass clinked against the table. "Perhaps I heard wrong."

"What else did they say?" Major Reed asked, his voice a steely calm.

She glanced up at the carvings on the plaster ceiling, pretending to think again. "Something about the Americans attacking by land and then the French—"

"What about the French?"

"Why, they were going to attack by sea."

He swore.

She shrugged again. "I thought you knew."

Father pushed back his plate. "'Tis only a rumor."

"Aye," she agreed.

Major Reed's chair scraped across the floor as he stood. "We must be going."

Mother set down her fork. "So soon?"

Lydia took a big bite of her toast to hide her smile.

"I fear so," the major said.

"But what about the purchase of slaves—?" Father started.

Major Reed motioned for his men to follow. "That will have to wait."

Their footsteps echoed back into the dining room as they stomped across the hall and then outside.

Hannah threw her napkin onto the table. "They are leaving."

Lydia didn't hide her smile this time. "I believe they are."

"Father," Hannah insisted, "you must hurry after them."

Mother patted her hand. "They will return soon enough."

Hannah turned toward Lydia. "Why did you have to say that about New York?"

"I didn't realize it was pertinent."

Father stood. "You must stay out of the affairs of this war, Lydia."

"I was only repeating a rumor." A rumor she had heard from Nathan, but still, a rumor. It seemed to her that the major had heard it from others as well.

"What you hear in town must stay there. I do not want our family involved."

Mother sighed. "We are already involved."

"It seems I was helping them." She paused. "And helping us as well."

Her father might never understand her desire to protect all of them.

She glanced over at Mother and saw the slightest of smiles mirrored on her face. At least one of her parents was pleased with her.

Father glanced at Lady Caswell. "You cannot approve of this."

"I approve of the soldiers going to New York."

"But they must win the colony of Virginia to win the war."

Mother stood up. "I no longer care who wins this war, Charles. I only want the madness to end."

CHAPTER 34

*T*he leaves in Williamsburg were melding into the golden colors of fall, the pleasant chill of autumn a respite from the summer's heat. Nathan rubbed his hands together as he walked up Duke of Gloucester Street, toward the brick home of George Wythe, the esteemed professor of law at the College of William & Mary.

A messenger had brought word that his uncle and Comte de Rochambeau—the leader of the French army—would arrive today.

There had been no resistance as the Americans and French marched south toward Virginia. The deceptive seeds about the opposition in New York had rooted firmly, and much of the British army traveled north by ship and land to defend the city. The remaining British soldiers camped near the town of York under General Cornwallis.

General Washington and Comte de Rochambeau would have stayed at the home of James Madison, the president of the College of William & Mary, but before the redcoats left Williamsburg, they burned Madison's home. The Wythe house would accommodate the generals well enough, though. Both

George Wythe and his wife were ardent supporters of freedom. Only the trusted servants and a few key officers would be allowed access to the generals here.

Nathan stood outside the front door of the Wythe home as the whistle of fifes and the steady beat of drums preceded the magnificent horses carrying the generals. The corps of fife and drums marched down the long street and onto the Palace Green that stretched across the front of the Wythe house, the lawn reaching up to the old Governor's Palace.

Governor Jefferson had never wanted war. He went into hiding after the British invaded Richmond, but there would be no hiding the arrival of Washington and Rochambeau. Not when thousands of infantrymen accompanied them.

When Nathan and Mr. Wythe stepped out to greet the generals, he scanned the crowd of men behind the generals until he found Seth— Captain Hammond—in the third row of the brigade.

Did his friend have news of Sarah and Grayson?

Nathan's anticipation at seeing his friend was dampened by the realization that Seth was now just a few miles from the woman he planned to marry.

He wished he could tell Seth about Lydia and how she had rescued him. He wished he could tell him that she risked her life to help their army. When Seth returned to her, perhaps Lydia herself would tell him.

Captain Hammond had succeeded as an officer, and he would be a successful planter like his father. Nathan should be pleased for him and for Lydia, but he couldn't conjure up any pleasure at their upcoming marriage.

He escorted Washington and Rochambeau up the steps and into a private chamber, where they would be well protected while they conducted their planning and business. Washington surveyed the chamber and turned to him. "You have done a fine job, Nathan."

"Thank you, sir."

"If your father were still alive, he would be quite proud as well."

Nathan hoped so.

Washington sat in a plush chair beside an antique writing table, and Rochambeau sat across from him. The French general wore a blue dress coat with a silver medallion stitched on it. His face was thin, and yet—just like Washington—his presence commanded attention and conveyed importance.

"We have business we must conduct," Washington said.

"Yes, sir," Nathan said, stepping toward the door.

"This involves you, Nathan." Washington tapped on the table. "What can you tell us of this town they call York?"

Sarah Porter slipped a shilling to a man at the docks in Newport News. "I am looking for your silversmith."

The man scrutinized her. "What do you want with the silversmith?"

"That would be my business and his."

"He works only with the finest of clientele."

"Aye, that is good," Sarah said, reciting her carefully rehearsed words. "I work only with the finest of smiths."

He eyed her again and then pointed toward a door.

Hunger was a powerful deterrent to a soldier who was supposed to fight. Even with the French helping them and the British army scattered, the Patriots still didn't have enough troops to fight the men in York. But if she and Grayson could help keep the American soldiers fed, perhaps they would have the strength to defeat their enemy.

Sarah waited only a few minutes before being escorted to the back room. The man known as "the silversmith" was a freed Negro, a short man who looked as unlikely as she to be a conduit to supply the Patriots. But Grayson and his men were unable to come into Newport News unnoticed, and she blended in well with the women, as she had done outside York.

Her head reeled for a moment, and she caught herself on a post. Ever since she'd escorted Grayson and his men off that dreadful ship, her body had seemed to war against her. She couldn't tell her new husband about her spells of weariness or the persistent thirst she seemed unable to quench. There was too much for him to concern himself with at present, and his own health was still recovering.

She pushed a list across the table to the silversmith. "My husband is looking to obtain flour, coffee, and ammunition."

The man's eyes widened as he read her list. "Two hundred pounds of coffee?"

"He said you had plenty to share."

"Aye. I suppose if you have enough money to spend, we have enough to share."

"If we keep our men fed well," she said, "they will fight well for all of us."

She paid the man half the money before slipping out the door. The rest they would pay when the supplies were delivered.

Grayson met her back at their fortress of trees and branches, and she fell into his arms.

"I was so worried about you," he said.

"You needn't have worried." She smiled. "Our friend will have the supplies waiting for us at an abandoned homestead a half mile north of here."

"Good work, Mrs. Porter," he said, and then he kissed her.

How grateful she was to have this man she loved as her husband.

Between the supplies still hidden in the cave, the supplies Nathan said he'd already hidden on Hammond Plantation, and now these new supplies, the colonists might be able to finish this war.

~

Nathan stepped into R. Charlton's Coffeehouse, near the old Capitol.

The main room was crowded with patrons speculating on the strategy of the soldiers, and he heard the hope in their voices. American soldiers camped outside town, and when they'd arrived, townspeople had rushed out to bring food and clothing. With the appearance of Washington, many were swayed again to the cause of independence.

Rochambeau and his fleet of ships meant they had a greater chance of winning Virginia, but even though they'd sent reinforcements up to New York, General Cornwallis and his army remained strong.

Nathan stepped into a back room and sat at a round table by a window. A man wearing a white apron set a porcelain cup before him and filled it with steaming black coffee. Nathan lifted the drink and inhaled the dark aroma before he sipped it.

They must defeat the British before the entire colony swam in the color of red.

He took another sip and listened to two men shouting on the other side of the wall. He couldn't see the Wythe house from this window, but Washington and Rochambeau were there, discussing the future with several key officers. They'd been consulting for two days now.

When his uncle had first begun talking about war back in 1776, Nathan knew there would be battles. He just never realized how much waiting and planning would take place between them. After a lifetime of working as a planter, planning was ingrained in Washington. Everything was being assembled together. The supplies and ships. The men. The strategy.

Many of the Patriots demanded immediate action from General Washington, but Nathan's uncle was never persuaded by passion, no matter how deep, and he was rarely swayed by immediacy. His contemplative process annoyed many who were akin to action, but in his thoughtfulness, Washington made choices that saved lives.

Nathan was grateful for his uncle's deliberate decision making, but he also knew they must act soon before more British troops arrived. A Loyalist from Williamsburg would surely have alerted Cornwallis of the army's arrival, and they would be preparing to fight at York.

Nathan untied the ribbon that had loosened at the back of his neck and retied it.

Did Lydia know that the Patriots occupied Williamsburg? The time for procuring information from her was past, and Nathan had no other work at the moment. His uncle had already sent scouts up north to report on the progress of the British troops. When the British reached New York and learned they still firmly held the city, they would surely march back south.

The Patriots had no time to delay. They must take York before it was too late.

A group of women huddled together outside the back window of the shop. He recognized Mrs. Pendell among them, but he didn't raise his hand to greet her.

Mrs. Pendell had known the Washington family when she was a child living near his uncle's home at Mount Vernon. Since the beginning of the war, she had managed to get them the information they needed as well as deliver information to men such as Dr. Cooper and even George Wythe and James Madison.

When the war was over, it would be fascinating to learn the different roles people secretly played. After choosing sides for so long, how would they all come together to form a unified country?

Someone pulled out the chair across from him, and then Seth reached for his hand. Nathan shook it. No matter what happened, Seth would always be his friend.

"It has been much too long," Nathan said as his friend sat.

Seth placed his musket against the wall. "It's good to see you."

"You've finally made it back home."

Seth glanced out the window. "Aye, but it no longer feels like home to me."

"I fear it will be difficult for many of us to find homes when this conflict is done." Nathan pointed toward his cup. "Would you like some coffee?"

Seth nodded, and Nathan motioned for the keeper.

Seth took a long sip after the man poured his drink. "It won't be long now before we fight, will it?"

"I don't believe so."

"Has the French fleet arrived?" Seth whispered.

"Yes. But we need more than just ships. We need supplies."

"If we wait too long, I fear winter will be upon us again."

Nathan nodded. None of the soldiers wanted to relive the deplorable winter they'd spent in Valley Forge.

"I received permission to go home today, as long as I return by the morrow," Seth said.

Nathan's heart began to race. Would he return to Hammond Plantation, or would he visit Lydia?

Nathan set his cup down. "Have you heard from your sister?"

"My aunt wrote to say that she is thriving in Philadelphia."

Nathan looked down at the coffee. Should he tell Seth about Sarah's involvement in the attempted rescue of Porter and his men? He decided against it. Without news of her success, Seth would only worry.

"Surely there is someone here you would like to see." Nathan paused. "A woman, perhaps?"

He was fishing, but he desperately wanted to know whether this man still cared for Lydia.

"The woman I plan to marry resides up north."

Nathan fought back his urge to smile. He had refused to let himself hope that Seth's intentions toward Lydia had changed, but it was as he initially suspected. Seth loved the daughter of Colonel Fielder.

"Has the colonel granted you his permission?"

Seth grinned. "He has. The moment we win this war."

Would Lydia be devastated at the news, or relieved?

He prayed for the latter.

CHAPTER 35

*W*hen he was young, Grayson had thought marriage would confine him to the mundane life of a planter, but the fears of his youth melted away as Sarah worked alongside him to prepare for the arrival of the troops.

Her courage shone as she secured important supplies in places he was not welcomed and slept in obscure places he would never have imagined a woman to sleep. She was still weak from her gallant rescue, but she continually assured him that her health was in good order.

No one knew how long the battle would last in York. Zadock and Elisha and the rest of his men had emptied their newly acquired boat of its supplies at the Hammond plantation, where Grayson and Sarah now stayed. They hid the supplies with the others that Nathan had rescued from the shipyards, and then the crew left to retrieve one final shipment from near Richmond. They would wait until the war began before delivering them to York.

Sarah sleeping beside him, Grayson rolled over on the mattress he'd concocted from straw. The British had destroyed her house, but the barn and other flank buildings remained. He wished he could take her to one of the grand homes in Williamsburg, but instead he'd built a fire in her family's washhouse, and the room made for a cozy home during the cool autumn nights.

He had never imagined such joy as he now felt. Sarah looked so peaceful in her sleep. The washhouse was hardly an elegant place for him to house his bride, but she seemed as contented as he, and he hoped their time here would help her rest. He had enough money from privateering to establish a comfortable home for her after the war, but Sarah had told him she didn't want a large house. She wanted to travel with him.

So they would travel. To the West Indies and France and Italy. Until now, the king had required the colonies to send their main exports to England, but once the war was over—if his father would consent— Grayson could expand the Caswell exports far beyond.

Grayson gently nudged his wife. "The sun is shining, love."

She opened her eyes and smiled weakly as she looked out the door of the washhouse. "It's lovely. I only wish I weren't so tired."

He kissed her forehead. If only he knew how to care well for her. "We've had a long journey. Perhaps you should continue to sleep."

"I'm terribly thirsty."

No matter how much water he retrieved for her on this journey, it never seemed to quench her thirst. She'd lost a great deal of weight in her quest to find him, but no matter how much she ate, she always seemed to be hungry as well.

"I'll fetch you some water."

When she returned to her sleep, he slipped out of the washhouse and walked to the well. After his crew arrived with the remaining supplies, perhaps he would take Sarah to Williamsburg for a real meal and a comfortable bed for them both.

He turned the crank on the well and lowered the bucket.

When he brought it up again, he tipped back the bucket and took a long sip. After his seemingly endless days in shackles, parched beyond what he thought he could ever bear, it seemed to him that he couldn't drink enough either. He would never again take water for granted, the freedom of the river or the life-giving drink from the well.

His gaze wandered up to the black remains of the grand house that once overlooked the river. Why must so much destruction precede freedom? But then, if the British hadn't burned her home, Sarah would never have left here, would never have gone to her aunt in Philadelphia. Without the destruction, he supposed, they might never have found one another. Or married.

Their love had emerged from the fire, with a promise of freedom to come.

He dumped the water into another wooden bucket and lifted it. Should he wake her to give her the water, or should he let her awaken on her own?

The thunder of a galloping horse startled him, and he looked up to see it moving toward the house. Then he saw the blue coat of the rider, the yellow cockade of a captain in the Continental Army displayed on his black hat. The captain dismounted, and when he took off his hat, Grayson rushed toward the man. Sarah's brother stretched out his hand, and Grayson set down the bucket of water and shook it.

"I've missed you," Grayson said.

Seth took off his hat. "It has been much too long."

His brother-in-law scanned the remains of the house behind Grayson, his eyes reflecting the destitution.

"I'm sorry about your home."

Seth stepped forward, his eyes still on the house. "I once had grand plans for this place, and to be honest, I once had plans for your plantation as well."

"You can rebuild," Grayson assured him. "And perhaps you and Lydia can still—"

"Much has changed in the past three years." Seth brushed off his sleeves as he faced Grayson again. "I have new plans now."

Grayson nodded. "We are all on a new journey, I suppose."

Seth unbuttoned his coat and strung it over his arm. "What are you doing here?"

Grayson smiled. "I have a surprise for you."

"I fear I've not had a good experience with surprises."

"I hope this will be a good one."

Grayson picked up the bucket again and the two men walked toward the washhouse, talking of all they had seen in the past years since leaving Virginia. Seth had survived both the frigid weather at Valley Forge and the defeat at New York. Grayson told him of his night runs delivering supplies and his time in the British prison.

Seth blinked. "I thought no one ever escaped a British prison."

"They don't, unless someone comes to rescue them."

"Who rescued you?"

Grayson opened the washhouse door. "Madam Knight."

He thought Sarah would wake when the sunlight flooded into the room, but she didn't seem to hear him. He set down his bucket, motioning for Seth to wait outside even as he moved to their bed of straw. "Sarah—your brother is here."

Sweat had returned to her face, along with a gray pallor. He shook her gently. "Sarah?"

Then he shouted for Seth.

Sarah's brother rushed inside, eyeing Sarah asleep on the mattress before his eyes narrowed at Grayson. "What have you done?"

"We have married," Grayson insisted. "A month ago near Newport News."

Seth knelt by the mattress and took her hand. "Sarah?"

This time she opened her eyes slowly, and the cool green in them warmed when she saw the men. "Seth—you have returned."

"I didn't know you were here," he said softly. "Grayson said you have married."

"Aye." She smiled at Grayson, and his heart seemed to explode with relief. He didn't know what he would do if he lost her again.

Seth's smile was strained. "Shall I call you Lady Caswell?"

She shook her head. "We are no longer Caswells. My name is Sarah Porter."

He brushed his hand over her hair. "You are ill."

Grayson dipped a tin cup into the bucket and brought the water to Sarah's lips.

"I am only tired. We've had a long journey." She guzzled the water. "It is nothing to fret about."

Seth glanced back at him, and Grayson saw the worry etched deeply across his forehead. Something was terribly wrong.

"She must have something to eat as well."

"Of course," Grayson said, feeling like an idiot.

In the corner was a crate he'd filled with food, and he retrieved an apple, slicing it quickly into small pieces with his knife. While Seth cradled Sarah's head, Grayson fed her. She ate the apple and then asked for another.

When she finished eating and drinking another cup of water, Seth lowered her head back to the pillow. As her eyes drooped shut once more, she reached out and took Seth's hand. "I'm so glad to see you."

Then she slept again.

When he and Seth stepped outside, Seth slapped his hand against the side of the building. "She's terribly ill."

"I thought it was exhaustion." Grayson wrung his hands together, and it felt as if his heart was wringing as well. "But she is worsening."

"Why is she not sleeping in a real bed?"

"We're waiting for supplies for York. I thought about staying in Williamsburg, but I—we didn't want anyone to recognize us in town."

"Don't go to town, Grayson. Go home. Your mother and Lydia will care for her."

Grayson pinched the bridge of his nose. He wanted to see his mother and Lydia, but Lord Caswell would not be happy to see him.

For Sarah, he must swallow his pride and go to Caswell Hall. "I'll leave right away."

"Unless the British took it, there should be a canoe in the boathouse," Seth said as he rushed toward the door. "I will fetch Dr. Cooper."

When Grayson lifted Sarah from the straw, her eyes fluttered open.

"Where are you taking me?" she asked.

"You once asked me to trust you." He kissed her forehead. "This time, you must place your trust in me."

CHAPTER 36

*D*ust billowed along the road, and Lydia turned and
squinted in the sunlight, hoping to catch a glimpse of
the riders as they approached where she and Hannah and the
field slaves worked.

Hannah stood up and pulled her hat close to her eyes. "Perhaps Dalton has returned."

Lydia stood up beside her. She hated the delight in her
sister's voice, when the thought of the major and his men
returning made her skin crawl. Last she'd heard at church, the
Patriots were supposed to confront the British army at York,
but there had been no word of a battle. Perhaps these men had
news for them.

Her sister ducked down again as if the leaves could hide her.
"We mustn't let them see us like this."

Lydia looked at her filthy hands and the dirt that stained her
petticoat. Except for perhaps Nathan, she didn't much care what
anyone else thought of her appearance.

Two men galloped by them. They were much too far away to
be recognized, but she was relieved that neither man wore a red

uniform. In fact, one of the men seemed to be wearing the gray-ish-blue of the Continental Army.

Was it possible?

As dust dissipated into the fields, she felt like sinking into the soil as well and lying dormant among the harvested leaves. A long time ago, she had dreamed about what it would be like for Seth to return to her. He would apologize for his anger, and she would apologize for not supporting him. They would marry at the river's edge in a grand ceremony of family and friends reconciled after the war.

But she hadn't thought about Seth in a long time.

Was he riding one of the horses? If so, what would he do when he saw her?

"I will shoot him if he tries to step on my property."

Father was currently in the barn, hanging the leaves they'd harvested earlier in the day to cure them. If it was indeed Seth who had arrived, she must warn him before her father returned to the house.

She fled to the drive and then ran as fast as she could toward Caswell Hall. She was already covered with dirt from her field labor; it wouldn't matter how much more dirt and sweat she accumulated in a run. The elegant, gentle lady that Seth left almost three years ago was no longer.

It was possible that the rider wasn't Seth at all, that another man in uniform was coming to visit. But she didn't know another Patriot soldier who would risk visiting them.

When she reached the house, she breathed deeply and fanned herself with her hands to cool down. Then she ascended the steps into the hall.

Prudence stood at the doorway leading to the library, her face grave. "They are inside with Lady Caswell."

"Who is it?"

"Master Seth and Dr. Cooper."

She leaned against the staircase, wiping her forehead with her sleeve.

After all these years, he was finally back.

Was it possible for them to rekindle what they had lost? But how could they rekindle even their friendship when her heart now belonged to another? She'd run all the way to the house in case it was Seth, but now all she wanted to do was hide.

"Father might harm him," she said.

Prudence shook her head. "Lady Caswell would never allow it."

Perhaps not, but she still must tell him what Father had said.

She walked toward the door, but Prudence stopped her. "Lady Caswell requested a private interview with them."

Private? She was the one who had waited all these years to see the man she was to marry. How could they exclude her?

But then again, if Dr. Cooper had accompanied Seth, something might be wrong.

Or had the war ended? Perhaps Seth and the doctor had come to warn them.

Prudence eyed Lydia's dress. "Might I make a suggestion?"

"Of course."

"We could change your wardrobe while you wait."

Lydia glanced down at the dirt stains on her soiled skirt. Her face must be drenched in sweat, her hair atrocious.

"We must hurry," Lydia said.

"We will."

If only she knew why they must wait.

Twenty minutes later, Lydia started back down to the stair hall. She gasped when she saw the man in the entry, and then joy flooded her heart.

"Grayson?"

Her brother was alive.

But even as Grayson looked up at her, she saw fear in his eyes. And she realized he was holding something in his arms. Someone.

Lydia hurried down the steps at the same time Mother rushed out of the library.

Her brother held Sarah Hammond, her body wrapped in a cloak on this summer day, her head limp against his chest.

Mother kissed Grayson's cheek and quickly directed him toward the library. Lydia followed them, her heart aching and her mind whirling to make sense of it all.

What had happened to her friend? And how had Grayson found her?

Grayson gently laid Sarah on the chaise lounge, and then he held a tin cup to Sarah's lips. Her eyes fluttered open and then closed as she sipped of it.

Seth draped a blanket over his sister, but he didn't acknowledge Lydia.

Dr. Cooper listened to Sarah's chest. "I must examine her in private," he replied. "Her husband can stay."

"Husband?" Lydia blurted as she glanced toward Grayson. When had he and Sarah married?

She wanted to rejoice at the news, and yet she was still trying to understand all the pieces.

"Might Lady Caswell stay as well?" Grayson asked. "I will need her help."

The doctor nodded.

Lydia moved toward the hall, and Seth stepped beside her. She motioned him toward it as if he hadn't been there hundreds of times. Inside, they stood in awkward silence. Her dreams long ago of becoming his wife, her anger at his leaving—it all seemed surreal.

The anger was now gone, as were the dreams. She and Seth were two strangers, the experiences of these past years alienating them. They both might desire liberty now, but they would never enjoy their freedom together.

She stared at him, unsure of what to say. She only hoped Father's work in the barn would deter him from returning to the house until late tonight, but even if he walked through the door at this moment, she doubted he would threaten Seth's life. Their old quarrel seemed irrelevant somehow, now that Grayson was back—and married to Seth's sister. No matter how they differed with Lord Caswell, Sarah and Seth had become family.

Seth rested his hand on the back of a chair. "The last time I was here, we exchanged words I regret."

"I regret them as well, but my father does not. When he comes, I fear he will not welcome you."

"I fear only for my sister at present."

Lydia's heart quickened. "What happened to her?"

"I'm not certain," he said. "Did you know your brother was a prisoner of the British?"

Her chest clenched. "The British?"

"He has been working for the Patriots since he left here."

She thought Grayson had fled because he feared the rebels in Williamsburg, but it shouldn't surprise her. While she had always prized security, Grayson had desired the liberty of being able to go where he pleased.

She sighed. "I did not know."

"Sarah helped rescue him from his captors, but Grayson said she has been weak ever since. They slept last night on our property."

Her stomach rolled at the mention of his plantation. "I'm so sorry about your home."

"'Tis not your fault."

"I fear some of it is my fault. British officers stayed here, and Hannah told them—" She hesitated. She didn't want to talk of their proposed marriage. "I told them you were fighting with the Patriots."

His eyebrows rose. "You once called me a rebel."

"I have learned much since then."

His fingers clutched the back of the chair, his knuckles turning white. "After the war, I shall not return to Virginia."

She took a deep breath. "I see."

He glanced down for a moment, and when he looked up again, she could see the conflict in his eyes—and a hint of the boy she once knew. "I have decided . . ."

At his hesitation, she prompted him. "What is it, Seth?"

"I have asked the daughter of my commander to marry me."

Perhaps her heart should ache at the news, but Lydia felt hollow instead. "And she has accepted?"

He nodded. "I'm sorry, Lydia."

"There's no reason for you to apologize," she assured him. "The years have propelled us apart."

"I hope we will remain . . . That is, I suppose we are more than friends—almost brother and sister now that Grayson and Sarah have married."

"I suppose we are." She managed a wan smile. "I wish you well, Seth."

"Truly?"

She took a deep breath. "Truly."

"I wish you well also."

Mother stepped into the room. "The doctor would like to speak with all of us."

Lydia and Seth joined her in the library. Both Dr. Cooper and Grayson looked grave, and Lydia didn't know if she could bear what they had to say.

Seth reached for his sister's hand as she slept. "What is wrong?"

Dr. Cooper replaced his tools into a small bag. "I fear she might have diabetes."

Lydia swayed. *Diabetes?* There was no cure for that disease.

"If she does—" Grayson stammered over his words, his voice distorted by pain. "If she does, how long will she be with us?"

"I have pills that may prolong her hours, but I fear it will not be long now."

Not days or weeks or months. They had only hours left with her.

The doctor lifted his bag. "A coma will overtake her first, so you will want to say your good-byes soon."

Lydia looked at her brother, at the agony etched on his face. Long ago she had wondered whether he loved Sarah Hammond. Now she knew—Grayson loved his wife with everything in him, and if the doctor was right, he must now say good-bye.

Sarah's eyes fluttered open, and she smiled when she saw Lydia. She reached out her hands, and Lydia went to her.

"Have you any water?" Sarah asked.

Grayson filled a glass from the pitcher, and Lydia sat on the lounge and helped her drink it.

"I'm sorry. I am so thirsty."

"No need to apologize," Lydia said. "We have a river full of water."

And then Grayson gave her more.

Sarah glanced up at her husband hovering over her. "I'm dying, aren't I?"

Seconds passed as Grayson stared at her, as if time could change the answer to her question. "I am—" His voice cracked. "I'm so sorry."

"Please, don't leave me," she said, her voice small.

Grayson sat beside her and brushed her beautiful hair away from her forehead. "I will not."

Sarah's eyes found Seth. "But you must leave and continue your fight, for all of us."

Seth embraced her. "I shall stay until morning."

Sarah kissed his cheek. "Please tell Father that I did my best."

"He would be so proud of you," he said as he fought his tears. "We are all proud of you."

Seth hugged her one last time before retreating into the hall. Lydia stood to leave Sarah and Grayson alone for the night, but Sarah reached out to stop her. "Lydia?"

Turning back, she fought against her tears as Seth had done. "You have been the best of friends," Sarah said.

Lydia kissed her forehead. "We are friends and sisters."

Sarah smiled weakly. "I want you to know, I have forgiven those men who killed Thomas and burned my home."

"I'm very glad."

Her smile grew stronger. "Do you remember how we used to dance?"

Lydia nodded. "There were no cares for us then."

"After I die, I want you to dance for me." Sarah leaned forward, coughing, before she rested back on her pillow again. "Dance as if you haven't a care."

Lydia kissed her friend's damp forehead once more. "I will dance."

"Do you want more water?" Grayson whispered.

"Aye," Sarah said as he sat beside her, holding the glass for her to drink. Her body could hold no water or sustenance—at least that was what Dr. Cooper had told them. Hers was a thirst that could never be quenched in this life.

After she finished, Grayson lay down on the lounge beside his wife and gently wrapped his arms around her waist. She clung to his arms as if they could hold her back from leaving.

He was the one who was supposed to die, back on the ship. Sarah was full of life and love and hope for their future. A future they were supposed to share. If only he could rescue her as she had done for him. He knew he should pray that God's will be done, but he couldn't bear to offer that prayer.

He pulled her closer to his chest. "I have taken your life."

"No, Grayson, you gave me life."

He trembled. "I never should have left you."

She stopped his words with a gentle squeeze. "This is no time for regrets."

But his heart was full of regrets. For leaving her the first time and then for traveling with her these past weeks when she was fighting to live. He'd begged the doctor to tell him what to do—he could travel to wherever necessary to find a cure for her—but Dr. Cooper said there was no cure. Her body was flushing out her life.

"Do you think I will see angels?" she asked, her soft voice blending with the night.

"I believe you might."

"And perhaps I shall be able to fly with them."

With her wings spread, her smile a reflection of the glorious, she would be radiant.

"I believe you shall be able to journey wherever you like."

"I am ready to be with my Savior."

"I love you, darling."

"You must call me Madam." She squeezed his arm again. "Madam Knight."

He kissed her hair and then carefully rolled her toward him so he could see her face in the starlight. "I love you, Madam."

"I may be leaving, but you must live, Grayson. You must buy a new ship and sail away."

He brushed her hair over her ears. "I will not talk of sailing without you."

"You came back here for me, but I don't want you to stay. You must be free."

"I don't want to be free without you."

Her body shook as she gasped for air. For a moment, he

thought he'd lost her, but she spoke again. "Perhaps He will let me sail with you."

"I pray He will."

She closed her eyes. "Until we meet again."

"We shall meet again soon."

As he told her of his love, Sarah slipped into a deep sleep. And he held her close to him until dawn.

CHAPTER 37

*E*veryone was asleep when Lydia snuck into the great hall.

The light from her lantern spilled over the freshly waxed floor, and she breathed deeply of the sweet scent of the flowers Mother had clipped from the formal garden. Flowers and the accompanying weeds were the only things on the plantation that seemed to thrive without much care.

The room had been scrubbed clean, the broken glass swept, the curtains washed. But the success of their work didn't diminish their family's sorrow.

Sarah's funeral had been a small affair. Their family and Seth had gathered at the family plot on the Hammond property this afternoon for the burial.

Father had the grace to tell both Seth and Grayson that he was sorry for their loss. But after the burial, Father insisted that Grayson help him harvest the crop on the plantation. In his grief and anger, Grayson stormed away from the Hammond plantation, and with great sadness, Lydia knew she might never see her brother again.

But tonight she must stop thinking of conflict. Tonight she would remember Sarah.

Lydia didn't want to think about her friend—her sister—being deceased. Sarah was one of the most alive people she knew, and tonight she would celebrate her life.

Tonight she would dance.

As the music played in her head, Lydia curtsied to the shadows and took an imaginary hand. She held out the sides of her linen shift as if it were made of the finest satin from Paris, and then she and her partner swirled around the floor.

Couples dressed in the finest of velvets and taffeta danced around them, but she only had eyes for her partner. She couldn't see his face, but it didn't matter. She knew who she danced with. He would never be welcomed into this house, but she could pretend that he had been invited to one of their grand balls.

The music ended, and she stepped back.

"Thank you, Mr.— " She paused. It was strange, not knowing his last name. "Thank you, Nathan."

The next song began, a country dance. Sarah would be pleased at the faster pace. The dancers looked so elegant in her mind, as if the troubles of today evaded them. That is what she loved about dancing. There was no sorrow when she danced, no regrets. She could lose herself in the beauty of it.

The shadows on the floor flickered, and the music faded in her head.

Had Hannah or someone else come downstairs?

Quickly she extinguished her lantern as she listened for footsteps. No sound replaced the music at first, but then she heard the low rumbling of voices outside the door.

"This is a fine place," a man said.

She held her breath. Who was in their house?

"It should make a decent summer residence." She recognized

Major Reed's voice, and relief washed over her for a moment. At least she knew who intruded upon them.

"You sound as if you already own the plantation."

"I am only acting on behalf of the king." Major Reed paused. "I do think it would be a tolerable dwelling for the governor of Virginia. Do you agree, Captain?"

"Indeed."

Tolerable?

How dare he presume to secure her family's home before they even won this war! Was he planning to take it by force or, heaven forbid, marry Hannah and claim it for himself?

It was a pleasure to call Sarah *sister,* but the thought of having to call this man *brother* made her stomach turn.

The footsteps grew louder, and she moved toward the servants' closed door beside the fireplace.

"Why are you still in Virginia?" the captain asked.

"General Cornwallis requested that I return to Virginia in case of a disturbance."

"What of your men?"

"Most of them went with General Arnold to defend New York, but a few dozen have stayed with me."

Before they stepped into the great hall, she slipped through the servants' door. Her face pressed against the frame, she peered through the crack to see the men. Major Reed was easily distinguishable by his short stature and white wig.

The captain wrung his hands, his voice filtering clearly into the narrow hall. "Why have you summoned me?"

"I feared the news had not yet reached Richmond of the arrival of General Washington and his men."

"W–Washington?" the man stuttered. "I thought he was preparing to attack New York."

"It seems as if the approach of our reinforcements has deterred this attack. Now, I fear, he is focused on attacking our troops on the Chesapeake Bay."

The captain paced across the floor. "What is required of me?"

Major Reed sat in one of the chairs that lined the room. "The general is staying in a private home owned by one of the men who signed the statement for their independence."

"Our enemy is being careless."

"Not as careless as we would like. No one has access to Washington except for a few slaves and his top advisors."

The captain moved closer to the fireplace and then paced back toward Major Reed. "Can any of these slaves be bribed?"

"I believe a man named Samar can. The promise of freedom is the greatest bribe of all."

The captain shook his head. "The slave will be stopped before he can shoot the general."

"There will be no guns," Major Reed insisted. "He will simply mix a tablet into the general's drink."

Lydia slumped against the wall, her hands trembling. She couldn't allow them to kill General Washington.

"And who will help him escape?" the captain asked.

"I said the promise of freedom," Major Reed replied, the icy cold in his voice sending a chill through her skin. "He will have to escape on his own."

"You want one of my men to contact him?"

"I want you to contact him in Williamsburg, dressed as a Continental soldier, to blend in with the others."

The captain rubbed his hands together again. "If this Samar succeeds, do you think the Americans will continue their attack on York?"

"It is doubtful." Major Reed's laugh was dark. "If they do, we will reciprocate as we did in Savannah and Charles Towne."

The man joined him in the laughter.

"I will travel to Williamsburg tomorrow," the captain said. "Do you plan to spend the remainder of the night here?"

Her eye at the crack, she tried to see if he nodded his head, but his face was darkened by the shadow.

"You can bed down in the parlor if you'd like," Major Reed replied.

As if it were already his home.

The major continued. "I have other business to attend to before morning."

He stood, his heels clicking as he crossed the floor toward the fireplace. She gasped; then, praying he didn't hear, she hurried down the narrow hall and rushed up the staircase, not stopping until she was safe inside her chamber on the second floor.

She locked her door and paced by the fireplace. Should she awaken her parents?

No, the men might guess she'd spied on them, and that would ruin everything. Father trusted the major, and even if Mother opposed what they planned, Father might applaud the assassination plot.

She must get a message to Nathan, but it was much too pressing to hide her message in the brick wall. She would have to write a letter to Mrs. Pendell, using the ink Nathan gave her, and deliver it herself.

By candlelight, she began to write of the plans on one side of the paper. On the other side, she wrote a letter to Mrs. Pendell about material she wished to order for a winter dress. Then she tumbled into her bed.

At first light she would devise a way to deliver her message, hopefully before this captain arrived in Williamsburg.

It was well past ten when a knock jolted Nathan from his reading. Few had access to the Wythe home, and anyone who knocked on his door at this hour must have a good reason.

Perhaps it was time for him to go to York.

He opened the door, and in the narrow hall stood an officer he didn't recognize.

"What is it?" Nathan demanded.

"Yesterday morning, one of my best men went to visit his home. He was supposed to return by day's end."

Nathan raked his fingers through his long hair. "Captain Hammond?"

"Aye. I am told you might know where he is."

"Perhaps he lingered near his home."

"I need him right away. We are preparing to march to York."

Goose bumps covered Nathan's arms. The battle for Virginia was about to begin.

"I will search for him at first light."

CHAPTER 38

A noise startled Lydia and she sat up in bed, listening to hushed voices in the hall. She clutched her bedsheet to her chest as the clock outside her room chimed thrice.

Was Major Reed searching their rooms? Her letter was written, and she had hidden it in a place she hoped no man would ever look, but she feared Major Reed might still discover it.

The whispering continued as Lydia padded slowly toward the door.

Had the major awakened her parents? And for what reason? Perhaps he wanted the last of their horses, the dwindling storehouse of food, the barn filled with curing tobacco. Or perhaps he wanted Mother to retrieve fresh linens for a bed.

Then she heard the sound of Hannah giggling, and she leaped from her bed.

Major Reed had paid a visit to her sister.

Wrapping a blanket over her shift, she rushed toward the door, but by the time she opened the door, the laughter had stopped. Hannah had dreamed of a wedding, but Lydia feared the major wouldn't care much about such things.

She hurried down the corridor, toward the grand staircase

that led downstairs, and opened the front door. In the faint light, she saw the outline of a horse galloping away. Running back upstairs, she yanked open the door to Hannah's chamber, hoping she might be mistaken, hoping that Major Reed had left without her.

But Hannah was gone.

Turning, she rushed toward her parents' chamber. Not only had her sister compromised herself, but she'd compromised the reputation of their entire family. A marriage to a British officer might offer some sort of protection after the war, but the mistress of a British officer could only bring shame.

Foolish Hannah.

She'd found her way off the plantation, but to what end? Her life would be ruined.

"Mother," Lydia cried, pounding on their door.

Father opened it, and in the moonlight from the portico window, she could see his nightcap slightly askew. "What is it?"

She looked over his shoulder at Mother, sitting upright in bed. "I believe Hannah has left with Major Reed."

Father swore. And then he was gone, down the long hall to check for himself whether what she said was true.

Lydia collapsed against the doorpost. "He will not treat her well."

Mother squeezed a pillow to her chest. "I fear you are right."

"And then she will return to us."

"There is no reason for her to return." Mother began to cry into the pillow, and Lydia moved toward her, wrapping her arms around the woman who'd worked tirelessly to make it all right. But she could not control the battle within. Their country might be divided between Loyalists and Patriots, but they were all free, in a sense, to make their own choices. The consequences were beyond Mother's control.

As Lydia hugged her mother, her own tears spilled down her shift. "You have loved our family well."

Mother wiped her tears on her sleeve. "Sometimes love is not enough."

Lydia moved to the edge of the bed. "Indeed, but that does not mean you shouldn't love."

"It hurts terribly." Mother's tears flowed again. "I tried to protect Grayson. For all those years I knew he had escaped, but I was afraid to tell anyone. Now he has left us for good, and Hannah—"

Lydia stopped her. "You knew Grayson was alive?"

"I knew he left, but I didn't know if he had survived."

Lydia slowly processed this news. "Why didn't you tell me?"

"I didn't know what those men in town would do if they discovered he had run," Mother said. "I couldn't ask you to bear that secret with me."

If only her mother knew what secrets she had borne these past months. "You protected him well."

Mother trembled. "But I can no longer protect my family."

Lydia wished she could assure her that she could keep her children safe . . . .

When Father returned, his forehead was covered with sweat. "She left with him."

"Are you going after her?" Lydia begged.

He shook his head. "There is nothing to be done."

"You must go." Mother tossed her pillow to the end of the bed. "Straightaway."

But Father didn't move. His eyes were stoic, looking back at the door as if Hannah might appear at any moment.

"You must detain her—" Lydia began.

But he stopped her. "She has chosen her route."

Lydia sprang from the bed. "You went after our Negroes when they ran away. You must go after your daughter as well!"

He collapsed onto a wooden chair. "She is not bound to stay with us."

"If you do not stop Major Reed, the British are going to destroy our family and probably take our plantation as well."

"They will not take the plantation," he insisted. "We are English. Subjects of the king."

"I am not English, Father." She stepped toward the door. "I am an American."

Father's fist slammed against the bureau. "I will not have treason in my house!"

Lydia's heart lurched, her mind tangled. She didn't want treachery; she wanted truth.

She fled into the corridor but stopped when she heard her mother calling her name. She would not run away like Hannah. She desired freedom, but she didn't want to break her mother's heart in pursuit of it.

Father stood by the window, staring down at the river, when Lydia walked back into their room. Leaning over the bed, she kissed her mother on the cheek. "I will search for Hannah."

Mother grasped her hand. "Thank you."

In her chamber, Lydia retrieved her sampler of the river and began stitching again. When she finished, she tossed it into a valise along with a few toilet items and an extra petticoat.

Hannah had chosen destruction.

Grayson, Sarah, Seth, Nathan—they had chosen freedom. It was time for her to choose her route as well.

CHAPTER 39

*B*efore the sun began to rise, Nathan borrowed a horse from the livery, so when the first light danced on the horizon, he and his barber's kit were already headed west toward the Hammond plantation.

He hadn't been able to sleep much the previous night, anxious about what might have happened to Seth. All he could imagine was Seth changing his mind and returning to Lydia.

Nathan could hardly blame his friend if he deserted the army to marry her, but Seth's commander wouldn't be as forgiving.

A small band of British soldiers were camped near the main road. Though disguised, Nathan avoided the men altogether with a detour south, hugging the bank of the river. All he had for protection was a pistol and the knife in his shaving kit, and he preferred not to use either one.

There was no movement at the Hammond plantation, and the supplies he'd hidden in the barn were gone. He glanced out at the river as a British ship sailed east toward York. Hopefully Sarah had directed Grayson and his crew to the supplies.

He stroked the black fur on the horse's neck. Perhaps he

MELANIE DOBSON

ought to return to Williamsburg and report that Seth wasn't at the plantation, but his mind raced.

What if Seth had changed his mind about Lydia? Or decided to marry her out of obligation?

Taking the main road, he turned toward Caswell Hall. The horse trotted between the tobacco fields as he pressed toward the house. Instead of Seth or Lydia, he found the man he assumed to be Lord Caswell working the fields with one white and three Negro men.

Lord Caswell looked up with his knife in his hand. "What are you doing on my land?"

Nathan pulled back on the reins. "I'm looking for Seth Hammond."

Lord Caswell's eyes narrowed. "What do you want with him?"

"It's personal business."

"Take your business off my land."

Nathan eyed the tobacco leaves at their feet. "You will lose these leaves if you do not harvest them straightaway."

Lord Caswell hesitated, and when he spoke again, Nathan glimpsed the man's broken heart. "I am keenly and painfully aware of all I am losing."

Nathan dismounted. "If you can tell me where Seth is, I will work alongside you for the rest of the day."

Lord Caswell eyed the shaving kit at Nathan's side. "What does a barber know of harvesting tobacco?"

"My uncle is a planter."

The man seemed to contemplate his words. "If you are a rebel, it would be detrimental to harbor you on my land."

"On the contrary, sir, it might benefit your position."

Lord Caswell continued to study him. "I don't think I want to know your political leanings."

"Then I won't tell you."

Lord Caswell turned and eyed the acres upon acres of

310

unharvested tobacco. He must know that Nathan wasn't a Loyalist, but if he didn't pursue the truth, he wouldn't have a moral obligation to demand Nathan stay off his property. His cash crop wouldn't be worth any cash at all if he didn't get it into the barn soon.

Perhaps Lord Caswell did rely more on his own kingdom than on his king.

"I'm willing to work hard," Nathan offered.

Lord Caswell leaned to clip a leaf. "As far as I know, Seth returned to Williamsburg after his sister's funeral yesterday."

The declaration stunned Nathan. "His sister died?'

The man nodded. "Of diabetes."

Nathan looked toward the trees, the line between the Hammond and Caswell properties. Sarah's death would devastate both Seth and Lydia. And Grayson...

No wonder Seth had lingered here. It wasn't to see Lydia. It was to say good-bye to his sister.

Perhaps he and Seth had passed each other on the trail this morning.

He wished he could ask Lord Caswell if he'd received word from his son, but he must pretend to have no knowledge of this family's personal affairs.

"Did he leave by himself?" Nathan asked.

"Aye."

Nathan patted his horse as relief mixed with the sadness. Lydia was still here, but how would he find her? He hesitated as a plan formed in his mind, a way to see Lydia tonight without compromising her role— or his. "Perhaps you could provide a meal as well, in exchange for my work."

"Where do you come from?" Lord Caswell asked.

"North of here."

"Did your uncle teach you how to harvest?"

Nathan nodded. "He did."

"I let the leaves wilt on the ground until dusk."

Nathan flung his cloak and scarf over his saddle before he tied the horse to a tree. Then he removed the knife from his kit before he joined Lord Caswell again. "Where would you like me to begin?"

Lord Caswell directed him to another row, and Nathan moved steadily along, cutting off the leaves that were ready to cure. As he worked, pleasant memories returned of working alongside his father before he had died.

Nathan had taken pleasure in this work of growing and harvesting first tobacco and then wheat. It was an honest way to make a living, planting seeds in the fertile land and then watching the magic begin, the water and sun transforming each seed into a healthy plant. He loved to watch things grow—but a few years after he'd gone to live with Uncle George and Aunt Martha, his uncle needed his help in overseeing the family's business affairs.

He sliced off another leaf.

Perhaps when this war was over, he would return to what he loved—the life of a planter.

Lydia scooped a handful of water from a stream and unwrapped the cheese and meat that Mother had wrapped for her. She wouldn't linger long in the woods, only enough time to eat before continuing to Williamsburg.

She wished she had been able to say good-bye to her father, but he'd left for the fields before she dressed. His determination to provide for his family was admirable, but she couldn't understand why his work was more important than finding her sister.

Perhaps he thought it was too late to retrieve Hannah, or maybe he was relieved that she was gone. Or perhaps—and she hated to even consider it—perhaps he thought Hannah's choice would protect his family, so he let her go.

Lydia wouldn't tarry in Williamsburg. She would deliver her message and then find out where Major Reed had taken her sister. If she hurried, it might not be too late to rescue her.

Something stirred in the trees, and her heart quickened as she turned. There was a flash of red among the green, and a British soldier emerged from the forest. He towered over her by a foot, and the ruddy color of his face matched his uniform.

"What are you doing out here?" the soldier demanded.

"I'm traveling into Williamsburg." She straightened her petticoat, trying not to appear as alarmed as she felt. If only Mother were here to deter them as she had before. "To visit a friend."

"I am under orders to search all persons coming into the town."

She sighed. "Will it take long? I would like to join my friend for tea."

Another soldier joined him, but he continued to speak. "Where do you come from?"

"Caswell Hall. My father is Lord Caswell."

She could see a hint of approval in his eyes. "We are familiar with it."

Did every British soldier know of the gracious accommodations at her home?

He opened her valise, and she cringed as he riffled through her belongings. When he picked up her sampler, examining it, she held her breath.

Then he tossed it back into her bag.

He eyed her. "I'm sorry. I shall have to search you as well."

It was what she'd feared. And what she had prepared for. "I pray you will be kind. Major Reed is a personal friend of our family's."

The man stepped back. "Major Dalton Reed?"

"Yes, sir."

He studied her face. "You do not fancy the man, do you?"

She forced strength into her voice. "What business is it of yours?"

"My wife works for the household of Major and Mistress Reed."

Her strength faded. "Major and Mistress?"

"Has he not told you of his wife?"

The world seemed to tilt. "I am afraid he has not."

"Mistress Reed worries about him."

The heat of anger rushed to her face. How dare Major Reed impose upon her family, suggesting that he might marry one of them, if he was already married—

Dear God, what would happen to Hannah?

She reached for the horn of the saddle and pulled herself up on the horse. "I must go."

Neither man stopped her.

There was no time to linger. She must deliver her message and then steal her sister away from that man.

Their political views might differ, but Nathan couldn't help but admire Lord Caswell. He had thought most British supporters to be stubborn, ill-tempered men who expected others to do their work, but Lord Caswell worked as hard as any man who loved his land.

Nathan eyed the fields one last time in the fading light before he turned toward the house. It had felt good to be working the land today alongside this man. It fit Nathan much better than clerical work ever did.

He stopped at the base of Caswell Hall and looked up at the three stories of brick and windows. "Did you build this?"

"My father and I."

"It is very impressive."

Lord Caswell motioned him up the stairs. "Perhaps. But there shan't be any pomp and circumstance tonight."

Nathan wasn't the least bit concerned about pomp and circumstance, but he feared what he might do when he saw Lydia. How could he be indifferent toward her?

If he spoke first, said it was nice to meet her, surely she would join in the facade—as she did when he pretended to be her servant.

Lord Caswell instructed him to wait in the library while he changed his clothing for dinner. As he waited, Nathan examined the pictures on the wall. One was a boy—Grayson, he guessed—when he was seven or eight years of age. He had an ornery glint in his eye, as if waiting to play some sort of prank on the unsuspecting artist.

Next to him was a young girl with chestnut hair the same color as Lydia's. Nathan didn't recognize her, but the woman in the last portrait captured his gaze and wouldn't let it go. Lydia sat alone in the gazebo, her strong beauty radiating from within her, and Nathan stared up at her, admiring the soft light on her hair, the fire that sparked in her lavender-blue eyes.

He backed toward the door.

What had he been thinking? Over the past two years, he'd feigned all sorts of professions and facades, but he could never hide his feelings for Lydia. Lord Caswell might have compromised his political leanings temporarily for the sake of his crop, but he would never compromise his daughter.

Nathan stole one more glance at her portrait.

"It's time for—"

He whirled at the sound of a woman's voice, and she stopped, staring at him before she spoke again. "Why are you here?"

It was the woman who'd fed him in Elisha's room. Prudence. "I was searching for Seth Hammond."

Prudence clutched her hands. "You must leave. Immediately."

"Lord Caswell has invited me."

"But he doesn't know who you are. You will bring trouble to our house."

"I only want to see Lydia."

"There is much that has happened. You do not know—"

Panic swelled in his chest. "Where is Lydia?"

Prudence shot a glance toward the door and then looked back at him. "She has gone after her sister."

"What of her sister?"

"She—"

Lord Caswell stepped back into the library, his work clothes replaced by a black waistcoat and jacket. "Are you coming to dinner?"

Nathan nodded. "I am."

A hundred questions brewed in his mind, but Prudence lowered her head as he walked by. If only he'd had another minute to speak with her.

Where had Lydia and her sister gone?

Lady Caswell nodded at him as he sat down in the dining chair. Her eyes were swollen, and when she spoke, her tone was as frosty as the James River on the night he'd plunged from the ship. "My husband does not seem to recollect your name."

Prudence was waiting in the corner, and he caught her gaze over Lady Caswell's shoulder. Then he focused once more on Lydia's mother. "I go by Nathan, Lady Caswell."

"Nathan?" Something shifted in her eyes as she studied him, and her demeanor slowly changed. Not to friendliness, but at least to tolerance. "Where is it that you come from, Nathan?"

"The northern part of Virginia. My father was a planter, and so is my uncle."

Lord Caswell lifted his goblet. "You learned well from them."

He thought of the hours his father and then his uncle had

spent with him, teaching him all there was to know about how to plant and harvest and sell what he'd grown. "My uncle may not agree about how much I have learned, but he would thank you for the compliment."

"I saw your cloak by the door," Lady Caswell said. "Where did you purchase your lovely scarf?"

Nathan set down his goblet, not certain how to answer. He had worn Grayson's scarf whenever the weather was cool—he hadn't considered the possibility of someone recognizing it. Why hadn't he left it with the horse outside? "From a friend."

She tilted her head. "It looks very familiar to me."

Prudence set a platter of ham in the middle of the table and then another platter of beans.

Lord Caswell lifted a slice of meat and served it to Nathan. "Where is your family?"

"My father has passed on, but my mother is living with my aunt."

"And your siblings?" Lady Caswell asked.

"I had ten brothers and sisters, but only five are still living."

"It is a tragedy to lose so many children," she replied, and he heard the empathy in her voice. She seemed to be well-acquainted with the sorrow.

He ate a bite of ham before he ventured, "How many children do you have?"

"Three. But they have all left us."

"I see." He took another bite. "Where have they gone?"

Lord Caswell glanced at his wife. "We do not know."

Nathan looked at Prudence again, but she ignored him.

"The weather is changing again," Lord Caswell said.

"Aye." He could feel the chill in the air as they'd worked.

"Can you help again in the morning?"

Nathan shook his head. "I'm afraid I must return to my work."

Lord Caswell sighed. "It is not safe for you to travel at night."

"I—"

"You must at least sleep in our servants' quarters. It is empty these days."

Nathan wanted to laugh at the irony. If only Lydia were here to share in the amusement. "That is kind of you, but I must leave this evening."

He hoped Seth was preparing to leave for York, but he must make certain.

Lord Caswell spied the lowering sun outside. "I have one more favor to ask of you."

"What is it?"

"You must understand, I cannot leave the plantation until I have harvested all I can."

Nathan nodded his head in understanding. If the man didn't harvest now, he might lose everything he and his father had built for their family.

"Could you search for my daughters in Williamsburg?"

This time Prudence met his eye, and he saw her nod.

"I would be glad to, sir."

CHAPTER 40

$\mathcal{L}$ ydia had to proceed cautiously as she walked through the remaining forest toward Williamsburg. The fate of General Washington was in her hands, and if she was detained or her things confiscated, all would be lost.

If they killed the general, she feared the British would take Virginia for good.

When she reached town, soldiers wearing blue and gray seemed to be guarding every corner. After spending hours wandering in the woods, trying to avoid any other contact with British guards, relief washed over her.

Perhaps it had been impossible for the captain to bribe the Wythes' slave, with so many Patriots occupying the city.

Night had begun to fall when she stepped onto the Pendells' porch and knocked. After she delivered her message, she would search for Hannah.

Mrs. Pendell's eyes widened with surprise when she saw her. "Is your mother with you?"

Lydia shook her head before reaching into the valise for her sampler of the river.

"I have brought you a gift."

Mrs. Pendell took the sampler and then turned it over, examining the white cloth that sealed the letter inside. She lowered her voice. "That is most ingenious of you."

"The contents are urgent." She stepped back. "If Mother knew I was here, she would send her love."

"And I would return it. No matter what happens, I will always consider your mother a friend."

Lydia left quickly, but when she reached the end of the street, she realized she had no idea where to look for her sister. Hannah would follow Major Reed wherever he traveled, but how was she supposed to find him?

She approached a soldier in a blue uniform. "I'm searching for my sister. I fear she is with the British camp followers."

The soldier hiked up his musket. "I regret to hear it."

"Do you know where the followers are?"

He shrugged. "Probably near the town of York."

More than ten miles from here.

"I thank you."

"It would not be safe for you to travel alone," the man said.

She walked a few more steps down Duke of Gloucester, the lanterns over the tavern doors lighting her way. Then she leaned against a hitching post. Where was she to stay for the night?

The stench of a nearby tannery choked her, the energy that had driven her to Williamsburg draining away. She could risk her life to walk to York tonight, but even if she made it in the darkness, was there any hope of finding her sister? Or should she go home and tell Father about Hannah's location? Perhaps he would search for her now.

She stepped away from the post. It was either walk east or back west.

She shivered at the thought of meeting the British guards in the darkness. Then her stomach rumbled. All she had left to eat in her valise was a small chunk of cheese. Mother had given her a little money as well.

She should buy something to eat before she left Williamsburg.

"Lydia!" She turned to see Mrs. Pendell running down the street, the edge of her petticoat balled in her hand.

Lydia glanced around her nervously. Their friendship wasn't a secret, but they didn't want to make a spectacle, either.

Mrs. Pendell reached for her arm. "Please, come back to my home."

She shook her head. "I must be going."

Mrs. Pendell whispered, "I cannot deliver this message myself. He will have questions."

Wagon wheels groaned behind them. "Your contact?"

"No, the general. He will want to know details."

"I do not have more details."

A cart passed, and the horses splashed mud toward them. Mrs. Pendell took her arm, guiding her away from the street into the shadows of an alley. "Are you afraid to speak with General Washington?"

"It matters not what I fear. My family has other pressing needs."

"There is little more pressing than this," Mrs. Pendell said.

Lydia debated whether to tell the woman about her sister, but Mother would be mortified if anyone, including Mrs. Pendell, discovered that Hannah had run away with a married officer.

"The British will win or lose Virginia in the coming weeks, and then our work will be finished," Mrs. Pendell said.

"But what if they lose?" she asked. "No one but you and Nathan know about my work."

"Then you must choose, Lydia. Truly choose."

She had already chosen what she believed. Like Seth and Nathan and Sarah. And her brother.

"They will find out about you as well," Lydia said.

"I am prepared for it."

Lydia pressed her palms together. Perhaps after she gave him the information, the general would help her travel to York. "If he wants to see me, I will speak to him."

Mrs. Pendell led her back to the street. "We will go there now."

~

Nathan handed the reins of his horse to the stableman and hurried into the Wythe home through the back door. He had thought a British guard might detain him in the forest for questioning, but none did. If all the British soldiers were marching toward York now, they mustn't delay any longer.

One of the servants took his cloak and shaving kit, and he changed quickly in his room before joining his uncle and the other men in their office. The men had spread two maps across the table and were in heated discussion about how to attack the soldiers at York. He wasn't sure where to find Lydia and her sister, but he would begin his search once General Washington dismissed them for the night.

The general glanced at him. "Captain Hammond has returned."

Nathan nodded. "He stayed to bury his sister."

"'Tis a terrible loss for all of us."

Someone knocked on the door, but the general returned his focus to the map. "We cannot be interrupted," he barked.

Mrs. Wythe inched open the door. "Mrs. Pendell is still waiting to see you."

Nathan looked up at their hostess. "How long has she been waiting?"

"For nearly two hours. She says it's urgent that she see the general tonight."

"Then we must see her." Nathan tapped the map. "She has been a most important contact for us."

General Washington turned back to Mrs. Wythe. "Please tell her she must be quick with her words."

Mrs. Wythe nodded. "Of course."

Before she left the room, Mr. Wythe stopped her. "Would you also send a servant up with coffee for our guests?"

Mrs. Wythe nodded again before she shut the door, and Nathan thought the woman must be part saint.

Seconds later, the door reopened and Mrs. Pendell walked inside. Behind Mrs. Pendell stood Lydia.

A half-dozen men filled the library, and in front of Lydia was one of the tallest men she'd ever seen. His hair was a reddish-brown, his eyes a cool blue. As Mrs. Pendell introduced her to General Washington, she wished Sarah could have joined her in meeting this great man.

The general stepped forward, extending his hand. "It is a pleasure to meet you, Miss Caswell."

She returned his handshake. "It is a pleasure to make your acquaintance as well."

"My nephew tells me I owe you a debt of gratitude."

She dropped her hand, confused, until Nathan stepped out from the shadows. But instead of wearing a laborer's clothes, he was dressed in a fine black coat and white breeches.

"Your nephew?" she asked.

General Washington looked between them. "Did you not know?"

"I did not, sir."

When the general eyed him, Nathan shrugged. "It was not pertinent information."

Mrs. Pendell wrung her hands together. "We have a most

urgent matter to discuss with you, sir."

General Washington's gaze became serious. "What is it?"

Mrs. Pendell prompted Lydia forward, but she could hardly speak. Her eyes were on Nathan, General Washington's nephew. He had said he was working for Washington, but she had no idea just how closely.

Why hadn't he told her?

The door opened behind her, and she turned to watch a dark-skinned man walk into the room with a silver platter. He was dressed in formal attire and white gloves, but he didn't hold his head high like a gentleman. Instead, his eyes were focused on the ground.

Mr. Wythe moved one of the maps. "You may set it here, Samar."

As he began to pour the coffee, a surge of compassion rushed over Lydia. This man desired freedom, just like everyone in this room, but he wouldn't obtain it by poisoning the general.

Samar held a cup out to General Washington, but Lydia stepped forward, waving her hand. "Don't drink that."

Nathan's face was as grave as the general's. "What is it, Lydia?"

"Major Reed returned to the plantation last night for a meeting. He told another officer of a plot to assassinate you, sir."

The general took the proffered cup. "Every British officer seems to have a plot to do away with my life."

When Samar began backing toward the door, she turned to him. "What did you put in his coffee?" she demanded.

"I—I don't know what you mean."

How she hated this. She didn't want harm to come to this man, and yet he had chosen this course.

She glanced back as General Washington lowered his cup onto the platter. Then she turned again toward Samar. "I know you poisoned the drink."

Samar swore before he turned and ran.

CHAPTER 41

*C*annons blasted around Grayson. The battle had begun early this morning, and, frankly, he didn't care whether he lived or died. The Americans had all the supplies they needed, and now he and his new ship must fight for his country. For Sarah.

He could never return to Caswell Hall. The memories of his wife were too strong and the rift between him and his father too deep to heal. While he loved his family, he would never conform to Lord Caswell's expectations for him to run the plantation, nor could he oversee his father's slaves.

Hours after Grayson left Hammond Plantation, Elisha found him and insisted on helping him fight the rest of this war. Today might be the end for them both, but they would remain strong until that end.

He scanned the ships in the waters around him. There were two French ships on their left, battling what seemed like half the British fleet. With the Grand Union flag high on their mainmast, he and his crew were focused on a ship waving the King's Colours.

Or at least, he was supposed to be focused. Even as he called for the men to load the cannon and fire, even as the blast echoed through his skin, he couldn't escape the memories of the woman he'd loved.

Through the smoky air, Grayson turned toward the shore. Near here was the wharf where his schooner had been docked, where in his hunger and thirst and complete deprivation, he had thought his life would never get any worse. And yet it had.

If only he had died back when he was on the boat. If only Sarah had never found out about his imprisonment. Perhaps the stress of living the past month without a home wouldn't have taken its toll on her. She might still be alive.

Would she have grieved the loss of him as he did for her? Perhaps not, since she had already grieved for him when he left the first time.

At the time, he had wanted to protect her by leaving quietly, but it had been cruel not to tell her good-bye.

Through the smoke, he searched the hills above the bank, the red uniforms and the blue, neighbors fighting against neighbors, fathers against sons. Many would lose their lives in this battle, but Americans well understood the cost of freedom. They were willing to risk everything for it.

Often he wondered if their enemy, given the opportunity to consider it, would choose freedom as well.

Instead of blasting the cannons again, Zadock and four other men prepared the cylinders they'd filled with arrows. They lit the pitched tips of the arrows and gunpowder propelled them forward. Some landed in the bay, but Grayson watched through his looking glass as dozens of the arrows found their mark on the deck of the ship in their sights. Minutes later, the ship hoisted a white flag.

Grayson should have celebrated his success, but victory no longer felt sweet.

"Hold your fire," Grayson commanded.

Zadock stepped up beside him. "I think she's burning, Captain."

He picked up his looking glass again and saw what appeared to be a fire on deck.

He lowered the glass. "Where is Elisha?"

"I'm right here."

"We must ready ourselves for prisoners."

The crew lowered a rowboat into the water, and Elisha rowed him toward the burning ship. "They still might shoot us, Master Porter."

"It makes no difference to me."

Elisha rowed again. "It does to me. I need to find Morah and Alden."

Grayson glanced back at this man who had labored for his family for thirty years, the man who had taught him to carve and swim and ride a horse. The man who had suffered through Grayson's whip and then forgiven him for a punishment he hadn't deserved.

The man who had saved him from the British.

"If we survive—" He paused. "When we survive this, we will find your family."

As they drew closer to the ship, a curtain of haze and smoke engulfed them. If there were any survivors, they were impossible to see, and he didn't want to get too close to the sinking ship for fear it would take their boat and Elisha down with it.

Elisha stopped paddling. "Listen."

Grayson listened, but all he heard was the blast of cannons and the distant popping sound of guns on shore. "What is it?"

"Someone is calling for help."

And then he heard it, a voice—no, two voices—calling out. It sounded like a woman and a child.

He pointed to his right. "That way."

Elisha dipped his oars back into the water and paddled right.

Through the haze, Grayson saw two people clinging to a barrel. He reached out and lifted the boy up first and then the woman.

The woman pulled the boy close to her, huddling over the child like a hen with a broken wing trying to protect her chick. Her sleeve crept up, and Grayson saw the dark skin underneath. He looked across the boat at Elisha and saw the man's eyes widen.

"Morah?"

The boy and woman both looked up at Elisha, recognition spilling into their eyes. Then Grayson watched as the woman collapsed into his arms.

"I thought I'd never see you again," Elisha said, kissing her wet hair, her cheeks.

She smiled at him. "We were coming home to find you."

Elisha reached for his son and engulfed him in his arms as well until another cannon blasted near them. Then he straightened. "I must paddle."

Grayson carefully moved past Morah and Alden. Then he motioned Elisha away from the oars. "Let me paddle now."

Elisha hesitated.

"Your family has come home to you," Grayson said. "You must be with them."

Elisha slipped from his seat. "Yes, Master Grayson."

Grayson took the oars.

The family huddled together, whispering and weeping with joy as Grayson turned the boat. Either they would find his ship, or they'd find shore.

Moments later, Elisha stopped him. "Morah says Commodore Hammond is here."

Grayson stopped paddling. "Commodore Hammond?"

She nodded. "Master Hammond found us at an auction. He bought us back so we could come home with him."

Groaning, Grayson squinted across the murky water and smoke.

He'd just sunk the ship of Sarah's father.

If he must, he would search all night to find the commodore.

When General Washington and the men who guarded him left for York the next morning, Lydia joined their entourage. The general asked Nathan to remain in Williamsburg to serve as a courier, but Nathan promised that he'd assist her after the battle if she could not locate Hannah.

Her world felt as if it had tipped once again.

How was she supposed to explain to her father that she'd begun caring for the nephew of George Washington?

The camp followers of both the British and American armies waited together on a hillside near York. Some of the women prepared food while others watched the fight as if the battle were a game in the Colosseum of Rome.

Lydia stood for a moment in wonder.

Cannons blasted from the web of sails and masts in the harbor below. Muskets and men volleyed on land. All the Americans had been doing to win their freedom—all she had been doing—came down to a battle along an otherwise peaceful bay.

Turning, she searched through the crowd of women and children until at last she found her sister sitting on a blanket. Hannah's dress was torn, her hair covered in the dust and sand blowing from the beach.

Neither Lydia nor her sister resembled the British ladies they'd been groomed to become. The war, the tobacco fields, and Major Reed had stolen everything from them.

And yet it wasn't too late for her sister to leave behind Major Reed.

Now Lydia could tell her the truth.

She sat on the blanket next to her sister, and Hannah looked over at her in surprise. "Why are you here?"

"I have come to escort you home."

Hannah returned her gaze to the battle. "But I have only just arrived."

A wagon filled with injured soldiers rumbled past them, several men screaming in agony. "This is not the place for you."

"It is better than working in those fields. The war will be over soon, and when it is, Dalton will care for me."

She took a deep breath. "He will not."

"You're jealous."

Lydia shook her head. "He cannot care for you, because he must return to his . . ."

"His what?" Hannah insisted.

"His wife."

When Hannah looked back at Lydia, her eyes were filled more with anger than surprise. "Wife?"

Lydia nodded. "One of the major's officers told me he left Mistress Reed back in England."

"He is not returning to England." Hannah's gaze fell upon the smoke again. "I will be Mistress Reed in Virginia."

"But he—"

Hannah stopped her. "You're wasting your time. I won't go back to those fields."

In the distance, Lydia saw flames engulf what looked like a ship. "I want the Americans to win."

Hannah balled up the edge of the blanket. "Because of Seth?"

"Because I believe in independence."

Hannah looked back at her. "So I suppose that means we are enemies forever."

"We are sisters, Hannah. No matter who wins this war."

Hannah took her hand, and together they listened to the roar of the battle.

Lydia knew not the location of Major Reed or Nathan or their brother, but for now they had each other.

And she hoped that one day her sister would change her mind.

～

A storm forced Grayson and the rest of the fleet to break from the battle. When they dropped anchor north of York, he hurried below to visit Commodore Hammond in his chamber.

Three days prior, he and Elisha had found the commodore clinging to a plank, barely conscious, and Elisha had hauled him into their small boat. Grayson rowed the man back to the ship, where he was tended to while Grayson and his crew continued to fight.

The ship rocked in the winds, but he was grateful for the respite the storm provided. None of them knew how long the battle would last, but it seemed to him that the French and American fleet remained strong.

Grayson knocked once on Commodore Hammond's door before he unlocked it.

The commodore sat up in his bed, staring at Grayson as if he saw a ghost. "My eyes seem to be playing a trick on me."

Grayson sat on a stool by the bed. "There is nothing wrong with your eyes, Commodore."

"But they tell me that Grayson Caswell is standing before me."

"It is true."

"You and your men have taken my ship?"

"I'm afraid that is correct." They'd sunk it, to be exact, but he didn't say that.

The older man leaned back against his pillow. "I suppose if I am to be taken, I'm glad it's by a neighbor."

"We are more than neighbors, sir." He took a breath. "A minister near here also made me your son."

In the hours to come, Grayson told Sarah's father of her last days and her death, and inside that tiny cabin, Commodore Hammond's grief mirrored his own.

As the crew waited above, the commodore clung to a locket Sarah had given him, and Grayson mourned with him, mixing tears of anger and sorrow. Morah had already told her master about his ruined home, but the loss of his ship and then the news of his daughter was almost too much for him to bear.

Commodore Hammond turned the locket in his fingers. "They have taken everything from me."

"The Americans?"

"Both the British and the Americans."

"Aye." Grayson stood and watched the rain through the porthole. He would need to give orders to the crew soon. "You can rebuild your house."

"The house was my grandfather's dream, not mine." The commodore coughed. "What news is there of Seth?"

Grayson turned back to him. "He is planning to marry the daughter of an American colonel."

"Ah. A planter?"

"Yes, sir."

"That will be good for him," Commodore Hammond said. "Do you still have your schooner?"

He shook his head. "It is the property of the British now."

"They have taken much from you as well."

He nodded.

Commodore Hammond folded his fingers over the locket. "I can no longer determine exactly what England is fighting for."

"She is fighting to win."

The chamber door burst open, and Zadock rushed inside.

"What is your news?" Grayson demanded.

Zadock glanced between the two men, his hat askew. "Cornwallis has called a cease-fire."

CHAPTER 42

NOVEMBER 1781

*L*ightning flashed across the steely blue waves on the James River as Lydia slipped out one last time to the gazebo. She watched the display as she strolled through the gardens, waiting for rain.

Three weeks ago, Cornwallis had surrendered at York. The Americans had yet to win their war, but they had won Virginia, and as the British retreated to New York, defeat seemed inevitable. Soon the colonists would rule themselves.

Father had resigned himself to the colonies' independence. Without income to run their plantation, a return to England seemed like his only choice. Even if her parents decided to embrace the new country, the little money Father had made from his tobacco crop wouldn't be enough to sustain the family for another year in Virginia. There was enough money, though, for passage for their family along with Prudence, Joshua, and Deborah. Once they reached England, Deborah would be promoted to a paid servant.

Tomorrow morning they would leave their beautiful home to journey to London. Her mother's parents would welcome them, and Lydia imagined that the days to follow would be filled with various gatherings as they tried to piece back together their place in society.

Even though she'd declared her desire for freedom to her family, she would never tell them all she had done during the war. Nor would she ever expose what friends such as Mrs. Pendell and Dr. Cooper had done to support the Patriots' cause. She'd become a keeper of secrets in the past months, and as they started a new life, her secrets must remain.

The dark clouds sparked again.

She should be excited about her prospects, but the country she loved, and the plantation where she belonged, was on this side of the Atlantic. She only wished her family would remain here as well.

Mother had resigned herself to Grayson's departure—his final hug was the consolation she needed to leave for England. Hannah had returned to Caswell Hall more than a week ago. Once she discovered that Major Reed had no intention of taking her as a second wife—and once the British lost the battle at York—she'd decided that the tobacco fields offered more comforts than a camp of women following a defeated army into winter.

Lydia shuddered to think what would happen if rumors of Hannah's indiscretion trailed them back to London. Father would do everything he could to prevent the rumor as they introduced her to society, but heaven forbid that she repeat her folly in London.

Thunder shook the gazebo as Lydia stepped inside it, and she pulled her shawl close around her shoulders.

In London, Father would be heralded as a hero for standing firm in his loyalty to King George, and the king would probably grant him land. If not, Mother's parents had more than enough to support all of them.

Lydia, however, hadn't stood firm in her loyalties for the king, nor did she want to spend her life serving him.

She had no choice but to leave with her family, but how would she survive in London when her heart belonged here with Nathan? A hero. General Washington's nephew. A Patriot heralded in the land she loved. Her gaze wandered to the riverbank where she'd found him so many months ago, nearly drowned in the willows. The place where her life began a course she'd never imagined.

The formal good-bye she and Nathan shared at the Wythe home was the last time she had seen him, and no matter how much she'd allowed herself to hope in these past weeks, he had not returned to her. Thousands of wounded American and French troops remained in Williamsburg, but Washington and much of his army had traveled back toward New York. Nathan had likely gone with him.

She had thought that perhaps he might care for her as she cared for him, but she had been the fool. If nothing else, perhaps her heart would heal in London.

Lightning illuminated the gazebo again, and by the column, she saw a cane with a worn yellow ribbon tied around it.

She inhaled sharply. It looked like the cane Elisha had carved for Nathan. And the ribbon she had given him.

Her eyes squinted toward the dark gardens that led toward the river, her heart racing. There had been no cane here last night or the night before last. Someone had left it today.

Perhaps Nathan had come with another message for her.

Rain began to fall as she took the cane and hurried away from the gazebo toward the orangery.

Oh, that he had delivered the message in person instead of leaving it for her.

Her hand shook, wet locks of hair falling into her face as she took out the brick. There was an envelope inside, sealed with a stamp, and she hid the letter under her arm to protect it from the storm. There were no British officers left to find the letter now, but the rain could easily erase the message.

Opening the door to the orangery, she slipped inside and tossed her wet shawl onto a table. Dried vines hung from the rafters around her, and brown plants wilted in their pots along the counters. Raindrops pelted against the glass roof as she looped the crook of the cane over her wet sleeve and turned the letter over.

This message was addressed to her.

Thunder rattled the glass above her as she pressed into the seal with her fingernail, sliding it back and forth until it loosened. Then she waited for the lightning to read the simple note.

My dearest Lydia,
Will you dance with me?

Her heart quickened as she looked up and then slowly turned. And there, as if by a miracle, stood Nathan.

Her voice trembled as she spoke. "What are you doing here?"

"I have come to dance."

"How did you know—?"

He brushed her wet hair back from her face. "Sarah once told me how much you love to dance."

She lifted her arm. "What about your cane?"

He smiled down at her. "I don't need it anymore."

He placed his wet cloak beside her shawl and offered her his hand.

When the light flashed again he drew her close to him, and warmth permeated her wet skin. The chill turned to fire as he guided their dance under the rafters, a symphony of harps and flutes and violins playing beautiful music in her mind.

He bowed to her, his hand still clutching hers as he spoke. "I met with Seth in Williamsburg."

The music began to fade as she wondered what other secrets he'd kept from her. "You know Seth?"

"Aye. And I knew I could trust the woman he was to marry."

"Seth and I will never marry."

"I know," he said as he pulled her close to him again.

This time he didn't dance. This time he held her in the shadows and she slowly melted into him. No longer must she fight what welled in her heart. This man cocooned around her, this man who fought the war for independence with intelligence, was the one she wanted to spend her life with.

Perhaps he had loved her for a long time.

She thought she must have loved him since she found him with the blanket draped over his arm, pretending to be her servant.

Nathan leaned down to her, his breath warming her neck, her ear. "You rescued me, Lydia."

She shook her head. He was the one who had rescued her.

"You saved my life," he said again, stroking her hair. "And you helped us win this war."

She looked up at him, his handsome face masked by the darkness. "You're exaggerating."

"Because of your courage, General Washington has pledged to protect your plantation and your family."

It was as she'd hoped, but her parents had already chosen a different road.

"My family is preparing to sail for England."

"Can we convince them to change their minds?"

She thought of how Mother longed for England, of how Father refused to submit to a government he was convinced would fail. "I don't believe so."

He kissed the top of her hair. "And what about you, Lydia?"

"What about me?"

"Can I convince you to change your mind?"

It felt as if she couldn't breathe. "Perhaps."

He stepped back, his hands clenching both of hers. The rain had stopped, and a glimmer of moonlight shone through the clouds. "Stay with me, Lydia."

She wasn't like Sarah. She would never run a plantation on her own, nor did she dream of traveling around the world. And yet she had taken risks these past months, more risks than she'd ever dreamed she would. Staying with him, with most of her family in London, would perhaps be the greatest risk of all.

A tremor of fear suddenly ran through her. He'd asked her to stay in Virginia, not to marry him. Nathan's position in this war had been based on deceit. Perhaps he, like Major Reed, had a wife somewhere else.

He squeezed her hands again. "Lydia?"

"There must be no more deception between us."

He nodded his head slowly. "I pray neither of us must ever deceive again."

"Have you ever married"—she paused—"or promised to marry another?"

He held her with his gaze. "Never."

Her shoulders relaxed. He had always trusted her. She would trust him as well. "I cannot simply—stay with you."

"I didn't mean stay, I meant—" He sighed. "I am making a mess of this."

Her heart quickened again.

"Lydia, would you do me the honor of becoming my wife?"

She smiled, and then she wrapped her arms around his neck, pulling his face to hers. His kiss warmed her to her toes.

Now he smiled at her. "Does that mean you will marry me?"

The rain started again. "I will."

He lifted her up and twirled her around. "Be careful of your leg."

He was grinning when he set her down. "See how much I need you?"

"I don't really know anything about you, Nathan." She paused. "I don't even know your last name."

He bowed again. "I am Nathan Washington Lewis, former business manager and spy. My mother is Betty Lewis, the younger sister of George Washington, and my father is deceased. He was a planter who sent me to Yale for school."

She laughed and curtsied. "It is a pleasure to make your acquaintance, Mr. Lewis."

He took her hand in his. "And I am about to marry the loveliest lady in all of Virginia."

"Then I suppose I haven't a chance."

He grinned. "It's too late for you to change your mind, Miss Caswell."

The war for the colonies might not yet be finished, but this man in front of her, Nathan Washington Lewis, had won her heart.

"And it's too late for you to change yours."

He pulled her close to him again. "I will never change my mind about you."

EPILOGUE

The fragrance of garden flowers sweetened the light breeze as it cooled the back portico of Caswell Hall. Nathan rested on the bed their grandchildren had made for him outside, and when his eyes fluttered open, Lydia reached for her husband's hand.

The house behind them could tell hundreds of stories, but Lydia loved the people who'd lived with her there much more than she loved the building. Most of all, she loved her husband.

Forty-four years of marriage, and they'd been together every night but one, the night of the great snowstorm. The president at the time—Thomas Jefferson—had called for Nathan, and he'd gone without her since she was about to birth their second child. After missing Micah's birth, Nathan vowed never to miss the birth of any of their other children, and he had kept his promise.

A host of people circled her and Nathan. Six of their eight children who had survived to adulthood stood on the portico along with fifteen of their grandchildren and four great-grand-children, as well. She sometimes mixed up the names of her great-grandchildren, but Nathan never did.

Their oldest grandson brought hot tea to his grandfather.

Even though the July temperatures were hot, Nathan couldn't seem to get warm. It reminded her of that night so long ago when she'd found him half-frozen on the riverbank.

He might not remember much about that night, but she would never forget. It was ironic that she was now the one to use the cane Elisha had carved, but it was a constant reminder to her of new beginnings and her husband's love.

The night Nathan remembered most fondly was the night they'd danced in the orangery, the night she'd agreed to become his wife. They'd rushed up to this house after the storm passed and surprised her parents. She had been just as surprised when she discovered they already knew Nathan. She hadn't requested permission to marry him, but Father gave it anyway. When he found out that General Washington had personally given his pledge to protect Caswell Hall, Father asked her and Nathan to care well for his plantation.

For almost fifty years, her husband had cared for their home, his country, and his family. Before they married, he told her he would never purchase a slave, and he never did, hiring field workers and servants to work with them instead. He'd served as a Virginia senator until he agreed to become the young nation's secretary of state. Lydia had traveled with him to England and France and the West Indies, and whenever they went, she thought of Sarah, her sister, sailing with her.

In 1785 Mistress Reed died of a mysterious illness, and Hannah became the official wife of Major Reed. Mother wrote Lydia of the marriage, and it grieved her heart. Lydia visited her parents once on their estate outside of London, and Mother seemed content in loving the Reeds' three children. Hannah died in 1802—at the age of thirty-six—and Lady Caswell died soon after. Lord Caswell remarried and lived until 1811.

Grayson never married again. He and Commodore Hammond started a shipping company near Seth's plantation in Maryland, and it quickly became the most profitable shipping company in the colonies. For Elisha's service with the Continental Army, General Washington freed him from slavery, and Commodore Hammond freed Morah and Alden. Even with their papers, Elisha didn't want to remain in the United States of America. He and Morah took the last name of Hammond and, with Grayson's help, purchased land in Canada.

Through the years, Lydia corresponded with Morah and then with Sarah Hammond—Elisha and Morah's youngest daughter—as she ran her father's successful plantation, harvesting wheat for Hammond and Porter Shipping Company.

Seth's oldest son, John, came back in 1809 to take over the Hammond plantation. He built a home even larger than Caswell Hall, and then he married Dotty, Lydia's and Nathan's second daughter. Glancing over at John Hammond and the grandchild in her daughter's arms, Lydia smiled. God had redeemed their families and reunited them. Any animosity that lingered from the past had been obliterated by love.

As far as she knew, Grayson was still off sailing somewhere. In spite of his declaration to never return, her brother came back to Caswell Hall about once every five years for a visit that lasted a day or two. He never stayed long in one place. He'd found freedom, but peace continued to evade him.

After sipping the tea, Nathan clenched her hand again. "Do you remember when we danced in the orangery?"

The clatter around her quieted before she spoke. "I will never forget it."

He glanced around at the faces of the men and women, the boys and girls, who loved him. He'd fought for their freedom, and he'd won it. "Tell them our story."

"I will, my love."

"I would not have changed a thing."

He squeezed her hand one last time before his eyes fluttered shut.

She looked up at the faces of all those she loved, at the tears in their eyes, and her heart felt both empty and full.

She would tell his story—their story—again to their children and their grandchildren. She would tell them, and then she would write it down so the generations could share it with their children.

Freedom had come at a price for those she loved. None of them could ever forget Sarah and Grayson or Elisha and Morah or the man who'd jumped overboard on that snowy day to save Virginia.

She might have rescued Nathan once, but he had spent a lifetime rescuing her.

AUTHOR'S NOTE

War lingered in the new United States until the Treaty of Paris was signed in 1783. Even though the nation won independence from Great Britain, Americans lost twenty-five thousand of their men as they battled for the freedom to speak and write what they believed, elect leaders, own land, and worship as they pleased.

While this story and characters are fictional, I've attempted to preserve the historical accuracy of events that occurred during the Revolutionary War. Many citizens of Virginia kept their loyalty to King George or their passion for independence a secret during the war, fearing repercussion from both sides. Families were often divided with fathers and sons fighting for opposing armies, and sentiments swayed depending on who was occupying the town.

Heroic women like Elizabeth Burgin, Lydia Darragh, and Nancy Hart played a critical role in the victory of the Americans while other women ran family plantations. General Washington relied on a network of both male and female spies and couriers to garner and distribute intelligence for the army.

Through the deception of his operatives, Washington fooled

the British in 1781 into strengthening their position up north. While the British prepared to defend New York against a ghost army, General Washington and Comte de Rochambeau marched their troops down to Virginia and ultimately defeated General Cornwallis and the remaining British army at what is now called the Battle of Yorktown.

George Washington Lewis, the son of Fielding and Betty (Washington) Lewis, was born in 1757 and purported to be General George Washington's favorite nephew. George Lewis assisted his uncle during the war as an aide-de-camp, working as a courier, secretary, and officer in the General's Guard. He escaped imprisonment by the British and married Catherine Daingerfield before the war ended. Together George and Catherine purchased a plantation home in Virginia.

Benedict Arnold's role in Virginia fascinated me. After he betrayed his country, Arnold joined the British army as a general, and in 1781 he and his fleet of ships and soldiers wreaked havoc along the James River. After plundering Richmond and setting it ablaze, they continued their destruction in Virginia, burning plantation homes, military supplies, and the shipyard on the Chickahominy. Also, after writing the final scene in George Wythe's house, I discovered that George Wythe was actually poisoned to death by his grandnephew. It is believed his grandnephew put the poison in his coffee.

On October 7, 1783, the House of Burgesses in Virginia granted freedom to slaves who served in the Continental Army. After the war, more than a thousand freed slaves established Freetown in Sierra Leone, and fifty thousand Loyalists and former slaves settled in the Canadas, a collection of colonies that gained independence from Great Britain in 1867.

The Imposter opens on July 4, 1826, as the United States of America celebrated fifty years since the Declaration of Independence. While the country commemorated the anniversary of freedom, July 4, 1826, was also another significant day in history: Patriots Thomas Jefferson and John Adams both passed away.

One of my favorite parts of writing historical fiction is the research and then the wondering—what would happen if . . . ? This story began brewing in me long ago, when I was a graduate student in Virginia Beach. Often I would escape to the quaint cobblestone streets of Williamsburg and feast on Welsh rarebit and cider at Chowning's Tavern. One of my favorite memories of my time near Williamsburg, though, was staying at an old plantation home along the James River. As I wandered the banks, my mind wandered as well, dreaming about what might have happened on that river years ago.

To research this novel, my daughter Karly and I returned to Virginia to explore. She was fascinated by the work of the blacksmith and wigmaker in Colonial Williamsburg, and we both enjoyed touring the Governor's Palace and George Wythe's home. Our favorite shop was the restored R. Charlton's Coffeehouse, where two women in colonial dress shared stories as Karly and I sipped dark chocolate mixed with cinnamon, cayenne pepper, nutmeg, and vanilla.

Many people helped me tell this story about our country's birth, and I am grateful to each of them. Most of all, I am thankful to my heavenly Father who never leaves or forsakes us. He is the same yesterday, today, and forever.

With joy, ~Melanie

LEGACY OF LOVE SERIES

Legacy of Love by Melanie Dobson is a historical romance series based on the courageous people and significant events that wove together the rich tapestry of America's freedom and faith.

Now Available:
The Masquerade (Gilded Age)
The Runaway (Underground Railroad)
The Imposter (Revolutionary War)
The Christmas Bride (Colonial America, Moravians)
The Journey (Oregon Trail)
The Society (Civil War, Amana Colonies)
The Stranger (Amana Colonies)
The Silent Order (Prohibition)

THE CHRISTMAS BRIDE

PROLOGUE

May 1754

Susanna couldn't concentrate on the Count's eloquent words, not when her groom stood just four paces behind her. Everything within her wanted to glance over her shoulder to see the color of Christian Boehler's eyes. And to see if there was a hint of love within them.

But she couldn't turn around. Her curiosity would only embarrass her future husband, with so many brothers and sisters behind them watching the great wedding, solemnly attentive, while her mind danced around the possibilities of life with her new husband and the adventure before them.

Instead of turning, Susanna fiddled with the ribbon that zigzagged up her bodice while trying to listen to Count Nicholas Ludwig von Zinzendorf as he performed the ceremony from the front of the castle's great Saal. Even as she tried to cherish the significance of this day, the beginning of her marriage, and her journey as a messenger, she couldn't concentrate on what the Count was saying.

Her laboress had told her stories about Christian Boehler's dedication to their Savior and of his burden to share their

Savior's love with the Indians in the Colonies. Her burden was the same, but she also wanted to love her husband and be loved by him.

Susanna rocked back on her heels. God had given her a man who served Him, but would he love her as well, in their journey together, like a man should love his wife?

Eleven other brides were fanned out beside her in a giant horseshoe for the Great Wedding. Their grooms stood in a curved row a few steps behind them, and then at the back of the large hall were a hundred brothers and sisters on benches, witnesses to their matrimony.

Morning light stole through the lofty windows on both sides of the room, trailing like a veil down the ancient castle's hall. Outside the windows, rolling hills surrounded the German community and castle, blooming with the purples and yellows of spring color.

As Count Zinzendorf spoke to them about the blessed society of marriage and the beautiful mystery of it, Susanna's mind wandered far from the walls of Marienborn. For a moment, she longed to be roaming through the coolness of the hills this morning and talking to the Savior instead of marrying a man she'd never before spoken with.

If only she knew why Christian had selected her to be his wife.

Couples were divided into pairs for the wedding, and in front of each pair of couples stood an elder who would speak to them when the Count completed his sermon. She and Catharine Weicht and their grooms had been paired with Elder Seidner, a young minister who shifted the book of marriage vows back and forth in his hands as if the words burned his fingers.

Beyond the rows of grooms and brides and six elders—the leaders of their community—the regal Count Zinzendorf continued to speak. A large, imposing man, the Count had black hair and an aura that spoke of both power and love. Other members of the German royal court powdered their hair white, but the Count rarely powdered his. Even without the powder and robes, his demeanor could intimidate his subjects if necessary.

The Count was a man who pursued the heart of God, and as part of this pursuit, he had opened up his estate to those persecuted for their faith, those known as the Unity of the Brethren. During the past thirty years, he had been leading all of them into deep, fulfilling relationships with their Savior.

Each bride was simply dressed, with a white cape draped over her bodice and a petticoat dyed blue or green. They all wore white haubes—caps with delicate pink or white ribbons tied under their chins. Widows wore white ribbons while the single sisters wore pink.

Susanna's ribbon was pink.

She blinked in the sunlight, her hands brushing the smooth ribbon that would change within the hour. If only her mother could have been here for her wedding day. She could almost hear the soft but determined voice of her mother, calming her fears, reminding her of her dedication to the will of their Savior and not to herself, reminding her of their Savior's love.

Her mother knew firsthand of this love. Their Savior had taken her to Him eight years ago while she served alongside Susanna's father as a messenger of the Gospel to the African people.

As Susanna stood before the elder, she pretended that her parents were sitting on the benches behind them. Her mother to comfort her. Her father to tell Christian about the Fritsche family's past and to talk to him about the future.

But she stood today in the company of her sisters instead of her family.

When she glanced to her right, Catharine Weicht winked at her, and Susanna smiled at the boldness of her friend on this somber day. In spite of her plainness of dress, Catharine was anything but plain. The waves of her auburn hair were pinned up neatly under her cap. Her ivory skin was as pure and pretty as the edelweiss that bloomed wild in the hills around them. Instead of the humility borne by the other sisters, her friend's presence breathed the air of aristocracy that ran through her veins.

On Susanna's left side stood a young widow, a white ribbon tied under her chin. With her dappled skin and slightly crooked nose, Rebecca wasn't nearly as pretty as Catharine, but Susanna admired Rebecca for her devout relationship with the Savior. Even though she was just five years older than Susanna, Rebecca had already lost her husband on a mission to Greenland, and she'd made it clear she would never marry again. Yet here she stood, chosen like the rest of them. No one argued with the lot.

The Count had divided their community into groups and called them each a choir hoping, perhaps, that the many different personalities in each choir would learn to live in harmony. There were choirs for both married men and women as well as single choirs. Boys and girls choirs. The widows choir and the choir for widowers. Each choir was led by a laborer or laboress, and they lived, ate, and worshipped together like a family, separated from the other choirs.

Women remained with the Single Sisters Choir until one of the single brothers conferred with their laborer about the possibility of marriage to a certain woman. The elders prayed about their request and then put it before the lot, just as they did with every major decision in their community.

Sometimes the chosen lot was a blank piece of parchment that simply meant to wait. Sometimes the elders picked the paper that said "no," and sometimes they selected the paper that confirmed the marriage. The requested woman was then given the option to decline or to accept the proposal.

Together, Catharine, Rebecca, and Susanna had faithfully

served in the Single Sisters Choir in Marienborn for more than
two years until the lot matched them with a man to wed. After
the lot matched her with Christian Boehler, Susanna was given
the opportunity to reject their marriage. But who was she to
reject what God had so clearly ordained?

Even though she'd never actually spoken with Christian, she
had watched him from afar. He was a respected member of their
community, but even more than that, her heart sparked with the
possibility of going with him to the new colony. She could roam
the wilderness with Christian Boehler and share Jesus's love
with people who might never have heard of Him. She would
befriend the Indian women and be the best possible companion
to her husband.

Behind her, the congregation began to sing "Oh Creator of
my Soul." As Susanna mouthed the words, she glanced over at
Catharine again and saw the graceful smile on her friend's face.

Catharine was the daughter of an English noble, her father
once a member of Parliament who had left his esteemed position to join the United Brethren. He and Catharine's fashionable
mother now traveled around Europe, sometimes alongside
Count Zinzendorf, to speak with leaders about their church.

Even though she lived in the common room with all the
sisters, Catharine still treated her sisters like servants. Susanna
didn't fault Catharine for her upbringing or her demands—the
Savior was transforming all of them—but she tried to gently
remind Catharine that they all lived and served in humble
circumstances. The sisters slept on the same straw mattresses
and ate the same soups and breads at mealtime and worked side
by side.

No matter how or where they had been reared, all the sisters
were clothed in modest apparel today—though Susanna knew
that Catharine wore maroon stockings under her long dress
while the other women wore gray or blue.

Susanna hadn't been educated like Catharine. There'd been

no governor for her or years of training at an exclusive boarding school to teach her how to handle stress with dignity and grace. She often wrestled with the jealousy that conflicted with her devotion to both her Savior and her friend.

She wasn't jealous of the fine home where Catharine had been reared or the lofty manners that embarrassed the other girls. Susanna was jealous of Catharine's vast knowledge based on years of education in the finest schools for girls. Catharine could read and write and paint, and she knew about faraway peoples and places.

It was Catharine who had told Susanna about the town of Philadelphia and the wilds beyond in the tiny community of Nazareth, where Susanna and Christian would live when they weren't visiting the Indians. Catharine told her about the fierce warriors in the Colonies and the Indians who sought peace by sharing and even selling their land to the white men.

Susanna and Christian. Catharine and her betrothed, Elias Schmidt. They had all been selected to travel to the new colony of Pennsylvania after their wedding.

"Be content again my soul, for the Lord does good to you," the Count said when the singing ended, sharing the watchword for their wedding. "Do not forget it, oh my heart!"

Susanna's gaze wandered over the shoulder of Elder Seidner, out the wide window behind him to the hills. She knew she shouldn't wonder at Christian's feelings, not when she didn't even understand her own.

She wished her heart were filled with love for Christian, like what some of the other brides felt for their betrotheds, but fear filled the hollows of her heart instead. She admired the man behind her greatly, had admired him since the moment he'd marched through the gates of their castle five months earlier. Though she'd admitted it to no one, she thought him to be one of the most handsome men she'd ever seen, and she respected his strength and his passions and his desire to serve their Savior as a messenger in the Colonies.

But she didn't know why he'd chosen her.

The Count paused, and Elder Seidner motioned Christian and Elias forward. She felt Christian step up beside her, saw the outline of his shoulder beyond her own.

What would it feel like to have Christian Boehler take her in his arms and kiss her, as the laboress in their choir house described? What would it be like to lie next to him in the bedchamber? She trembled at the thought, not knowing whether it was from pleasure or from fear of the certainty that she would fail him.

She wasn't educated nor was she beautiful like Catharine. She didn't have the manners of politer society or even the knowledge of how to speak with a man. Her father had left for Africa a decade ago, and her memories of him were pleasant but few.

Every day in Marienborn, she saw both the married and single brothers—she sat across the aisle from them at the love feasts and the foot washings and the quarter-hour devotions—but she never spoke with them and certainly had never touched one of them. She didn't know how to be this man's—or any man's—wife.

Across the room, a minister began conducting the marriage vows to one of the other couples, and then all the ministers began to speak as they joined the men and women in front of them. Susanna listened as Elder Seidner joined Elias and Catharine in marriage. Then he turned to Christian.

"Brother Boehler, will you love Sister Susanna Fritsche as thy wedded wife, to live together in holy wedlock?"

As she turned, Susanna was close enough to see Christian's light brown eyes that were tinged with yellow in the sunlight. But she didn't see the hope in them that she desired. Or love. Instead, she saw regret.

Her gaze dropped to the hem of his black coat, and her entire body shook from disappointment. Already she had failed the man, before she even married him.

The vow hung between them, waiting for his response.

Was it too late for them to change their minds? Maybe Christian could ask for another spouse before he left for Pennsylvania and Susanna could travel as a single sister?

She clenched the seams of her dress as she waited for Christian's refusal, but instead of rejecting her, he vowed to love her as his wife. Her stomach twisted like the cotton in her fingers.

How could Christian agree to to marry her when he regretted his choice?

The elder nodded at Christian's words and then looked to her. "Sister Fritsche, will you love Brother Christian Boehler, honor him, and be subject unto him in the Lord?"

Susanna's gaze wandered back to the window as she pondered the words. She could honor this man and even be subject to him, but why did the elder ask her to love him when Christian clearly didn't share this love for her?

She scanned the hills in the distance and wished again that she were outside so she could think, breathe. Just days ago, she'd been dreaming about marriage to a man like Christian Boehler, but she wanted her husband to look at her the way Elias Schmidt looked at Catharine—like a thirsty soul who'd discovered a desert spring. A spring he would drink from for the remainder of his life.

"Sister Fritsche?" the elder whispered.

She lifted her eyes, not to Christian but to Elder Seidner. How could the Savior require this of her?

The elder nodded at her again, urging her to answer. The other elders in the room were quiet, the vows of the other couples complete. Everyone in the room was waiting for her now. Watching.

Susanna took a deep breath. With God's help, she would

learn to love this man. And maybe one day he could learn to love her as well.

She summoned up the strength within her to match the confidence in Christian's voice.

"I will," she finally said. And she meant it.

Elder Seidner smiled. "I now pronounce you Brother and Sister Boehler."

Sister Boehler. The name echoed in Susanna's ears.

She had a new name now, a new identity.

But what would this new name require of her?

The Count began to pray. "Lord our God, You who have Yourself established and blessed the holy marriage, You wanted these husbands and wives to be bound together through the band of holy marriage, in order to do Your work together."

Beside her, Elias took Catharine's hand as the Count prayed. When Christian didn't reach for her hand, Susanna rubbed her fingers together. Even if her husband didn't love her, their marriage was blessed as holy, to work together as a couple to fulfill the greatest commission of all—to take the Gospel into all the world.

"In the name of Jesus Christ, our Head, Bridegroom, and Elder," the Count announced. "And in the name of our dear Father in heaven, we bring you honorably together and commission you to the colony called Pennsylvania."

The bell tolled above them. Trumpets blared in the court-yard below. One of the married women stepped forward and placed a haube over Susanna's hair, a white cap with blue ribbons, to set her apart as a married sister.

Catharine's parents gathered around Catharine and Elias to offer their congratulations. Another married sister kissed Susanna's cheeks, saying how blessed she was. And in the midst of the kissing cheeks and shaking hands, Susanna glanced across the room to search for her new husband.

She found him near the doors, shaking the hand of one of

the other newly married brothers, and she longed for a simple word from his lips. He didn't have to call her "beloved" or even "wife"; she would be content with just a kind word from a brother.

As she watched, Christian turned and searched until he found her face in the crowd. The clamor around her seemed to silence, and though he stood far from her, in that moment it seemed as if they were alone.

His hat against his chest, Christian slowly nodded to her. Then his broad frame disappeared out the door.

ABOUT THE AUTHOR

Writing fiction is Melanie Dobson's excuse to explore abandoned houses, travel to unique places, and spend hours reading old books and journals. She enjoys stitching together historical and time-slip stories, and her novels have won awards for historical romance, romantic suspense, and historical fiction. Melanie has published almost thirty books including *The Silent Order, Catching the Wind, Chateau of Secrets, and The Curator's Daughter.* Her Legacy of Love novels have been revised from her previously published Love Finds You and American Tapestry books (legacyofloveseries.com).

Melanie loves connecting with readers! The best places to find her online are:

www.melaniedobson.com
comments@melaniedobson.com
facebook.com/MelanieDobsonFiction

Made in the USA
Las Vegas, NV
13 February 2022

43620236R00215